CYGNUS CURSE

Poppy Rose Solomon

First published by Poppy's Pages in 2023

www.poppyspagesediting.com

Written by Poppy Rose Solomon

Edited by Pauline Menchavez and Ellyssa Paik

Cover art by Robert Ixer

Cover design by Haylee Buswell (HB Pencil Designs)

Paperback ISBN: 978-0-6456986-2-6

eBook ISBN: 978-0-6456986-3-3

A catalogue record of this book is available from the National Library of Australia

The author acknowledges the Gubbi Gubbi people, the traditional owners of the land this book was written and published on. Respect and gratitude are extended to elders past and present.

Bob, thank you for the art and for the wonderful memories. I miss you.

MAP

The World of Woken Kingdom

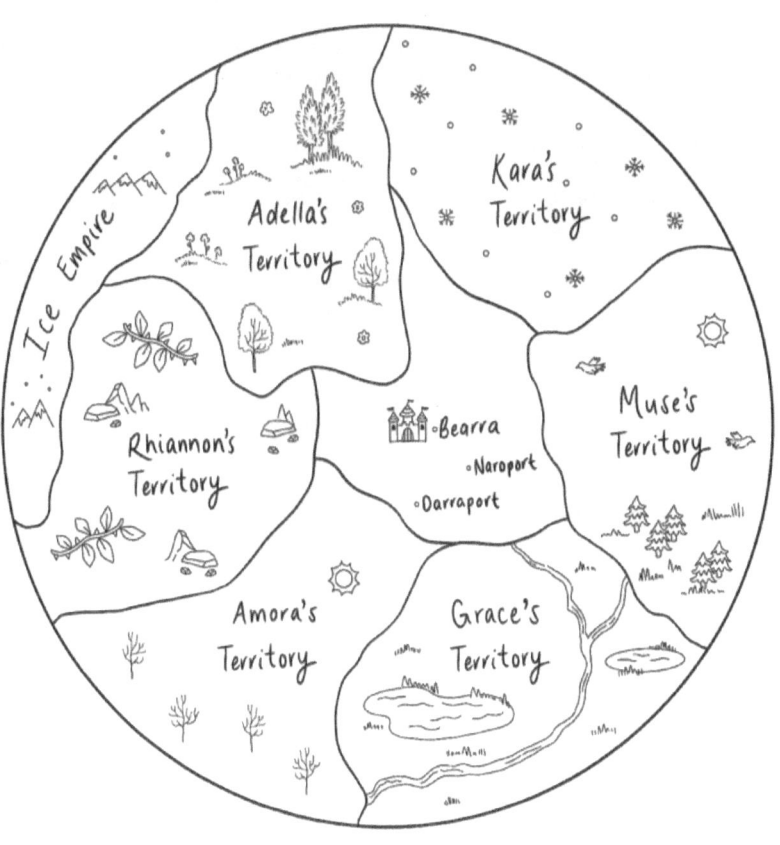

PROLOGUE

Sierra laughed as she spun and ducked under the pirate's sad attempt at a punch to her face. He was a big, brawling figure.

Strong? Yes. But any match for *her*?

She whipped behind him like wind and shoved him over the side of the ship. Sierra howled with delight as the pirate struck the water so forcefully that droplets landed on her hair.

She flicked the dark strands over her shoulders while she caught her breath and studied the stars. The sounds of her sisters fighting the other pirates dimmed as adrenaline took its thrilling course through her body.

It was nearly dawn, but the full moon was bright in the sky, illuminating the waters beneath her: a lake fed from Grace's crystal fountain itself. Clear. Pure. Beautiful. Sierra would die to protect it.

'Such a lovely night for murder,' she whispered to herself.

She'd kill for Grace's Territory, too. With a grin, she scanned the ship – smaller than the Reeds', but a decent pirate vessel nonetheless

1

– for her next opponent. Bruises were already forming on her arms, but she didn't care. She'd heal. She'd show her sisters and her parents her wounds, and prove to them her worth.

This was the perfect opportunity for it: one of the rare patrols her sisters actually allowed her to join.

The eldest, Irene, shot Sierra an impatient look from across the deck as she punched a young man in the face so hard they both recoiled. Irene steadied herself expertly; the pirate dropped unconscious to the wooden floor.

Sierra yawned. Nearly all the pirates were down, and how long had it been, ten minutes?

She wasn't sure why people even bothered to fight the Reeds, but pirates *were* known to be idiots. These were people who weren't smart enough to work legitimately – cowards who ran from honour.

The other five sisters danced around the boat, battling its remaining crew. Sierra had seen these pirates before – they were a small, in-significant group who mostly relied on stealing quickly and minimally, or doing odd jobs for bigger criminals. Their enchanted ship – the *Neptune* – piloted itself, which was the only reason their measly crew of six had survived this long. Most appeared to be around Sierra's age, though the youngest couldn't be older than thirteen.

Sierra tapped her foot and impatiently pondered as to why had they chosen now to attack the protectors of Grace's Waters. Everyone knew Sierra's family ran the territory. They controlled the trade, protected the waterways from crime. And they never failed. These seven young women alone – the infamous Reed sisters – had seen to it that no pirate had found any success near Grace's Capital in years.

Sierra was a major part of that, though none of the others would admit it. The *six* Reed sisters were a perfect machine, while Sierra was an extra cog: an unwanted baby sister who, for years, was only a burden. But she was useful enough now. Sierra would prove herself in time.

She spotted Emika – the youngest of her older sisters, who still had a whole decade over Sierra – wrestling with a red-haired pirate. She struggled slightly under his weight; Emika must have been wounded, because although the pirate was tall, he was slim and flimsy.

Bored and ready to maim someone, something, *anything,* Sierra grabbed him by his neck and yanked him off her. Something cracked – nothing *fatal* – and the pirate thrashed around in shock, hurtling backwards.

Oh, it was always too easy.

Emika glowered at Sierra, as if she'd taken something from her. A kill? Yet she didn't refuse Sierra's help in tossing the young man off the boat.

Maybe it was for the best that Sierra's sisters refused to work with her. It added some difficulty to each fight, keeping her on her feet. If she relied on others, she might become complacent.

But sometimes she wished for a *real* challenge, for something to hurt, and make her adrenaline race as it had when she first started training herself. She knew she was cocky; her sisters told her constantly. But she didn't care about that. She was going to be the best of them, so what did her attitude matter? They wouldn't love her any more if she were kind, humble, or fair. She'd tried that. One could not find any place in the world that way.

Sierra knew that if she wanted something, she had to take it.

Sierra swore as pain seared the side of her calf, and she spun to watch with pure fury as one of the pirates' swords sliced her leg. She screamed at the girl responsible and used her boot to knock the sword from her hand. Sierra groaned as her weight fell back on her wounded leg, but she managed to kick the girl in the ear, bowling her over.

In retaliation, the youngest pirate ran at her, twisting knives around her fingers like a tiny assassin. *Fairies.* Sierra was nearly spent. The hot blood dripping down her leg was burgundy in the moonlight, and if she didn't find a way to bandage it soon, she'd be in serious trouble.

But she couldn't call for help. She wouldn't.

The young girl tossed a knife, and Sierra dove out of its way just in time. It grazed her arm instead of slashing the artery in her neck.

This child was becoming a problem. Sierra didn't want to hurt someone so young, but if it was Sierra or the girl, the girl or the territory, there was no choice. Besides, Sierra had been killing by this girl's age, and she wouldn't have wanted anyone to go easy on her just because of her youth.

Sierra's sisters shouted around her. She didn't know who they were fighting, but there was a strange panic in their voices. Had more pirates boarded? Was anyone else wounded?

She shrugged and refocused. She had to concentrate on keeping herself alive.

Sierra screamed and lunged at the red-haired girl. Sierra's fingers were cut open as she wrestled the second knife from her hands and flung it into the water. She was about to pull the little pirate down and bash her head against the wooden floor when the ship lurched to one side.

Sierra went flying, barely noticing her sisters shrieking and lashing out for grip. She whacked the ship's barrier with a crack that knocked the wind from her chest. People shouted in an incoherent roar as her head spun.

The stars cleared from her vision and her jaw dropped. The *Neptune*'s captain had climbed halfway up the sails. Bright blue magic swirled out of his hands in massive streams, flowing and crashing like glowing waves. The black-haired young man stared at the Reeds with a laugh on his lips, and his magic wrapped around the boat again, threatening to capsize them all.

'*Thief!*' Irene screamed at him. 'You are not worthy of Grace's magic!'

He raised a brow and drawled, 'That's too bad.'

Sierra whipped her head around, trying to account for all her sisters. Each lay on the deck, bleeding and struggling as much as she was. When had the pirates gained the upper hand? Had this fight been too easy for a reason?

Sierra didn't know what to do. She couldn't fight. She'd faced battles with magic before, but this man had a lot more power than most humans could get hold of. *Fairies.* The pirates had not been trying to win; they wanted all the sisters weakened, together. They were only biding time until the right moment to use magic to kill every Reed at once.

So Sierra chose her last resort. She decided to be a coward. Heart racing, she bit her bottom lip to hold back a whimper. While the pirate was busy arguing with Irene, preparing his magic, Sierra picked herself up and slipped off the side of the ship.

She landed as soundlessly in the lake as possible. She was trained to dive into water with barely a splash – but injured as she was, it was impossible to be discrete. She couldn't help but gasp as cold liquid hit the open wound on her leg, the sting enough to make her scream. Luckily, the water muffled her cries.

She let out all her breath through her teeth and sunk as deep as she could, using the light of the moon to see through the murky lake, freshly churned up with mud. The pirates had made a mockery of Grace's crystal water.

As the pirate's azure magic spread out above her, she thought of her sisters. Were they all going to die tonight? It didn't seem possible. Not the invincible Reeds. To her left, a warm light began to shine through the lake. Morning. Had they been fighting this long?

She was weak for hiding like this. But she would rather drown in the water with her dignity than be killed by a pirate. Sierra could hold her breath for a long time, and she would not return to the surface until either she was dead or the pirates were gone.

His magic arced over the ship in a tidal wave of blue – a killing blow. Sierra's heart hardened as she imagined her sisters caught in the power. Dying. Yet her limbs relaxed with relief, knowing she would be spared. She just had to hope the pirates forgot about her.

But the captain's magic dove into the water, illuminating, rippling, bubbling as it snaked around her. Sierra tried to swim away, but her wounds ached in protest. The magic engulfed her, and it was *cold*. So much colder than the water.

Her body froze all over and she shook her head frantically. She did not know she could feel fear like this. She thought she'd lost the ability to. Not just the quick breaths of a near-miss, but a raw, thundering terror. And more than that: something in her heart felt a sense of *wrongness*. A gut feeling, as if her body could already feel the magic willing her to transform, begging her to fight it.

Sierra's eyesight snapped into sharp clarity. As the sun made its way over the horizon, she could see every beam of light bursting through the water.

Then, her body started to twist and pull, cave and grow. The pain in her leg was gone – but so were her *legs*. She tried to breathe, but her lungs were . . . were . . .

It happened in seconds, but she remembered every detail.

Sierra's body was her legacy, her tool. It protected people. Now, she no longer had hands or arms, which she had relied on for strength and agility. She no longer had strong, agile legs to run. Different colours entered her sharp eyes, and it was difficult to make sense of the images before her.

Her webbed feet kicked and pushed her through the water; her once silky but scarred skin was covered with feathers that bristled as she swam. Her mind tried to make her gasp, but her pointed beak only let out a heaving screech.

She tried not to twist her impossibly long neck, tried not to open her massive wings, tried to pretend it was all a dream, because that's what it felt like. Sierra had never felt so far from her surroundings, from her own body. Because this *wasn't* her.

Her chest constricted. In the seconds that passed while the sun rose, the original Sierra Reed was lost forever. She rose to the top of the lake and pulled in a sharp breath. When her eyes opened, she finally saw herself reflected in the rippling water.

A black swan.

＊◊＊○ ⚔ ○＊◊＊

Sierra scanned her surroundings for the pirates, hoping she could attack them somehow, seek revenge, but they were already gone. She did not yet know how to use her new body well enough to chase her enemies. Only the Reeds' ship remained on the lake.

She watched the six white swans who had appeared on the deck. When she tried to approach them, they pecked and screeched. Of course, swans were not known to be friendly creatures, but at least one thing was certain: these creatures were what was left of the Reed sisters.

They didn't seem as confused as Sierra, and they had more control over their bodies. She could see in their eyes that they no longer had their minds like she did. As Sierra stumbled and struggled to breathe, her sisters airily flapped their wings and hopped into the water. If they knew themselves, they would never give up so easily. They would already have flown home if they were capable, searching for help. They wouldn't be meandering like brainless birds.

Sierra did not want to leave them, or their ship. Who knew what might happen? But there was no choice. She had to return home and seek her parents' help. Grace could reverse this magic. The fairy would *have* to.

But how would Sierra communicate with anyone? They wouldn't know her in this form.

On her clumsy feet, she waddled across the ship. She would find something to bring back, to prove to her family that she was a Reed. But – *fairies* – she couldn't open any doors. She couldn't get below deck, so her only idea was immediately ruined.

All their clothes, jewels, everything the women had been holding when they transformed seemed to have changed along with them. If those things hadn't, Sierra likely would have drowned, caught up in her fighting outfit.

And Sierra looked *amazing* in that outfit. She had better get it back once this was fixed.

Sierra bowed her long neck, using her wide wings to shield her eyes from the early morning sun, hearing her sisters cawing as they flew off together to explore the lake. She wanted to cry, but this body was even worse at feeling emotions than her natural one. So, exhausted, she gave in and let herself rest until the sun was high.

By then, she felt more comfortable in this new body. She expanded her wings, feeling the warm midday light reflecting off her black feathers. Of *course* she would be the black swan, distinct from her pure-white sisters. And the only one to remember she was human. Even cursed, she was apart from her family.

She let out a long, pained shriek – and then choked, horrified at the sound.

Sierra flapped her wings and craned her neck like she'd watched the swans around her do for years. It took her the entire journey home to learn to fly, but by the end, it was easy. It did not matter what body Sierra was in. She was adaptable. A fast learner. She would not be stopped by a simple curse.

Still, as she returned home and her family's great, grey manor came into view, she had no idea what to do. If she tried to enter the house in this form, she would be expelled immediately. How could she get her parents' attention without them shooing her away?

At a loss, she spent an hour floating sorrowly in the canals around her home, passing the moat and the garden creeks, the sparking fountains, the hedges carved into creatures of the water. She nearly screeched when she came face-to-face with a topiary swan, its wings outstretched.

Fairies.

Sierra's mother and father exited the wide front door, their white clothes reminiscent of their daughters' white feathers, their faces pale with an expression that might have been worry or concern. She'd never seen that look on her parents before. Did they already know what happened? They weren't sentimental people, but even they knew the consequences for their family and the territory if something happened to their daughters.

Someone was talking to them. A fisherman. Sierra swam closer, craning her neck to listen.

'We found their ship abandoned,' the fisherman said. 'Nothing stolen or wrecked. They were all just . . . gone. I'm sorry.'

Sierra's heart rate slowed as she realised she could still understand human language. That meant someone might be able to get through to her sisters. Yet, even when they were human, they were difficult to communicate with. Whether or not they could understand speech, would the soulless women respond?

Sierra's mother gave the fisherman a hard look. 'Impossible. Why would they leave their own ship? And if someone took them, why not take anything else?'

The fisherman stammered, clutching his hat. 'Well, it did look as if there'd been a struggle. There was fresh blood on the deck.'

'No.' Sierra's father rubbed his temples. 'They'll turn up.'

'Could they have run away? Staged all this so you wouldn't know?'

'Don't you dare,' Sierra's mother hissed, her face reddening, '*ever* suggest our daughters would be capable of such a thing.'

The fisherman recoiled.

'They'll turn up,' her father repeated. 'They will. They will explain everything soon. That, or we'll receive a message for ransom. Either way, I won't waste my time on it. We have a territory to lead.'

With a dismissive wave, he stormed back into the manor, and Sierra's mother followed coldly.

Sierra let herself drift with the weak current of the moat. Of course her parents wouldn't care about her sisters – only the consequences of their disappearance, and how it made them look. They were deep in denial, and even once the truth hit them, they wouldn't be upset. They wouldn't grieve. They would only be ashamed.

She understood. They had a responsibility to the territory. As its protectors – the warriors whose very existence struck so much fear in most criminals that they didn't even try to attack Grace's Waters – they could not look weak for a moment.

But Sierra's heart sank with the realisation that her mother and father wouldn't be coming to save her. She didn't even know she'd had hope, but now that it was gone, all she could do was lay on the shore and let her swan eyes spill with tears.

⋆ ◊ ⸰ ⃝ ⚔ ⃝ ⸰ ◊ ⋆

It was early evening when Sierra's parents finally left the house to collect the ship. They couldn't be seen searching during the day. If anyone knew the girls were gone, chaos was guaranteed. Besides, they probably still thought the women would show up. Sierra took to the skies and followed their small boat closely as they travelled to the part of the lake where the fisherman found the ship.

The sun touched the horizon, and the waters became harder to see. Sierra sank lower as she followed the boat, soaring just above the rivers, following closely. After a while, she impatiently overtook, flying ahead as if that would get them there faster.

What would they think when they arrived? Would they understand that the swans were their daughters? Would the swans even still be there?

Sierra cawed ahead of them, and her parents peered up from their seats. She flapped her wings and spun around, trying to point them towards the ship. The sun descended, its last beams gone.

And as her mother and father watched, Sierra's body became her own again. Her wings disappeared, and, flailing through the air, she crashed into the water.

+ ◊ ˚ ○ ⚔ ○ ˚ ◊ +

The first thing Sierra heard was the familiar sound of her parents' yelling. As she came to, she realised she had swallowed water when she fell, and she coughed it all up at once. Someone must have dragged her out of the river; she had fallen unconscious the moment she landed.

Her parents' faces appeared above her. Their black hair glinted in the night, and as Sierra's eyes focused, it was like she was seeing them for the first time. Through the eyes of the swan, everything was so clear, but felt almost far away. Through her normal eyes, everything was close-up. Blurrier, maybe, but with so much more meaning.

When her gaze focused enough, Sierra was met with the cold, expectant stare of her parents' unflinching eyes, void of any love or concern. Her gut wrenched with real pain. But this, at least, felt human.

'What is going on?' her mother demanded.

Sierra sat upright, her body sore from landing so awkwardly. They were on the riverbank, sand running softly through her fingers. *Fingers*. 'We were cursed,' she whispered, her mouth moving in strange ways as she became accustomed once more to the ability to talk. She stammered through an explanation, recounting the events until she came to the present moment: the pirates, the magic, becoming a swan and then human again.

'So the curse was lifted?' Sierra's father had no sympathy for her story. If anything, he looked disgusted. His daughters did not show weakness. Not like this. 'It can't have been that much magic if it barely lasted a day.'

Sierra let out a sigh of relief. It seemed like a lot of magic at the time, but surely her father was right. He had to be, and she held on to that hope, desperate for something to tether her to normalcy. She was free. This nightmare was over. Her sisters must be out there somewhere, also returned to normal. Still, she kept her face neutral. 'I suppose so.'

She tested out her hands and feet, stretching out her featherless arms. She breathed oxygen into her deep lungs, brushed her hands through her long hair. The wound on her leg was gone, as if the transformation had healed her.

The desire to cry had turned into a desire to sob, but she wouldn't. No. She was Sierra Reed once more, and Reeds did not cry.

• ٥ˈ۝ ⚔ ۝ˈ٥ •

It took hours to find Sierra's sisters. Their small boat wasn't meant for these larger lakes, and it was especially perilous in the dark. But since they had to remain inconspicuous, this was all they could use. Sierra had never spent so much time alone with her parents.

She found that she did not enjoy it very much.

She also found, with every passing minute, that she wasn't sure she even wanted to find her sisters. Surely they would find a way to blame all of this on her, and punish her for it. And, of course, endlessly abuse her for hiding under the water.

But eventually they happened upon a small group of swans, six of them, their white feathers glowing in the night, and Sierra called to her parents to stop the boat.

No. She would not be punished by her sisters – but this was far worse.

'That can't be them,' her mother said. 'You told us the magic wore off. There are hundreds of swans in Grace's Waters.'

Sierra shook her head. 'I *know* that's them. I—'

Her father grabbed her wrist and spun her to face him. 'What have you done?'

'*Me?*'

'You! Why you?' he shouted through flared nostrils and gritted teeth. He was angrier than she'd ever seen him, and she'd seen him in a million rages. His entire body shook. 'Why are you the only one the curse didn't affect?'

Sierra's jaw hardened. 'I don't know . . . I was . . . I was under the water when it happened. They were all on the deck. I didn't think the pirate saw me.'

'You *hid?*' Her father's voice was low and terrible. He raised his hand as if to hit her. It would hardly be the first time, but that didn't make the thought of it hurt less. To Sierra, a hundred wounds in battle were nothing compared to the deep scars that came from her family.

Hands trembling, she forced herself to look him in the eyes. Why hadn't she just lied? 'I was too hurt to fight. I thought if I could get away, I could get help.'

Her mother watched the swans, not even bothering to look at her. Somehow her cold indifference stung worse than her father's anger.

'You are a coward, Sierra. You've been a burden on this family since the day you were conceived. Small, timid, weak – a stain on our bloodline. First you took me off the water, and now you've ruined your sisters, too.' She sneered at her youngest daughter.

Once again, Sierra was filled with shame. Her mother's life was ruined by the complications of her last baby. They tried to terminate the pregnancy, knowing it was a risk, but Grace forced the Reeds to keep Sierra and raise her. Worse, Sierra was a sick child, needing extra help and attention when her family already wanted nothing to do with her.

The Reed warriors went from seven to six, and though Sierra tried to live up to her mother's legacy, she was stained by her family's resentment. To the Reeds, Sierra was not only a mistake – she was a parasite.

'And yet,' her mother finished, 'you're still here. You'll pay for that.'

Sierra's bottom lip quivered, but she was used to this, she would not cry. Her father raised his hand, and she knew what was coming. She squeezed her eyes shut as his palm came down on her cheek.

Her skin seared, but at least she was human. At least this pain was hers.

＋◊✦◯ ⚔ ◯✦◊＋

Sierra's parents went to Grace first, rushing before the sun rose so they would not be seen going to beg. Sierra was not allowed to attend. Not the youngest Reed, the disgrace of the most important family in the territory. Not the girl who had failed so terribly.

But Grace refused to help. She would not interfere in their problems.

And, to Sierra's dismay, as soon as the sun rose she once again became the swan. Disgusted by the bird they saw, her parents cast her out of the manor and forced her to wait outside, swimming in the nearby canals, until she turned human again.

When she did, at the fall of night, she knocked on the manor's door, sopping wet and fighting tears. This time the transformation had been easier, but with the deep shame in her heart, she almost hadn't wanted to turn back.

Her father threw open the door and she stumbled backwards. She had no idea what to say or do. So she stood there gaping, waiting for him to start.

Her mother appeared next to him. Fire glowed inside the house, illuminating them from behind. 'You are not welcome here anymore,' she said. 'Leave.'

'What?' Sierra nearly reached forward; she longed so terribly for the manor's warmth.

'She said that you aren't welcome,' warned her father. 'Do not return until you find a way to fix the curse. Don't come back until your sisters are human. We would rather people think you've all been taken for ransom than let anyone realise *this*.' He gestured in Sierra's direction. 'I won't have a cursed, broken girl in my household. Not when we never wanted you in the first place.'

'If you come back without a cure,' her mother added softly but venomously, 'you will wish you hadn't.'

Sierra had not cried in front of her parents in many years, but with nothing left to lose, she let her tears flow. They were so hot on her cheeks that they burned her eyes. Why was crying such a fiery pain? 'You're . . . banishing me?'

Her father lifted a fist. 'Must I make myself clearer?'

'But—'

He grimaced at her, stepping back into the manor as he waved away an approaching servant. 'They say that the kiss of a royal – a kiss of love – can break a curse. Find yourself a prince, Sierra, and if he kisses Irene, the curse *might* be lifted for you all. Though I would not count on it.'

Sierra reached for her father, fell to her knees to beg. 'I don't know how—'

Her mother slammed the door in her face.

CHAPTER ONE

The jungle is bearable this time of year. Warm, but not stifling. The trees are thick and green, and the sounds of life are clear and crisp in my ears. I fly high above the canopy, dipping occasionally to keep sight of the river I know he'll be following.

One pirate ship. One captain. One curse that only he can break. And I know where he is. I *always* know where he is.

But finally, it's time to strike. I have not failed many times in my life, and I do not intend to fail ever again.

Weeks ago, I was given three blessings: a blessing of Strength from Rhiannon, a blessing of Justice from Grace, and the ability to transform into a black swan at will, even if my curse is not yet broken. The latter came from a boy called Teddy – another person I intend to strangle as soon as I get the chance. And I will.

Right now, I have the most power I've ever had. I'm going to use it.

My wings expand as I soar through the skies of Rhiannon's Territory, tracking my target: the *Neptune*. The pirate ship glides through a stretch of river so wide it isn't covered by the canopy of trees. Its tall sails wave in the hot air and the deep, dark-wooden hull creates a heavy wake in the river. With my sharp bird's eyes, I can see all six pirates on the deck. The *Neptune* isn't large – my family owns much larger and more stunning vessels – but this one pilots itself with magic, cruising along without the inhabitants needing to put in any effort.

Typical pirates.

Something *whooshes* right by my head and I tumble.

Fairies, was that an arrow? I regain my balance and widen my wings before I hit the water, then take the wind upwards again.

Another arrow shoots straight for my heart. I beat my wings and rise just in time for it to sail beneath me.

So the pirates have spotted me. But they've never attacked me as the swan before. I've watched them many times without them realising who I am, or at least not seeming to care – what's changed? Why are they already attacking, when they don't know I'm planning to attack *them*?

Sinister excitement flows through my veins. Why do they think they have a *chance*?

I spin away from another arrow and continue towards the ship, my neck outstretched, wings pulled in. I swing left and right, up and down, to hinder the archer's aim. The arrows are enchanted; I can feel the magic. It ripples against my feathers like sparks on the breeze.

Magic is rarely enough to stop a Reed – *rarely*.

The captain's magic must be weakened by now. Even with his five crew members, I can defeat him. But, unfortunately, killing them is not my plan. Yet. If I'm going to fix the curse, its creator must reverse it. Which means I'm taking over the ship, forcing the pirates to accompany me to Grace's Territory, and having them fix my sisters.

Simple.

When I've almost reached the back of the deck, swerving past another spray of arrows, I turn human and roll onto the wood in a smooth landing. It takes a second for my mind to clear – for me to accustom to my different body and senses, to the black fighting outfit that clings to my skin, the scratches the deck leaves on my knuckles – but I don't have the luxury of time.

They're already on top of me.

The big one grabs my arm, tries to pin me down, but I pull myself out of his grip and slide underneath him. The small one prepares her knives, ready to slash at me like she did a year ago – *fairies*, she's improved; I can sense her confidence – and this time I don't underestimate her. To combat her nimbleness, I use Strength to hit her wrists and weaken them enough that the knives drop. I pick one up from the ground and point it at the next pirate who tries to attack; she has the arched nose and medium-brown skin of an Amoran, with a heavy sword at her side.

I swallow at the sight of the weapon. It glimmers with magic. Everything these pirates have teems with enchantment. She swings the sword, then narrows her eyes, seeming to think better of it. I'm distracted for a second as the weapon transforms into a smaller knife, like the one I'm holding.

She lunges at me but I step aside and let her fall onto the big one. The small one glares at me, angry and calculating. When the big one and the Amoran stand, the three circle me.

I try to track the six pirates. Where's the archer? The captain? There's a second Musan, too, one that looks like the older brother of the young girl. Still, the only real threat seems to be the Amoran. She has training – real training – the others are only masquerading as warriors.

An arrow misses me by a splinter. I gasp and step to the side. My heart is racing, but I grin. Now it's getting interesting. *Fairies*, I've been waiting a long time for this.

Please, at least let this be slightly *challenging, or it won't even feel worth it.*

The big pirate jumps as the arrow I dodged sails past him, and I use the distraction to kick him in the chest. He falls with a thud, his pale face reddening.

With a sigh, I remember that although I so desperately want to, I can't murder anyone today. *Ugh.* 'All of you calm down,' I order, pulling back my small knife. 'I'm not here to hurt you.' They glare back at me in disbelief. 'Okay,' I add with a sneer, 'I'm not here to *kill* any of you. Yet.'

The little one comes at me anyway, but I block her with a punch to the chest. She reels and steadies herself on the big one.

I finish, 'I've come to demand that you right the wrong you brought upon my family. You will travel to Grace's Capital with me, bring your magic, and break the cygnus curse.'

It kills me to say it, to ask them for help – it's absolutely foul, really; why can't I just murder them already? – but I can't maim them beyond capacity if I need them.

There's a laugh behind me, and I turn to see the captain, finally revealing himself. He has dark hair and eyes like me, a sharp face, and I wonder if he grew up in Grace's Territory. If he did, despite appearing my age, I never knew him. 'The princess of Grace's Waters has finally come for her revenge, has she?' His lips curl into a violent smile.

I hold the knife in his direction and raise a brow.

He swings a pretty sword – stolen, no doubt, though it's the perfect size for him. He stands lazily, boredly, an irritating reflection of the nonchalance *I* work hard to maintain. 'Go on, then. Do your worst.'

I growl. 'I *will* have my revenge. But not before you turn my sisters back.'

'Unlikely.' He squints into the sunlight, wiping sweat from his forehead, and leans against the barrier that surrounds the *Neptune's* deck. His white button-down billows in the breeze like the sails; it's a nicer, cleaner shirt than I'd have expected on someone of his sort. 'Your family terrorised Grace's Territory for long enough, and I did the world a favour by stopping them.'

'Terrorised!' I laugh humourlessly. 'You would say such a thing, wouldn't you? We *protected* the territory from filth like you. And we will again once you use your stolen magic to break the curse.'

The big one snickers, his skin nearly as white as his teeth – which aren't as cracked and rotten as I'd have expected. I've been watching these people for a long time, but up close, they aren't the disgusting creatures I imagined. 'Great idea,' he says, 'but to do that, we'd still need to *have* the stolen magic.'

My muscles tense. 'You'd need to . . . excuse me?'

'Ah, well,' he says, staring me down, 'our brave, fearless, valiant captain lost it.' He's still laughing, and I resist the instinct to punch the wind from his chest. 'It was stolen from us several weeks ago. You'll likely never find it now.'

'How dare you— You can't mean—' I shake my head and push back the urge to vomit. And the urge to break someone's arm. 'Do not lie to me. Do not presume to trick me so I'll leave you alone. I am not stupid. And, and . . .'

'It's true,' says the Amoran girl. 'It was our captain's fault.'

'I don't care whose *fault* it was.' I slam my palms on the wooden railing. 'You're supposed to break the curse!'

'But it *was* Arden's fault,' says the archer.

'Enough,' orders the captain, his cheeks turning rosy. He attempts to hide his embarrassment by sneering at me, but there's a sudden youthfulness I see in him now he's been unmasked by his own crew. 'Could we not point fingers in front of the enemy?'

I take another note of the pirates' locations. The captain is in front of me, with the big white one and the Amoran fighter by his side, and the small red-haired girl behind the Amoran. The archer is above, poised at the mast, waiting for a signal to shoot. The sixth pirate, the young girl's older brother, appears on the far side of the deck, with only a small sword at his side. He holds it with a wobbly timidity. They all stare at their captain with anticipation and, it seems, impatience.

As if he knows they're punishing him, the captain rolls his black eyes. 'Fine. It was my fault we lost the magic. But we don't need it anymore. Now we can finally sail Grace's Waters without being attacked by Reeds, everyone's better off.'

'You truly believe you've won?' I say quietly, stepping towards him with my shoulders back and chin high. 'In the last year, all you have done is steal scraps, just like always.'

'I don't need to explain myself to you.' He moves the hilt of his sword into his other hand. Is he scheming how he might take me down? How hilarious. 'Poor Princess Sierra, the lonely Reed our curse didn't quite take to. It took us a long time to realise the black swan following us was *you*. A Reed who could still turn human. You are more than an inconvenience to us. But you're used to that, aren't you? I've seen how your family hates—'

'Are you attempting to distract me? Anger me?' I spit my words without letting my voice falter, not letting the sting show. 'It isn't working.'

'Okay,' he says, crossing his arms. 'No more games, no manipulation. Let's do business. We can't beat you, and you can't kill us. I've been waiting for your return, Sierra Reed. How can we resolve this so we never, ever have to see you again?'

I run a finger down the cool metal of the girl's knife, still clutched in my hand. 'Considering that you can't help me, I would love to kill you without delaying any longer.' I glance at the girl, making the pirates shift. 'All of you.'

Her brother steps towards us. 'Are you so certain you could kill us all?' The red-haired Musan isn't a fighter, but I won't make the mistake of underestimating him – Musans are adept at using their words as weapons. 'It's six against one, Sierra.'

I flinch at the use of my name, again. Like they *know* me. It's a tactic, certainly. They want to catch me off guard, show me how much they know, show me I should fear them. They may be young, but like me, I doubt they were ever children. Six pirates against one Reed aren't bad odds. They're placid now, but there are ploys behind each of their eyes. If I don't prove immediately that I'm capable of killing each one of them – *painfully* – they won't help me. *Fairies*, if they even can.

So I gamble. I spin and land behind the captain, yanking one of his arms back. My knife meets his throat and his sword drops from his grip. He grunts, but I've got him so he can't move. If any of his friends try to stop me, the knife will open his bloodstream *spectacularly*.

'This also feels like our captain's fault,' says the archer, hurrying down the mast in a flurry of skirts. She's very overdressed for pirating, but I respect it. I'm looking forward to killing her, but it is so nice when other people remember that looking good and murdering can go hand in hand.

The crew stand to attention, waiting for orders, but none move.

'How do I know you're not lying?' I wrap my leg around the captain and stand on his foot, pressing down hard with my boot to add impact. It feels *so good* to hurt him. 'How do I know you really don't have the magic?'

'If I had it, would you be winning this fight?' As he speaks, the knife nicks his skin.

I almost let the weapon slip as the truth sinks in. 'You . . .' Oh *fairies* oh *fairies* oh *fairies fairies fairies*! 'You really lost it.'

'Unfortunately,' he says slowly, deeply, so I can feel his breath on my hand, 'yes.'

I stare around the group, the six pirates, five of them glaring at me from various positions on the deck, weapons ready. 'I did not expect a slaughter today,' I snarl, 'but if you're telling me there is no way to save my family, I'll be incredibly happy to start the bloodshed right this second.'

'Wait!' says the soft Musan boy. His eyes have a strange warmth to them, and I'm reminded of Teddy, which angers me even more. 'There's still hope, if we can just find the magic.'

'Find it?' his sister argues, as if he's told her they can't have ice cream for dinner. 'It could be anywhere in the world, or already gone forever.'

'*Wren*,' he scolds her, then speaks to the captain. 'I warned you that we shouldn't cross the Reeds, but we did, and now we have to face the consequences. If we can work together and undo the curse, it could save us all.'

The captain groans in my arms. 'It took *everything* to create that curse. I'm not sorry the Reeds paid the price.' His voice lowers, making my heart rate jump. 'Sierra, what did they do to you? Kicked you out. Blamed you. Hurt you. Why would you want to save them? You have power now. You don't need anything from us.'

I twist my grip on his wrist. My stomach is at my feet, but I refuse to listen to his manipulation. 'Do you really consider yourself a hero? You ruined my family. You're going to fix it.'

The archer wanders around to face my hostage. I was already admiring her outfit, but up close I see that she's covered in expensive jewellery, and her dress is made of fine material in puffy layers of rich yellow. She's striking, her large eyes the same deep brown as her skin and set perfectly in her round face. Adellan, most likely. 'Lark is right. This is our fault. When we cursed that family, I didn't know they had any humanity to take. But look at her.' She cringes at me. 'She's hurt. We should help her.'

'You think I care about her or her family?' the captain says, and I wish I could see his face. I want to see it twisted in agony. 'They're killers! Gatekeepers to a city we should all have access to. They deserve pain! If it were them who had the magic, they would have done far worse than what we did. We didn't even take their lives. We showed mercy.'

The big one watches the scene analytically, and I realise he isn't just muscle – there's intelligence behind his eyes. These certainly aren't the sort of pirates I'm used to. 'Arden,' he says gently, 'pride is not going to help us today. If we go back to Naroport and start looking for clues to find the magic, this could all be over. No more looking over our shoulders for vengeful birds. We can break the curse, then run as far as we can before the Reeds can kill us. We'd be free again.'

I squint against the bright sun. They can't be agreeing with me, can they? I thought I'd have to best them all before they would give up. Now they're admitting they wronged me, and they're willing to help? What kind of trick is this?

'Are you all forgetting that I'm the captain?' Arden, evidently, says. I begin to place the names I've heard. Arden the captain. Lark and Wren, the brother and sister.

Wren is shaking her head. 'I haven't. We'll never find the magic. And the Reeds don't deserve our help.'

I make a show of twisting her knife against the captain's throat. A drop of warm blood rolls satisfyingly down my thumb. 'You understand that you either agree to help, or I murder you, don't you? Is your pride worth more than your lives?'

'Mine is,' Arden says coldly.

'We should vote,' says the Amoran. 'Raise a hand if you agree we should help the Reed.'

She begins to raise her hand, but Arden cuts her off. 'Vote? *I* am the *captain*!'

'Really, it's a formality,' says the sparkly Adellan archer. '*Neptune* knows we're equals.' She raises a hand, along with everyone except Arden and Wren.

The captain goes heavy in my arms, exhaling. 'The *Neptune* doesn't— *Fine*. We reroute to Naroport. But don't expect any guarantees, Reed. Even if, miraculously, we get the magic back, I don't know how to reverse what I did.' He risks shaking his head. 'This is going to be a nightmare of a quest.'

I let him go and push him to the deck. His knees scrape against the wood, and I allow myself a smile. It seems stupid, releasing my leverage, but it appears they all agree with Lark. This isn't a fight any of them want to chance. At least for now, they aren't going to try anything.

But I'll be ready if they do.

Arden stares at me, his black eyes boring into mine. It isn't just his angular face that gives him a serious look – it's the years of anger hidden in the lines of his eyes and mouth. With a wave of nausea, I wonder if we're more similar than we want to admit.

Still, I offer a confident grin. 'It's wonderful to officially meet you, *Captain*.'

CHAPTER TWO

'I'd had a bad day,' Arden explains, pacing the room. His straight black hair falls over his eyes, and he avoids everyone's gazes. His tanned arms are bare, sleeves pushed back for the hot weather of Rhiannon's Jungle. What I'd give to see the white of his shirt soaked with the red of his blood. 'We stopped in Naroport to get supplies. There was a bar . . . I'm sure I could find it again, see if anyone knows anything. I drank. A lot. After an indeterminable amount of time, I blacked out completely. I woke up on the ship the next day with no idea how I got back. Magic gone.'

My head falls into my hands, my hair streaming across my arms. I want to flick it all away in a giant fit of rage. But I steadily drawl, 'Were you hit on the head a few too many times, with all the pirating you've done over the years? Because that is the *stupidest*—'

'I'm aware,' the captain says bashfully. At least he can admit to his failures, even if he is the worst, most useless, disgraceful person ever born.

'Hm.' I lean back in my chair, at the head of the long wooden table below deck.

It's more like a small house down here than the inside of a ship. These pirates don't just use the *Neptune*, they live in it – and they aren't slumming. Having such a small crew means they can have a full kitchen and dining area, and comfortable bedrooms, while above the enchanted ship sails automatically, taking us steadily along.

The kitchen and dining space is cosy and warm, filled with candlelight and the smell of simmering sugar. The long table is made to accommodate many more crew members, and the space not taken by the pirates is covered in piles of books, jewellery, loose papers, maps, trinkets, shells, and myriad other pieces of junk.

The big pirate – Levi – nods. His pearly skin glistens even in the dim hull. The young man must be from the edges of the world to be that pale all over, even his hair white and eyes icy blue. 'We're with you, Reed. We almost booted him off the ship after that.'

'Why didn't you?' I kick my feet up on the table so they block the view of Ebony – the crooked-nosed Amoran who keeps glaring at me. She's the only one I find myself slightly threatened by. Aren't her people supposed to be all about loving and drinking?

'Because we've all made mistakes,' says Opal, the pretty, dark-skinned archer. Her tight curls are braided back from her face on either side, each braid ending in a pink ribbon.

She seems to be my age. They all do, except Levi and Ebony, who must be a couple of years older. And the little one, Wren, who can't be more than fourteen. Realising they're so young – realising they're *people* – makes it harder to utterly loathe them. How on earth did they all end up here? Where are their families?

Arden gives Opal a cynical smile, his eyes creasing at the corners. 'We didn't *need* the magic after the curse,' he says. 'More often than not, having a lot of something only makes you a target. Maybe I gave it away on purpose. We'd had it too long.'

'Excuses,' chides Levi, and I note the northern lilt in his accent. Could he be from Kara's Territory?

'Regardless, our only option is to go back to that bar.'

I nearly laugh. 'You think they'll remember you from one night, weeks ago?'

'I tend to make an impact,' he says, and Opal winks at him. I wonder if they're a couple. Ebony and Levi certainly are, but can pirates feel . . . *love?*

'Especially when he's an intoxicated clown,' says Ebony. She tosses her knife in the air and it turns into a smaller, double-edged dagger before she catches the hilt. She points it at the captain, finally shifting her scowl away from me. 'If they remember you, they'll remember kicking you out. They would have no reason to help us.'

'But it's our only lead,' Lark says, his wide Musan eyes narrowed as if in deep thought.

'Is there a way to track it?' I ask. 'That much magic stands out. It may have become weaker by now, but there would be clues, ways to find it.'

Arden's face passes through shadows made by candlelight as he paces. 'If there is a way to track it, Naroport would still be the first place to look.'

'Agreed,' says Ebony. 'Any other suggestions before the *Neptune* travels too far towards Naroport?'

'Only that we take the north route,' Opal offers. 'We've made enough enemies going the fast way. And I want to get a new dress from this little village that has the most gorgeous—'

'This isn't a shopping trip,' Arden says tiredly.

Opal frowns. 'I wasn't going to *buy* the dress.'

'This isn't a stealing trip, either.'

'Blah, blah. We should still go north.'

Levi clears his throat. 'There's also the matter of actually undoing the curse.' His big, pale arms are folded over the table. 'Finding the magic will be difficult enough, but we still have to get back to Grace's Territory and use it to fix those girls. Then we'll be in for a big fight.'

'Women,' Ebony says under her breath.

He swallows. 'Right. A big fight with those *women*.'

'A fight you won't win,' I add. I allow myself a small smile at the idea. My sisters and I, tearing the heads off these wretched pirates.

Wren crosses her thin arms. 'Then just kill us now. At least that way we don't have to undo all our hard work *and* spend weeks travelling with a bird monster.'

I scoff. '*Well*—'

'We'll take those extra weeks,' says Lark, with a reproachful look at his sister. 'That buys us time to figure out how to help Sierra without being killed. Doesn't that sound like the best idea?

Arden glances off with a despondent expression, but he doesn't disagree.

· ◊ · ○ ⚔ ○ · ◊ ·

Though I don't like the idea of leaving the pirates alone to plot against me, I fly overhead for a few hours. I need to be alone, clear my mind. See things from a wider perspective.

We're leaving the jungle I gained my Strength blessing in. A place I was supposed to return to, victorious, to show Rhiannon I'd won. Instead, I did something I'm starting to really regret: save Maya.

Save Maya? What was I thinking?

She needed the crown more than me – didn't she? Or did I only give it to her out of spite, to punish Teddy, because I knew it would hurt him more? I don't even know if Maya succeeded. I don't know what happened with Teddy's mother. Maya and Teddy might both be dead.

And what can I do about it? I could try to check on them, see if Maya is okay. But I don't have the time, and I don't care *that* much.

I breathe deeply and soar through the warm air. Rhiannon's Jungle thins as the ship sails west, the rivers narrowing until they're softer, less rapid. The air loses its thickness as the heat turns dry and searing. The plants become a softer green, and the birds start chirping instead of screeching.

Realising I've been flying a long way without rest, I dip back down to the *Neptune* and land beside Arden. He's sitting in a small spot of shade below a sail.

Although it's early evening, the sun is yet to set here, near the centre of the world. Still, the pirate captain has the dark, despondent aura of a night sky. He groans and turns away when he notices me, so I hop towards him, following his gaze to make him watch as I turn human.

When my eyes are my eyes again, we glare at each other. I get the feeling he's expecting me to leave, so I decide to stand and cross my arms, hoping my presence tortures him to the depths of his very soul.

He ignores me, though he can't hide his grinding teeth. Eventually, he says, 'I don't regret what I did to you.' He picks at a chip in the deck's wood, barely looking at me. If I weren't the only one here, I wouldn't realise he was talking to me at all. 'I've only agreed to helping you because it's what the others wanted. Sierra Reed, I hate you as much as you hate me. I'm going along with this for the sake of my family, not yours, and I won't pretend to be happy about it. That's all I have to say to you. Do with it whatever you like.'

Fairies, he's annoying. 'I don't care. Do you think *I'm* happy about this?' I sit across from him, stretching out my arms and legs, somehow stiff from flying. It's been a long day in the air, and I could use an argument to make me feel better. Arden's presence makes me thunderously furious – one of my favourite emotions. 'Do you think I enjoy dragging you along on this quest? I only have to because *you* lost the magic I need. If you weren't able to help me, you would be dead. Every second I spend near you, all I can focus on is not ripping your head off. It's exhausting.'

His lips quirk into a small smile. 'At least we feel the same in that sense.'

I huff. 'Well, I doubt there are many people in the world who could sit across from each other while plotting how to kill each other.'

'That's the problem.' He brushes a hand through his black hair, far too dramatically. 'I'm not plotting how to kill you. I can't.'

'Oh, I know you couldn't.'

'That's not what I mean. I could, I'm sure, if I truly wanted to. In fact, I do. I've been fantasising about it all day. But my crew would never forgive me.'

I lean back against a mast. 'Not much of a captain, are you? Nor is your crew much of a crew. Six of you on this boat, and everyone seems to do what they like. You don't even pilot your own ship. You just argue with each other and commit crimes. They all resent you for losing the magic. You get no respect.' I look him up and down, trying to speculate what makes him so special to his five friends. He's decent with a sword, sure. He's muscular, and he probably has a lot of experience with crime. He's good looking enough to garner attention from those who can't see past facades. Cocky, audacious, and self-obsessed enough to make it this far. But he's just some stupid *boy*. 'I have to ask, how do you all figure that *you're* the captain?'

'Because the *Neptune* is *my* ship.' He sneers at me. 'Well, it was my father's before I took it and ran. Everyone else joined me because they had to. No, we aren't much of a crew. We're a family. None of us wanted to be pirates, but we found freedom in this lifestyle. I'm sure that sounds foolish to someone like you, but it is what it is, and—'

I reply with a yawn, because he seems like he's about to tell me his life story, and I truly could not care less.

But the utterly evil pirate continues. 'Opal and I met because we were both running from bad situations. Between her charm and her skill for stealing, and my understanding of the world's trade systems, we survived – but barely. Ebony and Levi wandered in when we were so lost that I didn't think anyone would be able to help us. Then, Lark and Wren . . . Lark would have done anything to keep his sister safe, and we could offer them that safety. The six of us are everything the *Neptune* needs. Our family is balanced, just right. Perfect. Before you hijacked us, at least.'

I genuinely don't think I've ever been this bored in my life. 'Family? How sappy.'

'Like I said, you wouldn't understand. We chose freedom. We chose each other. That's why we had the brilliant idea of getting your family – our biggest threat – out of the way. But *I* ruined everything, and now my life is conveniently falling apart.'

The sun falls below the horizon, and with its loss comes a cool breeze. I bring my knees to my chest and fold my arms over them. 'You deserve it. To have your life fall apart. For what you did.'

He shakes his head, mouth open in disbelief. 'This is why I hate your family – and *you*. I'm trying to *explain*, to make you understand, but— There's something broken in all of you. Like you can't feel. I know what it's like to pretend you don't have emotions, to block them out and act fine. Yet you . . . You're incapable of a single thought that your parents didn't put in your head. You have no concept of empathy.'

I grimace. As if he knows. 'Well at least—'

A *boom* sounds in the distance – and my grimace spins into a smile. *Thank the fairies* for a way out of this conversation. 'You have enemies around here?'

'Probably.' He's already standing, and he reaches out a hand to help me up.

'Wait here,' I order, cringing at his hand. 'Tell the others to prepare for a fight. I know that sound.'

Not giving him a chance to reply, I turn into the swan and launch from the deck, wings beating powerfully. I travel up, and up, getting a good view of the river. In the near distance is a ship with a big crew. And, to my dismay, a giant blue flag flying from the mast.

I dive back down to the *Neptune*. The rest of the crew are already prepared, holding their weapons – some nervously, some with a hint of eagerness.

'It's Grace's soldiers,' I tell them breathlessly. 'Their ship is heading right towards us. They could recognise the *Neptune*. Even if they don't know what you did to my family, you're all criminals. We get caught by them, and people are going to die.'

'We can fight them,' says Wren. She's holding her knives just like Arden, copying the way he moves his hands.

'I know we can,' I say. 'But I'm not killing soldiers I've fought alongside if I don't have to.'

Arden, with half-lidded eyes, offers, 'Be ready to.'

I should've kept that *fairy's forbidden* crown.

CHAPTER THREE

SOMEWHERE, SOMETIME ...

Maya strode up and down the throne room floor, Teddy and Dawn seated patiently as she click-clacked her shoes along the marble and tried to think. The huge room, in all its moonlight and ornately carved triarue, had still not been fully repaired from the fight which occurred there weeks before.

Although the blood had been cleared – by some unfortunate maids, Maya guessed – she still felt as if she could see it sometimes, out of the corner of her eye. So, rather than let herself look at the floor, she gazed through the massive windows, trying to make out the constellations. The shape of a swan stretched through crossing stars – *Cygnus* – and Maya, reminded of Sierra, itched to be so free.

'*Please,*' she said to the princess, 'try to explain this in a way I can understand.' Maya's sharp face became darker and deadlier with every sleepless night, her ashy hair growing long and limp. Gone was the child who had escaped Bearra. She was something new now; still angry, but wiser. 'After everything, after more than a year, how can you still refuse to open Bearra?'

'I'm sorry,' Dawn replied, smoothing her saffron gown from atop her mother's throne. Golden curls bounced beneath her tiara of twisted triarue as she lightly shook her head. 'I'm aware that we can't stay hidden forever, but with no idea where Lire is, or what she's planning, we must keep ourselves protected. For now, that means keeping our people safe inside the kingdom. If that isn't enough for you, then I don't know how to make you understand.'

Maya huffed. 'With your thick castle walls and trained guards, I'm sure *you* believe we're safe here. I can't remember a time I've ever felt protected in Bearra.'

Teddy pushed back his hair, dark red in the night. Black circles ringed his eyes, which darted nervously between the two women. 'We can only do our best, Maya.'

She gave him a harsh look.

The evening was young, but Maya, Teddy and Dawn knew they would be up late as always, none of them willing to rest. There was too much to do; Bearra's problems never ended. Since the fight with Lire, the queen and king had all but disappeared. This left Dawn to act on their behalf as Bearra's leader, without the wisdom of a fairy to guide her.

Maya knew that Dawn needed to be crowned queen and find a partner to rule by her side. But she had no crown, and no one to help her. Her parents had relied on Lire alone, and any remaining influential Bearrans were too invested in their own interests to be fair advisors.

All the princess had were Teddy and Maya – a fake prince and a bookmaker – who couldn't be less qualified to help run a kingdom. Still, although she often felt that she caused more problems than she solved, Maya was glad to have something to do. Something to keep her mind off her grief, her hurt, her fears. She hadn't seen her face without bloodshot eyes since her sister's wedding.

And it didn't help that after each long night in the throne room, Maya so often found herself in Teddy's suite, where rest was the last thing on their minds.

She kicked at the floor, hoping she could either scuff her irritatingly nice shoes or the marble. 'So we sit and wait for Lire to attack? You know we have no hope against her, whether Bearra is open or not. Keeping us hidden from the world is only making us less prepared to enter it again. It's only making the people resentful. I speak from experience, Princess.'

Dawn's voice remained flat. 'Your experience as an individual does not equate to the needs of the kingdom as a whole.' Her posture didn't fall. It never did. Maya wasn't sure how it was possible. Even on their worst days, the princess's hair would stay perfectly in place, her bronze skin never tiring, her sweet hazel eyes never losing their gleam. But in that moment, the princess's gaze met the floor. 'There just isn't a blameless way to do this,' she said. 'All I can do is try to shield everyone. If they resent me for it, I can't blame them. If *you* resent me for it, I can't blame you. It doesn't change my mind. We've not only been left without a fairy to protect us, we're under attack from her. As soon as those outside Bearra find out, they are going to come for us too.'

Teddy nodded, tapping his foot. Maya could tell he was trying to look collected, but his shoulders were always tight, and he was constantly jittery. Half his shirts – *princely* silk shirts that could buy a Bearran family's meals for a week – were falling apart at the seams from his incessant picking and pulling.

If the stress of leading Bearra wasn't enough, he still felt guilty about what happened with his mother. With the crown.

And Maya was still working on forgiving him. Truly, forgive *and* forget? How about, *people shouldn't wrong people in the first place?* Why was it her job to do the work of forgiving everyone, just to give them the chance to hurt her again? But when she looked into his warm, brown eyes each morning, the sun rose inside her, and all her distrust made way for love. She'd work on the rest later.

'We have to widen our focus,' Teddy said. 'Not just worry about holding Bearra together, but how to get its power back. The reason this kingdom survived as long as it did was because of its massive hordes of triarue. Without Lire to guard and utilise the crystal, we've lost the advantage it gave us. What we need is a new weapon.'

Like you, Maya thought. But she was well aware that Teddy wasn't a fighter, despite his power. He was pure to a fault.

Dawn replied, 'I don't have the luxury of searching for a weapon. My hold on Bearra is weak as it is. This place is quite literally crumbling around me. All I can do is control what I can and help who I can. I do not have time to think ahead.'

Maya threw her hands in the air. 'Then what do we do? How can we make this better? If we could just get your parents back, they could be dealing with all these petty ruling things. Then the three of us could be working on ki— *stopping* Lire.'

Dawn gave Maya an impatient but sympathetic look. 'You know more than anyone that my parents aren't capable of that. They ran this kingdom successfully only because they had Lire telling them exactly what to do. Even then, calling their rule "successful" is generous.'

A cloud passed over the moon, and the throne room darkened. Maya squinted and said, with a hint of sarcasm, 'But now we have two people who are *blessed* with *Wisdom* taking care of things. Surely between the two of you, you can think of something.'

'What we need is a new fairy,' said Teddy. 'Surely one of them—'

'Would do what?' Dawn said. 'Take Bearra for themselves the way Lire did, forcing us to wait for their inevitable betrayal? Any of the fairies would happily help us. That's part of the problem. They want our power, and we can't let it fall into the wrong hands again.'

'We don't need a fairy,' Maya said. 'What about the independent cities? Darraport? Naroport? I know there are more. And they're fine without one. They have their trade. *We* have our mines. We just need to know how to integrate into the world again. Couldn't one of the cities' leaders step in to advise us here?'

Teddy rapped the arm of the king's throne. 'I wouldn't trust them any more than the fairies. Why wouldn't they be just as corrupt? I trust power less than I trust magic.'

Dawn nodded, but all Maya could think was, *it's all the same.*

She wanted to smack someone. Not them, but someone. These late nights of scheming – and almost nothing to show for it – were wearing on them all. Maya could be curled up at home with a book, she could be painting, braiding Briar's hair, baking bread with her mother. But Maya had, despite hating the royals only weeks ago, become vital to them.

She rambled, 'There are too many threats. The fairies, the cities, the Ice Empire. Magic and thieves everywhere. People within Bearra's walls that would betray us as well. We're running out of time – we need something big. *Fast.*'

Teddy gestured Maya over to him, and when he took her hands in his, he pulled her into his lap and pressed his forehead into her back. 'We didn't go through all we did just to lose now. We'll find our way.'

Dawn watched them with a raised brow. She often found the couple's displays of affection off-putting. Maya didn't care. She'd been through enough lately that she figured she deserved as much love as she could get. She wouldn't hide that.

Teddy, however, must have sensed Dawn's discomfort, because he reached out to take Dawn's hand. Maya's heart warmed. She felt no jealousy towards their friendship; she knew they both needed it. And, although they argued, she'd also come to see the princess as a close friend. Dawn was, after all, as much a victim as anyone else – and a prisoner in her own kingdom until she could find a way to open its borders.

But when Dawn reached back to squeeze Teddy's hand, he screeched. '*Fairies!*' He snatched his arm back so fast Maya nearly jumped off him. 'You burned me!'

The princess's mouth opened in utter offense. 'I did not!'

Maya stood, considering shaking Teddy. 'What's wrong with you?'

He ignored them both. He was staring at Dawn's wrist. 'Your bracelet,' he whispered with a frown.

'I know it's pretty,' Dawn replied, 'but you can't have it.'

He eyed her seriously. '*Iron.*'

'Huh?' Maya didn't think it was a very nice bracelet. Dull and plain. Not something she would have expected to see on royalty.

The princess tilted her head. 'Yes, iron. A gift from . . . *Oh.*' Her eyes widened. 'The legends about iron harming fairies . . . they're true? And if *you're* half-fairy . . .'

Teddy's eyes turned distant, as they so often did at the mention of his magical side. 'My mother tries to keep those legends secret.' He rubbed his hand where it was burned. 'While triarue enhances magic, iron rejects it. For those of us who have a lot of magic within . . .'

'It's like poison.' Maya glanced at the window, her mind working quickly. 'So it hurts your mother, too?'

'Of course. Why do you think it's so rare? She and the other fairies made sure it was all but eradicated from the world.'

Maya resisted the urge to grin. 'Well.'

'I know what you're thinking,' said Dawn. 'You want a weapon, you want to use it to hurt her – it won't work. I can tell you with utter certainty that there is no iron in Bearra except for this bracelet.' She observed it, taking a long breath. 'Lire gave this to me. I'd forgotten, I have so much jewellery.'

'Poor princess,' Maya teased. 'It must be hard having so much—'

'To protect *her* princess from the other fairies,' said Teddy. 'If anything happened to Dawn, Lire's plans would have been ruined.'

'Yes, exactly,' said Dawn. 'But—'

'That's perfect,' said Maya, pacing once again. Something fluttered in her chest: her hatred of Lire, her instinct to do something, anything, that might hurt the fairy and protect her family. 'If Lire had enough iron to give you that bracelet, it means the fairies never entirely eradicated it. And why would they, when it's the best weapon they have against each other? If they kept their own stores of it, hidden away from the world but ready in case they ever needed it . . .' She stilled. 'We need to find what they have.'

'I don't need to remind you again that we can't leave the kingdom,' said Dawn.

Teddy cringed. 'We might not have to. I'm sure my mother has some hidden away in Bearra.'

'And if we need someone who can travel and search for it,' Maya said with a grin, glancing back at the *Cygnus* constellation, 'I know a very capable huntress.'

Chapter Four

'Grace's ships are much faster than the *Neptune*, so there's no point running. You're going to sail past, right under their noses, and hope they don't recognise you. Do *not* try anything. I'm going to fly onto their boat and listen for any useful intel.'

Arden nods, which is strange. I almost want him to disagree with me, just to have an excuse to throw insults at him. Or just throw him. Can't *anything* go right for me?

'Don't be suspicious,' Opal agrees. Her voice is low and harsh, but she gives me a mischievous smile. 'You included, Reed. If they know about you and your family, they'll suspect a lone black swan in this region.' She tucks her bow under one arm and fixes the pink ribbons securing the braids either side of her head.

Lone black swan. How did that become my classification? I tell her, 'If I'm recognised, they have no reason to fight me. If they do, I can handle them. What concerns me is being seen with you.' I gag. '*Pirates.*'

I turn to go, but Levi calls me back. He crosses his enormous arms and stares down at me. Ebony nods at his side, her enchanted sword gripped tightly. 'If we do get caught, what do we do?' she asks, and Levi adds, 'What are their weaknesses?'

'Good try.' I scoff. 'I'm not telling you the weaknesses of Grace's army.' I transform into the swan and take to the air without turning back.

Grace's ship is close, and the soldiers are milling about on top, piloting it expertly. It takes so many of them, and so much effort. How Arden and his crew got the magic to enchant their entire ship – and have the magic not fade over time – makes no sense to me.

Based on my knowledge of the small crew, I'm not convinced they would know how to run the ship if it *weren't* enchanted. Arden said the *Neptune* was his father's . . . so was it already magical when he stole it?

I perch at the top of Grace's ship's foremast, trying to stay discreet, but a couple of soldiers have already spotted me. There are at least twenty of them on board, with a captain dressed in all-blue standing at the wheel. The vessel itself is painted the colour of a clear sky. Good camouflage on Grace's Waters, but as obvious as a flag anywhere else.

I strain my ears and stretch out my neck, but although my swan hearing is strong, it's difficult to make out any words. Since Teddy – ugh, *Teddy* – changed my curse, my experience as the swan has been different, as if my two halves are more separated than before. In this form it's more difficult to think, to remember my human body, to avoid animal instincts. When I listen to human speech, it takes all of my concentration to understand it. And every day it gets worse.

I think of my sisters, all their humanity lost . . . How close am I to becoming like them? What if one day I turn into the swan and I forget who I am, never to turn back?

Fortunately for me, these soldiers are loud and expressive. Gracians are usually reserved, but the military receives all kinds of perplexing, power-hungry creatures that act larger than they are.

'. . . to bring back good news,' a soldier near the captain says. Like many of the others, his uniform is white and stainless, perfectly pressed. 'If we cannot form an alliance with Rhiannon, we'll be punished. I can't go back to scrubbing out lavatories.'

The captain stands boredly by the wheel at the quarter deck. 'Yes, yes. You don't have to tell me how dire the situation is. But I'm not concerned about failing. Rhiannon is much closer to the Ice Empire than we are – she needs an ally against them more than we do.'

'What of Lire's army?' The soldier brushes his hair from his face as it blows in the wind. 'Rumours say she's looking in unusual places for soldiers. Strange allies, strange magic. Violent, ancient things. No one knows the state of Bearra. And who knows what Kara is doing in the north? Surely preparing for her sister's attack. I wouldn't be surprised if, while Lire's supposedly making all these moves, the dark fairy is securing an alliance with the Ice Empire.'

'Kara couldn't do that. The empire wants to eradicate every fairy and replace them with their own. Candace may not really be a fairy, but word has it she's getting there. And her daughter, General Isla, is a military prodigy.'

'But with the prince returned, circumstances have changed.'

I crane my neck. The empire's prince returned . . . Maybe it's the confusion of my swan brain, or the confusion of my own emotions regarding Prince Zeus, but I can't decide if that's good or bad news.

'Everyone is becoming desperate,' says the captain. 'Alliances are being made that ten years ago would've seemed ludicrous. No one thought Bearra would be back, at least in our lifetimes. If all we can do is our best to protect our home, then that is what we must do.'

'And if it's futile? If the fairy war becomes so terrible that there's no one left once it's over?'

'Then at least we tried.'

Their conversation drones off. Or, I just don't understand it, busy trying to make sense of what I've heard. Lire building an army, the possibility of Kara siding with the Ice Empire, Grace trying to make her own alliances.

What has the world come to?

However . . . I'm in a unique position of knowledge. With my connections across the world, I know more about the war, and the politics and people behind it, than almost anyone. I'm one of few who knows the truth about Lire, about Teddy and his brother, and Bearra's conspiracy. I have Rhiannon's blessing, and Grace's. Soon I'll have my family back, with all the most powerful people in our territory on my side. *And* I happen to know the infamous Ice Empire prince, since I'm the reason he went missing for a year in the first place.

I've always been powerful, but I can use my knowledge to make a real difference in the oncoming war. Just the thought of it makes my heart race with excitement. Unfortunately, before I can save the world, I have to break my curse.

'Ship ahead!' a soldier calls. 'Watch for pirates!'

'Pirates up this way?' Another soldier offers a snarky laugh. 'Doubt it.'

As we round a bend, I expect to see Arden's ship speeding by – headed in the opposite direction. But instead, through the bright sun, I see the still silhouette of the pirate ship sitting anchored in the river.

Are they trying to get themselves killed?

We approach fast, but . . . the pirates aren't even on the deck. They're hiding in plain sight. Pretending not to be home. *Fairies.* I suppose it's a better idea than acting as if they're sailing their obviously enchanted ship. If Grace's soldiers notice the magic, it'll be a dead giveaway.

Grace's ship sails right past, with only a few strange looks in the *Neptune's* direction. The soldiers must figure that someone left it there to visit a nearby village. It can't be a threat, because who would be stupid enough to leave their boat all alone?

My muscles relax, my wings falling. We're going to be fine. The pirates haven't been caught; I still have my chance to save my family. We're rounding the next corner, safe. I'll just stay a moment longer to make sure they're far ahead before the pirates move again.

One of the soldiers takes a last look at Arden's abandoned ship. 'Hold on,' he says. 'That looks familiar. Anyone else think that ship looks familiar?'

Oh, no.

The captain stares down his nose at the soldier below. 'Let's not waste our time.'

'No – no, I *do* know it. I've dealt with those pirates enough times to know their ship! Rumour has it they had something to do with the Reed sisters' disappearance!'

'Then we'll tell the Reeds we spotted the ship upon our *successful* arrival home.'

'And if the Reeds have our heads for not looking into it?'

The captain grunts. 'Fine. Make it quick.'

I hold in a squawk as the ship lurches to the left, readying to turn in the river.

After some wobbly manoeuvring, Grace's ship stops right next to Arden's, and soldiers begin tentatively hopping over. I find a spot to perch on the *Neptune,* watching them. Could it be that Arden's crew are good enough at hiding that they won't get caught?

For a moment I'm relieved at the idea. Relieved for *pirates?*

Then Opal appears out of the shadows and sends an arrow straight into a soldier's shoulder. Ebony jumps up beside her, her enchanted weapon also in bow form as she notches an arrow and fires at a soldier hopping ships. He tumbles into the river as it hits him in the leg.

Fairies. Of course this couldn't have been easy. Of course the pirates wouldn't turn down a fight.

One by one, the rest of them appear. Arden with his knives; Wren with hers; Lark with a sword; and Levi with his bare fists. If they still had magic, this fight would be easy. But they don't, because they *lost it.*

What are they planning, exactly? They might win with some luck, but how much damage will they cause?

I hate pirates.

So much.

The soldiers, far outnumbering the pirates, whip into action. Chaos breaks loose as weapons are slashed and punches are thrown. Shouting and screaming grates on my ears, but I stay in place. I can't get involved without revealing I'm working with Arden, and if these soldiers tell that news to my parents . . .

No. I watch from above, knowing the pirates will manage. I've fought them enough times to know I'm one of the few people they lose against. Besides, if they get maimed a little, what do I care?

Wren cries out, her voice so pained I recognise her terror even as the swan. My eyes dart to her and fear burns my gut as two soldiers pin her to the floor, throwing her knives to the side. Her friends are desperately trying to break out of their own fights and help, but they're too busy.

If I could sigh in this form, I would. *Fairies.* I can't just let her die. Can I?

Ugh. No, I need to help.

I spread my wings, knowing I'm going to regret this, and wondering why I'm even doing this. Because my emotions are so off as the swan? Because my Justice blessing wants me to save innocent lives? The little pirate is only a child. Someone I'm supposed to protect. I can't help the pull I feel to help her.

She screams again, and I swoop down to her, animal instincts taking over. I turn human just in time to kick one of the soldiers in the face, hard enough to knock her out and probably break her nose. She falls with a thud and I manage to land on my feet. The other soldier is too stunned to even attempt to attack me, so I promptly pound him to the ground with a punch to the stomach.

Wren scurries away, already launching herself at another soldier without stopping to thank me. Smart girl.

'Sierra Reed?' a voice says from behind me as I stand there, chest heaving. The soldier has a frown on his pale face. I recognise him – we've fought together.

Fairies, indeed.

Before I can reply, come up with an excuse, or simply hurt him, he lurches forward and falls on his face. Arden stands in his place, rolling back on his feet as he rebalances from the hard kick he gave the soldier. Arden grins as he sees Wren, just fine, then he gives me a soft look that almost, *almost* says 'thank you, and you're welcome'.

Without time for a breath, the fight returns to us.

'Retreat!' I yell at Grace's people as they come for me one by one, only to get thrown to the deck. 'You won't win! Not against me!'

Of course, they don't listen.

So I fight with the pirates. Me. With them. Together.

Disgusting.

I switch between swan and human as I take each soldier that comes my way – while trying my best to keep my fighting non-lethal. As much as I love a good kill, Gracians are the people I fight for, not against.

Arden isn't so generous. He slashes his knives around, seriously wounding some of the soldiers. As he swings, his blood-drenched shirt billows, and I— *Oh.* I absolutely *don't* look at the tanned muscles that glow beneath. *Fairies.* Not even a little.

Still, no kills. Wren copies her captain, fighting strong but not disfiguring anyone beyond repair. The three of us fight together as a team, and the soldiers slowly drop around us.

When I get a chance to scan for the others, I see Ebony and Levi have jumped onto Grace's ship. Back-to-back, they face the soldiers as a deadly pair. The soldiers on the *Neptune* who can still move crawl back to their own ship, and Ebony and Levi give a final beating to any that aren't yet battered enough.

Levi knocks one of them down with a single punch, and with his height, none are able to topple or restrain him. Ebony, meanwhile, weaves between the soldiers with the agility of a dragonfly, her weapon changing in her hands to whatever will best defeat her opponent – and she uses each weapon with absolute expertise.

I loathe the Amoran girl, and I doubt she would even pay me enough attention to loathe me back, but I think she might be my favourite person. Of all time. She's ethereal.

The pirates work together seamlessly the way my sisters do, but it's different. Rather than keep me out of their circle, they invite me in. We've known each other less than a day, and they're already watching my back. I don't have to fear any small mistakes on my part – not that I *ever* make mistakes – because I'm not alone.

It's working. We've nearly won.

But the Gracian captain refuses to surrender. He grabs at Opal, trying to steal her bow. She struggles against him. Lark scrambles to help, his red hair flying as he swings his sword more assuredly than I expected of the quiet young man, but the enemy captain easily pushes him away.

I scream in the face of the soldier I'm fighting and, in her moment of distraction, become the swan and fly to Opal and Lark. I peck at the captain's face until he lets Opal go, then I turn human again and tackle him down.

I get on top of him, pinning his arms at his sides. 'Retreat!'

'Sierra Reed,' he spits. 'Of course you're here, with *them*. Your parents were right about you.'

I exhale deeply, fighting not to lose my temper. Or worse, embarrass my family even more. I have too much adrenaline to feel the burning shame yet, but I know it'll come. 'Give. Up.'

He goes still. He may think little of me, but now he's certain I'm against him, he knows surrendering is his best move. No one wins against a Reed. 'Very well,' he says quietly. 'But next time you or your pirates are in our waters, you'll pay with your lives. Especially after what they did to your sisters.'

I dig my nails into his skin. 'Yet I am the only Reed still standing,' I heave. 'The *only* reason I'm sparing you is to honour our alliance under Grace. I expect you to run, Captain, and keep my family's name out of your mouth.'

He sneers. 'Whatever you demand, black swan.'

It's against every instinct within me, but I let him go. He shouts to his soldiers to retreat. I tilt my head back, wiping sweat from my brow. Mercy. I showed mercy. That's good, isn't it? My parents, my fairy, my people would be proud.

I slump on the deck and catch my breath. It's over. We won. And I feel *good*.

The soldiers start meandering back to their hulking ship, hunched solemnly. Some are still scrambling to their feet, but at least they're alive. We got through this. We all did. This wasn't nearly as bad as it could've been.

I sigh in relief.

And then, Opal sends an arrow directly into the captain's heart.

CHAPTER FIVE

The soldiers promptly and shamefully remove their wounded from our ship, their faces in numb shock as they carry away their captain, who just finished bleeding out on the deck. Although we won, it takes a while for the fight to truly be over, and even once the Gracian ship is far behind us, the *Neptune* and its crew are still splattered with blood.

Fairies, I know this will get back to my parents. I've lost any hope of ever gaining their acceptance. A captain of Grace's army, murdered by me. At least that's how it'll seem.

Why am I so shocked at Opal? I could have killed him. I want to kill her. I'm shaken, and I don't like it. It was a mistake to jump into that fight. The pirates might have won without me.

Now, even saving my sisters might not be enough to gain my family's favour.

The *Neptune* unanchors itself and sets sail as we descend to the kitchen to lick our wounds. As always, all I have to do is transform and my body renews. The others will suffer, though, at least for a few days.

Levi has a significant gash on his thigh, and his knuckles are scraped raw. Wren has bruises all up her arms.

They'll be fine. But some of those soldiers won't. The pirates made sure of that. They may have the faces of teenagers, masked with innocent youth, but they're bad to the core. I can't let myself forget that. If I hadn't risked so much to rescue Wren, the captain of Grace's ship might still be alive.

'Are they going to come after us?' Ebony asks, and it takes me a few moments to realise the question is pointed at me.

We quietly eat pasta with plain cheese and fried crab, which Lark cooked up far too quickly, especially considering he's as injured as everyone else.

Is the kitchen magical, too? Or is he just that good? If he's been taking care of Wren for as long as I assume he has, he must be well used to taking on parental roles like cooking quickly and effectively.

I force myself to straighten my back and look Ebony in the eyes, pulling myself from my thoughts. 'They were already after you. You just got unlucky today. It's me who's really in trouble.'

'You?' Opal fixes a ribbon that untied during the fight. '*The only Reed still standing?*'

'Yes, me. Because now those soldiers are going to tell Grace that I'm working with pirates. Pirates who killed a captain of her army. And she'll tell my parents. If it's possible to be banished twice, consider me banned from returning home for two lifetimes.'

Arden watches the ceiling with disinterest. His right eye is purple and swollen. 'Don't be so dramatic. They'll forgive you when we break the curse.'

'Oh, you wouldn't understand,' I snap at him. 'You don't have a family. You don't have a reputation, or responsibility, or—'

'The family I *have* wouldn't reject me for trying to help them.'

'We didn't even kick him out for losing the magic,' adds Levi.

I lean over the table, shaking my head. When I talk, I can't meet their eyes. I don't know why. 'You are so naive,' I say, as firmly as I can. 'Love and affection? Forgiveness and gratitude? Those aren't *family*. They are friendship. Blood is duty. You don't have the luxury of choosing your family, and you do not have the luxury of expecting them to love you.'

Wren stares at me through a judging cringe, scratching the table with a knife. 'If Lark hadn't chosen this family for us, we'd have nothing else. Anything is a choice if you *choose*.'

'How *beautiful*.' I ready a new speech, but something touches my leg and I leap out of my seat. '*Fairies!*'

Opal bursts into laughter. 'Junie!' She crouches to touch a small black cat, its bright green eyes narrowing as the girl pats its head. 'She's finally come to say hello. June, meet Sierra. She's a bird, but please don't chase her.'

'Why . . .' I stutter. 'How . . . How on earth do you keep a cat on a ship?'

Opal shrugs, smiling, and scratches June between her fluffy ears. 'We don't *keep* her. We found her under a bed one day, started feeding her, and that was that. In exchange for food and cuddles, she keeps rats off the ship. Sometimes she disappears for a few days, a few weeks, but she always comes back. Between the rocking of the ship and the sunny spots on the deck – and all the fish, of course – this ship is a cat paradise.'

'And when you're fighting?'

'She goes for a nap down here,' says Wren. 'But she does have sharp claws . . . Could we use that somehow? Arden—'

'Let's get back on topic,' he says, though even he spares a moment to give the cat a loving glance and make kissing sounds. Catching my eye, he clears his throat. 'Sierra needs a place to sleep. We don't have any spare rooms, and I doubt anyone wants to volunteer to share. Opal and I are the only ones not already doubled-up. I certainly don't want Sierra in my room. But Opal could stay with me, and Sierra could have her room?'

Opal's teeth and eyes glow in the candlelight as she grins at me. 'Oh, I'll share with Sierra. That way I can keep an eye on her, and we can stay up late gossiping and giving each other makeovers.'

No. Oh, *fairies*, no.

'Poor Sierra,' mumbles Ebony.

'It's a *joke*,' says Opal. 'Mostly. Sierra can have the hammock I use for my coats, and I won't disturb her unless she asks for it.'

I should demand better – I could take every room and force them all to sleep on the deck – but I slump in my chair and give in.

When did I become so soft? I should kill one of them tomorrow. That'll make me feel better.

Opal's tiny room is painted bright pink, and her things are thrown everywhere. There are several hammocks, because the cabin is meant to house many more people. It would, if the ship wasn't enchanted to run itself. But because the crew is so small, they've managed to divvy up the space quite comfortably.

The way these people are living is . . . impossible, and almost *nice*.

The temperature down here is pleasantly cool, and I wonder if that's another perk of the ship's magic. It sways ever so gently, a soft lull that I'm sure will send me to sleep instantly. I've always been able to dream best on rocking water.

Opal heaps blankets and pillows onto my hammock after pulling the piles of clothes off. 'That should do,' she says, patting it.

I hop into the hammock and let myself sink into the plush covers. If there's one thing I already know for certain about Opal, it's that she *only* does luxury. I nearly nod off right away, but she clears her throat. I prop myself up to face her. 'Mmh?'

'You know,' she says, 'I have a complicated relationship with my family, too.'

'Okay. Thanks for sharing.' I move to go back to sleep.

'Family's a strange thing,' she continues, undeterred. 'It should be impossible to both love and hate people at the same time. To be so connected and so disconnected, to want to run and hide from a person while wanting their attention. To have someone know you better than anyone else, while also not really knowing your true self at all.'

I sit up, narrowing my eyes. 'I didn't know anyone else felt that way.'

'Of course they do. I didn't run away from home to be a pirate for no reason. I had to get away. But everyone feels that way a little.'

Hm. Not Maya. She risked everything out of love for her family, to keep them together. Is she the outlier, or are we?

'Maybe you'll find you don't mind our lifestyle so much.' Opal tucks the coats from my hammock into a drawer. 'I already like you, and I have a feeling you'll be with us a while— Oh, don't look at me like that. We're going to be best friends, and it's stupid to waste time denying it. The others will come around too. Even Arden. Our family isn't full, Sierra, and your sisters aren't worth saving. Instead of chasing them, you could be one of us. In fact, I know you will.'

Hot anger swells in me. How could she be so presumptuous, so condescending? But I'm too tired to bother arguing, so I change the subject. 'Why did you leave your family?'

She slumps into her hammock, almost disappearing amongst her soft blankets. She stares at the ceiling, the candlelight bouncing off her round, dark face. 'I'm from Adella's Territory,' she says, clearly more than happy to talk about herself again, 'where everyone is more concerned with selflessness, with giving, than *anything* else. Where nothing is really your own. Everyone there is painfully nice.' She scrunches her face. 'My own family thought me a narcissist. Maybe I am. I don't like to give, I like to *take.* I like things to be my own. I like to hold emotions within myself that are real – anger, jealousy, longing . . . In Adella's Territory, you can't be that way. But I couldn't change who I was.'

She wraps the tassels of her knitted blanket through her fingers. 'So I left, and I found Arden – another lost runaway. I knew I had to take my chance with him. Now I don't have to compromise, to share. We don't pretend to like each other because of our blood, and we aren't bound together because we have no choice. Think I'm crazy, if you like, but life's better when you stop trying to fit someone else's mould.'

Sure. She wants my sympathy, she wants to change my views because of her oh-so-inspiring life story, but who does she think she is? Opal is a pirate. She's the *enemy*. 'Oh,' I reply.

'I've created my own happiness, Sierra, while you keep fighting for approval you will never, ever get.'

I grind my teeth. 'Good night, Opal.'

• ◊ʼ◯ ⚔ ◯ʼ◊ •

Opal is swishing blush across her cheeks when I wake. I shifted into the swan in my sleep, and I squirm under the blankets drowning me, my neck and wings caught beneath layers of fabric. Opal says something, but I don't understand her. I force myself back into my human body once I feel secure, but still nearly rock myself off the hammock.

Opal snickers. 'I was quite shocked to wake up to the smell of bird in my room. Luckily for me, there wasn't a loose animal – it was just you having dreams about killing me.'

'I'd never dream about that,' I grumble, shaking my head as if it'll help with the disorientation. 'It would ruin the real thing.'

'Well, when you weren't the bird, you were talking in your sleep about murdering *someone*.'

She pouts as she applies a layer of pink lipstick. It's pretty; I'll have to ask her where she steals it from. 'Lark will have made breakfast by now,' she says. 'Which means Arden will want to have a meeting soon. You should go and eat.'

I nod, my stomach rumbling. Usually if I eat as the swan – which is far easier, since I can munch on water grasses and insects – my human body stays full enough. It doesn't make sense, but it's convenient. I can travel far without having to pack supplies. Still, I'll always prefer a tasty human meal, and this morning I'm ravenous for the sweet scent wafting from the kitchen.

I hop out of the hammock, rubbing my eyes and running my fingers through my hair, and make my way to the open area that serves as the kitchen, dining room, and general meeting space. Lark is frying something over a small fire that does not look very safe – again, the magic of this ship is the only thing holding it together – and I take the head seat at the dining table. Arden and Ebony are already strategising, heads bent over an old, torn map.

'I'm concerned about not knowing what to do with the magic,' Arden says, speaking to me without looking at me. He's wearing another billowing button-down shirt. How are his shirts always billowing? We're *inside*. This one is navy, matching the dark circles below his eyes. *Wow*, he's so *beautiful* and *tortured*. 'Even if we get it, which is still highly unlikely, I don't know how to turn a group of swans into women. Can magic like this simply be reversed? The curse may have burned out all the humanity the Reed girls had. Not that they had any. Now there could be no souls left within them to bring back. None of us know enough about magic to do this safely.'

I shudder at the thought of turning them back just to be . . . *empty*. What would that make them? Less than ghosts?

Ebony's hard eyes meet mine. 'We aren't trying to stall you,' she says, 'but we can't go on without knowing the damage we could cause.'

'What we need,' Lark calls over the sizzling of his cooking, 'is to talk to someone who actually knows about magic. We need advice.'

'Change course,' I say. A smile creeps onto my face as an idea forms. 'We're going to Bearra. Someone there, if he's alive, owes me a favour. If I can resist the urge to irreversibly batter him.'

Besides, I would love an excuse to see what's become of Maya.

'In Bearra?' Ebony's brows knot. 'No one knows anyone in Bearra.'

'Oh, he's not just anyone. He's half a *fairy*.'

CHAPTER SIX

SOMEWHERE, SOMETIME . . .

Sierra was in the air, so Arden was in the kitchen – always as far from her as he could possibly be. When she was close, he couldn't think. He could barely breathe. But the pirate captain, when left alone, at least had the mental space to strategise ways of destroying her.

In Arden's imagination, he was back in the night he cursed the Reeds. He recalled the high of his magic, the raw power and adrenaline within him as he took down the seven sisters who had tortured his territory for years.

The black swan, however – Sierra Reed – wasn't like her family. She was Arden's age, and there was something so much more human about her – he could see it, sense it. Still, the heart within the girl made him resent her even more, because she *could* be better. So why did she choose to be a villain?

'Salt,' Lark said airily – he was always happy when he was cooking – and Arden passed the shaker to his friend with a grumble.

Although the pirate captain couldn't tell a pot from a pan, Sierra probably couldn't either, so the kitchen was safe. Unfortunately, being here meant he had to help make dinner.

'Thank you, Captain,' Lark said, with a significant air of sarcasm. 'That is, in fact, pepper.'

Arden threw his head back and passed the *other* shaker.

He wasn't always like this. In fact, Arden very much resented the person he'd become. Especially the angry, miserable man he was around Sierra Reed. He took his friends' teasing in his stride, knowing he deserved their resentment for losing the magic. He even let Sierra throw him around a little, just to keep her attention off the others.

But he longed to be the free, happy teenager he was before the curse. Before he lost himself to power and magic. All he had ever wanted to do was protect his family. His small crew. Yet he lost his way, and continued to lose, lose, *lose.*

Arden rubbed his eyes, only to make them sting from the juice of a diced onion still on his fingers.

When would his luck turn around?

Lark whistled while Arden wrung his hands together, taking deep, calming breaths. The pirate captain had always been prone to anxiety. It had taken him years to stop jumping at every sound, flinching at any unexpected touch. In his line of work, fast reflexes served him well. But it was as if his mind was an endless loop of urgent music, drums beating and violins screeching.

Arden was cursed with a torturously strong sense of responsibility. He *had* to look after those he loved. And it was haunting. Especially since . . . since . . .

He splayed his fingers over the warmth of the stovetop.

No, now was not the time to lose himself to grief.

'So, Sierra is lovely,' said Lark, stirring the pot. Figuratively and literally. Arden glared at him. 'Sorry. But you're so quiet. It's uncomfortable. If you keep letting her get to you like this, you'll only be letting her win.'

'I'll stop being angry with her when I watch her take her last breath.'

'Then I will poison her crab.'

'She's probably immune to poison. Like a snake.'

'I don't think that's right.'

Arden looked at Lark. How was his friend so . . . unbothered? Why did none of the crew seem to care that Sierra Reed was amongst them? They wanted to roll over and let her have her way, because they saw no other option.

But if they could just hatch a real plan to get rid of her—

'Stop scheming, and get some bowls out.'

'Okay, *mother*.'

Arden set the table, muttering techniques for murder under his breath. He was no killer, but when it came to the Reeds . . . He didn't want to take Sierra's life, but since she was always threatening to kill and torture him and his crew, what choice did he have?

The others wanted to act friendly and change Sierra's mind. *Befriend* her. For the crew's sake, Arden would try as well, but he didn't have much hope. His friends weren't from Grace's Territory. Their hatred of the Reeds stemmed from his, and from the trouble they'd caused in Grace's Waters, but Sierra and Arden's hatred of each other was *territorial*.

The hairs on his arms stood up and he whipped around to catch her coming down the stairs. 'Reed,' he sneered. He could always sense her in the air, like a bad smell. It was as if some magical force repelled them from each other.

'*Captain*,' she sneered back, in her lilting, horrendously sweet-yet-raspy tone. Her hair was glossy and brushed out, reaching her waist, and she flicked it back with her long fingers. Her red lips were pouty and her cheeks were flushed from the wind on the deck. *Wow. She's so beautiful and so perfect.*

The way she filled every space she entered with her ethereally deadly energy, it was no wonder everyone fell at her feet. But not him. Never him.

Thankfully, she entered Opal's room and slammed the door shut behind her. Arden mimicked her door slam, and as if she sensed it, she poked her head back out the door to growl at him.

He rolled his eyes and she went away for good.

'Spices, please, Captain,' called Lark.

Arden reached to the cupboard. It opened on its own, and once he retrieved the pots of spice, the *Neptune* shut it again. *Fairies*, he loved living in an enchanted ship. If only it had a way to forcefully eject Sierra.

'Once we've finished with the Reeds,' said Lark musingly, adding a pinch of paprika to his dish, 'I think we should take the time to really consider where we want to go next.'

'Somewhere warm,' offered Arden.

Lark sighed. 'Not where *physically*.' His tone turned awkwardly serious. 'What we want to do. I'm thinking of Wren growing up around all this violence, and I'd like to see if we can find a way for her to get a proper education. Or at least a way for her to live her life legally and safely.'

Arden tensed as if ready to fight a horde of soldiers. 'But she hated school, and she loves being a pirate.' He knew Lark wanted what was best for everyone, but Arden wasn't only defending Wren – he didn't want Lark to get any ideas about separating this family. Surely he wouldn't send Wren away? Maybe it would be better for the girl, but Arden couldn't go on without her. She was like a sister to him. She was his family, and he didn't want to let her out of his sight. Nor Lark, or any of the others. '*Lark*. What is this?'

'Fine,' said Lark. 'I'm still right, but I'm only using Wren as an excuse. I want—' He exhaled. 'I love you, but I don't want this life. I want an education. I want to make art, and have a family. I'll follow Wren until I die, but if it were up to me . . . I know I can't be a pirate forever.'

Arden started, offended. 'But— We aren't even that bad of pirates. We just do odd jobs and mug people every now and then. We aren't going around murdering and pillaging. You can take a break! While we work, you can stay down here and read books.'

June, Arden's fluffy black cat – the crew thought the cat everyone's, but Arden knew she was his first, and he was the favourite, wasn't he? – curled around his ankles, and he let his shoulders drop.

June always calmed him down. Like an anti-Sierra. Unfortunately, she sneezed from the spices in the air and sprinted into his bedroom.

'*Junie* . . .' Arden murmured, begging her to return and distract him from this conversation.

Lark tasted from his wooden spoon, then went back to stirring gently. 'We could be so much better,' he said, and Arden could hear the heartache in his voice. His friend was hurting, and Arden wanted to help, but he couldn't help him *leave*. 'I'm not making any decisions, Arden. I'm only saying that we need to think about our futures. I'm the only one of us who ever does.'

Arden swallowed the lump in his throat. Despite popular opinion, he worried about the future all the time. The past, too. Though he was usually more concerned with the next few days, the next few seconds, and tried not to ponder about coming years. What was he going to do, plan a *career*? He wanted to be free, on his ship, with his family, *without Sierra*, and never worry about paying a tax or passing a test.

It seemed simple to him, but the world thought otherwise.

'We keep making enemies for ourselves, all over the world,' Lark added. 'And if we don't stop, one day we'll have nowhere left to run.'

But Arden loved running, and he thought his friends did too. Opal and Wren surely did. Did the others want to throw away the lives they'd built just to be . . . normal?

Maybe this new quest with Sierra wasn't such a bad thing, if it meant distracting his friends from their thoughts of leaving.

'Just think about it,' said Lark, but Arden couldn't meet his eyes. They'd always been close. Brothers, for years now. Lark was wise, and caring, and creative, and— and Arden couldn't live without him. Tears pricked at his eyes. With a smirk, his Musan friend said, 'And, *Captain*? Go call the others down for dinner.'

CHAPTER SEVEN

It takes us two days of sailing to reach Bearra, since there are certain waterways the pirates are hesitant to pass through. Two days of infuriating arguments, scheming that leads nowhere, and not a single person I get to punch in the face.

The *Neptune* pulls into the closest river system to Bearra that isn't blocked, and anchors itself. As the crew and I crowd the deck and shield our eyes from the sun, the old kingdom rises tall and foreboding in front of us.

I've never been this close before, never been able to imagine what's inside except for what I've seen in illustrations. The walls are even taller than I pictured, decaying beneath the thick vines that wrap around and through the light-coloured bricks. The vines themselves are a vibrant green seen only in Rhiannon's Territory; they're utterly out of place in the centre of the world.

This is unfamiliar territory, and my only hope is that Maya or Teddy are still alive. I can just see the top of the plain castle sticking up in the centre of the round city; if Teddy is still posing as a prince, that's where they must be.

'Reed, I'm going in with you,' Arden says. His arms are crossed, eyes squinted in the harsh sun. There's a glint of sweat on his brow – it's hotter here than the jungle, but it's a drier heat. On this side of the vines, the landscape is like a desert, unable to produce more than some rare spots of yellow grass.

I shake my head and lean over the edge of the ship to get a better look at the vines. 'Oh, will you, Captain? And how would you get in? I can fly over the walls and right into the castle without anyone batting an eye. You, on the other hand, can *not* pass for a Bearran.'

'That's offensive.'

I glare at him. 'Bearra isn't like the rest of the world. All the people there are . . . How can I say this politely? They aren't used to people who don't look like them. A small kingdom like that will be able to spot a stranger, especially a Gracian stranger.' I run my fingers down my arms, musing about how they'll soon be wings. I can't wait to be away again – if I can get this conversation over before next year. 'Our advantage – and it does not please me to say this – is the curse. I can fly in as the swan. It's a perfect disguise.'

Levi cocks his head. 'How many black swans are in Bearra? Would you not still stick out?'

I wave a dismissive hand. 'I'll be fine. Once I'm at the castle, I'll eavesdrop until I hear news about Teddy or Maya, then I'll ambush them.'

Ebony thumbs her enchanted weapon, gaping at the towering walls – almost close enough to touch if she were to lean over the ship's railing and reach out. 'This half-fairy boy beat you before. Are you certain this is safe? If just one of us went in to watch your back—'

'It would be one more person we're putting at risk. Though I'm flattered you want to protect me.'

Wren adds, 'I want to go too. I don't care about protecting you. But I want to see what's in that mysterious old kingdom.'

'Because you're such a historian,' her brother says with a laugh.

She rolls her eyes.

I force back a smile. 'You won't miss any action. I'll tell you everything. And so you don't get any ideas and run off, I can make you a promise. While I'm in there, I'll get you something worth your while.'

'Like what?' Arden asks, brow furrowed. *Had* he been thinking of running?

The water flows gently beneath us, murky and lifeless. Untouched for a century. While all is dead out here, what treasures does the woken kingdom hold?

I smirk. 'How about the most precious substance in the world, which happens to be this city's greatest fortune? I'll get you *triarue.*' With that, I transform, spread my wings, and aim for the top of the vines.

The height of them, which would strike fear in anyone without wings, makes me glad for all my practise flying over the past year. As I ascend, beating my wide wings with power that forces me against the air, I'm reminded of being shakily flown by Teddy into Grace's Fortress. My way is *far* superior.

Soon, the ship and river are in the distance, and I circle in the air to glance back at the pirates, now just small dots. I flip over to show off, then soar past a flock of tiny birds, leaving them tumbling in a wake of wind.

That's right. *Fear Sierra Reed.*

As I float across the thick vines and into Bearra, the kingdom's canals shine blindingly in the sun. Within them, boats carry people and resources through villages, and between the waterways, dirt roads are dotted with terracotta roofs. Farms sprawl through the outskirts until they touch the walls. Bearra is nothing like a city; it's a big, ancient town, with houses, shops, carriages – and of course, the hill in the centre.

I make a beeline for the hilltop castle, with its squared walls and wide windows, my neck outstretched and wings tucked in. As I approach, I can feel the magic in the air – the layers and layers of triarue built into the castle and deep within the earth. No wonder Lire closed Bearra off for a century. Who wouldn't take this power for themselves?

Yet the fairy has clearly not succeeded in her plot. I don't know what normal looks like in Bearra, and my swan senses may struggle to make out the emotions on people's faces, but this old kingdom is certainly not apocalyptic.

The castle gets closer, and I circle it for a few minutes, taking in the flat rooftop and thick, beige bricks while I scan for the best way in. Guards line every entrance. Every *human* entrance.

I finally come across an open window on one of the top floors. It leads to a bedroom that overlooks the sharp cliff face on one side of the castle's hill and across to the flat expanses of land beyond Bearra's walls. I flap in front of it, see no one inside, and squeeze through the opening. I roll onto the floor and turn human, standing up, ready to explore—

And Teddy stumbles right through the bedroom door, breathing heavily, with Maya in his grasp as he kisses her.

With a strength I didn't know he had, he presses her against the wall and she laughs in delight. He pushes her sleeve to the side and kisses her shoulder. She shudders, tucking her hair behind her ears, then slides her hands beneath his shirt. They don't even notice me standing there – which ruins my relief at seeing Maya alive, and shocks me out of my anger at Teddy.

I clear my throat and raise a brow. 'So you two made up, then?'

They jump apart with a synchronised scream. Teddy already has magic pouring over his fisted palms, that lilac purple which sends a shiver up my spine. When they realise it's me, their faces display a mix of relief, embarrassment, and fear. Are they trying to make my day? The scarlet flush on their cheeks nearly makes me cackle.

Maya tugs her shirt back into place, flipping her light-brown hair over her shoulders. Though there are dark circles around her grey eyes, she appears healthy enough. Well-fed for the first time in over a year, I imagine, if she's gotten this cosy in the castle.

Maya has always been pretty, but in the weeks since I last saw her, it's like she's grown into herself even more. She seems older. Or, maybe it's just that I walked in on her about to do something particularly *adult* with Teddy.

'You're alive,' she breathes.

'So is he.' I gesture to her red-haired prince. 'Unless you'd like me to fix that?'

Maya grins, her eyes gleaming at me. *Me*. 'It isn't that I haven't thought about it,' she says, 'but no. We have bigger problems.'

Teddy eyes me. His hair is dishevelled, and I don't like the fancy clothes he's wearing. He looks too much like the powerful man he pretends he isn't. 'Why are you here, Sierra? Did you break your curse?'

I meet his gaze. Maya told me not to kill him, but what about just a *little* bit? 'No,' I tell him, 'I haven't, thank you. Actually, I came here to—' I wince '—to ask your advice.'

'Mine?' he says, at the same time Maya mumbles, 'His?'

'Unfortunately.' I take a seat at the end of the bed and stretch my legs. They're both still gaping at me. Honestly, are people really so fragile? 'So, I found the pirate who cursed my family, but when I demanded he undo the curse, he revealed he'd lost the magic – which apparently we need. Now we have to track down the magic and steal it back, *and* work out how to undo the curse without causing harm to anyone. Myself included.'

Teddy's warm eyes line with crinkles as he frowns. 'Did you just refer to yourself and a pirate as *we*?'

I give him my deadliest glare – the one I've been reserving only for Arden. 'Will you help me or not? You owe me, fairy child.'

'I'll have to think about it.'

I turn to Maya. She really should ditch him and come on an adventure with *me*. 'Well, at least the two of you are enjoying yourselves. I wouldn't have expected that, considering everything.'

'Trust me,' she says, fixing her hair, 'being together is the *one* thing we get to enjoy. The kingdom is falling apart.'

'How awful.' I don't bother trying to sound genuine. This is already becoming boring.

Her eyes sparkle and she chews on her bottom lip, then she says, 'Actually, Sierra Reed, we were hoping we might find a way to get in touch with you, because we could use your help.'

'No.'

'We found a way we might be able to fight Lire, and since you're with pirates now . . . you might be the best person to source it.'

'Maya. *No*,' I insist. She pouts, and I groan. '*Fine*.'

They catch me up on their lives – and the dramas of their kingdom – as we amble to the throne room to find Princess Dawn. Last I heard, Maya hated her, but the three of them are apparently inseparable now. Except, of course, when Maya and Teddy are tearing each other's clothes off.

They destroyed the crown, which makes my skin prickle with irritation after everything we went through to get it. I'm mildly surprised to hear that Teddy's brother is dead, and his mother, Lire, is missing. And I'm very curious to know more about the weapon they seem to have discovered.

It's strange, walking with these two through their home as if we're friends. Well, maybe not friends, though Maya is one of the few people in the world I don't actively despise. Should I have hugged her? *Ugh*, no.

They lead me to the throne room, which is unexpectedly grand for an old, unassuming kingdom. The large windows let in pools of light, showering the room in gold and highlighting the bright blue triarue inlaid in the walls. Every decoration points to the throne at the very end and the princess atop it.

She's unmissable, maybe the most beautiful person I've ever seen. I'm tempted to turn into the swan just to get to see her from another, sharper pair of eyes. Certainly the princess is as blessed as people say. She's all gold and bronze, shining hair against brown skin, a tiara on her head, and a pink and green dress falling in swirls down her arms and legs – a dress, I note, which Opal would die for.

'Dawn,' greets Teddy as we reach her.

The nearby guards exchange uneasy glances, presumably at the casual way he addresses her. Do they know, yet, that he isn't really a prince? And worse, that he's the son of their enemy?

The princess rises and nods at Teddy, glancing at me with an expression of distrust thinly veiled by royal politeness. Teddy motions to me. 'This is Sierra Reed, of Grace's Territory. She might be able to help Bearra.'

I offer a slight bow, and the princess gestures to her guards. They filter out of the room.

Princess Dawn steps down from her throne and stops in front of me, looking me up and down through her hazel eyes. 'I've heard a lot about you, Lady Reed. I met your great-grandparents a handful of times, though the Reed name was still making a name for itself then.

I did not like them, but I had to appreciate their ferocity, and their determination to protect Grace's Territory. You look quite a lot like your great-grandmother, actually.'

I keep my face blank. 'I've been told I have her eyes. And her taste for violence.'

'I shall ask you to remember,' she says, without losing her air of politeness, 'that you have entered this kingdom illegally, and the only reason you are unguarded and not in prison is because Teddy and Maya trust you.'

'I wouldn't say trust,' Teddy says.

I glance at his hands. 'And I wouldn't say I'm unguarded.'

'Enough,' interrupts Maya. She seems small, inconspicuous in this room, with these people – but I must remember who she is and what she's capable of. 'Sierra's come to Teddy for advice, which he's going to give. But we think she may be able to return the favour.'

I sigh with boredom. 'Because apparently I have nothing better to do than *search for your weapon*. Which is . . . ?'

'Iron,' offers the princess, more frankly than I'd have expected. She must really trust Maya and Teddy to extend that trust to me so immediately. 'The metal hurts fairies and dampens magic. With enough of it, we can use it against Lire.'

'Yes, fantastic idea.' *I could be a swan right now, soaring through the air.* 'Except that's why the fairies had it all eradicated centuries ago.'

'We don't think so,' says Maya. She stalks over to the throne and sits on it cross-legged. No one bats an eye. *Fairies*, that girl is equally as perplexing as she is astonishing. 'We think the fairies must have hidden it somewhere, each having their own secret stores of it to use against each other if needed. Why destroy the greatest weapon you have against your greatest enemies? We don't destroy swords just because they can cut us.'

'Poetic, Maya, and an interesting conspiracy,' I say, 'but I'm not sure how you think I can help with this. Or *why* I would.'

I have no loyalty to Dawn, to Bearra. Teddy is the one who owes *me*. And if I did find iron, why would I deliver it here, and not to Grace? Her territory is where my loyalties lie. Their optimism is sweet, but if they're going to win against a fairy, they need to be realistic.

'Because there's a war coming,' Maya says. The change in her hits me even harder than before. Where is the girl who was so headstrong, so selfish? That adorable, naive brat? The woman in front of me now is an exhausted leader. No wonder she went back to Teddy – she isn't in her right mind. 'I'm sure you've heard whispers, if not more. Lire is out there, readying her army, while we're stuck here just trying to survive. But this war isn't just between us and Lire. It's between all the fairies, all the territories, and maybe even the Ice Empire too. We're doomed, because we all know even an army is no match for a fairy. We only won against Lire last time because of the crown. But Sierra, if you help us find this iron, we will finally have a small advantage over them. We'll have a chance at killing Lire.'

My eye twitches. *What?* Knowing Maya, she isn't interested in power at all. She just wants to protect herself and the people she loves. Teddy and Dawn, however, are more difficult to read. I'd hand Maya the world – I already did, once – but I don't have any faith in the others.

'Even if it comes to a war,' I say, 'why would I side with you? Why not Grace?'

Princess Dawn tilts up her chin so she can look down at me, despite being shorter. 'As Maya said, this war may seem to be between the fairies, but it will affect us all. Every human is in danger. Helping us is helping to stop countless lives being lost. Helping us is stopping a few beings from having so much power that we lose all of our own. Not even Grace should be able to decide the fate of the entire world.'

I exhale, understanding her point even though I dislike it. My job is to protect Grace's Territory, but if helping Bearra means helping the world, isn't that what I should do? I don't know exactly what Grace would want from me, what my parents would want, or even what I want.

Maya is looking at me expectantly, so I tell them, 'Grace plans to build an alliance with Rhiannon. I overheard her soldiers talking about it in Rhiannon's Territory a few days ago. They didn't seem to know the truth about Lire, but the world knows a war is coming. They also mentioned Candace. She's growing more powerful, and rumour has it the Ice Empire is allying with Kara.'

'Perfect, more trouble,' Teddy says, spinning the yellow ring on his finger. 'But at least Kara hates Lire.'

'While you're searching for the iron,' Maya says to me, 'keep listening for information on Lire. Where she is, the army she's building, what she plans, when she plans to strike.' I grind my teeth; I *hate* being ordered around, even when it's Maya. 'I know you can spy better than anyone else, and we can trust you. We need you and your skills.'

I nearly throw my hands in the air. Bearra's hot air is getting under my skin, along with the bright light of the throne room. 'How many favours are you going to ask of me? I have my own quest. The curse I have to break, Maya, have you forgotten? Forgotten how I gave up my cure for *you*? I can't just sail around the world looking for things you need.'

Maya bites her lip, giving me a hard look.

'We can't force you to help us,' Dawn says, stepping between us. 'But I hope you can see how this will help the world. We would not ask you if we had another choice. I need Maya and Teddy here with me, and outside of them, there is no one in Bearra who knows the new world. You are all we have, Lady Reed. And when we win the war, we will be happy to repay you however we can.' She daggers me with her regal stare. 'And if you do not help us, and that is why we lose . . . that will be on your conscience.'

I give her a short laugh. 'If you knew me, you would know I don't have a conscience.' I smile sweetly at Maya. 'But since I'm already going to be travelling looking for the pirates' lost magic, I'll see if I feel like *thinking* about *maybe* helping with your things. Only because my close friend Maya asked so politely.'

'Thank you,' the princess says, and she looks as if she really means it. As she should.

I dismiss her, and instead speak to Maya. 'Are you safe here? Is your family?' I don't bother to lower my voice when I add, 'And is everything okay with *Teddy*? I don't know if you remember, but—'

'Don't waste your limited conscience worrying about me,' she says with a grin. 'No, nothing's okay. But I'm working on fixing things, and if we can win this war against Lire, there's a lot of good I can do. I can make sure no one has to quest across a foreign world to rob a grave ever again.'

A tension I didn't realise I'd been holding releases at once. Was I *that* worried about her? It surprises me to notice that my admiration for Maya runs deep and true. She might have just evaded the truth, but she's being genuine and optimistic. Her struggles have never stopped her, and of course they won't stop her now.

And I want to help her build her utopia. I'm still furious with Teddy, but if Maya has forgiven him, I suppose I could *consider* removing him from my mental list of people to murder. They do make an adorable couple, and I want Maya to be happy.

'Alright, since it's my duty to protect Grace's Territory,' I tell them, squinting through the gleam of the triarue throne so I can stare everyone directly in the eyes, 'I have to do my best to stop Lire. Protecting the world means protecting Grace's people, and if helping you is how I can do that, fine. I'm going to get this iron and see what I can find out about Lire – and I won't fail. Once I've broken my family's curse and gotten what you need, I'll come back and fight alongside you.'

'Oh Sierra,' Maya says, reaching out her arms. 'I've missed you.'

'I have *not* missed you. Allies only, remember?' A real smile fights its way onto my face, from the depths of my warming heart. *Ugh.* I wave away her hands. 'Now can we talk about me?' I turn to Teddy. 'How am I breaking this curse?' He cringes. '*Teddy.* Remember the only reason I'm asking for your help now is because you took away my only chance before. I know you feel bad about it. Make it up to me.'

Dawn perches on the arm of the throne, next to Maya, and the two of them watch Teddy expectantly. How I love to see them torturing him.

His cheeks go pink, and it bothers me for a moment, seeing how little energy he has, how little charm he bothers to use – the energy and charm that were effortless in him last time we saw each other. Not that I care.

'Yes, okay, fine,' he stutters. 'First you need to find the magic used to create the curse. That might already be impossible, since there's no way to track it. I don't know for certain, but I would guess that you also need to have the curse reversed by its caster. Depending on who has it now, if it still exists, you might need a . . . a *creative* way to steal it back.'

I stomp and roll my eyes. 'That's all you have for me? Everything *I already know*? Thanks, fairy baby.'

He shrugs, his hair falling over his eyes. 'I don't know! Follow the clues. Talk to people. Look for magic everywhere. Try to feel it. Your curse is part of you, so the same magic runs in your veins. You might know when you sense it. The pirate might, too.'

'Easy. What next?'

'You could try to experiment with it. The pirate can do some tests on only you to see what works to reverse the magic. Like you said, things could go wrong. Once you know if the swan can be removed from *you* safely . . .'

'I'll know if my sisters can become human again.'

'I can't make any promises,' Teddy says, siding up to Maya as if she'll protect him from me, 'but I'm sure their human selves are still alive inside them. There may be some psychological damage, but I think they'll be okay. Magical transformations aren't concrete – the magic is still brimming inside them, holding the transformation together. Once it's gone, they should turn back to their usual, unmagical selves.'

The shadow of a cloud passes over the sun, dulling the glittering triarue, the marble floor, and the princess's hair. With the shininess gone, I'm reminded how depressing this all is. I want to sit down. I want to be home. I want to be *done*. Why am I still so far from success?

'And if they don't?' I ask. 'If we turn them back and their minds are gone? What do I do?'

He looks down. 'If that happens, then you have my condolences.'

I arrange my expression into an ice-cold mask, because what else am I supposed to do? Cry about it? 'Well, thank you for nothing.' I glance at Maya, then back at Teddy. 'I still don't trust you. Maya might have forgiven you, but I haven't. And I want you to know, before I leave, that if you hurt her again, you'll wish you were dead *long* before I'm finished with you.'

Before Teddy can respond, Maya raises her hand to silence him. 'Sierra,' she says fondly, 'it is so hard to believe we ever weren't close friends.'

'Allies,' I reply, and Dawn giggles, so I make sure to glare at her to make sure she knows I'm certainly not friends with her, either. 'One more thing. I need something to bring back to the pirates. I promised them I'd make this visit worth their while. Give me some triarue.'

Teddy scoffs. 'We can't just give you—'

'I know you have plenty of it, and if you're expecting me to travel around looking for iron, spying on Lire – *dangerous* and *time-consuming* tasks – it's the least you can do.'

'Of course,' says Maya. 'Come on, Dawn. We need to show our loyalty to our allies. We aren't using the triarue, anyway.' When the princess doesn't argue, Maya winks at me.

Dawn exhales deeply, as if tired, though her perfect face shows no indication of fatigue. 'Of course. I'll have it organised immediately. Lady Reed, would you and your friends like to stay overnight in Bearra? We can ensure you're well fed and comfortable before you leave tomorrow.'

'No.' I consider the pirates waiting for me, wondering where I am, how much triarue I'm getting for them, imagining how they might kill me, or how I might kill them. Oh, we have such fun. 'We should be on our way.'

'But promise you'll return soon.' Maya touches my arm, and this time I don't push her away. She's warm, and she cares, and . . . I'm going to miss her. 'I mean it. Save your family, then come back and tell me all about it. I . . .' She releases a long breath. 'I need you, Sierra. I want you by my side, so win this time. You deserve to.'

Chapter Eight

Opal scrunches her nose. 'Naroport. Darraport's slimy little brother. I loathe this city.'

She doesn't have to tell me. It's like the air itself is sticky.

Levi nudges her, nearly knocking the much smaller young woman over. 'You only hate it because you're banned from it.'

'Who bans a person from an entire city?' Holding up the hem of her soft-green lacey dress, she kicks at the loose gravel of the street.

'When you're a known thief,' says Arden, 'such things happen.'

'Don't be smart with me, Captain.' Opal gives him a smug look. 'You're the one who lost our magic here. If anyone, it should be *you* this city hates.'

'He didn't mean to lose the magic,' Wren says. '*You* broke the law on purpose.'

'We all break the law,' Ebony says. 'All the time. Why are we arguing?'

'Arguing?' says Arden. 'I thought we were bantering.'

'Still a waste of time.'

'It's okay,' mediates Lark. 'I'm sure we're all a little afraid of what we could find here.' He places an arm around Wren's small shoulders. Though he can't be more than three years older, the way he acts like a parent to her makes the siblings seem many more years apart. It's difficult not to see Wren as a child and Lark as an adult, when in reality they're both teenagers.

'I'm not afraid,' Wren mumbles, shrugging his arm off her. But Opal puts her arm over the girl too, and suddenly they're all teasing Wren by pretending to protect her. Levi picks her up and dangles her upside down, then Arden holds her beneath the shoulders while the others tickle her stomach. 'Sierra!' Wren calls to me as they stifle her, trying not to giggle as the others howl with laughter. 'Tell them to s-stop! Aren't you supposed to be our new leader now?'

I shrug and grin as they ruffle her hair. 'What the six of you do is none of my business, as long as it doesn't get in my way.'

It's a drizzly day, terrible for flying, though I would rather be human in this city than any other animal – except maybe a rat. The buildings are tall and grey above us, without Darraport's natural vibrance. Instead we're met with the aura of poverty, stink, and grunge. To be banned from a place like this, Opal must have stolen something *really* significant. Surely only the worst criminals would visit such a repugnant city.

The seven of us loiter on a dilapidated street, our heads turned down against scattered droplets of rain. Arden and Levi finally put Wren down, and I watch the pirates talk and go back to bickering.

I feel so outside of it. This shouldn't bother me, but it does. They remind me too much of my sisters; a unit of six I could never break into. And, once again, it hurts more than I want to admit to myself.

I pinch the skin on my forearms to bring me back to reality, and I remind myself that soon, these pirates will all be murdered at my hands. The tightness in my chest softens.

Still, I wish Maya were here. Even Teddy. Our history may be beyond complicated, but at least I know where I stand with them. We've seen enough of each other – the best and worst – to allow us to speak and act freely.

Here, with this crew of pirates I barely know, I'm so alone. They're only here because I'm forcing them to help me. But why do the people I see as enemies keep surprising me? Why do I keep finding myself wanting them to be my . . . friends? Am I ill?

I must have been away from my family for too long, because I really am losing it.

'Where's the bar?' I ask.

'Yes, drinks!' Levi claps.

I nearly throw myself to the ground and bang my head against it. 'The bar where Arden lost the magic.'

The huge, snowy boy slumps. 'Ah.'

Arden's dark eyes meet the street. He's been cold as ever to me, even after I gave him that bag of triarue courtesy of the princess. I could give him the world and it wouldn't ease his hatred of me. It's fine. I feel the same way about him. But I'm the one in charge here, so he could at least pretend to be nice.

He pulls his coat over his shoulders to protect himself from the rain. 'I barely remember this city,' he says. 'If you think I know where the bar is, or even what it looks like . . .'

'I'm not sure I've ever met anyone quite as useless as you,' I tell him, pulling my own coat around my body.

'What about a name?' Ebony asks. 'If you can think of the name of the bar, we can ask people if they've heard of it.'

He runs a hand over his jaw. 'I don't know . . . Something crude, probably. Something—'

'Wait,' Wren says, her face pursing in concentration. She's wearing a blue raincoat that makes her really look like an adorable little bird. 'That night, when you got back, you were talking in your sleep. I thought it was nonsense, so I didn't say anything, but . . .'

'What?' I press.

She smirks, though her cheeks begin to mimic the red of her hair. 'Well, I thought it was a different word, but now I think about it, he kept moaning something about a . . . glass hole?'

'The Glass Hole Bar!' Arden nearly cheers.

Half the crew's expressions turn to impatience while half of them shriek with laughter.

'The Glass Hole it is.' Opal snickers. 'I'm picturing something dark and sticky, in a basement.'

Ebony goes pale. 'We're going to ask people where to find the *Glass Hole*? A place like that, imagine the state of the people there – and we have to visit it?'

I tilt my head, taking in the crooked-nosed girl. Sometimes it's difficult for me to match up the pirates' true personalities with their, well, *pirate* sides. Ebony is both a socially hopeless intellectual and the scariest Amoran fighter I've ever met. I'm surprised even she's put off by the thought of this bar.

'We'll survive,' I say, though I'm not looking forward to it either. 'Let's split up and each take a section of the city for our search. Meet back here at midday. Don't forget to keep our other missions in mind.' I already told them about the favour Princess Dawn asked of us. I also told them there'd be a decent reward for our work if we find anything. Incentive from a princess who's already offered them a bag of triarue must be enough for them to do good work.

Arden nods. 'Okay, two groups of two, one group of three. Ebony and Levi, Lark, Wren and Opal, and Sierra with me.'

Levi dips his head onto Ebony's shoulder, and she turns and kisses his cheek. Again: the pirates' strongest muscle and leanest fighter don't match the snuggly couple I'm seeing before me.

Wren groans. 'Can't I go with you, Arden? I'm always stuck with my brother.'

Lark blinks slowly, tilting his head. Strands of ginger brush his eyelashes. 'I'll pretend I didn't hear that.'

'Opal needs supervision,' Arden says to Wren, followed by a guilty glance at Opal. 'You and Lark have to make sure she doesn't get banned from this city. Again.'

Wren points. 'Then it can be you, me and Opal. Lark can take Sierra. *Please.* Lark won't let me have any fun in the city.'

'Exactly,' says her brother. 'I have to babysit the two naughty children to make sure there's no trouble.'

Wren fumes, and I try to give her a sympathetic look, which probably comes across more as a grimace. 'Arden has to stay with me,' I tell her. 'We both want to keep an eye on each other. The rest of you are . . .'

'Less important,' finishes Levi, with his dog-like grin.

'So it's settled,' Arden says, pressing his words through grinding teeth. He's less excited about being partnered with me than Wren is. 'We meet back at this exact spot at midday. If anyone isn't here, assume there's trouble and go straight to the ship. Good?'

Wren rolls her eyes but keeps her mouth shut. Opal throws an arm around Wren and scruffs the younger girl's hair. With their pale complexions, Wren and Lark always look as if they've been dipped in snow beside Opal, with her deep Adellan colouring – and her vivid outfits. She leads the siblings down the street, and Lark politely links arms with her. Wren follows close behind, walking with a distinct sulk.

Ebony pulls Levi along with her as they saunter off, holding hands. Anyone would think they're just a couple on a romantic walk – and, well, aren't they? None of us look like pirates, like criminals. Like teens on the run, trying to save ourselves and the world.

Once we're alone, Arden meets my eyes, his mouth in a flat line. 'This way?'

I begin walking without answering, and he matches my pace. Step by step, synchronised, so neither of us is behind the other's back.

He's only slightly taller than me when I have my heavy boots on. Slightly. And I only notice him *that* much because I'm observant. Strategic. It's important to know one's enemies' builds.

Though I'd be lying if I said he was disgusting to the eye. It could be his quiet confidence, his strong jaw, his mysterious black eyes, or his voice, soft but commanding. *Fairies.* If I could see him only for those things, I might not hate to look at him.

Instead, when I see Arden, that blue magic that cursed me lights up in my mind's eye, and all I feel is rage. Fear. Even now, I want to hurt him, push him to the ground, punch and slash and cause him any pain I can. I want to kill him. But I can't. It's the most frustrating thing I've ever felt.

After a while of this co-ordinated, painful pacing, I ask him, 'What were you even doing in this city? You'd had months, nearly a year of good luck since cursing my family. Why did you sail all the way to this city just to get drunk and throw everything away?'

He stares ahead, pretending to focus on shop signs, and I notice his long eyelashes, framing those eyes so deep and dark I can hardly see the pupils. I want to tear them out of his head. 'I don't owe you an explanation, Reed,' he snaps. Then he seems to change his mind, his features softening. He must realise at the same time I do that a distraction from this disgraceful city might be welcome. 'It's a long story. Are you sure you want to hear it?'

'No, but there's nothing else to do.'

For a moment I think he might strangle me, but then he explains, 'I made a mistake, but I'm not a drunk. That day was just . . . I was weak. It was a family thing. My blood family, that is. My father, who I stole the ship from, had shown up after I hadn't seen him in years. I'd tried to keep the curse quiet, because we didn't want the consequences of being found out, but rumour spread that we had something to do with the Reeds' disappearance. We were trying to hide out in this horrendous city, but the rumours reached my father and he eventually found me.'

'So?'

As we turn a corner, the now brick road becomes more uneven, the day even greyer and darker; I have to watch each step carefully. A couple of drunk men shout at each other in an alley, and not for the first time, I'm glad I know how to defend myself. If the Glass Hole is anywhere, it would have to be in a decrepit area like this.

Arden and I follow the odour of debauchery.

He presses his lips together for a moment, then lets out a deep breath. While he speaks, he walks straight ahead, never for a moment looking at me. 'My mother died a few years after I was born. I have no memory of her, and—'

'Oh, the story is *that* long?'

'*Fairies*, Sierra.' He clenches his fists before continuing. 'So, my father raised me alone in a small town in Grace's Territory. But it wasn't enough for him. He resented having to bring up a child by himself. He started drinking, and then he started gambling. He became addicted to risk, to rush. By some miracle he won our ship, already filled with magic. Priceless. I don't advertise this for obvious reasons, but the reason the *Neptune* doesn't run out of magic – like most vessels would – is because it's *made* of triarue. The wood of the ship is infused with it, and it keeps the enchantments strong.'

I refuse to let my jaw drop, but I still ask, 'That's . . . possible?'

'You've been on it, you know it is.' He gives me a quick irritated look. 'Don't ask me where it comes from or who made it, because I have no clue. Anyway, my father wasn't interested in using the ship. He only wanted it as a trophy. So I began taking it out. I learned how it worked, and that I didn't need a crew to use it. To make the money we desperately needed, I got work doing jobs like fishing, transporting goods, trading. Then jobs no one wanted to do, because it was dirty, grimy, or illegal. That's when I learned about your family. They only stopped me once, and I managed to hide what I was really doing, but I knew after that I needed to watch out for them.'

I kick a piece of broken brick, and a couple of filthy children cringe at me through a shop window. 'That's why you hate my family. We made it more difficult for you to break the law. You poor, sad, little pirate captain. How my heart breaks for you.'

'You are so ignorant. Your family controlled Grace's Waters, so you controlled the trade. If the Reeds didn't want someone making money, that person became a target. It was about keeping their rich friends rich, and gatekeeping resources.' His jaw tightens. 'The entire economy of the territory was under their control. The lack of goods they allowed in meant they could charge whatever taxes they wished. Tyrants love masking themselves as leaders and protectors when they're the reason we need protection.'

'Nonsense.' I roll my eyes and quicken my pace – a small show of dominance. 'The Reeds' only business in Grace's Waters is stopping crime and protecting the citizens of the territory. Anyone who thinks we wronged them, or played favourites, is simply a criminal.'

He shakes his head with that disbelieving look he loves to give me, eyes shadowed and lips turned down. 'You asked me a question, remember? How I lost the magic.'

Of course he wants to change the subject; he knows he can't win an argument with me. Because I'm so gracious, I allow it, waving him on.

'I was making money for us,' he continues. 'Enough even to help others in the village. But my father's addictions only worsened, and the more money I made, the more he could use to bet. I couldn't say no to him. I didn't know I could back then, and it was his ship I was using, after all. We fought. A lot. Sometimes it would be so bad, and we'd be raging so furiously, the fighting would get physical, and— It took me a long time, but I realised there was no fixing him. He wouldn't ever get better. And neither would—'

He pauses. 'I didn't want to be a slave to his mistakes anymore, when I knew I could do better on my own. And nothing was keeping me there after . . .' He matches pace with me, then walks just slightly ahead. 'Anyway, I didn't care to be part of Grace's Territory, knowing what the Reeds were like, and knowing Grace had no justice for me. There was nothing left for me at home. So one day, when I was only meant to be out on a fishing trip, I changed course. I made it to Adella's Territory, where I met Opal. We ran away together and became pirates, completing illegal work for cash so we could live the free lives we longed for. After a while we met Ebony and Levi, then Lark and Wren. We were all escaping something, and we found safety with each other. For a few years, we were actually happy.'

'Then you flew too close to the sun – or should I say sailed too close to the storm?'

'Say whatever you like, because I probably won't be listening, Reed.' He crosses his arms over his tight black shirt, and the bottom pulls up enough to reveal a slither of tan skin. Oh, wouldn't it be nice to *stab him right there.*

Luckily for him, we're distracted by shouting in the next street. People wave around sharply coloured signs that contrast the grey-brown city. Arden puts an arm out to— to what? *Protect* me? I force myself to take a breath and slow down to watch the protest instead of swiping the knife from his belt and stabbing him right where I fantasised.

Realising what he did, he lowers his arm and flushes. 'I— We don't want to get caught up in whatever that is.'

Still, I tilt my head for a better look. The people are yelling about fairies, and I realise the bright signs match the colours of magic. *Fear the Fairy War*, says one. They can't know about Bearra, but they can tell there's unrest amongst our world's powers. If even regular people are worried about a fairy war, things are even more serious than I thought.

'They're afraid,' says Arden, squinting at the protestors. We're still far enough from them to stay out of trouble, but he's right – the panic in the atmosphere is heavy. 'They have no fairy, and they know it's going to cost them.'

Above them rises one of the less decrepit buildings in the city, and I assume it's a government office. Shouts rise as someone – the mayor, maybe? – walks out of the doors and into a waiting carriage, guards protecting them from the protestors.

'Save us! Save us!'

'Surrender to Lire!'

I step back. *Huh?*

'Sierra,' Arden says seriously. 'Let's go.'

I want to stay and gather more information, but he's right. This isn't the kind of danger worth getting into. We continue along the street until the protests become a dull hum, my mind going over everything I've seen and trying to figure out what to do with it.

'So, skip ahead a year, and my father catches up to me,' Arden says.

'What?' I snap out of my thoughts to see his expectant face.

'You asked how I lost the magic.'

'We're still talking about that? *Fairies.*'

He sneers.

Flies waft over to us from a steaming butcher's, and we wave them away. As my arms move, I allow myself to accidentally slap Arden on the cheek. Only *lightly*.

He clears his throat. 'Anyway, nearly a year after the curse, my dad finds me here in Naroport, demanding the *Neptune* back. He was in a lot of trouble. Without me to provide for him, he'd gambled away everything he had, and as usual he was more often drunk than sober. He even begged me to use my new magic – which I'd only gotten by working for years to trade for it – to help him. We argued, I refused to give him anything, and eventually we parted ways as if he'd never come. No apology. He didn't even pretend to care about me. It *hurt*. I was so angry. How could he come all this way just because he wanted my power? I ignored my friends, knowing they wouldn't understand, and raced straight to the first place I could find that would make me forget it all. I got so drunk I blacked out.'

'And let the magic get stolen.'

The expression he gives me is almost begging for sympathy. 'It wasn't just a bad day. I saw my father, the man I thought I'd been free of for years, and suddenly he'd come to beg me for help. All the emotions I'd been repressing about my past came back at once. I wasn't in my right mind. I'm *never* as reckless as I was that night, but when you're in that sort of state of mind, you don't think.'

I exhale through my nose and wipe sweat from my brow. Is this talk over yet? It feels like he's been droning on for years. 'Who hasn't been through terrible things?' I argue. 'It doesn't justify making stupid mistakes.'

'I'm not you, Sierra,' he says, his voice deep and piercing; he rarely shows me true anger like this. 'I'm not an emotionless Reed. I'm just a man. Sometimes I make mistakes. I won't spend my life hating myself because of them.'

'Whatever, *Captain*.' I turn my eyes up to the tallest building above us to avoid looking at him. If that's what he thinks of me, so be it. I won't be upset for how he misunderstands me – why should I be? Why waste any of my energy on the insults of a man I don't respect? 'I'll make sure to spend the rest of my days hating you enough for the both of us.'

I expect a retort, but nothing comes. He's stopped a few paces behind me, and I turn to see his inquisitive expression. 'I know this street,' he says. His eyes flicker around, as if trying to catch hold of a memory. 'There!' He points down an alley. 'There's something down there – I remember it. I *know* that's it.'

I stride towards the dark alley, leaving him gasping in my wake. The dark clouds make it hard to see, but a small signboard, lit by magic, reads 'The Glass Hole'. Arden catches up to me and opens the large wooden door before I can, slipping inside first. He doesn't hold it open, and it just about slams in my face, but I catch it in time.

Sounds of music, chattering, and clinking glasses pound through the doorway. A rickety staircase descends immediately where the door opens, so if someone weren't paying attention, they might open the door, step inside, and fall all the way down.

We hurry in, both of us surefooted despite the unevenness of the stair placement. As much as I hate Arden, it *is* nice to be around someone who can match my pace.

Very quickly, I realise why this is called the Glass Hole. It isn't just a crude word to describe a crude place. The bar opens out around us like an iridescent cave, but the rounded walls, instead of being made of dirt, or even brick or wood, are a thick, steamy glass. People smoke from every direction, and a cloud of vile vapor envelopes my senses. It's like I'm suffocating inside a wine glass.

The bartender, an older woman wearing a silky purple dress, notices us, then takes a better look at Arden and groans. 'Not you again, boy! You aren't welcome here!'

Arden raises his hands innocently and steps slowly towards the bar with a friendly smile I haven't seen on him before. It's almost . . . pleasant to look at. I tear my eyes away – of course a pirate is skilled with masking their true nature so they can hurt more people.

'I'm sorry for whatever I did,' Arden says. He walks right up to the bar and leans over to speak with the woman. 'It was one of the worst nights of my life, and I don't remember a thing. That's why I'm back here. You may be able to help me – I need to know what happened.'

'Help you?' the bartender says with a sneer. 'You came in here alone at the beginning of the night – always a red flag.' She pours a glass of beer and slides it across the bar to an unsightly patron sitting in a choking cloud of smoke. 'Perfect customer for a few hours, spending plenty of money, sitting and keeping to himself. But after too much to drink, you started getting loud. You danced with a young woman – another drunken wreck – and after a while the two of you were jumping on tables, smashing bottles. Before I knew it you were picking a fight with my security guard. You were thrown out. *Banned.*'

Arden hangs his head. 'I really am sorry. It's my bad, ma'am. Truly. Do you know where I went next?'

She starts throwing together ingredients for a cocktail, taking her time to answer as glass clinks and liquor pours. 'Didn't know, didn't care. But it did look as if you were leaving with the girl.'

'Who was this girl?' I ask, my words sticking in the rank, humid air. I lower my voice, realising I look like a jealous partner – and I'm *not*. No part of me cares who he dances with, even considering how enticing he looks with that gleam of sweat making him look all *hot* and *alluring* in the low light of the bar. *Blergh.* 'What did she look like?'

'Not local. Like she could be from Kara's Territory, but with a Darraport lilt to her voice. Kept talking about her shop in the city. Usually I wouldn't remember these things, but because she ended up making so much trouble . . .'

'Did you get her name?' I press. 'What kind of shop?'

'What's it to *you*?'

'She might have stolen something from me,' Arden says earnestly. Even I'm starting to believe he genuinely feels bad about his misdemeanours here.

The bartender seems to go through an internal turmoil deciding whether or not to reveal the woman's identity, then must decide she doesn't care. 'Brown hair and white skin, average height for a young woman, and nice clothes. It may have been a bookshop.'

I turn to Arden, hope making my heart race. 'So we go to Darraport, look for a bookshop, and try to find this girl and get information from her about what happened. See if she's the one who stole the—'

'The *ring*. For our *wedding*.' He gives me a sweet smile that makes my stomach turn. Puts his arm around me. *Ew, ew, ew*! Is that really the best he could come up with? Just because he looks good does *not* mean I want him touching me. 'She could still have it. I could get it back.'

'Oh, my love,' I say, tasting bile as I resist the urge to throw him across the room. 'How *incredible*.'

CHAPTER NINE

Darraport isn't far from Naroport, so we've switched cities by the afternoon, the seven of us darting through the streets searching for clues about Arden's mysterious woman. Fortunately for the citizens of this city, and unfortunately for us, there are bookshops *everywhere*. And while we might be free of the horrors of Naroport, Darraport isn't the loveliest city either. The streets are crowded, and although it smells better than Naroport, there's still a dank, depressing fog. The windows of tall buildings reflect the sun in my eyes; not that there's anything interesting to look at. Fairyless cities have no culture. It's all business and bricks.

We've split up again, and this time I'm being babysat by Ebony and Opal – or as Opal put it, 'Girls' day!'

It hasn't escaped my notice that the crew never leave me alone with Lark or Wren – their two weakest. But I know from experience that they can protect themselves. They aren't deadweight or weak links. It's the rest of the crew that treats them like they're made of glass.

'Ebony loves books,' Opal tells me, a few steps ahead in a new flowy green dress that shifts in the wind. Her hair is tied up in one large cloud of brushed-out curls, and emerald clips hold everything in place. No matter the occasion, Opal does not dress down. And why should she? 'Don't you, Eb?'

Ebony keeps walking, with only a slight nod. Like Maya and me, Ebony doesn't talk for the sake of talking, and I quite enjoy it. It's so nice when people shut up. Yet I get the sense that in her case, it isn't just a distaste for politeness; Ebony doesn't always grasp social cues.

Opal presses her. 'Eb, tell Sierra about your books.' She gives me an apologetic expression, but I shrug. Why is Opal acting as if we're trying to become friends?

'History books, mostly,' Ebony relents, exhaling. Her dark, wavy hair is tied at the back of her head, and the outline of her enchanted weapon, in the form of a knife, is clear on her hip. 'I like to see how the world has changed. How it can be improved.'

Opal smiles. 'But particularly the books that talk about how women are better than men.'

'Yes, non-fiction.'

'You're onto something there,' I say. 'Men only pretend to be stronger and smarter than us because they're insecure cowards.'

Ebony allows herself a hint of a grin, her eyes brightening, and it shocks me so much I nearly stop walking. 'Exactly,' she says. 'At least the fairies are women. Before the territories formed, when royals ruled smaller kingdoms, it was mostly men in charge. The fairies may not be perfect, but when they established their power over the last century, they took down most monarchies and gave power to the people instead. More women were voted into leadership positions, and the world advanced quickly. But there is plenty more progression the world can make before there's true equality.'

Well, *now* she's started talking. I suppose one simply needs to find her interests. Opal may seem self-centred, but she's clearly an attentive friend.

'But you don't want equality,' Opal says as she stares lustfully into a luxury wedding dress shop. 'You want a matriarchy.'

'Of course. But we have to reach equality first. Once we have the opportunities that men do, they'll be utterly overpowered. We'll have no choice but to take charge.'

'You sound a little villainous, Eb.'

'I'm only ambitious, Opal.'

'Oh, certainly,' Opal replies, a finger to her chin as she muses on the idea. 'Though I don't see the point in all these gender discussions anyway. Men, women, who's better, who's stronger, who should be in charge, who should wear this or that, or do this or that. In the end, it isn't what you're made of that counts. It's the material possessions you possess – oh, and what you make of yourself.'

I blink, baffled. I'm not sure she's wrong, but I'm also not quite sure I follow her reasoning. Ebony, on the other hand, has already exited the conversation, scouring store window fronts, so I attempt to draw us back to our mission. 'So you like books,' I say, and that regains Ebony's attention. 'Are you any good at finding bookshops?'

She gives me a look as if to say, *Are you stupid?* 'What do you think I'm doing right now? I've been sourcing rare books for years. In fact, I got so good at finding them that I even found a picture book from

Bearra. *Pre-sleep.* And got a great deal on it, too. The owner didn't realise its value.'

Opal fluffs the layers of her dress against a patch of sunlight, making it sparkle. 'Oh, no. Don't get her started on her pre-sleep collection.'

I raise my brows. 'You don't have any old books by Maya Nova, do you?'

Ebony glances at me with wide, inquisitive eyes. 'How did you know?'

'She's my . . . Someone I'm acquainted with.'

'Your Bearran friend is an *antique author*? Reed!'

My ego grins inside me at impressing Ebony – someone I thought I would never win over. Not that I was trying. 'Maya would create children's books for her family's business,' I explain. 'She wrote them, did the illustrations, bound the books herself. But they went out of business after Bearra woke.'

Ebony stops entirely, right as another patch of blue sky appears, bathing her in light as if her excitement has brought real magic into the air. 'That . . . That makes my book even more valuable. Books aren't made like they used to be,' she says. 'It was a sacred art, in Maya Nova's time. Now it's all about speed and cash. Though of course, it's fantastic that books can reach more people and be available to promote education. As I say, ed—'

'Education is liberation.' Opal swishes her dress with one hand and pushes Ebony back into motion with the other. She does a terrible impression of Ebony's far huskier voice. '*We must free our minds from what we've been taught, and learn the world for ourselves.*'

'Yes,' Ebony says, not seeming to realise she's being made fun of.

The conversation is lost to a crowd we pass through; the people adoringly watch a screeching violinist playing in the street while utterly ignoring that others are trying to *move*. I shove a listener, and once we're finally free, I say, 'Enough distractions. Ebony, where are we looking? Do you smell paper and ink yet?'

Her nostrils actually flare as she glances around, then her eyes lock on to a young woman with an intricate blonde braid running down her back. Ebony beelines towards her and takes her arm. The woman nearly jumps out of her skin, but they have a short conversation that I can't hear, then she points east.

Ebony sprints back to us. 'There's a shop downtown with a worker who matches the description we have.'

'Convenient that this woman happened to know.' I frown at her doubtfully.

'Oh, no, it wasn't. The blonde braid? Her white cloak? You didn't notice? She's dressed like an old Ice Empire citizen, circa two-hundred years ago.'

Opal and I stare at her.

'There's a series of books set in that time period – very popular – and the most recent one was just released. I want to get a copy today if I can, but it's hard to find because everyone wants it. That woman, I knew she'd have been searching for the book, and therefore she'd know about the local booksellers.'

I can't help it. My face breaks and I beam at her. 'Ebony, that's amazing work.'

'Really amazing,' Opal agrees, patting her shoulder. 'That's my brainy friend.'

Ebony just raises a brow as if to say, *of course.* 'This way.' She gestures for us to follow. 'Arts district. A shop called Master's Manuscripts.'

'Wait,' I say, because we're already flying off, 'should we get the others first?'

'No.' Opal shrugs, her sleeves shimmering at the movement. 'Either they'll find it on their own and meet us, or we can find them later once we have more information. We can't waste the day looking for them.'

'And if she recognises Arden,' adds Ebony, 'she might not want to help us. So it's best we investigate first.'

'You would make an incredible spy,' I tell her.

It takes us an hour by foot to reach the bookshop: a small, quiet space tucked between big buildings. In this part of town, there are as many rats as there are people, and I can smell mould, but art covers so many of the surfaces that it doesn't feel depressing – it's vibrant. The bookshop itself has big windows that let in sunlight, and the dust from old books floats like glitter. A woman who matches our description – pale skin and long brown hair, tall and thin-lipped – is inside, stacking rolled maps on a shelf.

'Got her,' Ebony says.

'Should we go in?' Opal asks.

In answer, Ebony walks in.

The door jingles as we enter, and the woman glances up with a polite smile. She appears to be in her mid-twenties, and wears the classic light, silky clothing of Darraport. 'Can I help you ladies find anything today?'

Ladies. The three of us must look odd to her. From Opal's pretty dress to mine and Ebony's more comfortable, flexible clothes, we're all clearly from different places. We're also dishevelled and damp from our long day of chasing clues through steamy cities.

A trio of friends innocently book shopping? Likely not.

Ebony tells her, 'We're searching for a rare edition of a book, only we can't remember its name.'

'Well, that's my specialty. What's it about?'

Ebony gives her a serious look. 'A young pirate who has collected a large amount of Grace's magic, but on a drunken night loses it to a young woman. Sound familiar?'

Opal nearly snorts, then clenches my hand to suppress her laughter. I dig my nails into her skin to avoid a similar reaction. *Shocked* is the only way I can describe how I feel.

So we're leaning into being conspicuous, then.

The pale woman nods and eyes the ceiling as if trying to visualise the book. She takes her pile of scrolls off a nearby bench and begins slotting them into a shelf. 'I'll be honest, I've not heard of that one.'

'Oh, you know,' Ebony says, giving the shopkeeper her hypnotic Amoran doe eyes. 'The boy has a bad day, visits a city he doesn't know well, dances through the night with a girl, and when he wakes up, the magic and the girl are gone.'

Opal elbows her. 'Let the woman think.'

'Come on,' Ebony presses. 'Are you sure you don't know the story?'

The woman shifts between her feet. She places her remaining scrolls on the countertop and we follow her into another room, *fiction* marked above the door. It's dark in here, save for the few candles scattered about, the sunlight not quite reaching this deep into the shop. 'Oh, I hear plenty of stories. I try to keep track of them all, but sometimes they become lost in the mix. Do you know the author's name?'

'Nova. Maya Nova.'

The shopkeeper scans the *N* section silently, though her hands are fidgeting, and by the way her eyes dart around, I'm not certain she's actually looking.

'So . . .' says Opal, running her fingers down a book's spine just to quickly pull back and cringe at the dust, 'you like bookselling?'

'I love working at the bookshop,' she responds, but her voice has a mechanical tone, as if the words are well rehearsed.

'Travel much? Surely you enjoy a trip to Naroport every so often. It's very close.' This time Ebony nudges Opal. I'm not sure what their plan is, exactly.

The shopkeeper begins to peruse the next shelf. 'I'm very busy with the shop, and Darraport has everything I need,' she says flatly. 'I love working here.'

'You run the shop alone?' Ebony asks. 'That's a lot of work.'

'It is,' she says. 'But I inherited the shop from my late grandfather, and I've been making a good income from it since.'

'The bookshops in Naroport are very good too,' I add impatiently. Surely she's going to slip eventually, unless we have the wrong person. Does she have the magic I need or not?

'Hm,' Ebony agrees. 'They have a lot of rare editions passing through the city there, probably because of the trade routes. Surely you often visit Naroport to get hold of copies for your own shop.'

She opens her mouth, and *finally* it seems we're getting somewhere. 'Well—'

In an explosion of dust, Arden and Levi thunder through the door. The shopkeeper screams. She backs herself into a bookshelf when she notices Arden, which I take as proof she knows him. A book topples off the top of the shelf and nearly hits her head.

Fairies. Ebony, Opal, and I glare at the boys with red, deadly fury. We were so *close.*

The boys are flushed and shiny, panting.

'You loud, tactless males,' Ebony hisses, 'and your absolute disregard for—'

We both notice the shopkeeper fumbling in her pockets. Ebony and I rush to her and, realising we had the same thought, each grab one of her arms. The shopkeeper yelps – Ebony nearly has a better grip than me – and her hidden knife clatters to the floor.

'She's a spy,' Levi breathes, his head nearly brushing the ceiling of the small shop. 'Lire's spy.'

'*What?*' We all say at once.

Opal picks up the knife and presses the tip to the woman's heart. 'Speak.'

She grinds her teeth. 'I should've known, an odd group like you three passing through, obviously up to something . . .'

'That is *rude*,' Opal scoffs. 'I only stole one thing.' She holds up a small leather-bound book, which seems to appear out of nowhere. 'And it wasn't even for me. It was going to be a gift for Ebony, because I'm *such a kind person.*'

I stamp my foot to get their attention. 'Enough. Arden, what did you find out?'

The captain steps forward, closing our circle. 'Levi and I asked around about her. We went to the wrong bookshop, talked to its owner. They said this place only opened recently. It barely gets any business, and most of the books are old things people wouldn't buy.' He shuts the door to the small fiction room behind him, locking us in candlelight. It highlights him from below, making him truly look like a fearsome pirate. 'They thought it seemed suspicious, including the young woman who ran it. A woman who disappears for days at a time, leaving the place unattended.'

'Very suspicious,' agrees Levi, gleaming with perspiration. I pull my eyes from the muscles of his uncovered arms. I can see what Ebony sees in him, but *fairies*, he reminds me a little too much of a certain northern prince I've been trying to forget. 'We thought she could be a magic thief, some sort of black market trader.'

'Until the other shopkeeper told us this woman has a special interest in fairies.' My eyes flicker to Arden's hand, which menacingly thumbs the end of his sword's hilt. 'She always asks travellers about them, and has a particular curiosity when it comes to Kara's Territory and Bearra.'

'And whom would be after that specific type of information?' Levi provides – for dramatic effect, I imagine, because I'm not certain that's a valid use of *whom*.

Arden grins victoriously as he eyes the shopkeeper. 'Someone. Spying. For. *Lire*. Helping her build her army and gather information on her threats. A spy hidden within one of the world's biggest cities, where she could meet hundreds of people and find out all kinds of things.'

'Or find potential candidates to join Lire's army,' Levi adds with a proud smirk, as if he's finished a puzzle.

The shopkeeper squirms in our grip. 'Lire, the fairy? I'm a bookseller. I have nothing to offer her. I have no reason to know her at all!'

Opal grabs her chin, forcing her to make eye contact. 'Then explain yourself. The dinky little shop. Your interest in travellers. The knife hidden under your clothes.'

The young woman scans the room, probably pondering possible escape routes. Realising she's outnumbered, she sighs, deflating in my grip. 'Fine.' Her expression goes flat and her eyes darken. 'You caught me. *Congratulations.* What are you going to do about it?'

With her confession, it's as if the shelves of old books around us become nothing but a façade of crumbling paper. None of this is real; half of them probably came out of bins. The backrooms and tight spaces aren't for ambience. It's a spy's hideout. I wonder if she can even read.

'We don't care that you're a spy,' says Arden, but I certainly care, since I'm supposed to be helping the Bearrans. 'We just want to know what you did to me and what became of my magic. Did you steal it or not?'

'You lost your magic? How humiliating.' She laughs. 'No, I didn't steal it. I followed you closely because I knew you had a lot of it. Thought you might've been a soldier of Grace's. I was in the city looking for something else for Lire when I bumped into you. But you were so drunk, so deep in your own anger, it was impossible to get anything out of you. I walked you far enough back to your ship that you wouldn't get lost, then left. If anything, I'm the only reason you made it back to safety that night.'

Arden steps back, his shoulders dropping, and for a moment my heart pulls with sympathy. He failed his family, and I know what that feels like. We both live with guilt and shame.

But I'm not like him. He's a pirate – he failed because it's what he deserved. I failed trying to protect people.

He *should* feel ashamed.

'So you don't know anything about the magic?' asks Ebony, staring up at the shopkeeper.

She offers back a condescending stare. 'If I had it,' she says huskily, 'I'd be using it against you right now, wouldn't I?'

I chew my bottom lip, trying to repress the fresh ache in my centre. She doesn't have the magic, nor can she lead us to it. The only clue we had for breaking my curse is *nothing.* All this and we've gotten nowhere.

It isn't *fair.*

I tighten my grip on her arm and lean close to her face. 'If you can't tell us anything about the magic, you better at least tell us what you know about Lire. Where is she? What's she planning?'

She huffs. 'I'd die before telling you any of my fairy's secrets.'

'Then you'll die,' says Opal, pressing the knife's tip into the spy's sternum hard enough that blood seeps through her shirt. At first I think she's bluffing, but then I remember the way she thoughtlessly killed one of Grace's captains.

I consider stopping her, but I'm so disappointed about the shopkeeper not having Arden's magic that a bit of torture might cheer me up. Opal slides the knife slightly upwards, creating a vertical tear in the woman's shirt; more scarlet blooms through. 'Tell us something interesting. Now.'

She ignores the cut on her chest, her eyes flickering between us bravely. 'I have nothing to tell you. I don't know what happened to your magic. Clearly it was stolen from you after you got back to your ship. How do you know it wasn't one of your own crew who took it? You are pirates.' She smiles triumphantly. 'And as for Lire, she'll kill me for revealing anything to you. I couldn't hide it from her. The fairy of wisdom knows all. I would rather die now with my honour than be put to death in shame.'

'Sure,' Ebony says, nonchalant. 'Then one last question before we put you to death. Do you have any books on iron?'

'Iron?' The spy laughs, her dark hair falling over her shoulders. It's easy to guess why we're really interested in iron, but it'll be bad for everyone if Lire finds out. Ebony should've been more careful.

'It's for our . . . ship,' Arden says, clearly thinking along the same lines as me.

'You need an extinct metal. For your ship.'

'. . . Yes.'

'Which part of the ship?' The spy's eyes narrow at him.

Opal sneers, standing between her and Arden. 'You aren't in a position to ask questions, now, are you?'

I stifle a yawn. Though I don't loosen my grip, and try to remain menacing, I am becoming incredibly *bored*. How long has this interrogation dragged on? Why can't she just tell us everything so we can be on our way? This dusty old shop is not an exciting place to be, and we aren't even fighting.

The spy relaxes. 'Have it your way. If there's any iron in Darraport, I don't know about it. No one does. But . . .' She sighs theatrically. 'In the back room of this shop, there are maps and books I've been instructed to find and keep hidden. Some have certain topics that Lire would prefer stay unknown. I sort through everything that comes through here to look for them. You take as many as you want and I'll tell the fairy I burned them. On the rare chance that she believes me, I might live. You take what you want, and I won't tell her to come after you.'

'Key?' Levi says, already trying to jam open the closed door in the room's corner. I imagine the rickety lock is reinforced with magic if even Levi's huge hands can't break it.

It's also probably a trap, but since I want something interesting to happen, I'll let this one pan out.

'Under the front desk,' the spy says quietly, with a quick glance down to the knife at her chest. 'Top drawer.'

Arden hurries to get it, shuffling around for a moment before he returns and unlocks the door. 'It's a deal,' he says to the shopkeeper. 'We take what we want, and then we leave you alone. You don't tell Lire you ever saw us.'

'I swear it,' she says, snark in her voice.

As the door swings open, a mountain of maps, books, scrolls and loose pieces of paper appears. No, not just a mountain – an *avalanche*. The door flies open and dust and paper spew from the opening. Tomes slide across the floor as if they were barely being held in.

Levi takes the shopkeeper's arm from Ebony so she can help Arden sort through it all. I wait patiently, digging my nails into the shopkeeper's wrist. After what feels like hours, Ebony finally returns with a pile of books in her arms. Her face is blank in a way I'm learning means she's satisfied. She drops everything into an old sack Arden finds in the corner of the room, and he heaves it over his shoulder.

'Thanks so much,' Opal says, pulling back her knife only slightly. 'Lovely shop you have here. Impeccable customer service.'

I release the arm of the spy, my palms sweaty from restraining her. Ebony takes Opal's place, shifts her weapon to a sword, and pushes it out towards our enemy – enough length to give us space, while being able to do some damage if she tries anything as our backs turn.

We're nearly all out the door when Ebony stops. Her eyes dart from side-to-side, then she turns back and says to the spy, 'Why would Lire leave you defenceless in a bookshop? It was so easy for us to find you and overpower you . . . Why not leave you with a guard, or at least a partner?'

Too late, I realise she's right. *Fairies.* Ebony's unchecked curiosity could be the death of us all. Why waste time asking when we should be *running*?

Readying for a sprint, I catch yellow tendrils of magic snaking around the spy's fingertips, and I step in front of the others.

'Defenceless?' She laughs. 'Oh, sweet girl, no. I just wanted to see how much I could find out about your plans before I killed you. Shame you're so boring.'

There's a moment that I'm fine, brave, ready to fight – and the next I'm frozen, picturing lilac and blue magic, magic that can hurt me, just like . . . just like . . .

My breath hitches and I can't move. My feet are stuck to the brick pathway. I clutch my stomach.

Then Arden takes my shoulder and shakes me. 'Run!' he shouts, and I return to sanity.

We burst through the door and spring through the city, darting between people and through alleys, panting and flailing. But we're all strong, we can all hold our own. The crowds part around us, and Opal's dress flies like a green flag as she runs. Ebony's weapon is tucked securely into her waistband, and Levi thunders – every step of his huge body an earthquake. And *Arden*. Arden is swift as wind, agile as a river, stunning as—

I jump over a trunk as it's hauled out of a carriage, and my feet land smoothly back on the concrete. Through searing, exhilarated breaths, I shout, 'Anyone know where we're going?'

The spy must be long behind us. Each time I peek backwards, there's no sign of her or her magic. She mustn't want to lose her false identity by attacking us openly.

'Ship's this way!' Levi points in the direction we're running; I hadn't realised we *were* going in a particular direction. I was just racing, letting them lead me. Like we were one unit, like no one felt a need to keep an eye on the rest, because instinctively we were all heading the same way, the same speed.

Why is this . . . *fun*?

'It's okay,' Arden pants, suddenly at my side, though neither of us slows. His cheeks are red from running. 'She won't use her magic. Not out here. She can't lose her cover.'

I don't have the energy to reply. He's *pitying* me because he saw how scared I was. Does he think it's because of him? Because of *his* curse that I froze in terror? He doesn't know I've seen far worse things than him.

'If only we had some magic of our own!' Ebony says, laughing as she runs, alight with adrenaline.

We reach the city centre, closer to the ship, and the crowds are even denser. We're forced to slow to a speedy walk, weaving through the people, pushing past the city-dwellers and tourists.

Someone is shouting, 'Hey! Hey!' And we turn to see two orange heads zipping towards us. I'd been so focused on the mission that I'd forgotten we were missing Lark and Wren.

Fairies, I'm relieved. It isn't that I care for them, of course, but Lark is the only one of us who can cook. It would be highly inconvenient to lose him.

Opal takes Wren by the hand. 'Running away. Found the girl. She's a spy and she has magic. Will explain when we get back to *Neptune.*'

Lark's eyes widen and Wren's jaw drops, but they don't say anything. They match our pace and follow us all the way back to the ship. We jump up to the deck, and the ship's magic seems to sense our urgency, because the ropes pull in, the sails drop, and the anchor comes up all on their own before we've had time to crash and catch our breath.

It's only when we're pulling out of the marina and into the river-ways that I realise I could've flown the entire distance back to the ship. It never occurred to me, in all that time running, to just . . . leave them behind. For a while, I was so caught up in it all – so caught up in *them* – it was like I was human again.

Really human.

CHAPTER TEN

Three days later, we're sailing anywhere but Darraport, the *Neptune* drifting aimlessly. It knows we don't know where to go. But it knows we need to keep moving.

The more time I spend on the enchanted ship, the more I grow to understand it. It isn't simply an object; it has a heart and mind, a soul connected to the souls of the crew. The magic woven into its walls makes it part of the family, always listening, always helping. I can see why the pirates are so adamant about calling it home. It's more than a ship – it's a place they feel settled and comforted, no matter where in the world they might be.

We scour through the books and maps Ebony grabbed before we ran. I fly high in the air every few hours to make sure we aren't being followed. Though no one says it, we know there is very little hope of ever finding the magic. So we use our second mission – spying on Lire and searching for iron – as a distraction.

Well, maybe the pirates are only using it as a distraction for *me*, so I don't murder them for becoming useless . . . but it works. I need a break from disappointment. I need a fight I can *fight*.

At breakfast, Wren taps her fingers against her bowl and says, 'Can someone remind me why we're suddenly working for Bearra?'

We're in Amora's Territory, our eyes sore from reading small, faded text under candlelight. But despite the hard work, the magical haze of this area brings a relaxed feeling to the ship. Paired with the slightly cooler weather, the *Neptune* has become incredibly cosy.

'Because,' Opal says, 'Sierra says so, and we do what Sierra says.'

'What would be so bad about Lire winning?' Wren asks. 'She's already ran the world for centuries.' Lark clears his throat, and she adds, with deep sarcasm, 'I ask with respect and politeness.'

I stretch my legs and eye her impatiently. Wren is fierce, but the protectiveness the others have for her is fiercer. I can't bite back at the girl without getting the other pirates' wrath in return.

So, I keep my words soft and explain, 'Lire's influence has always been discreet. She's seen as a deity more than a leader. The fairies have too much power, but our history shows that being divided equally helps to keep them in balance. But if one fairy alone wins this war, they'll become so powerful we'll lose all free will. That's why we have to find iron to weaken the fairies, and can create a safer world where magic is controlled.' I glance at Arden. 'A world where no one has too much power, and magic isn't allowed into just anyone's hands for any use.'

Arden laughs under his breath, folding a crusty map. 'You just don't like magic because you got cursed. That doesn't mean no one should have magic, or that it should be controlled by a select few. That would only lead to more corruption.'

'You are so full of yourself.' I lean my arms on the table so I can glare at him better. 'I'm not wary of the dangers of magic because of *you*. Anyone with enough power can do magic like you did. Plenty of people have more magic and can do a lot worse. And they're smart enough not to lose it and be sent on a wild goose chase across the world.'

I seethe as fresh fury rises at all the stress we went through searching Naroport and Darraport for *nothing*. And it's all his fault. I finish, 'There is power stronger than you'll ever have, *weakling*. I've seen it.'

'Sure you have.'

'I am not a liar, *Captain*. When I was in . . .' I clench my fists. I hate talking about this, but I'd hate losing this argument more. 'When I was chasing the crown, the fairy's son – Teddy – he used his magic against me. Not just magic, but true power. Not just a child playing games, like you. I've never been in pain like that before, and I never want to be again.'

He glances off, unconvinced.

'You-You have no *idea* how it felt. Your curse was nothing. *Nothing*. Days, Arden. He left me frozen in ice for days. I couldn't move, breathe . . .' My voice is raised high, so I try to calm myself. I lower my shoulders, try to make my expression neutral, make my breaths even. All six pirates are watching me closely; even Arden appears taken aback, as if he knows he pressed too far. 'Magic is a danger. Fairies cannot be underestimated. If Lire's own son is afraid of her – and I'm afraid of *him* – I don't want her to have any more power than she already has. That's why we're fighting with Bearra. Discussion over.'

Lark places a hand on my arm and I almost rip away before I realise he's trying to be *comforting*. I loose a deep breath and shake my head lightly to pull myself back to reality. To remember I'm on this ship, with these people, and I am safe.

'I didn't know,' Arden says quietly and . . . earnestly? He places his palms out towards me. 'Sierra, you know I didn't know all that.'

'Maybe not,' I say, and the dark, curved walls of the ship's interior press cold claustrophobia into my skin, 'but it's your fault it happened.'

'Sierra?' asks Wren, eyes wide and voice small. June, the little cat, hops into her lap and purrs. 'If I'd known you would get hurt, I wouldn't have helped curse you. I thought we were being heroes, and you were a monster. I'm sorry. I didn't know you could . . . feel.'

My stomach drops. I swallow hard and try to offer a small smile in her direction. I don't forgive her, but how can I blame her? She was barely a teenager when it happened. Wren, at least, can't be held responsible.

And yet her apology means the world to me. The crew were clear that they regretted the curse, but for their sakes, not mine. For one of them to truly admit that they wronged me is freeing in a way I never anticipated.

Her brother nods, his face soft. Ebony and Levi lean into each other with sombre looks. Opal has her chin resting in her hands, eyes up attentively.

But Arden's expression stays dark, and he stands. 'Sierra, I'd like to speak with you alone.'

I want to refuse, but I'd also like to get away from these staring, expectant faces. The wooden floor groans as I ease out of my chair, and I trail Arden up to the deck.

The cool morning air hits my skin, easing my mind as I breathe it in. I push my hair behind my shoulders and turn my face up to the sun, staring through the pinkish Amoran air for a few seconds before closing my eyes.

I long to turn into the swan and fly – fly far away, and never look back. See if there's another world out there where none of the fear exists. Where I can start anew, be a different me. Be happy. Human.

Arden gently touches my arm and motions for me to follow him. I do, until we're sitting at the front of the ship, in the shade of one of the sails, watching the water break in two as the ship cuts through a river. Even at its slow pace, the *Neptune's* size creates chaos below.

A few large waterfront estates with their manor houses dot the shores either side of us, eerily reminding me of home. This area, however, is made of soft grasses, hills, and grazing sheep. Even the creatures seem drunkenly at peace. A pack of wolves eyes a herd of cows from across the river, while pink dolphins leap out of the low waves, squeaking at us.

I wish I could swim with them, but I can't take the time to enjoy things like that – especially not in front of Arden.

I rest my head on my knees, and he sits in front of me, his legs crossed. He runs his hand through his Grace-black hair. Stares at me with those unreadable eyes. The sun glimmers off the water around the ship, and Amora's Territory continues pleasantly floating past.

For once, I don't actively feel like murdering the pirate captain. 'Lovely to spend some time in the sunshine,' I say. 'But why are we really up here?'

He gives me a dead stare, like it should be obvious. 'You seemed like you needed space.'

'So you decided we should spend some time alone together?'

'Okay, it wasn't a perfect plan . . .'

'*Captain*, what has gotten into you? You aren't thoughtful towards me. You hate me.'

His eyes travel upwards in a lazy eye roll. 'I don't know, *Reed*.' He readjusts so his knees are to his chest, like mine. 'What Wren said, about us not knowing about the consequences of what we did to your family . . . I think I might have been unfair to you. We all have complicated pasts, and it isn't fair to judge you on yours, because I don't judge my friends for theirs. I'm not sorry,' he says, and for some reason he *keeps on rambling*, 'and I stand by what I did, because your family has done terrible things. But the more time I spend with you, the less *Reed* you are, and the more you're just . . . Sierra. You're just a traumatised child like the rest of us. Your family might be terrible, and you aren't a great person yourself, but am I? If you judged me by my father, you wouldn't think very highly of me, either, and—'

'Arden.' I hold up a hand. 'Stop talking. You've made your point.'

'I have?'

I let out a groan, softening a little – *only* a little. 'I know what you mean,' I say cautiously, 'because maybe, possibly, I feel *slightly* the same way. I still hate you too. And I'm not sorry for anything. But before I knew you, I saw you and your crew as soulless, hateful criminals. And what you did to my family felt personal. I know now that it wasn't, and that you're all better people than I thought. *Slightly* better.'

Truly, is it so bizarre? I once wanted to kill Maya, but we became friends. Getting to know her was the first time I realised that people could surprise me in a good way. That not everyone was ultimately against me.

Then again, Maya never cursed my family . . . though I wouldn't put it past her. That girl can be tyrannical when she needs to be.

'You and I can spend our lifetimes hating each other,' I continue, just to keep Arden in his place. 'But that doesn't mean we have to make each other miserable. I would rather we worked together to save my sisters and stop the fairy war. Not out of fear, but because we're allies. I . . . I'm tired of working alone. And this—' I gesture at the ship '—this could work.'

Maybe I've lost my mind, but my words are true. I want to rest, and to feel safe, for the first time in my life. Everything I've been through is catching up to me, and I need friends who can watch my back. I need a team just like this one, if they'll have me. At least, if I can resist the urge to strangle each of them, one at a time, as the others watch, whenever they annoy me.

He nods thoughtfully. 'I do want to help you. I don't want to bring your sisters back, and I don't want to do your family a single favour, but I want to make up for the hurt I've caused *you*. We've fought together now. I've watched you protect my family. And I trust you about this fairy war. If we can save lives by doing what we can for Princess Dawn, then we should do it. Even if we hate each other.'

I fight back a smile. I loathe him. I want him dead. Don't I? I *should*. This could all be a trick, some way to make me trust him just so he and his crew can stab me in the back. I'm sure most of them would. And yet I want their approval. I long for their friendship.

Six sisters. Six pirates. Same *fairies forsaken* story. Except, maybe this time, the ending could be different.

Oh, this has turned into a disgusting situation.

He reaches out a hand for me to shake, and the inviting smile on his face is one I've never seen directed at me before. It makes my chest fill with *warmth*. I take his hand, grip hard, and shake.

'Welcome to the team,' he says. But his smile fades as I yank on his hand and jump atop him, my arm at his throat, knee to his chest, keeping him down. 'What are y-you—' He struggles to choke out words.

I laugh and release the pressure. 'Just reminding you who's really in charge. And what will happen if you betray me.'

His face reddens. 'I didn't need reminding.'

I lean in close, threateningly, teasingly. 'Then maybe I just needed the ego boost, *Captain*.'

'I like you better as the bird,' he whispers, his eyes void-black even as the sun moves over us.

My heart races. *Why is my heart racing?* 'And I like you better,' I whisper back, 'when I'm thinking about destroying you.'

His head tilts, then lifts slightly, his mouth open. He's so close to me I can feel his breath on my lips. I can smell his cologne. See every individual black hair on his head. He glances at my lips.

What is he *thinking*? Is he . . . thinking about the same thing as me? *Fairies.*

My face goes warm. My whole body does. This isn't right. We aren't . . . We can't . . . But does it really matter? It's only a little . . . It would only be for *fun*. Everyone has these kinds of feelings sometimes. It means nothing.

I lean in, only as much as he has, and wait for him to fill the space. We're allies now, aren't we? We should be *bonding*. His pulse hammers beneath my hands as I clench his loose shirt. The fear drops from his face and he looks up at me through half-lidded eyes, and—

'Arden! Sierra!' Levi calls, his footsteps thumping up the stairs. 'We found something in the books! A lead for iron!'

I jump off Arden faster than I imagined possible, rolling back. I'm all flushed, so I turn away, pat my hair into place, and pull down my shirt where it rode up. I'm tempted to turn into the swan and fly away, but that would make things even worse.

Am I *insane*? What was I thinking?

It was like when I'm the swan, when all the thoughts leave my head. When I lose myself only to be overcome by instinct. *And* there's the air here. Amora's torturous haze of passion. Everything is working against me, making me lose my logic and give into these awful, repulsive *feelings*.

When I finally face Arden again, he only looks confused. He calls back to Levi, 'Stay there! We'll be down in a minute!'

'An entire minute?' I sneer at him. 'We aren't *busy.*'

He tilts his head and says innocently, 'Aren't we?'

Absolutely *not.* I can't be fooling around *kissing* people. Especially not Arden. *Anyone* but Arden. And even if it wasn't him, I still wouldn't do it. Intimacy always leads to chaos, or worse, love. The last time I kissed someone— No. That won't happen again.

That was different. But I'm still not about to let myself make the same mistake. I learned my lesson. From now on, I need to focus on controlling myself.

Before it's too late.

CHAPTER ELEVEN

SOMEWHERE, SOMETIME...

In the weeks after her banishment from the Reed manor, Sierra flew all the way to the Ice Empire and walked half the way back. She was shattered and drained beyond recognition. But she was determined.

At least the pale prince she now dragged behind her didn't particularly mind being kidnapped. He was less like a captive and more like a trouble-making puppy. When Sierra had broken into the empire's castle and took him, he exclaimed, 'You want to whisk me away to kiss a bird and turn her into a woman as beautiful as you? Why didn't you come sooner!'

Prince Zeus. She despised people like him. People with no sense of responsibility, no concerns about anything at all. Why care about being kidnapped, as long as there might be a prize waiting at the end? Despite his royal status, Zeus spent his days abandoning his duties in favour of partying and laziness.

Even at her worst, Sierra had *never* abandoned her duty as a protector of Grace's Territory. So how could a crown *prince* be such a—

'Moron,' she groaned at him, several times an hour.

Travelling with Zeus was like carrying an impossibly heavy, bulky bag. He could take care of himself, and he was fit enough to keep up, but he was always in the way, always talking, always shocked or excited or ridiculous. It had taken four days of trekking across the snowy, mountainous expanse of the Ice Empire for him to finally accustom to Sierra's curse. Woman. Swan. Woman. Swan. At first he would scream and run behind tall pines, scratching his arms and legs. Eventually, he would only watch her, staring as if she were a performer on stage.

Each day they fell asleep together, shivering and sore, somewhere they could find any semblance of shelter. When Sierra became human again in the night, they walked.

She knew Zeus liked her company, though she couldn't understand it. She'd turn around as they hiked and catch his clear blue eyes on her, a smile playing at his lips.

He was the same age as her, barely seventeen. Far too young for her eldest sister, but this was the way it had to be. Legend said a kiss between royal soulmates could break a curse, and he was the only prince left.

Sierra would try anything, go to any length to bring her sisters back. To be able to go home. Kidnapping royalty was hardly outside her limits.

So, Sierra had kidnapped Prince Zeus of the Ice Empire, and now *this* was her reality.

She knew she had impossible odds. What were the chances the legend was true, *and* that the idiotic prince would be her sister's soulmate? Irene wasn't even royalty, but as the eldest Reed sister, she held plenty of power. She was the one who received the brunt of the curse – it had merely reverberated to the rest of the sisters. It hadn't even properly touched Sierra.

She would have kissed Zeus the second she met him – repulsive as the idea was – if she thought it might help, but what if that only made the curse worse? What if it hurt the chances of him being Irene's soulmate?

This was already risky enough.

+ ◊†○ ⚔ ○†◊ +

When they reached Rhiannon's Jungle, they stepped over tree roots and through marshy dips in the ground.

Yes, the jungle was dangerous, but it was the fastest way from the Ice Empire – in the coldest outer reaches of the north-west – back to the centre of the world. They would cut straight through to Darraport, then head south-east to Grace's Territory. By taking routes along rivers, they hoped to find a ship to take them.

The prince did not care one bit about the walk, and was more than happy to experience the outside world without servants and responsibilities following close behind. All light hair and fair skin, Zeus was airy inside and out, like a soft cloud. He was handsome and strong, witty and charming, and yet utterly *dense*.

He had never had to work for anything, while Sierra had spent her life destroying herself for any recognition at all. Even when he had his luxuries taken away, Zeus followed the path laid ahead for him without a hint of stress. He was probably blessed by magic, too, as so many royals were.

Fairies, she hated him.

As they trudged through the jungle, Sierra's foot caught on a vine and she tumbled. Before she could right herself, Zeus appeared, his arms around her, holding her up. She gasped, threw him off – heart racing, ankle aching.

He raised his eyebrows flirtingly, rubbing his arms. 'Most people would say, "Thank you, Your Highness."'

'Am I a person?' she spat back.

Zeus swept a hand through his hair as he stepped away. His skin was pink from the heat and humidity, unaccustomed to being this close to the world's centre. 'I apologise if I offended you, Lady Reed.'

Sierra rolled her eyes and continued walking. 'You give yourself too much credit, believing that *you* could offend *me.*'

He sighed exasperatedly. 'Fine, Swan Maiden, whatever you like to think.'

'Don't call me that.'

'How I love your dark, bitter attitude,' he mumbled, a mischievous glint in his gaze. 'It makes your eyes sparkle. Don't forget that I'm *your* captive, here for *you.* Yet here I am being wonderful company, while you never cease to be rude. But you know, Swan Maiden, it only makes me like you more.'

'My apologies for having little experience with kidnapping over-talkative princes, *Your Highness.*'

'I only hope my people don't find me. I enjoy spending time with you too much.'

Sierra waved a hand dismissively. Jungle insects bit at her legs, buzzing in the night air, and all she could do was ignore them. Unfortunately, she couldn't ignore this *other* pest. 'Unless they come with an army, I wouldn't count on them getting you back.'

'And when I marry your sister, we'll get to spend even more time together! I'll have all the famous Reeds to protect me.'

She laughed humourlessly. 'Oh, yes. That's the only reason I kidnapped you. Not to save my family. Just to keep you forever.'

'You could, though,' he said seriously, stopping. 'You could marry me and forget about your sisters. We'd be very happy.'

'Funny, Zeus.' She kept walking ahead; she would *not* entertain this.

'You think I'm joking? Except for the swan situation, you're *perfect.*'

She laughed again, shrugging him off. But this was all part of the problem. Each day, Sierra could see the prince warming more to her. Brushing his hand against hers, asking her deeper questions, trying to get her to let him in. It was dangerous. The more she tried to push him away, the more persistent he became.

And here was her other problem: when she thought of giving him to her sister, a venomous feeling entered her stomach. Jealousy, or fear. Part of her *did* want him for herself. Why, why, why?

Fairies, she was in trouble.

When she woke the next night, she found his hand resting on her back. She stayed there for a few moments, careful to be still, not to stir him. She relished the feeling of his touch. But, eventually, she came to her senses and slipped away, watching the stars rise as he slept.

· ◊ ˚ ○ ⚔ ○ ˚ ◊ ·

They never found a ship to stow away on, so their trip took weeks.

Weeks together. Weeks alone, walking, talking. Endless nights of watching each other.

By the time they reached Grace's Waters, they knew each other intimately. She learned all about life in the Ice Empire; its cold weather equally as serious and harsh as the military culture. He learned all about her life as a warrior, about her infamous family. She knew how he moved, the shifting of his shoulders, the contours of his physique, whether shirtless in world-centre heat or covered in layers of fur at the world's edges. Every time he stripped his clothes to swim, she noticed her breath catching. She noticed the places her mind went.

And she knew that the way Zeus looked at her was becoming something other than lustful. He had always watched her with that flirtatious, hungry gaze, but now it seemed he was not only admiring her appearance. He knew her, he respected her. She was no longer another woman to win over, but his saviour from a life he never wanted.

She still did not respect him, but there were parts of Zeus – his perfect smile, his gleaming upper-arms on warm days, his optimism and carefree mind – that she had grown to appreciate.

They reached the edge of a river, its diamond-like water lapping at a shore of white sand. Sierra did not hesitate before ripping off her shoes and dipping her feet in with a soft sigh. Although it was early evening, the water was the perfect temperature.

Home.

This was where she had last seen her sisters – the six white swans. She was happy to be human in this moment. In this form, she felt less separate from the others. As the swan, the black of her feathers was yet another mark of her separation from her family – a mark of her shame.

Zeus stood behind her and placed his hands on her shoulders. She turned slowly, looked up at him. In the glow of the earliest stars of the night, he was like a deity, his white hair haloed.

'Concentrate,' she told him. 'Look for the swans.' Quickly, she averted her gaze. They were so close. She could not allow the confusion of her feelings to let her fail. Not now. 'They can't have gone far.'

'Then what?' he said, not moving his hands from her. They slipped down to the tops of her arms, brushing bare skin.

What if she just . . . killed him? That would fix *one* of her problems.

'I kiss one of them on the beak? What do you think will happen? I'm not in love with a bird.'

Sierra exhaled, her heart pulling with the motion. 'You could be. If my eldest sister is your soulmate . . .'

'She isn't.'

'Zeus.' She shook her head, and her eyes – pathetically – filled with tears. 'This is my *only* hope. Please – *please* do not ruin this.'

'I don't want to kiss her,' he insisted. 'I won't. What if she pecks me?' He lifted his fingers to his lips and cringed, then swallowed. 'That isn't the point. The point is, I don't love her. I've never met her. She isn't even human. This plan won't work.'

'Don't say that. We'll find her. We'll at least try.'

His hands slid down to her forearms, gripping her desperately, though he knew she was stronger. 'Sierra, please. Forget about them. I love *you*. I love you. You're all I want. Let me kiss you. That'll break the curse.'

She stepped back, knee-deep in the water, and finally faced him. Her chest iced over with anxiety. She'd be lying if she said she didn't return his feelings, had never wanted him to kiss her over these long, lonely weeks. But she had been strong, she had never let her emotions get in the way of her duty. Not like him.

'No,' she tried to command, but her voice came out weak. 'No, Zeus.' She glanced back at the river, as if that might break the spell they seemed to be under.

'I know you feel the same.'

Sierra's heart was breaking. Her sisters. Her family . . . But . . . *him*. He was right. She cared for him. She wanted him more than she wanted her family's approval. But she couldn't live with her curse forever, never feeling the sun on her real skin, never seeing the blue sky through her own eyes.

Not for something as pitiful as love. A love that would never even work.

Zeus leaned towards her. 'I love you. I love you. I love you, Sierra. Say you love me. I beg you.'

She blinked, and tears ran down her cheeks. Her fingers trembled, shivered in the night air. 'Of course I do.' Her voice cracked. 'Of course I do. But it means nothing.'

His face softened. 'Swan Maiden, it means everything.' His hands swiftly slid up her arms and around her jaw, cupping her head. Her body stopped her mind from making the rational decision to throw him away. Before she could think, they were kissing.

And it was the most wonderful feeling she'd ever experienced. She didn't know she could feel this way. She'd been attracted to all kinds of people, and kissed plenty of them, but *romance* was reserved for those who had the time for it. Never her. And certainly never . . . Never love.

'I adore you,' he whispered against her lips.

She could almost feel the curse's magic hardening within her as her chance of breaking it disappeared. She couldn't make herself care anymore. Her strength failed her, and she couldn't move from his grip.

Sierra's breath caught as they lowered themselves to the ground, hands never leaving each other. Their feet tumbled in the water of the shore, their clothes filling with sand. She wrapped her arms around his waist, then up his chest, over his shoulders . . .

'I love you too,' she whispered, and he shivered in response.

Then it all went wrong.

Zeus gasped, choking. He broke away from her, falling as he reached out, eyes wide with panic. With all his confidence gone it was like seeing a stranger. He grabbed at the air. Nothing was attacking him. Was he sick? Was he suffocating?

'Zeus!' she screamed, reaching down to him, knees scratching against the sand. 'What's wrong? Zeus!'

A cloud passed over the moon and the world became terrifyingly dark. Zeus thrashed, and when Sierra tried to touch him, to hold him still, sand slashed into her eyes. She turned, sputtering, blinking it from her blinded gaze.

He kept gasping for breath as if he were being strangled.

She rushed to the river to clear her eyes. She submerged herself in the water, renewing her spirit. But when she turned back to the shore, he was gone. None of that light hair, those broad shoulders, the flirtatious gaze or teasing grins. That beautiful voice with the soft northern accent.

In his place was a moonlit swan. It breathed heavily, its chest and wings expanding with every inhalation. Its long, white neck craned to look at its reflection in the river, and it fell over its own feet, wings flapping. Its black eyes gazed at Sierra with recognition. With *fear*.

She fell to her knees as everything within her broke at once.

She'd warned him to stay away.

She'd begged him to stop.

She had failed her sisters by taking their one chance at breaking the curse.

And to punish her for her mistake, the curse had passed itself on to the prince? Why. *Why?*

Sierra reached to him, but he staggered back.

Maybe in the morning, when she turned into the swan, she would have some animal way of communicating with him. She would fix this. She would get him back. Because losing him, like she lost her sisters . . . it was unfathomable. Yet she could see the intelligence in his gaze, the awkwardness of his body – it was still Zeus within the swan, unlike her sisters, who had nothing of themselves left. He was like Sierra.

When he flopped to the ground, shifting his wings over his body, she sat beside him. She could not leave Zeus alone like this – alone like she was. She waited up the entire night, not leaving his side. He stayed by her, shivering, and eventually let her stroke his feathers. After a while he calmed, and even fell asleep. She'd join him soon, and then she would think of the next step. She'd find a way to save them both, and her sisters.

As the sun rose, her black feathers appeared once more and she opened her eyes to bright yellow rays of light. She turned to Zeus, relieved and ready to communicate.

But Zeus was no longer beside her.

No, he was watching her from above, through his ice-blue eyes, running his hands over the bare skin of his arms. He pinched his cheeks, pulled on his hair. 'Sierra,' he rasped in deep terror.

She flapped her wings. She tried to speak with her eyes. *I'm sorry. I'm sorry.* It was no use. The squawk that came out of her beak only made him step back in fright.

She let out a screech. How could this magic, which already haunted her, be so cruel as to see her love and choose to increase her pain even *more?*

If their curses were opposite, if he was to be human in the day, and she at night . . . they would never talk again.

Sierra cried out, her throat scratching.

He reached to her, touched her neck. His eyes were filled with heartbreak. 'Sierra, it isn't your fault, you didn't know this would—' He choked on tears. 'I'm so sorry. I shouldn't have pushed you. I should have done what you said. I still love you. I love you . . .'

But she couldn't respond in any meaningful way. She cocked her head to one side, still trying to convey her sorrow. Trying to tell him she loved him. That he was the first and only person she had ever loved.

He stood, panting, pulling at the hem of his shirt. 'We . . . What are we supposed to do now? I can't— I can't . . . We'll never be together. Never again.' He turned away, trying to catch his breath, clutching his chest.

Sierra understood his panic. She'd lived it. She knew the magic of the transformation. The way it twisted her mind, destroyed her concept of reality. She couldn't bear to think she caused him the same pain.

'Sierra, I'm so sorry,' he said, his words barely audible through his quick breaths. 'I have to go home . . . They might be able to help me. Candace. She could have the magic to fix this. I can't live like . . . I can't. What am I supposed to do?'

She moved toward him. *Don't leave. We'll figure this out.*

'I love you,' he said again. 'I love you, but I can't do this.'

Sierra's insides were breaking apart, piece by piece. Yet as he turned and left, she did not chase him. She knew the prince. She may have fallen for him, but she knew what he ultimately was, and she should have remembered.

Shallow.

Weak.

And once more, she was alone.

CHAPTER TWELVE

We spend a week following a new lead on iron: a map that leads to an old mine in Adella's Territory. I mostly spend those seven days avoiding Arden.

Avoiding remembering that we nearly . . . we nearly . . .

Danger. That's all that could come from these *feelings* I've been having towards him. And out of anyone in the world I could be thinking of kissing, I won't let it be the person I'm supposed to hate most. The person I've spent over a year fantasising about *killing.* No. I won't let my focus waver. Not even for a second. Not until my curse is broken. Not until the fairy war is stopped.

We head to the deck of the *Neptune,* into the sweet, calming atmosphere of Adella's Territory. It's awful. In Grace's Territory, my mind feels clear and bright. In Rhiannon's, I feel stronger. But here, a place that makes me feel . . . kind? *Ugh.*

Still, compared to the haze of passion and laziness that covers Amora's, this is the lesser of two evils.

At least I don't feel like kissing anyone. Mostly.

'Lovely to be back,' Opal says, wearing a puffy lilac dress that touches her knees. Her hair is in two buns either side of her head, with several thin plaits framing her face. Her neck, arms and fingers are covered in silver jewellery.

The extra show is clearly to distract from her discomfort at being here. Her home territory has as many bad memories as the rest of ours.

'How about we say hello to your parents?' Arden teases, in his much plainer black button-down, the sleeves rolled up to reveal his tanned forearms, which I am not looking at. 'I'm sure they miss you.'

Opal rolls her eyes. 'More likely they miss the watch I stole from them on my last visit.'

'I thought everyone here was supposed to be nice,' says Wren, her red hair wrapped in a silk scarf to protect her from the sun. It is *adorable*.

Opal becomes uncharacteristically bitter, her lips turning down. 'There's a difference between being nice because you *are* nice, and being nice because you're *supposed* to be. Most of the people here are only pretending. They give and give to appease Adella, but I know what they're really like.'

'Like you?' I say.

She gives me a fake-sweet smile. 'At least I don't hide it.'

'Which makes you better than them,' says Lark, with a strong undertone of sarcasm.

'Exactly!'

Our fabled iron mine isn't near any river systems large enough for the *Neptune*, so we anchor with the plan to spend the better part of our morning hiking. The ship's sails flap in the breezeless air as we leave, as if saying goodbye. Knowing the ship, it's doing exactly that.

At least Adella's Territory is famously flat, beautiful, and accommodating. There's barely a cloud in the sky, and the temperature is perfectly warm. Whenever I begin to feel thirsty, we happen upon a flowing, clear stream, and whenever I'm hungry, we pass fruit trees. My body never tires or aches.

And this part of the territory is sparsely populated, so luckily Opal doesn't have to speak with anyone.

Wren is throwing walnut shells at her brother when we stumble across the mine. She stops dead at the sight of it.

A cavernous opening is left uncovered, scaffolding left behind, rusting as if the mine were abandoned at once. It's almost as if the friendly feeling of the territory evaporates the deeper I gaze at the hole in the ground, my stomach instead filling with the pull of dread. The area around the entrance is clear of trees, plants, and creatures, so we're left in direct sun; a bubble of eerily quiet, lifeless land in the centre of the territory's thriving surroundings. All that marks the cave's gaping mouth are piles of rocks and dirt amongst the scaffolding.

'*Fairies*, no,' Wren says, and her words echo through the mine below. 'When we said mines, I didn't realise it would be a *cave*. I am not going in there. Let Lire rule the world.'

I shift, wincing. 'I'll go down,' I offer. 'At least if I fall, I can fly back up.'

'Incorrect,' warns Ebony. Her clothes are all black, her hair in braids. Ready to explore in the dark. But even the unflappable Amoran doesn't seem excited about the mine now she can see it. 'Flying through open air is not the same as trying to fly through small tunnels. Your wingspan could be too large. I think we all expected the mine to be a little more . . . *Not* a hole in the ground.'

'Rope,' groans Levi. He's leaning on Ebony; he's always touching her in some way. 'Why didn't we think to bring rope? Torches? We knew what we'd be looking for.'

Oh. That *would* have been a wise idea.

Sheepishly, the seven of us continue towards the cave's mouth, our steps slow and cautious. I glance around for anything that could be of use. 'The miners must have left something. We'll find a way down.'

Arden frowns, his hands on his hips. 'No, I don't think they did. There's magic here. You can sense the wards, can't you? That's why there's no one – and nothing – here.'

He's right. That must be why the cave is so frightening to us all. We usually aren't bothered by something as measly as a hole in the ground. These wards aren't as aggressive as the ones around Maya's grandmother's mausoleum, but they have the same sort of ambience.

'Afraid?' Opal laughs nervously. 'Not me.'

'This isn't a good sign,' Lark says. 'If there were still any iron here, magic wouldn't work.'

'Well, that's fine, isn't it?' Opal says. 'Someone's already mined it, which means we don't have to go down there. We just have to find where they took it.'

'Where *who* took it?' I say, more than a little defeatedly. 'And *when*? The fairies had all the iron eradicated before even my Bearran friends' lifetimes. This mine could be ancient.'

A bat zips out, shooting towards us. We scream and duck as one, half of the pirates tumbling to the ground. It goes for Levi – *A bat attack? That's different* – and I become the swan on instinct, flapping my wings in its face before it can scratch his eyes out. Levi thumps to the dirt.

I screech in the bat's face, frightening it enough that it flies back into the cave.

Fairies.

Absolutely ridiculous. We have to deal with *bats* too?

I'm about to shift back when Arden appears by my side, reaching for me. 'Your wing!' Hot blood drips onto his hands, which are trying to cover the wound, and I stumble faintly. The pain only comes once I'm aware of the injury – a dull ache in my wing with a sting where it bleeds.

The bat . . . bit me?

'Sierra?' says Arden. It's hard to discern – I'm struggling to remember human emotions when I'm so distracted with the swan's discomfort – but he seems genuinely concerned.

Before I can faint, I manage to turn human and slump to the grassy ground. None of the pain lasts through the transformation.

It's just me again. Whole.

Arden gapes, still not-quite touching me, though it's the closest he's gotten in days. His eyes dart between mine and the blood on his hands. 'Reed, please don't pick fights with animals. That thing could've seriously hurt you. It— It did.'

I glare at him, rub my arm as I stand. 'Why do you care who I pick fights with?'

He scoffs. 'I suppose I don't. Forget I tried to care after you just saved my friend from a bird.'

'Bats aren't birds,' says Ebony, helping Levi up. 'They're mammals.'

'What else is lurking in there?' Wren shivers, staring at it wide-eyed.

'Nothing I want to deal with,' says Arden. 'It's too dangerous.'

I snicker. 'I thought you were supposed to be pirates. Isn't danger your whole . . . thing?'

'Not particularly,' says Opal. 'I just like pretty things.'

'Okay, Sierra.' Wren raises her ginger eyebrows at me. 'If you're so brave, then go in.'

I cross my arms. 'I already said I would.'

'And she's proven her bravery for the day,' Levi says. 'Uh, thank you.'

'You're welcome.' I approach the cave, goosebumps covering more of my skin with every step, until I can see right into the murky darkness. Arden and Ebony are the only ones who follow, staying close behind me.

As far as I can see, the mine drops steeply into nothingness, like a wide well. Except for a rickety, ancient ladder, there's no way of getting in or out without wings or magic. But Ebony was right. As the swan, I'm too big to fly through. The bats are made for it. Not me.

Arden sighs, swearing under his breath. 'Let's just get this over with.' He kneels down at the edge, climbing over so his feet are on the ladder.

'Wait! What are you doing?' Ebony reaches for him like she's going to yank him back up.

'We have to follow this lead. It's all we have. If you hear me scream,' he says to me, 'fly down and get me.'

'No. This isn't safe,' I say, my skin prickling. 'The ladder is ancient. The mine is full of bats. You have no light. Are you insane?'

He smiles awkwardly, continuing his descent. 'Yes? I thought you and I were together in that.'

The cave's void makes my legs shake. But – no – it isn't me that's afraid. It's because of the wards. 'Must I remind you that I need you alive,' I sneer, 'for any chance of you undoing my curse?'

He keeps crawling down, his head dipping below the bright sunlight as if sinking into shadowy water. 'Then don't let me die!'

Fighting the urge to simply give up and murder him, I manoeuvre onto the ladder and follow.

'Not you *too*,' Ebony whines, but I'm already down now, hurrying into near blackness so I can catch up.

He hisses. 'Watch my hands, Reed! You have big feet.'

I grunt. 'I should knock you down. Laugh as I watch you fall.'

'*I need you alive.*'

I shuffle my foot in his face – not *lethally* – and he sputters as he tries to flick me away. We both jolt at the sudden piercing creak of the ladder and nearly lose our grip for a heart-stopping moment, but we quickly recover, pretending it never happened, and continue climbing down in silence.

When there's no light except the shrunken circle of sun at the cave's entrance, Arden stops.

'*What?*' I whisper, my voice echoing.

His feet thud, echoing up the cave. 'The bottom!'

I hear him take a step back to give me room. When my boots touch steady ground, I sigh with relief. That is, until the cold air of the depths creeps over my arms.

He takes my hand. 'So we don't lose each other,' he explains. His hand is warm. Mine is sweaty and freezing.

I'm not afraid of the dark. I've swam in deep lakes much more threatening than whatever might lurk in this cave. But there is something off about this place. Magic may be the only thing I fear, and this . . .

We should call up to the others, tell them we made it, but I don't want to attract attention to ourselves. 'How are we supposed to find anything down here?' I whisper to Arden.

'You tell me. I can't see a thing.'

'This was a terrible idea. *Your* idea.' I shiver, unable to relax with the feeling of his hand in mine, but unable to let go. 'We can't move in case we lose the ladder. Or fall in a hole, or worse. You could have at least thought to bring matches.'

'But you didn't eith— Okay, okay,' he relents. 'I agree. Let's work with what we have. If you were to turn into the swan, would you have any better luck seeing?'

I swallow. If there's anything I don't want to be down here, it's a bird – with no hands to hold. 'No, I can't see much better, and I don't want to risk transforming down here anyway.'

'Alright then,' he says slowly, as if scheming. 'Okay, I want you to grip the ladder and get as low as you can to the ground.'

'Why?' I say, though I'm already doing it.

He follows me down. 'Do not, under any circumstances, let go of my hand. I'm going to inch out as far as I can and see what I can feel.'

'No you're not.'

'I'm already doing it,' he whispers.

'No.' I pull his hand, snatching him back. He groans. 'If you hurt yourself,' I explain, 'you can't heal like I can. What if you cut yourself on something? What if you fall? No. You hold the ladder. I'll search.'

He sighs. 'Fine.' And after a moment, 'I . . . appreciate that.'

Thank the fairies we can't see each other right now. I couldn't face him. Me trying to stop him getting hurt? Him thanking me? It has to be the Adellan air. The darkness. The wards.

I wait until I can sense his hand on the ladder, then get as low to the ground as I can. With one hand gripping his and the other stretched out in front of me, I scour the floor by touch.

The smooth rock is occasionally speckled with gravel. I comb over each section of the ground around us, piece by piece, mine and Arden's arms stretching until our fingers barely touch.

My hand slips over something sharp – I whip it back with a screech.

'You okay?' asks Arden, squeezing my fingers.

My cheeks heat. 'Fine. Just a scratch.' For now. *Anything* could be waiting on the ground to slice through my hand. *I'll heal*, I remind myself. We have to find the iron. We have to do something. Get somewhere. If we're really not going to find the magic we need for the curse, I need *something*.

Or I'm going to lose my mind.

'If you say so.' He doesn't let my hand move out of his strong grip again.

I continue patting the ground, my body tense with fear. One or both of our heartbeats pulses through our fingertips.

'Ah!' My hand curls around something. He shrieks in shock, but I hush him. The object's metal tip is cool, its wooden handle smooth. '*Hammer?* I found a hammer!'

'Yes!' He laughs with relief. 'Okay, it isn't what we came for, but—'

'If the hammer has a marking on it—'

'An owner, a maker—'

'We can follow that clue to the iron.'

We stand closer to the ladder once more, and I can almost feel his smile. He takes the hammer from me and his jacket rustles as he slips it into a pocket. Suddenly I'm not afraid of the dark, because there's a glimmer of hope – exactly what I needed. I relax into it, take a few deep breaths, my body pressed next to his against the rusted rungs.

I'm warm, and I'm elated, and Arden's hand is firm in mine, keeping me steady, and . . . Why don't I hate that? Grudgingly, I'm reminded of the feeling of touching him a few days ago, the way I felt like . . .

But we couldn't. Not then. Now, though? Now we're in the dark. Where we can't be seen. Where we can't see each other. Why do I want to throw my arms around him? And not in a violent way?

Why are his fingers lacing through mine so warmly, so softly?

Why am I pressing my body closer to his?

Oh, *fairies*, not again . . .

His hands travel up, one still gripped in one of mine, so my palm is brought up to my face. He feels around gently, curiously, cautiously, getting an understanding of my mouth, my nose, my eyes, where all the pieces fit. Brushing a finger over my lips in a way that makes me go weak all over.

For a moment I think to stop us. I really mustn't turn him into a swan. Funny as that would be, it'd be inconvenient.

But a curse-changing kiss has to be one of real love. At least, that's my theory. For something like what happened with Zeus to happen again, there would have to be a real connection. Not anything like what Arden and I have, which is pure hatred for each other. There couldn't be *less* love between us, so what harm could a kiss do?

Arden's breaths are heavy and slow, hot on my skin. 'Sierra . . .'

'Quiet,' I whisper past his hand.

He presses my hand against my cheek, our fingers still interlocked. He lifts my jaw, and when his lips reach mine, I don't know how the entire cave hasn't lit up with fire. I push my arms around his neck and curl myself into him, kissing his soft lips so hard that I'm not sure if I want to hurt us both. The heat somehow continues rising, an inferno blazing around us, and it doesn't matter that I can't see. In this moment, I can feel everything.

We could be anyone in the dark. No one has to know we're enemies. Not even ourselves. I'm not a Reed. He's not a pirate.

But one thing that's undoubtable? His lips are . . .

Fairies.

He kisses my neck and runs his hands down my back. I push my fingers through his hair, smelling the top of his head, pressing our waists together. He reaches under my shirt. The hammer is sharp against my chest, pressed against me through his jacket.

We found a clue. Everything is coming together. Don't we deserve a bit of . . . whatever this is?

I don't know how far it's going to go. I don't plan on stopping it, coming up for air. *Fairies.* I can't stop. And—

Flutter. Arden jumps and screams. 'Bat!' He pushes me away before remembering where we are and pulling me back into his chest.

Spell broken, I put my hands on the ladder and race up as fast as I can, Arden close behind. Every feeling I had a moment ago evaporates instantly. The emotional whiplash clouds my mind, but I'm not chancing another second down there.

The flaps grow louder and stronger in my ears, and I have to use one hand to dispel the little creatures while using the other to climb. A new kind of adrenaline – my *preferred* kind – swims through my body.

When we finally reach the top, I slump to the ground, pull up Arden behind me, and stare at my scratched arms. The crew stares at us disbelievingly. Then they notice the rising flurry of leathery wings.

Well, our kiss didn't turn anyone into a swan, or wake a kingdom, but apparently it roused an entire cave's worth of *bats.*

They reach us, screeching, and Levi lifts me to my feet. Ebony helps Arden, and the seven of us run for a good ten minutes before finally falling to the ground beside a stream of water, gasping for air.

Arden's face is flushed, his lips red from where I was . . . biting at them.

He doesn't look me in the eyes. What happened could be a dream. No one saw. No one will ever know.

And yet . . .

'What happened down there?' Wren asks. 'Did you find anything, or was your little bravery contest as useless and stupid as we all figured?'

Ebony has her hands on her hips. 'I thought you were hurt. I could hear you both groaning.'

Lark and Levi share a *look*, mouths open.

Fairies. 'I just scratched my hand,' I stammer, quick to change where their minds are, 'but we found something,'

Arden swallows, pulling the hammer from his jacket. 'It isn't much, but . . .'

Ebony snatches it. 'It has a marking in the metal! We can track down whoever mined the iron!'

I smile with the others, my heart still pumping loud enough it's nearly deafening. I smooth my hair down and sigh, but when Arden finally meets my eyes, a fresh bloom of hatred rises in my chest. Along with something else. And I know, somehow I just know, that he's feeling it too.

Oh no.

I glance at Ebony and Levi, their shoulders pressed together, and think about their – I wince – their *love* for each other. I never, ever want to be tied to someone like that. Especially not— *ugh*!

But a little bit of lust never hurt anyone . . .

CHAPTER
THIRTEEN

After spending the morning flying above, desperate for space and fresh air after that foul cave – and what happened in it – I float down to the *Neptune* and head below deck to find Ebony poring over books, searching for a link between the hammer's marking and any existing place or person.

The ship remains floating peacefully along the soft rivers of Adella's Territory – we don't see any point in going far, since the iron miners were most likely to be from this area. Besides, none of us are in a hurry to leave this beautiful weather. I just have to pointedly remind myself to *not* look at Arden's arms as he works on the deck in only his undershirt. Which is another reason I'm staying either below or up in the skies as much as possible.

Lark calls Ebony to have some of the soup he's reheating, his sister swinging her legs on the benchtop, watching him cook. Ebony waves him off, deep in her study, so I grab us both a bowl and lay hers in front of her.

'Found anything?' I ask, peering over the pages. She has the hammer in front of her, the inscription lit by a candle. *Peers Metal,* it reads with a small wood-burned logo of a necklace with a heart-shaped pendant.

She takes her soup and gently sips from the spoon. 'I'll never find anything if you all keep distracting me.'

I glance at Lark, who gives me a knowing look. 'Well,' I say to her, 'let me help.'

'You want to help.'

'It's *my* mission, isn't it?'

She shrugs. 'Look through the old newspapers for any mentions of Peers Metal. Or iron. Or the logo. Or any mines at all. The newspapers are probably too recent to give us anything, but it's worth a look. You can read, right?'

I huff. 'Obviously.' I tear a newspaper out of her hands and open it wide. It crunches under my fingertips, at least fifty years old. It's printed in faded, barely legible pink ink.

'I was only asking to make sure,' Ebony says, not looking up from her book. 'You grew up on the water, busy with fighting. How should I know if you're educated?'

I shoot her an offended expression, which she doesn't see, because she refuses to stop reading.

'I can't read,' Wren says from the kitchen bench, swinging onto her feet and walking behind me to look at the newspaper. 'It isn't so shameful.'

I spin to frown at her. 'What?'

She seems so intelligent, like the others. Though I'd never tell them that.

Wren hops down and moves to sit beside me, rapping against a pile of books, the hardcovers making a satisfying *tap tap tap* under her short nails. 'Lark knows enough to get by, but even he isn't good. Reading isn't really taught in Muse's Territory.'

'Ridiculous,' I say under my breath. 'And no one here has taught you?'

She wrinkles her nose. 'Ebony is trying, but it's like all the letters just jumble together.'

'Maybe you need glasses.'

'I can see fine,' she says. 'Like I can see all those worry lines on your forehead.'

I nearly smack her with the paper. 'Hey!'

She grins. 'We'll be alright, Sierra. Don't stress so much.'

I smile in return before I can help it, and suddenly it hits me that the hatred my sisters always showed me is absolutely nonsensical. I barely know Wren, but if she was my younger sister, I'm sure I would love her. There's a protective instinct I feel, even though she's only a few years younger than me.

So what's so wrong with *me* that my sisters despise me?

Before I can spiral, Arden, Opal, and Levi sprawl down into the cabin, dry, pink, and windswept. Opal claps when she sees Lark at the stove, her nostrils flaring with a sniff. 'Soup!'

Lark smiles at her. 'Pumpkin. Just how you like it.'

'Oh, my lovely Lark.' She pats him on the back and he blushes. 'I don't know how we ever survived without our chef.'

'Opal!' Arden feigns offense. 'My cooking wasn't *that* bad.'

'It really was. Sorry old friend.' Opal slumps next to me and nearly spills her soup.

Ebony screeches like a hawk over its nest. 'Watch the books!'

'I thought we were supposed to *read* the books,' Wren says, lightly. 'Not watch them. They aren't plays.'

Ebony responds with a dirty look, then reaches over the table to muddle Wren's hair.

When I laugh, Arden's eyes snap to me. Confused. Shocked. Because apparently even *now* he can't see me as human. I'm still not allowed to have any emotions, despite all we've been through together. I turn away, my smile gone.

We take a while to relish Lark's pumpkin soup, which tastes even better with his freshly baked bread. It's wonderful, and lifts everyone's spirits. Soon the group are all talking and arguing and laughing.

The conversations between the six go so fast I can't always keep up. There are over two years of friendship on this boat, two years of memories I'll never have been part of.

Why do I feel jealous? I hate them and everything they do. I don't wish for . . . *this*.

It's becoming a problem. My temptation around Arden. My warmth towards Wren. Ebony and Opal are becoming like *friends* to me, and Levi and Lark make me feel comfortable and cared for.

We're all getting too relaxed with each other. They were supposed to be scared. We aren't supposed to be friends. They're *my* crew. That's the deal. They know I could kill them.

But I'm starting to wonder if they're starting to believe I won't. If *I* believe I won't. And where does that leave us, if I no longer have any power over them?

I hate what they did to me. And yet . . . I can't make myself hate them anymore.

Even if they no longer see me as a threat, they're still here with me. They regret what they did. They haven't tried to push me away. They've invited me into their home.

Or is this what they do to everyone who crosses them? Prey on their weaknesses just to take everything from them? Do they laugh behind my back, like this is all a joke?

'Is there someone we can ask?' Opal says over a mouthful of steaming, soft bread. Her braided hair almost dips into the soup. June appears, trying to play with the braids, and when Opal settles her, the black cat lays in her lap. 'About the hammer. It could take forever trying to find information in books and maps. *Or* we could just find someone who might know about it.'

'Like who?' Levi says. His bowl looks like a teacup in his big hands.

'Like . . . I don't know. Surely there are still miners around Adella's Territory. Wouldn't they know? What's the closest village to the mine? We'll ask them.'

Arden puts down his spoon and, ignoring Opal's argument, shoots me the special gaze he reserves only for me: half-lidded, hateful eyes. 'What about your Bearran princess, who sent us on this quest?'

'If she knew anything,' I say, sending his look right back, 'she would have told me.'

'And we're certain we trust her,' questions Wren.

'I'm certain I don't want to lose a fairy war, so, yes.'

'No, Opal,' Ebony says, and it takes me a moment to realise the conversation has reverted. 'We can't ask just anyone about iron. That's a very fast way to get a target on our backs. I hope we're all in agreement there.'

'We could *try*,' Opal says, sitting back defeatedly.

'Ebony's right,' says Arden. 'If word spreads that we're looking for iron, that not only endangers us, but the entire world. Bearra has triarue. They just need iron, and then they might be powerful enough to actually fight. We can't take this lightly or mess it up. There's too much at stake.'

'Finally he says something smart,' I mumble under my breath, sipping my soup.

His spoon lands in his bowl with a splash. 'Are you really so surprised that I take saving humanity seriously? Do you still think so little of me?'

I raise a brow. 'Yes, *Captain*.'

'That's it!' Ebony shouts, and all eyes turn to her. At first I think she's trying to stop our arguing, but then I see her finger pressed hard against the yellowed page of a history book. She wasn't even listening, apparently. 'I found our miners. This company specialised in gold mining two hundred years ago. Opened mines all around Adella's Territory. When the fairies decided to remove all iron from existence, they were hired to dig it all up here.'

'Hold on,' Opal says. 'History lesson needed. *All* iron? What about everyday things it might have been used in? Because it was used before, wasn't it? How did the fairies *eradicate* it?'

'Plus the iron in blood,' adds Levi.

Ebony shrugs. 'They're fairies. Anything is possible, especially if they saw iron as a big enough threat that they decided to work together to get rid of it. They would have made it a worldwide excavation, forced everyone to destroy what they had, and then erased the entire thing from history.' She studies the veins on her forearm. 'And the iron in our bodies can't be enough to make a difference. Humans can still use magic regardless of blood. And we are not going to start draining people to make weapons.'

'Ew,' offers Wren.

'Iron can be eroded by rust,' Levi says distantly, as if accessing an old memory. 'Water and oxygen . . . Even if the fairies have it hidden, it could've been destroyed naturally.'

'I don't believe that,' says Lark. 'We know the fairies kept some for themselves, because it's in their nature to have insurance against each other. Not all of it – they would've had to show they destroyed the majority – but they'll have protected what little they have.'

'So where do we start?' I ask Ebony. 'What does this new lead tell us?'

'We have a place and a name,' she says. 'Peers Metal was based in a village called Wellmere, to the west of Adella's Capital. So we go there and see what we can find out. Those miners will have descendants, or the village will have records. If it still exists.'

'I thought we weren't allowed to ask people?' says Opal, pulling at the hem of her baby-blue dress.

'Ask them *subtly*.'

I ask, 'Can we reach Wellmere by ship?'

Ebony pulls open a world map, folding it out across the table as everyone scrambles to clear their soup bowls. She squints at the north-west: Adella's Territory. 'There.' Her finger lands on the old map. 'Not too far from where we are now. We'll be there in a day. The ship can get us close, but we'll need to anchor and walk some of the way.'

'I could fly ahead,' I say. 'Check it out before you arrive. There could be nothing there and we'll have wasted a day of travel.'

'No,' Arden says, his brows turned up in concern. *Fairies*, he's always scowling at me one moment, then trying to protect me the next. What am I supposed to think of that? 'Let's stick together. It's too dangerous for any of us to be alone right now. Especially if we're following a conspiracy like this.'

'I'll be the *swan*, Arden. No one is going to recognise me.'

The swan. I've barely thought about breaking the curse in days, we've been so focused on finding iron. It's a perfect distraction, isn't it? One that I need, since I'm sure we've lost all hope of saving me and my family. I'm grateful this mission gives me something to do. But every time I remember why we're chasing iron instead of magic, my heart aches a little more.

'Sierra,' Arden says. 'Please, just stay.'

When I realise he really means it, that he isn't just trying to prove he's in charge, I back down. 'Fine. How long will this walk be? Should we go this afternoon or wait until morning?'

'*Tuna's* already changed course,' says Opal. She's right – I felt the ship shift the moment Ebony mentioned the town's name.

Arden's jaw drops. 'You did not just call my ship *Tuna*.'

She throws her hands up. 'Just thought I'd try it! You don't think it's a cute nickname?'

'*No*,' says Ebony. 'Give the *Neptune* some respect, please.'

Opal looks around at the rest of us as if we'll agree with her. We do not. 'Okay, fine. *Neptunie* will not be a fish.'

Arden is still shaking his head disbelievingly when he answers me. 'We'll be at the best place to anchor within the next few hours, but it'll be too late to go. We'll wait until morning.'

'Oh, look at us,' says Wren, slopping soup from her spoon, 'saving humanity.'

Ebony smiles sadly. 'Somebody has to do it,' she muses, sounding as if she wants to do more. But what can a pirate do, other than scheme and steal?

Chapter
Fourteen

Wren kicks a stone across the path. Wellmere is a large village – a small city, almost – crisscrossed with streams and clouded with perfectly-white sheep. The seven of us walk as one, deciding to stick together in this unfamiliar village, even if we're a suspiciously mismatched group. At least Opal, with her deep-dark skin and Adellan accent, fits in here.

The weather is cool enough for jackets, so we have weapons concealed. Even so, we need to be tactful about what we look at and who we talk to. We plan to start by wandering the streets and hoping to happen upon a clue. It feels lame and hopeless, chasing something that could be nothing at all, but—

I stop dead.

'Peers Metal', proclaims a huge sign on one of the village's largest buildings, right in the town centre. The business has clearly not disappeared even after two hundred years. It's *thriving*. Their building is a storefront, warehouse, and office in one, and it's as if all of Wellmere is built out from it. Peers Metal isn't in Wellmere – it *is* Wellmere.

'This can't be real,' says Opal, eyes wide as she takes in the sparkling sign.

'Do we go in?' Wren asks.

'We can't *all* go in,' Ebony says. 'Just Levi and I will. We can tell them we're engaged and looking at gold for rings, then see if we can hint about iron.'

Opal holds up her hands. 'No. Why would two foreigners have come all the way here to ask for gold that can be bought nearly anywhere? I should go. This is my territory.'

'Then I'm coming,' Arden says. He gives her a funny look. 'We can play a couple, can't we?'

Opal bats her eyes. 'Of course, lover.'

'What about me?' Ebony complains. 'I found the place. I know the most about it. I should be there for the questioning.'

'And what would our excuse be?' Opal says. 'Unless you want to be our mistress?'

'Arden doesn't have to be there. Women can get married too.'

'Aw, you would marry me?'

Ebony looks Opal up and down. 'I could do better.'

Levi smiles stupidly.

I groan in frustration. 'Ebony and Opal go together. Tell them you're sourcing gold for a big wedding in the capital, for an anonymous wealthy family who will pay *generously*. They want precious stones and metal, the rarest and most expensive . . . Even, dare you say, iron.'

Opal takes Ebony's hand and begins dragging her away. 'Brilliant idea,' Opal says, kissing Ebony's fingers. Ebony tears out of her friend's grip. 'Back in a minute.'

Arden sighs when they're gone, and so we aren't loitering outside the building, we cross to a grassy park and sit under the shade of a bushy, emerald-coloured tree.

Wren picks at the soft grass and tosses the pieces in her brother's lap. He smiles at her.

I wonder how long it's just been the two of them. Lark is only a few years older – my age – but he's like her parent. Really, he's like a parent to everyone on the ship, making us food and being our empathetic sounding board. He's protective and calming; opposite to Wren, with her brashness. Yet they look exactly the same, both topped with that brassy hair.

Once again I find myself jealous of Wren. How different would my life have been if I had an older sibling, someone to protect me, like Lark? I have parents, but I'd have preferred a guardian like him. It isn't that I'm not proud to be a Reed, but . . . I wish they'd been proud to have me.

Arden starts picking at the grass too, also placing the pieces in Lark's lap. 'I hope they don't waste time,' he says, scrutinising the Peers Metal sign. 'I don't like this.'

'The girls can take care of themselves,' Levi replies, head tilted as he delightfully enjoys the weather.

Wren stifles a howling laugh. 'Ebony would slap you if she heard you refer to them as "the girls".'

Levi pouts at Wren. 'And that's why you're not going to tell her.'

'I'll slap you,' I offer. 'It feels only right, since she isn't here to do it herself.'

Wren grins and nods at me. Levi inches away.

'I know they're capable.' Arden upgrades from grass to a fallen twig, and snaps it into smaller sections. 'That's part of the problem. They're too smart, too strong. Sometimes they don't think about if they can really handle something before they jump into trouble. Especially Opal.'

'Opal's harmless,' Lark says with a wistful smile. 'We all get ourselves into danger. That's our lifestyle. If we couldn't handle it, we wouldn't be alive.'

'Don't overestimate yourselves,' I say, not to be cruel, but as a warning. Lark must know he's the weakest of them. Shouldn't he be the most cautious? 'The lives you led before were much simpler than now. Before, you only had to face the human enemies you made yourself. Now, if Lire finds out our plan, we'll all be killed and Bearra will lose its only hope. We risked enough interrogating the spy in the bookshop. There is no room for Opal's *harmlessness.*'

'I trust us, Sierra.' Lark says gently. 'We'll all do our best.'

His words are no comfort to me. I can only think of the day I joined the pirates, when Opal killed one of the soldiers who attacked us. There was no reason for that man to die. And, in the bookshop in Darraport, she stole things just for fun – even though we were on an important mission and trying to stay discreet. As much as I like Opal, she's a liability.

The pirates move on to a conversation of their own while I sit in contemplative silence. A few times, Arden and I accidentally lock eyes, just to glare at each other before turning away again.

A few minutes later, Opal and Ebony spot us in the park and hurry over. Ebony has a fresh pile of papers in her hands, and lifts them for us to see. 'Lots to tell you. Good news and bad news.'

'Bad news?' asks Levi. The only time he ever looks worried is when Ebony might be. 'How bad?'

Ebony raises a hand for silence. 'We'll get to it. First things first, we confirmed the company was hired to dig the iron mine two hundred years ago. After some persuading, they weren't afraid to admit it. Everyone in Wellmere knows some of the story. They had quite a few mines, got really rich from them, and built their business from there. Wellmere and Peers are still very wealthy. We hinted that we might be interested in iron for the wedding, and we'd be willing to pay a lot, but they insisted they couldn't source any. If it still existed in Adella's Territory, they'd know. And it does not, because someone already bought it all, a very long time ago.'

'However,' Opal says, 'we asked who the buyer was. They were adamant about not saying anything, since it was all confidential, but we got a few hints. There was a lot of iron, and it needed to be transported away from here. When Adella had it all dug up, she wouldn't have let it outside her territory, so it must be hidden here somewhere. But it wouldn't be in the capital, because it would affect her too much. And it would also have to be somewhere the other fairies wouldn't go.'

'So we only have to scour all of Adella's Territory except here and the capital,' Arden says. 'Perfect. Opal, can we stay with your parents for a few years?'

She sneers. 'You're going to be even more thrilled when we tell you the bad news.'

'Which we'll get to in a moment,' Ebony cuts in. 'We told them if they could just point us in the right direction for iron, we were sure our anonymous employers would reward them for their troubles. The manager said no at first, that he'd been sworn to secrecy, that it was against the Peers Metal code, and so on. But eventually he gave us three vague clues. First, if you're looking for something no one is supposed to have, try pirates.'

'Obviously not going to work, but we didn't tell him that,' says Opal.

'The second was that if it were buried somewhere, it would probably have a landmark so it could be found again. So we're looking for a place that isn't very populated, and has a landmark. Thirdly, we'll know it when we see it, because the lack of magic will be quite alarming. He said that if we have any magical items with us . . .' She lowers her voice. '. . . For example, an enchanted weapon, an enchanted ship, or a young woman who turns into a swan, the magic will stop working.'

My jaw drops. 'Even my curse?'

'Possibly. At least around the iron.'

'Maybe you'll *die*,' says Wren, laughing to herself before she sees the horror on my face. 'Sorry.'

'I suppose we'll see when we get there,' Ebony says.

Arden clears his throat. 'The bad news?'

'Oh, right.' Opal's face falls. 'Well . . . You show him, Eb.'

Ebony takes a sheet of paper from the bottom of her stack. 'Sorry, Captain.' She hands it to him, crumpled as if it were taken in a hurry.

Arden goes silent for a moment as he studies the sheet, his face blank. 'You were right, Opal. I am *thrilled.*'

Lark and Levi crawl behind him to look at the paper, leaves crunching under them, and their eyebrows simultaneously raise.

'What is it?' I shift onto my knees. 'What's on the paper?'

Arden turns it around: a wanted poster. It warns of Bart Lacerta, a known thief. But under the name is . . . a drawing of *Arden.* The image isn't quite right, though. I squint, taking in the extra lines, the thinner hair.

Oh.

'Your father is wanted?' I ask. 'What, for the gambling? Or for generally being an abysmal human being?'

He looks away, his expression still flat.

'Worse,' Ebony says. 'He went to Peers Metal and stole a lot of old documents. Which makes me think he's probably after the same thing we are. I don't know why. But the weirdest part was . . . well . . .'

'He has magic,' finishes Opal. 'Grace's magic. "Blue as water," they told us.'

'*He* stole our magic?' several of us say at once. I add, 'This doesn't make sense. Why would he have it? How? And why's he also looking for iron?'

'He could be working with Lire,' says Lark, eyes narrowed contemplatively. 'If he was in a bad place, in debt, criminalised . . . he could've been desperate for work and found a way to join Lire's army. So a few weeks ago, he meets with his son, realises he has magic, then later that night finds him and steals it. Now he's on a mission to look for iron, spying for the fairy. Otherwise why would he only steal documents, and nothing valuable? He's being taken care of.'

'Seems unlikely,' Levi says. 'What are the chances Arden's father can lead us to *both* the things we're looking for?' He glances at Ebony for confirmation, and she nods, as if they've both done the equations in their heads. One plus one equals *doubtful*.

'Whatever this is,' Arden says, crumbling the poster in his hands, 'we have to find him. I don't want to see him, but it's the first lead we've had on the magic in a while, *and* a solid step towards iron.'

'And how do we do that?' I decide not to be cautious of his emotions, because surely pity would only make him feel worse. Especially mine. 'Do you know where he lives? If he's spying for Lire, he could be placed anywhere.'

'And what about staying here and searching for Adella's iron?' Opal asks, twirling a curl of her hair. 'I vote that we leave as soon as possible, because I *hate it here*. But do we search here first, or go after Bart?'

'No one suggest splitting up,' says Wren. Her hair is fiery in the sun, and her face is pale with nerves. 'Please.'

Arden taps her knee. 'Of course not. But Ebony's right. We have to make a decision.'

'It has to be the iron here first,' Levi says. 'Bart could be anywhere. He has magic, and we don't know who his allies are. They could be far more than we can handle if they're Lire's soldiers. We don't even know where to start looking for the man. But here we have a real lead.

We can get the iron, deliver it to Bearra, then go back to searching for the stolen magic.'

'But,' Arden says, 'if we find my father, he might be able to help with both.'

'Are you sure we can find him?' I ask. The iron is important, but isn't the magic more important to me? This was always about breaking my curse and now, suddenly . . . there's a chance again. 'When you last saw him, where was he? How did you find him then?'

'He found *me* in Naroport. He could've been on Lire's side already. I didn't ask. Our meeting didn't last long, I was so concerned with getting away.'

'We've already theorised that he knew about the curse,' says Ebony. 'It's likely he knew you had magic and came to get it from you. Since then, he's been here and used the magic to steal from Peers Metal. These are good leads.'

I press my palms into my eyes. As much as I want to hunt down Arden's father, even I have to admit that the iron is our priority. Humanity first, Reeds second. 'No,' I say reluctantly, 'we should stay here. I have time to break my curse. Bearra needs us now.'

Arden shakes his head. 'We should forget this place and go after him.' Sometimes I wonder if he disagrees with me for no reason other than to disagree with me. There's no way he'd rather find his terrible father. 'We can keep looking for clues about the iron on our way, and we can always come back if we can't find my dad. But if our theories are right, finding him has three benefits. We'll get the magic back, we'll get him to tell us where iron is, and, potentially even more importantly, we'll have one of Lire's spies hostage.'

A door slams, and a trio of large, muscular men charge out of the Peers Metal building. The seven of us stand; they're coming right for us like beasts striking prey.

Fairies.

Levi steps in front of the rest of us, pushing his sleeves up his arms to show that he's just as big as them. 'Can we help you?'

One of the men points at Opal. 'That girl – the wedding planner – she stole from us. The gold we had on the counter is gone. She was eyeing it the entire time.'

'How *dare* you accuse a lady of such a thing,' Levi says. 'That's a terrible way to run a business.'

'Have her empty her pockets,' the man grumbles. 'If the gold isn't there, we'll leave you alone.'

Levi gives him an expression of pure repugnance. 'I will not allow you to dishonour my good friend—'

'Pockets.' He stares daggers at Opal. 'Now.'

She steps towards them and tucks her hair behind her ears innocently. 'One Adellan to another,' she says with a sweetened tone, 'I would never, ever steal. I'm here for work, just like I told you.'

He continues towards her, even when she tries to back up. '*Pockets.*'

'Stay back!' Arden shouts, getting in his way, but the far stronger man shoves him aside.

I look to Ebony and her eyes tell me to stay quiet. *Don't cause a scene if we don't have to.*

It might be too late – I barely blink and Opal is in the man's grip, with another roughly fishing through the folds of her jacket and dress.

Arden yells at them to get off, but it's no use. She's screaming as the man pulls a large chunk of gold from her corset.

Oh, Opal.

'One Adellan to another,' he says, watching the gold glint in the sunlight, 'you're in big trouble.'

'Just leave it!' Arden says. 'Take your gold back and we'll go.'

'Leave it?' He grips Opal's arm harder, and she yelps. 'Do you know how valuable this is? And she just *took* it! This could feed a family for a year. Understand?'

'I understand,' she whimpers as another man yanks her hair. 'I'm sorry!'

'Adella's soldiers will decide how sorry you are,' the third one says. 'There's a war coming. We aren't taking any chances when it comes to criminals. The rest of you should go before we bring you in too.'

Levi laughs humourlessly. 'You're not taking her.'

'You think you're going to fight us?'

'Actually,' Arden says, 'yes. So you'll want to leave while we're still giving you a chance.'

The man's fingers slip up Opal's arm and around her neck. 'Who has the upper hand here?'

'Is this your choice?' Opal chokes out. 'Is-Is this how it's going to be?'

'Come on.' He begins to drag her away.

Her feet kick against the grass, turning up dirt, but when they still don't stop, she drops her mask of fear. 'Well, you asked for it.' She drops, putting all her weight on his hand, and the shock is enough for him to let go.

She scurries off and teases the gold, back in her hand.

I blink slowly. Why. *Why?*

If we're going to get into a fight, can't it at least be an enemy I can kill, not some innocent business people?

'*Hey!*' says the man, the glint of the metal flickering in his eyes.

'Opal!' Arden shouts.

Before the miner can run back at Opal, Ebony is on him, pushing him to the ground while flipping her knife. Levi sprints to her side.

Now, it's war.

A rough hand on my arm spins me around – the second man is on me. I swing to release myself, but he lobs a punch towards my head. I duck, barely missing him, but he keeps hammering at me with his huge hands.

I inhale sharply as a punch lands on my stomach, and I stumble over. Dizzy, I blink to see Arden jumping in front of me and driving the man back. Arden's knives slash around, cutting deep into the muscle of his opponent's arms.

I turn into the swan, healing myself and regaining my senses, and fly directly up to assess the scene. Three men. Levi and Lark on one. Arden on another. Opal is on the ground, catching her breath, and the third—

A scream pulls my attention: Ebony, locked in a chokehold. At first I plan to let her deal with it on her own – when can't she handle herself? But Wren is thrashing at the man hurting her friend, trying to free her, desperation on her small face. Despite their skill, he's too strong even for them both.

And with the grip he has Ebony in, her face is going purple.

Fairies.

I dive to the ground and turn human, rolling to a stop. But before I can go to help, Arden's miner is on me, grabbing at my hair and pushing me to the ground. I screech, thrash around and bite at his arms, but I can't get away long enough to run to Ebony. But I *have* to get to her. I have to save her. I need to—

Pssh. I'm Sierra Reed. What am I dithering around for?

I turn into the swan again, ready to move, but before I can peck the man's eyes out, a whistle shoots through the air. *Arrow.* It lands in Ebony's attacker's neck, and blood fountains over us as it pierces an artery.

He tries to clutch at his throat, but it's no use. He won't survive.

Everyone freezes as he falls, dropping Ebony. Wren curls around her friend, holding her as she coughs.

I turn to see where the arrow came from, although I already know. Opal stands with her bow held up, her tattered dress rippling with her heaving breaths. No, not her bow, she couldn't have brought it – but Ebony's enchanted weapon, transformed. When did she get her hands on it?

Fairies.

Another reckless kill that could have been avoided.

I shift back to myself and groan. Seeing her with that bow, watching the man's blood turn the grass red as it pours like spilled paint . . . My stomach fills with acid. This is *wrong*.

One of the men has fallen to his knees, watching his ally bleed out. But the other – the other loses interest in everything but Opal. He charges at her, blazing with fury. She steps back, panicking; he's too close for her to shoot at him. Ebony's weapon transforms into a thick knife. Opal tries to stab him with it, but she doesn't have the aim. He twists her wrist and takes the knife for himself. It grows in his hand. She squeals. He's livid, no more bluffing. Going in for the kill.

Without thinking, my feet carry me towards her, and suddenly I'm flying – the swan carrying me faster than I could run – and I peck at his face until he backs away. I turn human again, land on his back. He keeps thrashing, trying to get his arms around Opal's neck. There's no slowing him down, and he's too big for me to knock out. I have to—

I have to. I know what I have to do. And with all my Strength, calling on Rhiannon's blessing—

I snap his neck.

We thump to the ground.

I watch in horror as the light leaves the eyes of the man I just killed. For Opal.

They attacked us first, but only because she provoked them. And now two people are dead because of *her*. I have blood on my hands because of her, and it isn't even *her* blood.

I heave, angry and nauseous. As much as I love murdering those who deserve it, I'm supposed to protect people. Not gallivant around the world helping pirates attack innocents.

I wipe my hands on my pants as if it'll undo the kill, and slump to the ground. My head hangs between my knees. Not long ago, I was going to kill the pirates. When did I become someone who would kill *for* them?

'I don't think we should stay in Adella's Territory,' Ebony wheezes, fingering her already-bruised neck.

Arden huffs, hunched over to catch his breath. 'Really?' he replies, then he turns to give Opal a dirty look. 'As if this weren't difficult enough. Now we'll be wanted for *murder* here.'

Opal wipes blood from her forearm. 'And that's my fault? Did you forget the part where I saved Ebony's life?'

'She wouldn't have needed saving,' Arden shoots back, 'if you weren't so careless.' He helps me up and squeezes my hand tightly, as if he knows how I'm feeling. But he doesn't. He's nothing like me. How can he understand what it's like to fall so far?

'Let's go,' he says. And together, we run.

CHAPTER FIFTEEN

SOMEWHERE, SOMETIME . . .

The downside to being perfect, Princess Dawn thought, was that one always, at every moment, had to uphold perfection. Mistakes, for most people, were expected – even accepted. *Perfect* people were given no room for error, and though Dawn was blessed, she was breakable. That's what everyone seemed to forget.

'Mum,' she said gently, standing over the queen and king's bed. Her mother had the same golden hair as her, sprawled over a silk pillow, though her already pale skin had become sickly and sallow from the weeks spent in bed. The closed curtains only made the air staler; her father's breaths were shallow and weak. 'Could you wake up, please? Dad?'

They stirred, groaned, turned away.

'*Please.* I need you.'

Her mother rubbed her eyes. 'Dawn, honey, why don't you go and talk to someone else?'

The princess exhaled and collapsed at the foot of the bed. She buried her face in her hands. 'I can't keep running this kingdom alone,' she whispered, nearly choking on the words. Couldn't they see how exhausted she was? Couldn't they see she was breaking? Things were supposed to get better once Jacob was gone. *She* was supposed to get better.

'You're doing so well, honey,' said the queen. 'You know what we've been through.'

What about what I've been through? she thought. *Don't you care?*

She didn't want to put any blame on her parents, but surely all of this responsibility shouldn't be hers alone to bear. They were the ones who trusted Lire. They let Jacob into their lives, and ignored Dawn when she voiced her concerns. They almost let her marry a monster.

Yet when Lire left, the queen and king were the ones who fell apart. They did not try to fix their mistakes, nor help their people. They went quiet. They disappeared. They were so consumed by their own grief and regret that they didn't see the pain their daughter was drowning in. Nor could they accept the impacts this all had on the kingdom. They couldn't even apologise.

And now? Now, Dawn was ruling a kingdom alone. Because Bearra had always relied on Lire's wisdom and power, the royals had no need for a court to assist them. Except for the richest, most influential Bearrans who always had something to say – something to benefit only themselves, of course – there were no advisors, generals, or guides to rely on.

All Dawn had were her friends, Teddy and Maya, but they knew nothing about leadership. They could only support her. And while the two of them had each other, Dawn had no one of her own. She couldn't even convince her own parents to get out of bed to help her.

'Please,' Dawn pleaded. 'Be the queen and king. Just for one day. Come to breakfast. Come to the throne room and meet with some of your subjects.'

Her father rolled over and blinked slowly at her. 'You're blessed, Dawn. We equipped you from birth to handle these kinds of situations. We aren't like you. We need rest.'

'*I* need rest.' Dawn's voice was an octave higher than usual. She swallowed the lump in her throat. She needed help. She needed someone to hold her hand. Why did everyone have *someone* except for her?

In her eighteen years – or, one hundred and eighteen years – the princess only ever had one person to herself. One love that encompassed everything, one love that was her whole world. But Relia was not in the kingdom during the sleep. Dawn searched everywhere for her. If she wasn't in Bearra, there was nothing left of her now.

Dawn had learned to live with this. It was always a possibility that she and Relia would be separated forever. They never had a real future, but they were undoubtedly, heart-breakingly in love. Although the girl lived far away – in a land that would now be considered Muse's Territory – with every letter, with every dance, with every conversation, hidden away in the gardens while music poured muted through the ballroom windows, Dawn's heart was full.

And that was how their story ended. One of Dawn's final memories before she woke from her century-long sleep was a single kiss at her seventeenth birthday ball.

When she realised her love was long gone, she'd been so sick that she almost wished to end her own life. But she could never do such a thing – because where would that leave Bearra? It didn't matter that there was nothing left for her.

Now, Dawn had to watch with envy as Maya and Teddy whisked each other away to bed each night, hand in hand. Even her parents, who slept all day and all night swaddled in their despair, had each other.

'Off you go, honey,' said the queen. 'We need to recover. Please, Dawn, don't make us feel guilty. You must realise how difficult it was for us to watch Prince Jacob die. How difficult it is for us now that Lire is gone.'

Dawn stood abruptly. 'How difficult it was for *you*?' Heat built in her throat, threatening an explosion. She had tried so hard for the past year to forgive them each day. But *this*? The well of resentment within her was overflowing – no, not just flowing. Bursting. She could not be perfect a moment longer. 'I was the one who had to *kill* Jacob. Do you understand?'

'Yes,' her father replied, but his voice was distant, as if he were still half asleep. 'You are so strong.'

'No. No, I am *not*. You don't care at all, do you? You don't know what I went through. You abandoned me. You let me think I had to marry that man – a violent man I was *terrified* of – just to appease Bearra. You could have put a stop to it, but you didn't even see it. I had to kill him because you didn't save me. He haunts my nightmares, along with his mother. Not that I get to have much sleep anyway, because I'm too busy doing *your* jobs.'

'You're so strong,' her mother echoed.

Dawn stormed out of the room, slamming the door in the least ladylike display she had ever shown, making the maids outside gasp. She sprinted all the way to her room, where she crumpled into her bed and descended into sobs.

'How were your parents this morning?' Teddy asked Dawn.

She smoothed her dress across her legs, which were too small for the throne she sat in. The oversized triarue seat was made for someone who could command it with more confidence than she could muster. 'They still refuse to get out of bed,' she replied flatly.

His question was well-meant, but she hated him for asking. People always wanted to know about the queen and king, and what was she to tell them? She was tired of making excuses. Teddy knew the truth, but sometimes his pity was even more exhausting than if she simply lied.

Dawn caught her reflection in a window. Flawless. As always. Who would know the blessed princess of Bearra was hanging on to sanity by a thread?

Teddy's hand shifted as if he were about to reach for her, but he pulled back. They had to be careful; rumours spread quickly. Although they meant only to comfort each other when they touched, people thought Teddy was a prince, and many Bearrans expected that Dawn would marry him now Jacob was gone. They couldn't understand why Teddy was with the 'poor bookmaker girl'.

Dawn made it clear many times that she would only ever marry a woman, if she had the time or inclination to form a romance at all. But in the people's minds, a royal was a royal, and she and Teddy were the only two in Bearra. Once, she *had* wished to marry him, if fate could switch him for his brother. Now that she was free, she had to keep the idea out of people's heads.

'They'll be better soon,' said Teddy, though he didn't sound convinced. Leaning against the throne, he tapped at the crystal armrests.

'They won't be.' Dawn kept her voice low so only Teddy would hear. 'The fairy war is going to be the end of us. We're barely making it now. When Lire comes back—'

'We've made it this far, and we don't need your parents. We're doing well enough. Probably doing a better job than they could. You know that.'

That was easy for him to say, considering he wasn't the one on the throne. 'Where's Maya?'

'With her family for the day.'

'Good. That's good. And you didn't join them?'

'*Dawn.* I love Maya's family, but I would not leave you to sit here alone.'

'I—'

His sweet brown eyes watched her, his brows crinkled. 'You're not coping.' It wasn't an accusation, not said out of pity, just a statement of fact.

'I'll be fine,' she lied, sitting up straighter. What was she to tell him? That she was falling apart? It wouldn't help anyone. 'I'll recover when the war is over.'

He nudged her elbow with his. 'I'm not okay either. None of us are. You don't have to pretend for my sake.'

Though the hilltop castle always remained warm, the afternoon had brought with it a spattering of rain clouds that covered the sun. The throne room felt dark and humid, and Dawn wished she had a comforting jacket to wear, like one of the soldiers'. But she couldn't be seen in anything less than a gown.

Teddy seemed perfectly comfortable, though she knew his mask was as good as hers.

'Life was so simple a hundred years ago,' she mused. If only Teddy could truly understand. She and him were so similar that she often forgot they came from entirely different worlds. He was never Bearran, and as much as she liked to think her kingdom had become a home to him, she wasn't sure any place – especially somewhere that now held such trauma for him – could ever convince him to stay long. 'Bearra isn't what it once was.'

He said, softly, 'I know it's hard to feel at home here after all that's happened. We've both wanted to run away. It can't be easy to rule from the same room where . . .'

'Where I killed your brother?'

He stepped in front of her, forcing her to meet his eyes. 'I didn't mean that, and don't say "killed" like Jacob wasn't a monster.'

She shook her head, resisting the urge to cover her face with her hands. 'The path is never clear for me,' she admitted. 'I keep making poor decisions. How can I be deserving of a blessing of Kindness if I can take a life? How can someone so confused and hopeless rule? Teddy,' she whispered, 'I can't do this. I'm not capable of saving this kingdom alone.'

'Shh.' He gently lifted her chin. 'You're Dawn, remember? Not just a princess, not just your blessings. You're my best friend, and I'll always be here to hold you together when you're falling apart.' Teddy smiled, and Dawn knew that smile could rule the world – it moved people like the moon moved the tide, and the princess was no exception. She already felt a little better. 'Oh, and so you don't have to settle for me forever, I'll help you find a princess to marry. I'm always keeping my eyes open. Who knows when she'll show up? You'll have your queen, Dawn, and even if that isn't for a long time, you are never alone.'

Her eyes stung once more. 'Thank you.'

'Sierra will get us a weapon,' he said, taking her hands, forgetting their onlookers. 'We'll make it through this war, because it's our only option. We'll heal later, rest later. For now, let's save Bearra.'

'And if Sierra fails? We accept death?'

Dawn wished to be optimistic, but in the weeks since they sent the Gracian warrior to find iron, they had heard nothing. Bearra was waiting for a crew of pirates, of all people, to bring its salvation. The princess could only hold the kingdom together with her bare hands until then. The Bearrans were becoming so restless; it was like wrangling a hundred small children fighting over a single biscuit.

'Maybe.' He offered a lopsided shrug. 'Is death so scary? You were asleep for a hundred years. You've had plenty of practise.'

Despite everything, she laughed. Teddy could always lift her spirits, from those early days hidden behind her dresses and hiding from his brother, to her worst days now.

'You're right,' she said. 'It isn't scary at all.'

'No, it isn't. So let's just enjoy the good times we have left, okay? Promise me you'll try to have some hope.'

'I'm blessed with Passion,' Dawn said with a sigh. 'I must.'

'And I'm the son of the fairy of wisdom, so I know what I'm talking about.'

In that moment, Dawn didn't care that Teddy wasn't all hers. She was grateful to have any part of him at all. Still, she wished the person giving her this talk was Relia.

If Dawn really was facing such terrible odds, if her life was going to be so short, couldn't she at least have *one* beautiful thing all for herself before the end?

CHAPTER SIXTEEN

'Have you all forgotten that we're pirates?' Opal says.

In the days since we fled Adella's Territory, Opal has taken no responsibility for her actions. She can't see anything wrong with what she did: the stealing, the endangering us all, the kill. The forcing *me* to kill.

'Robbery may not be anything new to us,' says Arden from his place at the head of the table, 'or other illegal activities . . . But we don't put ourselves and the crew at risk on purpose. Not like that.'

The sun is strong today, and since Wren burned some oil earlier trying to give her brother a break from cooking, the cabin has become stifling. And that's not to mention all the tension in the air.

Opal mutters, 'It was fine when you had the big plan to curse the Reeds.'

We've had this argument so many times now, and it keeps getting more tedious. Arden exhales impatiently. 'Okay,' he says. 'We don't put ourselves at risk like that *anymore*. The stakes are too high now, Opal. This isn't only about the sev— the six of us. We were clear that scouting Wellmere needed to be inconspicuous. We can't be caught looking for iron. So what do you do? You steal the biggest chunk of gold you can find!'

She rolls her eyes. 'Well at least now they aren't going to suspect us of wanting iron. They'll just think we're regular thieves.'

'But we've lost the option to search Adella's Territory,' says Levi, 'because they're all probably looking for us. You saw how powerful that company is.'

'*Okay*,' she says. 'Sorry no one told me we changed the rules. I won't do it again.' She doesn't even try to sound genuine. 'Nothing to be done about it now. So how are we getting to Arden's father?'

Arden stares at her as if to say *this conversation isn't over*. Still, he answers, 'We'll have to check Grace's Territory first. Go to his house and look for clues. The last place I saw him was Naroport, but I doubt he's still there.'

'Especially since Lire already has a spy there,' I add. 'The bookshop girl.'

Arden nods, then he gives me a strangely knowing look. 'So we're going home.'

'Back to where it all started,' I reply, very much without enthusiasm.

$$\cdot \, \lozenge \, \cdot \, \bigcirc \, \times\!\!\!\times \, \bigcirc \, \cdot \, \lozenge \, \cdot$$

It takes nearly a week to reach Grace's Territory, and the energy on the ship is significantly *off*. Arden and I don't talk to each other unless we have to, everyone is annoyed with Opal, and no one is excited about chasing down Arden's father, so we're left eerily quiet.

We have no idea what we're headed for in Grace's Territory, and I am not excited to visit. The last time I was there, I was getting Grace's blessing with Maya and Teddy, which I'm not sure has helped much. My fight to get justice for my family has seen very little success.

To repress the depression gnawing at me from the inside out, I spend my days flying, practising my sword fighting with Ebony and Lark, and trying to rest. Sharing a room with Opal, however, makes it difficult to sleep; she makes it clear she's becoming desperate for someone to give her attention again, constantly clearing her throat and jingling her bracelets.

'Nearly there,' Arden says on the final day, meeting me at the bow of the ship. The place we first decided to be *friends*.

My eyes flick to his lips. I vividly remember kissing them, but now, in the daytime, I can't place them. It was a half-kiss, stolen. How is the man who so hungrily held me then, the same moron before me now? *Fairies*, I swear I used to have better taste.

Actually, no. I never have.

'The ship will take us through the night into Grace's Territory,' he tells me. 'Then we'll go around the capital. We have to stick to back routes, since we're even more wanted here than in Adella's Territory – especially after Opal killed that general in Rhiannon's Territory – *fairies* – but soon we'll be at my father's town.'

'Are you surprised?' I ask. 'That it's all him?'

He takes a deep breath and leans against the side of the ship. His black hair flashes over his eyes in the wind. 'It isn't that I didn't think he was capable of terrible things . . . I've seen the worst of him, and I know how little he cares for anyone but himself. I just never thought he'd go this far. How could he join Lire? How could he steal my magic?' Arden shrugs. 'I know I stole his ship. And his money. But he deserved that.'

'He's certainly an idiot,' I say, leaning next to him. 'But at least the man we're chasing is someone you know. It's easier than chasing a stranger.'

He frowns. 'Easier, maybe, but not simpler. It hurts more.'

'What, he's a good fighter?'

Arden laughs, and I try to make myself angry at him for it, but I can't. He laughs around me so rarely that when it's genuine, my stomach flutters. 'Not that kind of hurt, you dense bird. He can't fight. Though we have to be careful now he has magic.' He sighs. 'If he still has it. But I'm not worried about fighting him. It's just . . . that's my dad.'

Oh. He doesn't have to tell me. The thought of facing my parents any time soon fills me with such deep dread that I want to cave in on myself. I try to give him a reassuring expression, though it probably comes out as a scowl. I can't help it. Around him, anger is muscle memory.

Arden picks at his fingernails, his brows furrowed. 'Last time I saw him, I was so angry that I had to drink until I blacked out to feel better. It wasn't only anger, though. It was – it *is* – sadness. It's too much for me, all of that pain, and the magic, and knowing he's a spy . . .' He meets my eyes with such real sorrow that I almost gasp. He never shows this side of himself – at least not in front of me. 'Reed, I'm going to be a mess. I know I don't have to ask, but I need you to take the lead here.'

'Of course.' I glance away. 'I don't get along with my father either, if that helps. Except in our case, it's him who doesn't like me.'

'That doesn't help, actually,' he murmurs. 'Just makes me feel sorry for you.'

'*Ugh.*'

'No, it's— It's nice to know someone understands.' He gestures to the hull, where the others are. 'They think they do, but they don't. I don't mean to sound harsh, but Opal, Ebony, and Levi's parents still care about them. They're just runaways. And Lark and Wren never had parents to begin with.'

He scratches at the wood of the ship. 'My father is my only family left, and he never even tried to be enough for us. But every time I've started doing well without him, he's tried to take it all away. I hate him so much, and yet I still fantasise about things changing, about him caring. Sometimes I wonder what my life would've been like if he at least tried.' He frowns. 'I feel insane for grieving a man who never, and will never, exist. But even now my heart says I could fix him if I was just good enough, important enough, to be worth his time.'

My body reacts before my mind does, my hand shifting to sit atop his on the railing. He flips his over and squeezes my fingers gently.

'*Grief,*' I whisper. I never had the right way to explain it before. 'I know exactly how you feel. It's grief, and denial. My family are probably over the moon that I'm long gone, but I still *have* to get back to them, make them accept me. I know it will never be enough, and I don't care. I keep trying to make them love me. I can't move on.'

He shuffles closer, but we both face forward so we don't have to look at each other. 'We can't choose who loves or hates us,' he says, 'and we can't change people's minds. I chose to give up on my father and create my own family, and it was the best thing I ever did. Even if he still haunts me.' Arden pauses, inhales. 'You can still save your sisters if you want to. But when it's done, you should stay with us. Or go out on your own, if that's what you want. Just get away from them. Forget them. If you don't, you're going to spend your entire life drowning for them.'

I swallow. How idyllic his idea sounds, how easy he makes it seem to be like him. To run away. 'My family has a duty,' I say. 'We protect Grace's Waters from bad people. It's what I was raised to do. I can't just give up my responsibility because my family and I don't like each other. A soldier doesn't leave their army just because they don't get along with their general. Soldiers stay because they believe in what they're fighting for.'

He lets out a short, disbelieving breath. 'You aren't a soldier. You don't need an army or a general, and you know that. You could do so much *more* good on your own than with the Reeds. And you could be so much happier with us.'

'And how do you know that?' I narrow my eyes and finally look at him – he's the most earnest and soft I've ever seen him. *Fairies.*

He turns to meet my gaze. 'The way you laugh with Ebony and Opal. The way you're so at ease with Lark and Levi. The way you look at Wren with such warmth. And you and I? We can be entirely open with each other. I never have to watch what I say with you, I never have to pretend. We understand each other without words, Sierra, and I . . .' He exhales, his black eyes locked on mine. 'I don't want to let you go now I have you.'

My heart swells even as my stomach constricts. This rawness is so much more intense than our kiss in the cave. This is everything I've ever wanted to hear from someone, and . . . I can't accept that. 'Even if I said I agreed with you,' I whisper, 'happiness isn't an excuse. It isn't a doorway out of duty.'

His face goes red. Is he *hurt?* 'Well, I can't stop you doing what you think is best.'

'No, you can't,' I tell him, though my heart is screaming, *I want everything you're offering. I want this life. I want you.*

'But I think you're worth more than just your duty.' His palm suddenly feels warmer against mine. 'You're more than I ever expected. Stronger and smarter than most people I've met in my life. If we help Bearra win this war, you will be so much more than *better.* You could lead armies. You've gone up against a half-fairy and won. Sierra, you're—' His gaze snaps up. 'That isn't right.'

I raise a brow. 'It isn't?'

'Not what I was saying about you. That *bird.*'

'Oh,' I utter, dizzy from the change in conversation. A small green bird flitters through the air above us, and I'm very irritated about its rude interruption. Still, I admit, 'Okay, yes, as someone who knows birds—'

'That isn't from Grace's Territory.'

We watch it for a moment before it soars down to us. We both press ourselves back against the side of the ship. Why we're so uneased by a tiny bird, I can't say, but I don't like it. It drops a rolled up piece of paper, then swooshes back up into the air and away.

Huh?

Arden and I glance at each other, then he picks up the note.

'How on earth . . .' I say. 'What is it?'

'Someone sent this to us. Somehow. I don't know.'

'What does it say?'

He reads aloud. '*Come find me in Muse's Territory. A town called Avaene. I'll find you there and tell you what you want to know about the fairy war.*'

'Well that's obviously a trap,' I say. 'Lire knows what we're doing and she's luring us there so she can kill us. Did you know there are talking animals in Muse's Territory working for Lire? That bird is probably one of her recruits. We have to stay far away.'

He raises an eyebrow as if *I'm* being ridiculous. 'No, we have to check it out. Let's go there first, then come back to Grace's Territory to confront my father. This person may have something we need. Something we can use against my dad, or even something solid to bring back to your friends in Bearra. If it isn't a trap, I think it'll be worth our while.'

A gust of wind blows his hair back from his face, and I nearly – *nearly* – brush it back into place. 'I think you've just found a miraculous excuse to avoid seeing your father.'

'Of course not,' he says. 'I think we're going to ask the others first and vote on it.'

'*I think*, I'm actually in charge here, and I don't care to put it up to a vote.'

His jaw tenses. 'Well, Reed, I *think* that right now we're chasing my father based on a wild theory that he might be the source of all our problems. I *think* that what we have right now is a real lead.'

'It's a note from a bird, Arden. A bird! And it's clearly a trap!'

He spins and saunters down to the cabin. 'You're a bird!'

'I'm going to kill you!'

'What, you're going to *stab me in the back*? I'm so scared.'

I hold back a scream as I follow him.

'What's all the yelling about?' Levi asks when we get downstairs. Everyone's around the table, as if we've walked into an intimate dinner party. Arden hands him the note. 'Huh. Where'd this come from?'

I slump into a chair next to Lark, and he pushes a plate of biscuits towards me, still warm. 'A bird dropped it at our feet,' I mutter through a bite of cinnamon. *Oh fairies, it's good.* 'And no, I'm not being sarcastic. Arden wants us to forget his father and go straight to Muse's Territory to look into this nonsense.'

'It's obviously a trap,' says Ebony, reading the note as Levi shifts to show her. 'Arden just wants to avoid his father.'

I grin victoriously. 'That's exactly what I said.'

'We need to discuss this seriously.' Arden glares at me. 'Forget my opinion. This calls for a vote. Either we stay in Grace's Territory and look for my father first, or go directly to Muse's, see what this note is all about, then come back.'

'I vote we don't go there,' says Wren, her face already paling. 'Too many bad memories.'

'Seconded,' says her brother. 'Nothing good comes out of that place. This isn't a lead we want to follow. If this person is that desperate to talk to us, they'll find a less suspicious way.'

'Sure,' Opal says, 'but you two are just as biased as Arden is. None of you want to face your tragic pasts. I know no one cares about my opinion, but I say we go see what this mystery person has to tell us. Unless it's Lire herself, I'm pretty sure we can handle them.'

Lark crosses his arms, glancing at Wren apprehensively. 'Fine. If it's what the rest of you want, I'll go. But Wren stays on the ship.' For once, she smiles warmly at his protectiveness. *Fairies*, how bad were their lives there that even Wren is backing down from possible action?

'Sounds fine to me,' Arden says. 'Eb?'

She shrugs. 'I'm with Lark. Whatever everyone wants. It sounds dangerous, but it could a strong lead. I don't mind a bit of danger.'

'Levi?'

'I'm with Ebony,' he says. 'Sierra? What's your vote?'

I glance around the room, considering their answers. We keep getting into trouble by being reckless – aren't we all still furious at Opal for making a bad decision that put us all in danger? And I was so certain this is a bad idea.

But if the crew are confident, I know we can face whatever danger this mystery holds. I know the terrors of Muse's Forest, but Opal and Ebony are right. This is what we do, and so far we've always made it out alive.

Need I remind myself that I'm *Sierra Reed*? Even if Lire herself awaits us, who does she think she is against me? Me *and* my crew.

'Let's go, then,' I say. 'But we stay careful, we make it fast, and we don't let Arden be a baby about confronting his dad.'

'Here, here,' says Opal.

CHAPTER
SEVENTEEN

Avaene is, thankfully, right on the river, just south of Muse's Capital. It only takes us a couple of days to sail there, the waters easy and the weather mild. Still, as soon as we enter the territory, we're all on edge. If the note wasn't suspicious enough, I've experienced the violent side of this place.

None of us are more anxious than Lark and Wren, though. Whatever they ran from here, it scared them as much as this place scared me. Between the talking creatures and Muse's cult of followers, there's an eerie, dark atmosphere in this idyllically-masked golden forest.

We anchor in a quiet – for Muse's Territory, at least – spot nearby Avaene, though not close enough that Wren might be bothered by anyone. Though it feels wrong to leave the frightened girl here alone, she stays behind with the *Neptune*. When my feet touch the ground, I ask the others, 'Should someone stay with her?'

'Wren can take care of herself,' says Opal, but Lark gives her an uncharacteristically dark look. Of course he would have preferred to stay behind with his sister – both to protect her and to not have to face his old territory – but he knew we'd need a Musan to guide us. If anything, we should have left Opal on the ship so she can't cause trouble again.

Already, the cacophony of the forest is making my ears sore, and I want to cover them. And it worries me, because if even the grass under my feet can talk and listen, what does it hear? Who might it tell? We're in a precarious enough position as it is.

I shiver. 'I know she can. I still don't like it.'

Arden puts a hand on my shoulder and nudges me forward. 'Let's just make this quick.'

We scurry along, not stopping for anything – *especially* not the snakes hissing at us to crawl into their burrows. But twenty minutes or so later, we halt at the sound of a strange hissing.

A fog-covered lake, dark and imposing, hits us with air thicker than in Rhiannon's Jungle. But it's cold, and goosebumps run up my neck. I take an involuntary step back, bumping into Arden. He takes my arms from behind me, and though I relax, he quickly lets go when he sees Levi's teasing eyes on us.

'Something's wrong,' Opal whispers.

The six of us inch towards each other. The talking of the forest is muted here, and everything is grey and dull, like we've stepped into dusk. If I would expect to find iron anywhere, it would be in a place as terrifying as this.

Could this be the trap?

'So creepy,' Levi says, wrapping a big arm around Ebony. 'Lark, do you know anything about this place?'

The Musan boy is pale and tense, more afraid than I've ever seen him. 'There are a lot of nasty things in Muse's Territory. Least of all a foggy lake.'

Our eyes remain fixated as the water bubbles, shaded by a thick layer of overgrown weeping willows. The fog seems to whisper, and maybe it really *is* whispering, that cold air conscious against our ears, caressing our skin. My eyes blur when I look at the ripples for too long, my mind mesmerised by the birds in the canopy quietly humming discordant melodies.

Opal shifts between her feet. 'You know what they say—'

'Even the dead speak in Muse's Forest,' says a small voice behind us, and we spin around so fast we nearly bowl each other over.

Acid creeps into my gut as a girl before us wavers, her hair and tattered dress splayed around her like she's floating in water. She's grey, almost translucent, hovering a foot off the ground. Her eyes are half-lidded, black around the edges. What in the *world* of *fairies*?

Ebony steps towards her fearlessly – though the rest of us are tensed enough to spontaneously combust. 'Hello, my name is Ebony,' she says to the girl. The spirit? Ghost? *Fairies.* 'Are you saying that you're dead?'

She nods. She might be a few years younger than me, maybe even younger than Wren. Too young to be dead. 'I'm Elsie.' Her voice is distant and airy, as if instead of coming from her lips, it surrounds us. 'I died very long ago. The forest brought me back.'

'And that's . . .' Opal searches for words, her bright yellow dress sticking out so sorely in the dull environment that she looks as if she's from another world compared to the ghost. 'That's alright with you?'

'Oh, yes. I like being dead,' she says. The girl twirls her hair. 'Living was too difficult. Haunting a forest in eternal misery is easy. Have you ever lured someone to their death? Driving people mad until they drown in the lake is very fun.' She grins eerily at Opal. 'You really should die.'

Opal looks her up and down, cringing. 'I'm fine, thank you.'

Out of the air, another spirit appears. Levi nearly screeches, and she gives him a soft smile. This one seems marginally less dead, with a little more colour and sharper edges. I imagine she had auburn hair once, and she appears to be my age. Her dress has the remains of pink lace snaking across silk.

Not to scare myself even further, but how many ghosts *are* there? Because one was already enough to make my stomach churn like a lake in a storm.

'Elsie,' the new one says, her voice soft. 'You must stop frightening strangers.'

'I didn't mean to frighten them!'

The second ghost wrings her hands. 'Well, we're dead. We frighten everyone.'

'Not L—'

'*Hush.*' She turns to Ebony, who's still the only one of us not poised to run. 'What brings you here?'

Ebony raises her chin to meet the floating girl's eyes. 'Someone sent us a note, telling us to meet them in Avaene. I'm sorry to have disturbed you. We were only passing through the forest so we could meet this person and find out what they want.'

'Who?' asks Elsie. Her eyes are unnaturally large, opened even wider with curiosity. *Creepy.*

'We don't know,' Arden replies unsteadily. I'm not sure he's blinked since Elsie appeared. Even though I don't *hate* him anymore, it still gives me some satisfaction to see him scared.

'How daring,' says the second ghost, 'visiting a place you do not know, to see a stranger. You must know it is especially perilous to visit a place like Muse's Forest.'

Ebony smiles at her, still seeming to miss that this is a real, proper, terrifying *ghost*. A ghost who is warning us of *more* danger. 'You could help us. Do you know if Avaene is safe?'

She considers for a moment. 'It is safer than here.'

'Any advice?' asks Opal, her face half turned away, as if she can't bear to look at them.

'Do not die,' says the ghost, 'unless you want to join us.'

Ebony steps between them, thank goodness. We can't have Opal getting too scared and causing a fight. 'Who are you?' Ebony asks. '*How* are you . . . I hope you don't mind me asking, but—'

'Muse's magic, of course,' says Elsie. 'The magic that makes the forest sing. There are pockets of the forest so thick with power that even the dead cannot remain silent. Many who perish here are forced to stay. Mostly girls like us, who died before their time. Some take their own lives here just for the chance to be immortalised, even if it is not much of a life.'

I rub my temples as my stomach flips. 'What about you?' I ask the second one. The *new* one, who doesn't seem to belong as much as Elsie.

Her eyes trail off, faraway. 'Call me Carlotta. As Elsie said, some people choose this end. I'm one of them. A very long time ago, I lost the person I loved most. I chose to rest here, in the hopes that I might see her again someday.'

Choose this life? My jaw nearly drops. This girl looks like she shouldn't be here at all. And how would she ever see this person she loves again if they're both dead?

'So, if you've been here a long time,' I say, trying to get back on track before I drop into crippling terror, 'you must know the forest well.'

'We see everything here,' she says, sending a fresh set of goosebumps over my arms.

'How many of you are there?' Arden asks.

'In the entire forest?' Elsie says. 'Maybe hundreds.'

I sense the blood rushing from my cheeks. These two may seem friendly, but there is something so *off* about them. They're dead. They shouldn't exist. They might be harmless, but if there are hundreds of them . . .

'Where are *you* from?' Carlotta asks, floating closer. Her coloured edges grow stronger, and her hair turns redder. She looks strange in the soft daylight as she moves further from the fog. Shouldn't a creature like this only exist in the dark?

'All over,' Ebony answers.

Carlotta muses over that for a while. 'What do you know of the fairy war?'

My breath hitches. 'No more than anyone else.'

'The fairies fear it too,' says Elsie, before Carlotta gives her a silencing look.

'We should go,' Arden stutters. 'But it was lovely to meet you.'

Carlotta hovers closer. 'No, no. Not yet.' She leans in, right next to me. The air in her wake is freezing. The forest grows darker. 'What do you know of Bearra?'

'No more than anyone else,' I repeat, my breath hot and my words weak. 'They only woke about a year ago, but as far as I know, they still haven't opened their walls to the outside world.'

'The princess,' she pushes. 'What about the princess?'

'Dawn? She . . . I don't know, how could I?'

'Anything. You don't know *anything*?'

I stumble. 'No. No, of course I don't. Please— I don't know what you want.'

The ghost falls back, her face dropping. She shimmers, her colours weakening. 'I am very sorry. Of course. I only . . . I miss Bearra. It is a beautiful kingdom.'

'I-I'm sure it is. I wouldn't know.'

She comes close again, and the cold air coming off her as she leans in burns my ears. She whispers quietly enough that I doubt the others can hear. 'You're hiding something. You know about Bearra.' Her voice isn't accusatory, but frantic. 'When you see the princess, tell her that her enemies are closer than she thinks. For her to make it through the fairy war, she'll have to make alliances with everyone she can, but under no circumstances trust *anyone*. Lire has a plan, a game, and if Dawn cannot learn to play by her rules . . .' She releases another breath that sends frost over my skin. 'The fairies already hate each other. Tell Dawn she must bend them to her will, manipulate them so they turn on each other. Humans cannot defeat fairies. Forcing them to defeat each other is the only way.'

I gulp, struck to silence. Why is she so concerned with the princess? Why does she care about the war?

Carlotta backs away, smiling softly, her mask returned.

'What did you tell her?' Elsie probes, her eyes darting between us.

Carlotta blinks. 'I told her what would happen if she ever disturbed us again.'

'Right.' Elsie nods innocently. 'Strangers are bad. That's what she says.'

'Yes, and I painted a clear picture for them.' Carlotta hooks me with her eyes. 'Did I not?'

'Y-Yes,' I reply. 'Yes you did.'

◆◊˙○⚔○˙◊◆

'Ridiculous,' says Opal, once we're far from the ghost lake. 'What did they think they were going to do, scare us to death? They aren't even people. They're echoes. Threatening us . . . *Ridiculous*.'

'Carlotta wasn't threatening us,' I say, still breathless. 'She was pretending.'

Ebony stops. 'What? Why?'

I've been going over that in my head for the last ten minutes, and I'm still no closer to understanding. 'She whispered to me that she knew I knew about the fairy war, about Bearra.' A couple of deer begin shouting at each other – something about apples and winter – reminding me that everything here can not only talk, but listen. I lower my voice. 'She told me to give a message to Princess Dawn. That she can't trust anyone. That she needs allies. That she has to turn the fairies against each other and beat them at their own game.'

The six of us stand in a tight circle. The sun is now high and harsh above us, though a cold wind rustles the singing leaves. A flock of birds soar overhead, singing harmonised songs of flight and skies. Songs I don't need words to understand.

Levi has an eyebrow raised, his mouth open. 'The ghost, she . . . *Huh*?'

'How would she know about any of that?' says Ebony.

'And why would she tell you?' Lark asks, biting his fingernails. If he was jittery about being here and leaving Wren before, now he really might be petrified beyond sanity. 'Whose side is she on?'

I glance around at the animals and trees; a patch of sunflowers have turned in our direction. 'I don't know. I don't know who she is, or was, or what she might hear in this forest. And try to be quiet. If the ghost means to help us, let's not give her away. She wanted to hide it for a reason.'

'Because of "she,"' Arden says, his eyes distant and thoughtful.

'Who?'

'Remember what Els— the younger one, said? "Strangers are bad. That's what she says." Who is *she*?'

'Their leader?' offers Levi.

'Whoever she is,' says Ebony, pacing, 'she must be who *our friend* doesn't want finding out that she helped us. She could be someone powerful, even Muse herself. If Muse is on Lire's side, and that's how the ghosts have information on the war . . .'

'Let's hope it's only Muse,' I say, 'and Lire isn't using the dead as spies.' My head spins. '*Fairies*. We can only hope she isn't. But . . .' The animals here have already been recruited by Lire. They were happy to kill for her. 'I'm going to be sick. Lire is recruiting the *dead*.'

Lark screws his face up. 'If the ghosts of Muse's Forest are working with Lire, why would one defect and warn us?'

Opal pats his shoulder. 'Someone she loved died, and for the chance to see her again, she died and became one of Muse's ghosts. She may not even be from around here. She just came here to die. Her loyalty isn't to anyone but her love.'

'Oh!' Ebony nearly jumps. 'She wants to help Bearra. She immortalised herself for the chance to see someone again. She didn't say her love died, but that she lost her. Therefore . . . ?' She waits for us, but no one follows her train of thought. With a groan, she says, 'Whoever she loved went to *sleep*. She was Bearran. The ghost died to wait for her, and that's why she wants to help Bearra now.'

'*Fairies*,' says Lark. '*Seven fairies*. You don't think she also sent the note?'

My mind is thundering so much that I have to resist the urge to turn into the swan just to quiet it. 'It's . . . It's beyond reason. We need to return to Bearra and tell Dawn about this. This might be more important than we realise.'

'No.' Arden has his hands in his pockets, and he faces me with a serious expression. 'We can't let this derail our mission. This was information from a girl who doesn't want to see someone she loves suffer, but what has she told us, really? We know Bearra is in trouble, and by getting the—' he lowers his voice '—*iron*, we're helping to save them. Whoever sent the note has more to tell us, so we need to focus on finding them and then getting back to Grace's Territory to confront my father.'

I exhale. Of course he's right. This isn't mind-blowing information; I'm just reeling because I saw a *ghost*. 'Okay. She may be on our side, but we should assume the other ghosts are working with Lire. I don't know what that means for any of us, but it's bad. That's one thing we really do need to warn the princess about.'

Arden meets my eyes, and for a moment the others disappear. It's only us, scheming, plotting, afraid together but fighting together. And I feel stronger, and . . .

What am I thinking? I give myself a light slap on the wrist.

'We need to be careful here,' Arden says, giving me a weird look as he watches my hands. 'We need to get what we came for, and leave as quickly as we can.'

'I did warn you,' says Lark. 'There's a reason Wren and I ran from this place.'

⋅ ◊ ⁺ ◯ ⚔ ◯ ⁺ ◊ ⋅

Avaene is safer than the forest around it, just as Carlotta said. *Slightly.* It's quieter, the houses spread out with no plants or animals in sight.

As if the people who live here have tried to banish all the horrors of Muse's Forest, and created a silent haven. The buildings are narrow but tall, sitting on sand streets. The deserted village is lifeless, bland, and bright.

I prefer this to all the noise, of course, but why don't these people simply choose to live in any other territory? Although, I haven't seen a single person here yet . . .

'They said they would find us,' says Ebony, kicking up loose dust.

There's no sign of whoever sent the note, which makes me wonder if it *was* Carlotta all along.

But as I'm shading my eyes from the sun and trying to study the village, a woman steps into the street. Her clothes are dark, her hair grey. In the golden forest, she would look sapped of all colour, but she matches the bleakness of the town. She watches us for a moment, then waves for us to follow her.

We stick together and pace cautiously as she leads us along the sand, past the thin houses. The deeper into the village we get, the quieter it becomes, until the silence makes my ears ring. We enter one of the houses and, because we don't value our lives, apparently, we follow the woman through tight hallways into a basement.

I press my shoulder to Arden's – because it's a small space, not because I want to. My stomach churns uncharacteristically, and I feel slightly faint. But I'm not nervous or ill. It's as if I have seasickness, and I can't tell why. Is there something in the air? I lean on Arden for support, hoping no one notices my strange reaction.

The room is dim and silent; candlelight shadows are cast across everyone's faces. Ebony stands in front of Levi, hand on her weapon.

Arden, to my surprise, presses his shoulder back against mine as we keep our backs to the wall. Lark wrings his hands by the doorway.

'Well?' Opal demands from beside Lark, her eyebrows raised at the pale woman. 'What's this about?'

The woman looks at each of us in turn. She's as pasty as Levi, with the colouring of someone from the world's outer edges. Even so, she's a rainbow compared to the ghosts we just saw.

As long as she doesn't have magic or backup, I have no doubt we can fight her. Yet, despite being outnumbered, she appears completely at ease. 'I thought there was another,' she says.

'That's not your concern,' Lark snaps. 'Who are you?'

'That,' she says, taking a seat on a grimy old armchair and crossing her legs, 'is not *your* concern.'

Arden and I glance at each other.

'Is this a trap?' Opal asks. 'If it is, you've got us now. You can tell us. I'm getting hungry and I'd like for this to be over.'

'Not a trap,' she says. 'However, I must be careful. Human enemies are one thing. Fairy enemies are another. I have my reasons for working against Lire. Those of us fighting the fairy of wisdom must be careful not to endanger each other by allowing anyone to know too much.'

'But you're going to help us?' I cross my arms. 'How?'

She laughs lightly. 'So impatient, Sierra Reed, just as I've been told. Alright, then. I can't tell you who I am, or how I know anything about you, but I can tell you there are people you may not expect who are on your side. My benefactor has had eyes on you for some time, knowing how useful you could be in the coming war.'

Eyes on *me*? The only person I can think of who might know this woman and myself is Prince Zeus – and only if I'm right that the woman is from the Ice Empire. Could Candace be recruiting allies against Lire?

But why be so secretive? Well, maybe because Zeus knows that if he shows his face I'll—

'The fairies have spies everywhere,' the woman continues, 'so it won't be long until Lire comes after you as well. She is building her army with people who long for the power she can offer. Like the intelligent animals of the forests here, who yearn to see the rest of the world.'

'And the dead,' I add.

'Yes. Anyone who could benefit from Lire's power is your enemy. That includes the other fairies. I can't tell you anything for certain, but I will give you the theories we have based on what our spies have heard. Listen closely.' She settles into her seat. 'Kara has always been against Lire, but it seems she is siding with the Ice Empire. They will soon control the circumference of the world. Muse already seems to be allied with Lire. Grace is looking for any allies she can get, but she won't side with Lire. She knows her sister already has too much power, and Grace wants balance. Rhiannon will likely side with her. Adella and Amora are anyone's guess. I believe they'll try to stay out of it and protect their own people. But they are fairies. They are too powerful to make any assumptions about.'

She pauses, allowing us a moment to absorb all the political theorising. I caught maybe *half* of it. 'There will be three major forces,' she says. 'Lire and her army. Kara and Candace. Grace and Rhiannon. If any of the other fairies join the war, it will tip the balance. Especially if Lire does secure Muse, since her people will follow her to battle. All three sides will be trying to get the undecided fairies to join them. All three will put all they can into taking Bearra. All three will be bringing out their hidden iron stores, once they're desperate enough.' She meets my eyes. 'But there is a fourth force, a hidden side of the fairy war. *Humanity.*' Hope is clear in her heavy gaze, and I find myself nodding despite my disbelief. 'There are many people like us who don't want the fairies to be any more powerful. We know that if their power becomes imbalanced, there will be chaos, and we – not them – will deal with the consequences.'

'So what do we do with this information?' I ask. In the end, it doesn't matter to me who our enemies are. If someone attacks me, or the people I need to protect, then I'll fight back. I don't care whose 'side' they're on. 'How can we protect Bearra? The world?'

The woman pulls a sword out from behind the chair. A dull thing. Nothing special. But as she stands and moves it towards me, numbness spreads through my body.

'What is that?' I sputter, my eyes rolling back. I lose balance and fall on Arden. He holds me up, his arms strong around my waist. 'What's . . . happening?'

Ebony reaches out and touches the blade. '*Iron . . .*'

'That's right,' says the woman. 'Which is why it's affecting your cursed friend. This blade will make anyone with even a small amount of magic uncomfortable. It will *burn* anyone with a lot of magic. If driven into a fairy's heart, it may kill her.'

Fairies, so that's why I've felt ill since I entered this dusty old room?

Lark cringes at the sword, fearfully stepping back, even though the woman holds it out horizontally, non-threateningly. 'Well, Captain,' he says to Arden, 'I bet you're glad you lost our magic now.'

Arden gives him a dry look. 'So this is our chance of winning the fairy war? One sword?'

'No,' the woman says. 'It's a start. It will protect you as you search for more iron to make more weapons. My benefactor wants you to have it. Consider it a thank you from the people who know you're fighting for us.'

Ebony takes it, weighing it in her hands. It's too big for her, but she holds it confidently. 'Thank you.'

'Don't thank me.' The woman returns to her chair. 'Kill Lire for me. For everyone. Help Bearra win the war.'

'We plan to,' I say, still eyeing the iron, pushing myself from Arden's arms as Ebony takes it away. It's still making me nauseous, but the further it is from me, the more my strength returns. 'Is there anything else you can tell us? Is there anyone else who works with you, who can help us?'

'Nothing that won't compromise our safety. But tell Bearra their army is bigger than they think. And tell Lire's son to be careful. That boy has spent too long running away, pretending to be someone he isn't. Now he wants to play prince. But he won't be able to protect the people he loves if he doesn't embrace the extent of his power.'

I shiver. 'I've seen the extent of his power. The war would have to become *very* bad for me to ask him to use it again.'

'It will. He and the Bearran princess have a tough job ahead of them. If the two of them work together, they might be able to save not only their kingdom, but everyone. *Only* if they make themselves powerful. You, pirates, know this well enough. No one reaches their potential by keeping themselves small. No one wins a war with gentleness.'

'And where do we fit into this?' Arden asks. 'Why not deliver this sword directly to the princess?'

The woman smiles. For the first time, I notice the dark rings around her eyes, the worry lines on her forehead. 'You may not be the ones to lead this war,' she says. 'But a skilled and powerful team such as yourselves may be the ones to save it.'

CHAPTER
EIGHTEEN

'It's making you sick, isn't it?' Wren asks, sitting across from me on the ship's deck. She glows in the sunlight, the scars and bruises on her face creating patterns. '*Neptune's* struggling too. It doesn't like the iron.'

I wipe sweat from my forehead, trying my best to look lively. She's right. Since we got that sword, I haven't been at my best. My head hasn't stopped spinning. It's hard to transform into the swan, and even harder to turn back.

Similarly, the *Neptune* is groaning and grinding, the triarue in its walls fighting against the metal infecting its system. We only left Muse's Territory last night, and things are already grinding to a halt.

'I'll be fine, Wren,' I say, forcing myself to sit upright. 'It's like that woman said – the sword affects anything magical. The curse has me run down. It's nothing life-threatening. We just have to get this weapon to Bearra as soon as we can, then we can get back to the business of breaking the curse.'

Despite the weeks of allyship between us, I'm still careful not to let the pirates see me as weak. If they realise how *run down* I really am, they could use it as an opportunity. They may seem loyal, but now more than ever, I must remember who they really are. If they had a chance, they would stab me in the back. Wouldn't they?

I want to trust them entirely, to feel safe with them, but there's always that doubt lingering in my mind. There's always the fear that no matter what, they'll only ever see me as a Reed.

'We'll have to get a different ship for the rest of the iron,' Wren says. 'Ours is struggling enough with one sword, and we need enough for an army.'

'We just have to find it. The princess can do the rest.'

'I don't think so,' she says, eyes wide. 'When that woman gave us the sword, she specifically wanted us to carry out this mission to the end. She gave us her best weapon. It wasn't so we would hand it to Princess Dawn, or she would've given it straight to her.'

Maybe so. Though I still suspect the Ice Empire is behind it – Zeus, particularly – and that's the only reason these enemies of Lire are trusting me.

Lark appears behind his sister and slides onto the deck, crossing his legs on the wooden slats. He greets me with a smile, and I recall that not so long ago, I was never left alone with these two. Now they sit with me like they feel more comfortable with me than without. And it's . . . not *awful* . . . to have someone feel safe around me, have faith in me to protect them.

'We have a decision to make, then, don't we?' Lark says, meeting my eyes. 'Go immediately to Bearra and deliver the sword, along with the ghost's warning. Or forget Bearra for now and go back to finding Arden's father so we can see what he knows about more iron – and if he has our magic.'

Fairies, I'm sick of making decisions. I wish to go back in time to chasing the crown with Maya. It was so simple: one fairy at a time, clockwise around the world. The last few weeks have been one wild goose chase after the next.

'We should look for Arden's dad,' says Wren. 'It makes sense, doesn't it? We have a weapon to protect ourselves against magic. Now is the perfect time to confront him.'

I twirl my hair as I contemplate – a habit I've picked up from Opal. *Fairies*, that's horrendously soft of me. I ball my hands in my lap. 'Bearra needs the sword too. What if something happens to us before we get it to them, and they're left with nothing?'

Lark gives me an amused look. 'I hadn't picked you for someone who would place the needs of Bearra over her desire to save her family, Miss Reed.'

'I—' He's right. What am I thinking? I have a weapon that can protect me against *fairies*. I'd never give that up for a kingdom I don't even live in, to protect people I don't even know. Looking for iron is a favour for Maya, nothing more. Breaking the curse is my mission. Of course, it is important that we win the war, but . . .

Honestly, it keeps slipping my mind that we have to break the curse, and it's even more urgent now that the iron is affecting me. *What* is happening to my priorities? Am I losing my mind?

'It isn't about Bearra.' I stare daggers at him, just to remind him to fear me. 'If we don't help Princess Dawn defeat Lire, the world won't be a place worth living in anymore. If we let Lire win, I may as well leave my sisters as they are so they don't have to suffer through the consequences. My job has always been to protect Grace's Territory, and that is what I am doing. It is *not* about some pathetic empathy for an outdated kingdom.'

Lark's jaw tenses and he puts an arm around Wren. His skin looks paler than usual, sickly, and if I didn't know he had a traumatic day yesterday returning to Muse's Territory, I might guess he was suffering from the same iron-based illness as me. 'Of course,' he says, his voice weak. 'Silly me.'

Wren leans between us. 'So what's our next step, Sierra? Bearra, or Arden's father?'

'Why don't we discuss it as a group and put it to a vote?' offers Lark.

I cross my arms. 'Vote? Are you not *my* crew, who is supposed to do what *I* say?'

I'm not sure if it's the iron making me feel so prickly today, or something else, but deep down I really feel afraid. I'm so vulnerable with this sword around, and if I don't show the crew who's in charge now, soon it'll be too late. Arden was right when he said they make me happy. I'm starting to truly, genuinely care for the six of them, and that's the worst thing I could do. Because if they take their chance and betray me . . . I'm not sure my heart can take it.

'Of course,' Wren says with a puzzled frown. 'Captain Reed.'

Lark watches the water in exasperation, communicating volumes with his silence. Trust a Musan to know how to speak soundlessly.

✦ ◊ᐟ◌ ⚔ ◌ᐟ◊ ✦

We call a meeting, the seven of us crowding around the table with the ship lurching around us. The iron sword lies between us all, and I lean back to avoid its power.

Arden meets my eyes, and there's an apology in them. He knows it's his fault this weapon is hurting me. *As he should.*

I explain our options, and finish warningly, 'We can discuss this as a group, but I'm making the decision.' Lark offers the slightest hint of an eye roll, so I hold his gaze until he sheepishly looks away.

Opal throws her braid over her shoulder. 'We should keep the sword. Permanently. It was given to us so we could use it, was it not? We need it for our own protection. Bearra will get plenty of their own iron when we find more.'

'That's true,' says Ebony. 'It's more important that we have it, at least for now.'

'But it's making Sierra sick,' Wren says. 'The ship, too. We can't carry the sword around forever. We need to change something. At least until Sierra's curse is broken.'

'That settles it,' says Arden, giving me a soft expression, which does not affect me in the slightest, though there is an entirely unrelated tickling in my stomach. 'We have to get this curse broken before anything else. Otherwise we're making everything more difficult for ourselves. It's clear we can't find more iron until we know Sierra is safe from it.'

I will my heart to freeze over, because his words – his desire to keep me *safe* – make my chest fill with warmth. *Pathetic.* He doesn't want to break the curse for my sake, but to make winning the war easier. To take the pressure off his ship. Or he only wants me alive now, staying with him, because he values the protection I can offer his friends.

I don't mention that Rhiannon and Grace's blessings will stay with me even when the curse is broken, but I can only hope they won't be a problem. They aren't *real* magic, and besides, iron didn't seem to hurt Maya or Dawn.

'Deal,' I say. 'We keep the sword until we've broken the curse and found more iron, then we join Bearra to fight alongside them.' I sharpen my tone. 'I am going to win this war, and you're all coming with me.'

+ ◊ ⊙ ⚔ ⊙ ◊ +

Arden finds me on the deck, clutching my stomach and rocking back and forth. I try to flatten my features, but I'm half-certain my face is green. The *Neptune* starts to turn a sharp corner, and I hang onto the railing so I don't drop to the floor.

'*Fairies*, Sierra.' His black eyes are wrought with concern, eyebrows peaked in the middle. 'You look appalling.' I give him an unimpressed glare, and he adds, 'Sorry. But I have an idea. To make you feel better.'

That same sickening warmth enters my chest again, worse than the queasiness. 'Why are you so concerned about my health?'

He scoffs. Standing in the afternoon sun, with the shadows highlighting his lean body and the brightness making his tan skin glow, it's hard to look at him without blushing. Oh, that stupid billowing button-down.

Remember who he is.

'Sierra, I care about you. I'm as shocked and sickened as anyone to admit it, but since we became friends – as per our mutual agreement – I've found myself concerned with your wellbeing. I know you've never had friends before, so it might be a little disconcerting . . .'

'Stop.' I keel over as the boat rocks and a fresh wave of acid enters my stomach. 'What's y-your idea.'

'Come with me.' He offers a hand.

I take it without thinking, because no matter what I want to tell myself, my body trusts him, and I need the help. 'Where?'

'Into the heart of the ship, where I can stab you in the back with our new sword while you're weak. No one will hear you scream down there. Oh – or I could lock you up and hold you for ransom. What do you think?'

I groan and follow him downstairs into his cabin. 'I could still kill you,' I say under my breath. Suddenly I can feel my heartbeat in my palm, and I drop his hand. 'Iron or not. Magic or not. I'll always win.'

He glances back at me. 'I know, Reed. Why do you think I cursed you?'

'Well, sorry you have to undo all your hard work.'

We descend to Arden's bedroom, and he leads me to a door beside his meticulously organised desk. As he opens it, a small set of stairs appears, leading into a tiny room that's pitch-black inside – a dark, dank, hidden part of the *Neptune's* core.

Arden lights a candle. 'I forgive you,' he says, smirking, then the guilt returns to his face. 'I shouldn't have ever had that magic. I was useless with it. I'm a better pirate when I'm just me.'

'You're still not a very good pirate,' I reply, but it hits me that he isn't a pirate at all, really. Well, he is, of course, but . . . he and his crew are just teenagers who made new lives for themselves because they had to. They steal, yes, and they cursed me, but otherwise they don't do *much* harm. Not like other pirates, who kill and kidnap for sport. Opal may be the most morally concerning, but the rest are just people who are doing what they can to survive.

Rubbing my forehead, I once again find it impossible to convince myself to hate them. But this is *Arden*. He ruined my life. He isn't sorry, not really. I have to remember.

He steps down into the room, and although the candlelight is dull, it's enough for the tight space – nothing more than a large closet. Maybe he really has brought me down here to kill me.

'What is this, Arden.'

'Relax, Reed. This room is where we store our most expensive, uh . . . *acquirements*. Jewels and things. Mostly a lot of triarue. It helps keep the ship running.'

'You brought me here to show off all the jewels you've stolen?'

'No, but you can stare in awe if you like.' He takes my arm and pulls me gently into the room. 'I thought, since the iron is making you sick, and triarue is its opposite . . .'

I let out a breath as I step inside; it's like a heavy cloud lifts out of my body. I feel warm and sleepy, and I want to curl into a ball on the floor and drop into lazy dreams.

'You okay?' Arden asks.

I note the caution in his gaze. 'Not to suggest that you were right, but I am more than okay.'

He smiles widely, then catches himself, and turns his face back into a prideful smirk. 'You're welcome.'

I lean against the wall, then slide down until I'm seated. 'I'm not thanking you.' I yawn through my words. 'It's your fault I'm in this situation at all.'

'I know,' he says, stepping back up into his room to grab some pillows and blankets. We spread them over the small floor, propping cushions against trunks of jewels, and he sits beside me. 'I don't expect a thank you. I just wanted to help.'

Help? *Me?* Doesn't he know we're nothing to each other? 'I don't understand you at all,' I tell him.

'I feel the same way about you.'

I sigh. 'I mean it. It disgusts me to say this, but you don't seem like such a terrible person. Misguided maybe, but not evil.' I'm dying, that's it. I'm sick beyond repair. That's why I'm being so nice. 'What possessed you to curse my family?'

He looks at the door. 'I've told you I don't regret it,' he says. 'Your family created its own enemies, then called us evil. So many people *had* to turn to crime. I just wanted to do something good.'

He ignores my cringing; why do I ever ask him questions? I know how he can ramble on. 'I started collecting magic,' he continues, *rambling on*, 'and at first I used it for small things, like cleaning, or helping Lark in the kitchen. Or . . . you know. Getting away with a *little* more thievery than normal. But the thing about power is that the more you have of it, the hungrier you get for more. I thought I had a chance to defeat the Reeds. Not just kill them, but really humiliate them. I dragged my crew into it – I shouldn't have, I know that now – and we somehow, miraculously, did it. Then I lost the magic.'

'Hm.'

'And then you showed up, ready for your revenge. I thought the curse was me doing something truly good for the world, but in the end it wasn't for anyone but myself. It was for my ego, my pride . . . It was to show my father how capable I was.' His breath trembles and his eyes bore into mine. 'So, yes, I'm sorry about it.'

I'm sorry. His words hang in the air as if written in front of me with magic, glowing and warm. Finally he's admitted it. Finally something shifts between us, a wall we built beginning to crumble.

'I helped a lot of people by taking out your family,' he says. 'I don't know if I would go back and stop myself, if I could. I told you I don't regret it . . . Or I do. I'm not sure anymore.' He inhales deeply. 'Well, I wouldn't give it a second thought if it wasn't for you. I didn't know I'd hurt someone worth protecting.'

'*Protecting.*' I laugh despite his sincerity. I can't break now. 'Yes, because I so desperately need you. Your curse may have once hurt me, but I learned to use it to my advantage. I believe that you're sorry, but don't pretend it's because of any amount of care for me that you're undoing the curse. It's because I'd kill your friends if you didn't.'

When he looks back at me, he almost seems . . . wounded? I have a revolting instinct to reach out, to touch his cheek and run my fingers along that sharp jawline, to wipe away tears that aren't there.

Arden brushes a hand through his hair, groaning. 'Why don't you believe that any of us care about you? It's your *family* we're against. You're barely a Reed. They didn't accept you. They didn't love you.'

'"Barely a Reed"? How dare you—'

He shakes his head. 'No— I— That isn't the point. You're one of us. You have been since the day you dragged us on this mission. We've all grown to care about you. Not because we have to, but because we've gotten to know you. Because we've all done things we aren't proud of, and we know better than to judge you for what you've done.'

I try to respond, but he keeps going. 'It doesn't matter whether or not you're a Reed. You're so much more than that, so much better than them. What matters is I hurt you once, and now I regret it, and you're my friend, and I'll do whatever I have to now to make things right. I'll keep you safe, keep you healthy, wipe your tears, just like I would anyone else on this ship.' He anxiously works his jaw. 'Sierra, if I hated you, I wouldn't have brought you down here.'

'To this dark, stinky closet?' My words are weak. *Please keep me safe, keep me healthy, wipe my tears.* He isn't lying, is he? If he is, I can't come back from that.

'*Fairies*, you're infuriating. If I didn't care, I would still be on the deck, laughing while watching you suffer. If it were a few weeks ago, I would have *loved* that. I would be planning ways to kill you.' He cringes softly, then gives me a sweet smile that makes my heart flutter. 'When you've never been cared for, care is hard to accept. I know that, because I've experienced it myself. But at a certain point you have to give in and accept the love that's being freely offered to you.'

I stay silent for a while, my mind both frozen and whirling like a storm, my chest burning with warmth, heartbeat racing. The triarue in the room works like a medicine, not curing me completely, but fighting the illness within, exhausting me. Making my mind all the more woozy.

'You don't owe us any love in return,' says Arden, his palms out. He watches me so sincerely, not breaking eye contact, and he has me in his grip – I can't look away. 'Of course you don't. I could give you the world and you wouldn't owe me a thing after what I did to you. But I want you to know that you have a family now who actually cares. Who wants you around, and who wants to do the right thing by you. We're honoured to be fighting alongside you to win this war, Sierra. We'd be honoured to have you on our ship if all you did was sleep and eat all day. Because, by some miracle, we *like* you.' He winces. '*I* like you. I've never been able to be so honest with anyone. I can tell you anything, and I trust you, and I want to be that person for you, too.'

I swallow the lump in my throat. 'I'm tired,' I whisper, not allowing my voice to crack. I close my eyes so he can't see that they're becoming glassy.

Still, I allow myself to rest my head on his shoulder, letting his warmth consume me. To the sounds of his breaths, I fall asleep, knowing he'll be in my dreams.

CHAPTER
NINETEEN

I spend each night sleeping in the dark room of triarue under the ship, and most of the daytime flying above. Protected from the sword, I slowly begin to feel better. But I need this curse broken *now*.

Not only is it going to affect me if we fight this war with iron, but the swan is getting stronger. Weeks ago I realised I was losing myself more each time I transformed, and began to fear never turning back. Now, after spending so many hours a day flying, it's only worsening. My proximity to the iron sword could be all that's keeping the curse from taking me entirely, even as it makes me sicker.

On our fourth day of sailing towards Arden's father's house, Lark waves me down from the air. Between flying or burying myself in the storage room, I haven't spent much time with the others lately. So it surprises me when Lark, of all people, is willingly trying to get my attention.

I float down to the ship and stretch my neck as I try to transform back to myself. I think of my arms and legs, how they feel. Remember what it is to experience my emotions, to string together coherent thoughts. Arden comes into my mind – I do *not* know why – and suddenly I find myself human again.

Still, it takes me a minute to adjust, and understand the nervous look Lark is giving me. 'Sierra,' he says, wringing his hands. 'I had a thought. It's possibly nothing. But I wouldn't want to keep it to myself in case it's *something*. Can you talk for a moment?'

My mouth struggles to form words, so I nod. We walk around to the other side of the deck, in a shady spot covered in cushions; Opal and I spent an hour here stargazing last night until I couldn't take the nausea anymore.

'What is it?' I don't do a good job of keeping the confusion from my voice. I'm still blinking to get my sight back fully.

'I was thinking about iron and triarue last night.' His light eyes squint against the sun, and his Musan hair looks so soft and warm I want to twist my fingers through it just to remind myself how it feels to touch silk.

Fairies. I really need to break this curse if I'm fantasising about *that.* Instead I run my hands over the grooves of the wood of the deck, and focus on my breath.

Lark goes on, 'Iron makes you weak, and triarue makes you better. But it isn't *you* that these things are affecting. It's the magic inside you.'

'The magic . . . Right.'

'Right. It started to make me think that maybe instead of breaking the curse – which could never happen – you could use iron to suppress it.'

I don't respond for at least a minute, rubbing my eyes. 'Sure. But how would we work around the iron hurting me?'

'I'm not certain,' he says with a shake of his head. His glowing red strands of hair shuffle around in the sunlight; my eyes blur and it's like a glittering fire. I'm only half-listening to his words. 'It's worth looking into, though, don't you think? What if we got to your sisters, and all it really took to turn them back was touching the sword? It could be that your body is struggling so much because the magic is fighting back, but with enough iron, if the magic was suppressed completely, it couldn't make you sick.'

I frown. 'Because the iron isn't making me sick. The curse is.'

'That's the theory. So if you touched the iron, what might happen? Would it burn you, like someone with a lot of real magic in them? Or is this sickness just the curse trying to convince you to stay away from it, when really it could be the cure?'

'The *cure* . . .'

'Like I said, I'm not certain. But Sierra, what if you just tried? I hate to see you so weak.'

I'm finally starting to wake up – even if the illness is getting worse the longer I sit here – and hope warms my chest. The earnestness in Lark's eyes is so sweet that I want to do it just for him.

Ugh, what sort of person have I become? It must be the curse, the iron, all these things against me . . . I'm not even mad at him for calling me weak. I tilt my head. 'I hope this isn't an elaborate plan you've come up with to try to kill me.'

He smiles. 'You may have to take that chance. I just hope the iron doesn't burn out your blessings too, though they don't seem to be doing much lately.'

I sit up sharply. 'What does that mean?'

'It means you're being a lot more friendly and reasonable. I'm not complaining, of course, but you aren't the Sierra I once knew.'

'I must be sicker than I thought, then.' I stand, a hand on my stomach. 'Fine. I'll touch the sword and we'll see what happens. But if it doesn't look like it'll work, we're dropping the idea immediately. And even if it does work, that doesn't free you from our mission to *properly* break the curse.'

'Of course.'

Together we descend to Ebony and Levi's room, where they're keeping the sword wrapped and hidden within a box of triarue. As we enter the small cabin, lined with piles of books and loose sheets of paper and not much of anything else, Lark explains his idea.

Ebony has her arms and legs crossed on the bed, her head tucked into Levi's shoulder. His large body makes a deep indent in the mattress. They don't sleep in hammocks like the rest of us, which at first strikes me as strange, until I remember they're the ship's only couple.

'Sierra,' Ebony groans. 'No. You're already sick enough. We are not risking this.'

I glance at the box at her feet. 'I'll only get sicker if we don't find a cure soon.'

Ebony and I stare each other down, but eventually she realises that I'm going to do this regardless of how dangerous it is, so she hesitantly begins to open the box. 'Be careful, and don't push yourself.'

Lark clears his throat. 'Back in a moment. Just getting some water. My nerves . . .' He wanders off quickly, his footsteps travelling to the kitchen.

'I don't know why he's the one who's so nervous,' Levi says, but even he's gotten up and started shuffling between his feet.

'Well.' I shade my eyes as the sword reflects bright sparks of orange candlelight. Ebony must have polished the iron. 'I'm only nervous to get this over with.' There's bile in the back of my throat, and with my churning stomach, I know I don't have long before I need to get back in the air or the triarue room. 'We need to know.'

'I think we already know this won't work,' says Ebony, cradling the sword effortlessly, as if it weighs nothing. I step back instinctively as the iron's power sends waves of weakness through me. Ebony rushes to put it back in the box. 'This is a bad idea. Let's leave it.'

'No.' I inch forward, fighting the urge to keel over. Determination fills my body with fierce strength. 'Hold it up for me. I'll just . . . We'll see how much I can handle.'

She sucks in her lips and holds the sword on her palms. Levi's eyes travel between me and the sword, as if we're two fighters in a ring and he's watching to see who'll strike first.

When I reach towards it, a powerful tension in the air pushes me back. Still, I force myself to take a step closer – even as my legs threaten to give out. I stretch my arm and let my hand fall on the sword, and—

The screams are deafening. *Screams.* My screams? Metal clashes to the ground, and it's then that I register the pain. Burning, searing, scorching my hand so deeply the feeling travels through my entire body. The tips of my toes and the depths of my lungs. On *fire*.

Ebony has let go – only the hilt fell – but my fingers are wrapped around the end of the blade, holding it – because I mustn't let go – that's all I remember – I have to know if I can get through this. But the flesh of my hand is burning deeper and deeper, eliciting more horrific screeches. Blood drips to the floor as the skin of my fingers melts off.

I heave, trying to get through the pain. *I'll heal. I'll heal.*

The magic inside me seems to simmer and rush, like dry leaves thrown on a fire. It's fighting back. I just have to hold on. Get past the pain. A little longer.

Burn the curse out of me.

I make the mistake of letting myself examine the state of my hand. Sores and blisters burst over peeling flesh. Red coats my arm. I scream again, and this time the pain is too much. I crash to the floor and the sword clatters somewhere away from me, my knees banging on the wood as I cradle my hand.

'Put it away!' Levi shouts. I feel his arms around me, and I'm being picked up, rushed up the stairs. He places me down on the deck, the hot sun making the burns throb. I can't look. 'Transform!' His face is right on mine, his eyes wild. I've never seen him like this, making full use of his size, his thundering voice, and for a moment I'm so afraid I don't register his words. 'Now, Sierra – heal! You're going to lose too much blood!'

I press my face into the floor, curl up into a ball and sob, and there are no thoughts, there are no instincts. I am nothing but pain. An intangible thing made living. I am a burning curse, a rage of magic.

'Sierra!' he shouts again. 'Transform!' I barely hear him, and I don't want to. I go still; my breathing all but stops. I'm floating out of my body. '*Fairies*, Reed.' He picks me up. I'm too exhausted to thrash and scream. I'm weightless in his massive arms. I squeeze my eyes shut. 'Sorry, but you have to wake up.'

Someone else is screaming. Ebony?

And then I'm flying. If I didn't know how it felt to be in the air, I might not even register it over the agony. Then I realise: I'm not flying. I'm *falling.* Time slows and I'm flailing and blood and skin fly around me, a fountain of burning flesh.

I splash into water. Sink down. Deep.

Instead of pain alone, I feel ice.

And I wake up.

The instinct not to drown is too strong – it's the first thing I learned in this life. I am a Reed. I do not drown.

What's happening? I thrash and panic before I remember. *The iron.* I have to transform before it burns me alive. The pain returns and I grit my teeth.

With all the power I can summon from my two blessings, from my soul itself, I turn into the swan beneath the water. My wings stretch out and—

The pain is gone instantly. I'm alive again. *Alive.*

But I need to breathe. I push myself through the water, towards the light of the sun. With another powerful beat of my wings, I burst up to the surface. I draw in fresh oxygen, starving for it, water falling off me in waves as I right myself.

I'll take a few breaths, calm myself before turning human again.

But, no, I don't want to. I want to stay as the swan, free of agony, free of coherent thought. I don't want to remember what it is to burn and burn.

Nor do I want to remember the endless *cold* of my human life. Frozen out of my family, frozen in ice, frozen in my own misery, forcing myself to freeze over my own heart. *Please, let me be free.*

Someone yells, to my left. My name, maybe. The word is slipping away from me. Everything is slipping away from me. I crane my neck to see a ship on the river. Humans – six humans – are leaning over the edge, watching me. One looks as if they're about to jump in, but another pulls them back.

A dark-haired man is calling, '—erra . . . *Sierra*!' and I remember he is Arden, and Sierra is me.

I have to turn human again. I have to return to him.

But I don't want to. I'm not human. This is who I am. What I am.

'Sierra!' he shouts, and suddenly I *want* to remember how he says my name when I hear it through human ears. I want to know the feeling of him beneath my hands, my lips. I want to remember standing beside him, pretending to hate him even when he's the only thing holding me upright.

So I shut my eyes and remember. Think of the pain – accepting it is the only way to be human again – and use the memory to bring me back.

My hands materialise, and my legs and my face and my mind as my wings, feathers, and beak disappear. Black clothes cover my arms and legs, weighing me down. Still, I breathe a sigh of relief and tread the water, healed, as if nothing ever happened at all. But I'm dizzy. So dizzy. I float, waiting for the pirates to pick me up. I could fly to them, but I'm too frightened to turn into the swan again so soon.

That was far too close to being the last time.

'Sierra, are you okay?' Wren yells down. 'Why on earth did you do that to yourself? Are you insane?'

Opal pulls the younger girl back.

'I'm fine!' I shout to them. *I'm not.* They lower a rope so I can pull myself up. I'm weak, but muscle memory allows me to yank my way back onto the deck.

Ebony takes my hand and inspects it closely. 'Are you certain you're okay?'

I glance at Levi, who has his arms crossed and his white-blonde hair dishevelled and stuck to his forehead. His breaths are heavy and he watches me closely as if I might die on the spot. It was him – he threw me in the water and forced me to transform. I nearly didn't come back from it, but if he hadn't . . .

'Thank you,' I breathe. 'That was . . . a good call.' It might be the most honest I've ever been with the brawny boy, but I don't say the words I really mean: *I owe you my life.*

And Arden . . . He brought me back. But he isn't watching me. He's watching the water, turned away from us, shoulders tense.

Levi shrugs. 'Water redirects magic, so it seemed the best way to ease your reaction – and give you a shock.'

I exhale, shaking my head and wondering how he and Ebony – the two smartest people I know – ended up being *pirates,* of all things. Then I give Lark a glare and point at him. He steps back, eyes wide with fear. 'You,' I hiss, 'are not allowed to come up with ideas anymore. Got it?'

CHAPTER TWENTY

Because I am such a kind-hearted person, I make a show of not being *too* angry with Lark – if only so I don't have to deal with him cowering every time I'm near him. Using iron to cure my curse may have been his idea, but I insisted on trying it. If everyone is mad at him, eventually they'll realise they should be mad at me as well.

The rest of the pirates, however, dote over me, constantly – and annoyingly – checking to make sure I'm okay. Especially Arden. My instinct to kill him is stronger than ever, because he just won't leave me *alone*. Though I imagine his attentiveness is also a distraction for his fear of returning to his childhood home and seeing his father.

At sunset we arrive in the small riverside town and make the short walk through marshy land to Bart Lacerta's shack. All the houses here are half falling apart and rotting away, sinking into the mud. The smell of the water is bitter and stale, and I crinkle my nose against it. How can a place in Grace's stunning territory be so . . . disgusting?

I suppose *this* is why Arden resents my family so much. Why he resents their wealth, their power. I've never even seen this part of the territory before. I've certainly never protected it from anyone.

Humidity threatens rain, and thunder rumbles in the distance, rolling along the rivers. The crashing sounds make me shiver.

Although my body healed days ago, my mind is still swaying after touching the iron sword. I've been close to death so many times, felt worse pain – how could it have been a piece of metal that nearly killed me? The way the iron curled into my soul, eating at the magic inside, a whirlpool of fighting forces inside me . . .

I can't explain it, and yet I can't forget it.

'So,' Opal says, carefully stepping across the marsh to avoid dirtying her shoes. Her dress is white, almost searingly pure, and she lifts it above her ankles. 'Are we sneaking in, or knocking?'

'There isn't much to sneak in to,' Ebony says. 'No offense.'

'Say whatever you like about this place,' Arden replies. 'I have no attachment to it.' His eyes travel over the tiny building, its second floor crumbling into its first. The aged, rotting wood is covered in moss, and any glass windows that aren't shattered are covered in a thick layer of salt. Arden kicks at a stone on the ground. 'I'll go in alone and see if I can find him. You can all stand guard out here.'

Snickering travels through the group. 'Don't even try,' says Levi. 'We'd never let you do this alone.'

'Really. Please,' Arden says earnestly. 'I'm not trying to be heroic. It's just something I want to face by myself.'

'I'll go with you,' I say. 'Just me.' I secure the knife at my belt. 'Just to watch your back. Everyone else can stay outside, or see if they find anything in town.' My jacket pockets are filled with triarue to lift my energy, and my hair is tied back. I'm ready for a fight, ready to face a man with magic. *My* magic.

When I receive strange looks from the others, I add, 'I'm not offering for Arden's sake. I want to get away from that.' I gesture at the iron sword at Ebony's side. I smirk. 'And babysit.'

Arden groans. He turns to me, shielding his eyes from the sunset. 'Babysit me? It's *my* house.'

'Aw.' I begin to walk so they know my word is final. 'Our captain is growing up so fast.'

Opal giggles behind me.

'Call if you need us,' says Lark, as if he would be the one I'd ask for help.

Arden takes me around the back of the shack to a decaying door. It isn't locked, and it opens with a crackling creak. Mud sticks to our shoes, but Arden makes no effort to wipe it away before stepping inside.

'Ew,' I whisper as I step in behind him; he takes my hand and guides me across the uneven entryway. It seems like we're alone, so I let him.

The house is dark, even with most of the windows smashed. The atmosphere is dank and putrid from the food left behind and the never-ending rot. Everything in this place is dead or dying, from the cobweb-covered furniture to the torn-up newspapers strewn around the floor, half wet and decomposing. A layer of grime covers every surface; I let Arden's hand go so I can pull my hands close to my sides, willing myself not to touch anything.

'My father's finances were always up and down, with the gambling,' Arden explains, his voice low. 'We weren't always living here. When he won the *Neptune*, I moved out of the house and lived on it, and he got a place in a nicer area of town. Obviously that didn't last, though.'

I can't imagine what it'd be like growing up never knowing how much money I'd have at the end of each day. If I would be living in a palace or a slum. Money has always been one of the few things I never had to worry about. I hated the pirates who did illegal, terrible things to get it. I prided myself on stopping them so that honest people wouldn't become victims to their thievery.

Now I wonder, as someone who has never *had* to steal, how I could judge anyone else for it. I have fought and killed, but I have always considered myself to be good. My time with Arden and his friends – people I never wanted to see as *people* – taught me that although we're pitted against each other, very few people truly want to do bad things.

Maybe it's the iron, or maybe I am really starting to . . . feel something for the crew. My mind seems to mellow, expand, lose its rigidity around them. Around others, too, because of them. They've forced me to see the world in shades other than black and white.

And they've made me realise that all the years I was hurting people like them, I should have been helping them. I should have given them opportunities to do better, not purposely make their lives even worse.

I take a long breath through my mouth, partly to pull myself out of my head and partly to avoid smelling anything. 'What's the plan?'

Arden places his hand on a half-full teacup. 'This is warm,' he says. 'My father is either in the house, or has been recently.'

'He was here for *tea*? Today?' My stomach turns. 'Are you sure the cup isn't just warm because it's been rotting so long there's something growing in it?'

He gives me an almost pleading look. He's afraid. This isn't time to make light of the situation.

'Arden,' I say seriously. 'We'll be okay.' Because for some reason, I feel afraid too. Maybe because I know what it's like to be hurt by a father. Maybe because if we succeed today, this could be the day the curse is broken. Maybe because everything could change, just when everything has started to feel right.

We search the house, tiptoeing and barely breathing. The house is so small that within a minute we're certain no one is home. The tension falls from Arden's shoulders, and his breathing steadies.

'We still need to be careful,' he says. 'He could be back any second.'

'If he is, the others will stall him,' I reply.

'Not if he has magic.'

'Ebony has the sword.'

'I know Ebony can protect herself,' he says. We step over a pile of unwashed, torn clothes, back towards the door we entered through. 'I just don't think she'd be capable of killing, if it came to it. But he wouldn't question it.'

He leads me up the creaky stairs, and I hold my breath the entire way. We pass through a narrow doorway and he takes a seat on a rickety bed covered in dust. The few objects lying around suggest this was his childhood bedroom. *Fairies.* I can't believe the pirate captain ever *was* a child.

I peer around, unable to meet his eyes. 'And you?' I ask him carefully, picking up a deflated ball and pretending to study it. 'Have you ever taken a life? Could you?'

In the corner of my eye, his posture shifts. 'Not entirely.' There's a layer of shame to his voice. 'There are many people I've hurt. Many whose lives may have been lost, and it was indirectly my fault. Your sisters lost their lives because of me, didn't they? But no, I have never killed someone.' He laughs humourlessly. 'That's what I have Opal for.'

My breath hitches, surprised at his rawness. Why does he seem so . . . soft? The pirate I thought was pure evil isn't even a *killer*? A killer like *me*.

My perspective of him keeps shifting as I try to push myself away from him. But every day, I find myself close to him again. One minute he's good, and sweet, and I care for him. The next I not only wish him dead – I want to be the one to kill him.

And what are we, now? I am a swan and a woman. A Reed but not a Reed. A killer who doesn't want to kill. A fighter tired of fighting. He is capable of so much more than what he is, but he never could be, because of the life he's had. Once, we were a girl and a boy who could never imagine the other was human.

Now everything has become so clear, the fog lifted, and yet I don't know what it means.

We lock eyes as he asks, 'Do you still have to kill me? When this is all over?'

'You heard the woman in Avaene.' I move towards him instinctively, wanting to be close, to show him I care. The memories of this room aren't even mine, yet I can sense the years of trauma seeping into the air. All I want to do is comfort him. 'Together we might be humanity's only chance of winning the fairy war. Even if I still wanted to, I couldn't kill you now.'

'And after we win?'

'If we both make it, then I'll re-evaluate.'

'How merciful of you,' he says through a smile. He musingly stares at a shelf, on which six wooden soldiers stand side-by-side. The faded-blue paint of their uniforms is chipping off, a layer of dust on each one's head and shoulders. Even in their disrepair, each is placed precisely the same distance apart. In fact, everything in this room is the same – falling apart, but placed in a just-right position, as if the smaller, more innocent Arden who lived here fought for just that small sense of control.

'Someone gave those to me out of pity,' he says. 'I would play with them all the time, not even understanding what soldiers were. I had no concept of an army. But to imagine friends, people I could trust, a team . . . That gift might have saved me.'

'Just like your crew?' I whisper.

'Yes.' He reaches out and takes a soldier from its place, gently brushing off the dust. Through the narrow, salt-covered window, I can just make out Ebony with her iron sword at her side, and Levi next to her as always. 'They saved me,' he says, 'but I learned that fantasies are never what you expect. To be a leader, you have to accept pain. Always worrying, always wishing you had more eyes so you could keep better watch of everyone you're responsible for. Sometimes I wonder if I should send them all back to where they came from, so they'd be safer. To this day I can't imagine why they chose me.'

My skin tingles. I know why. All I want to do is crawl into his arms, embraced by his care and protection. There's something about him that makes him feel so safe, so steady. Even I can admit that now.

So, I say, 'They're lucky to have a captain who cares about them so much.'

He shrugs, his eyes rimmed with red. 'I feel so selfish, keeping them close because I need them, when I know . . . I know they'd be better off without me.'

'They would never agree with that.'

He swallows, and sits on the bed sheepishly. I follow him down, crossing my legs on the dusty covers. 'I want to tell you something,' he says. 'Something no one else knows, so you have to swear not to share this, Sierra. Please. I don't want this to . . . to change the way the others see me. But I need to be honest with someone, and you're the only person I can tell these things to. Do you understand?'

'I— Yes.' I shift to face him better. 'What is it?'

'Before I stole the ship and ran away, I had . . .' He exhales, fidgeting with his fingers. 'The real reason I left was because I lost my little sister.'

I recoil. 'You— Your . . . Arden?'

'Kyla. She was five.' He pauses, as if waiting for me to jump in and stop him, or laugh, or cry, but I don't. I choose to listen, because I can see how badly he needs to talk about this. 'We had different mothers, though neither were around. Our father, of course, was . . . You know. But Kyla, she was so sweet, so perfect.' He smiles lightly. 'She looked just like me, though her hair would turn a lighter brown when she spent time in the sun, and her skin would go all dark and get covered in the cutest little freckles. She was warmth and giggles and love and . . .' His smile drops. 'And she was born with a heart defect.'

My breath stops. '*Arden.*' His protectiveness of his crew, his anxiety, the fears he hides from everyone but me. It all makes so much sense now. He already lost the person who meant the most to him, the person he was supposed to take care of. Of course he'd never allow anything like that to happen again. I don't know what to say. How could he have dealt with this? And worse, dealt with it alone?

'I was determined to keep her alive,' he continues, eyes on the floor. 'It didn't matter that she wasn't expected to live past age four. I was going to save her, and even if I couldn't, I'd make sure she had a good life. My father – he made it so difficult. I stole medicine and blankets for Kyla. I tried to give her some semblance of a happy childhood. But I was only a child myself. I couldn't . . .' His voice cracks.

'*Arden,*' I whisper.

'She was all I had, all I loved. I . . .' His breaths come fast, and he covers his face with his hands. 'When we won the ship, I moved her into it, hoping that the magic and the rocking of the water would help to heal her. We would spend days out on the rivers, and she'd follow me along as I did jobs, but I always made sure she was safe. Then, one day, when I was exhausted and sleeping at home, my father took out the *Neptune* with his friends. He likely didn't even realise Kyla was still on it.' He curls over, and I place a hand on his back.

I want to scream, *that fairy forsaken moron,* but I have a feeling my anger isn't going to help. Arden doesn't need that. He needs sympathy, and I want to be the person to hold his burdens, so I remain quiet.

'You know why he did it? He took the *Neptune* out fight *you*. He was drunk, and sick of the Reeds, and . . . I can never stop imagining the rough waters, the chaos. All the things I tried to protect Kyla from. She must have been so terrified.'

I shiver. He doesn't say it, and he doesn't have to. The reason he hates my family so much runs deeper than I thought. If we didn't exist, Kyla might still be alive. My skin crawls and I want to bury myself in the ground, never to show my face again. I can't even work up the will to say sorry. How terribly did it pain him to see my sisters and I alive and well, making his life miserable, when Kyla was dead? No wonder he cursed us.

He sobs, and his next words come out in a flood. 'Her weak heart . . . She wasn't able to take it. My— My father came back carrying her limp body as if it were a pile of clothes, not his daughter. I barely saw him after that. I couldn't bring myself to face him, and eventually I just stopped coming home.' He sits up to look directly in my eyes. 'That's why I protect my crew, Sierra. They're my family now, and I will not lose anyone I love again.'

I still don't know what to say, so I sit closer to him and put my head to his chest for a while, listening to his heart and his soft cries. Tears threaten me as well, but I try to hold them back, because this is his grief, not mine, and I won't allow him to comfort me when he's just told me this.

But after some time, I know we have to leave, so I sit up and place a hand on his shoulder. 'Your father isn't here. We should go, think of what to do next. He could be back soon, or he may already be off on a mission to another city. Wallowing in here isn't helping us.'

He nods weakly. 'I . . . I think I just needed a moment more. I haven't been back in so long, and I want to see her room. Can I have a minute alone?'

'Of course,' I say, and he leaves me on his bed. Alone, I let myself shed a few tears and hold myself around my stomach. *Fairies*, he's been so strong, for so long. He's made mistakes, but who hasn't? I've been filled with anger and grief like him. I know how hard it is to hold things together while fighting endlessly for a semblance of something lost, or something that never existed.

Arden returns holding a little doll. Its curly, dark hair is matted, and its yellow dress probably used to be orange or red. Strangely it reminds me of Opal; in another world, she and Kyla would have been sisters, the best of friends. Oh, *fairies*, why did I have to think of that?

I wipe my face – I can't let him see I'm upset – and stand. I just want to make him feel better. I want to fix this, but how can I? He's looking at me with such soft eyes, and I want to melt into the floor. 'We could break some things?' I mutter, and I start rambling like *he* usually does. 'If that'll make you feel better. We can steal your soldiers back? If you want to play with them for a minute, I can do a very convincing soldier voice. *Yes, ma'am*. Or—'

'No. But thank you.' His face cracks into a grin and he laughs, really laughs, a deep, lovely sound that breaks through the stale air and lifts my chest. 'I'm going to be fine. It's just shocking, being back here. Like my old self is threatening to creep back in.'

I try to smile. 'What, the boy who stole his father's ship and became a pirate, and managed to get six other delinquents to join him? Did your old self ever leave?'

'Six?'

I catch myself and cover by rolling my eyes. But then I decide not to lie. 'Well, I suppose I count as one of you now, don't I?'

He nods, smiling widely. 'I just wanted to hear you say it.' His head tilts, and he says, 'Thank you for listening to all of that, and for being here. I couldn't have told anyone else. You don't know how good it feels to let it out.'

'Of course.'

It's a strange thing, us being alone. We can't be like this, vulnerable, when the others are around. We have to show our strength for them. But these moments, alone in the dark . . .

I stand, about make my way downstairs when he clears his throat. 'Sierra. Wait.'

I stop, worried he may have heard something. 'What is it?'

He shakes his head. 'No, nothing bad, I just . . . I need to tell you something. Something else.' He sucks at his bottom lip nervously, but he's being serious. Not guilty. Not afraid.

'Then tell me,' I reply. It's difficult to look at his face this way. His eyes are so dark in this room, with so many emotions crossing between them – fear, grief, hope – as if he's debating whether he's going to regret his next words. I fight the urge to hold him, to tell him it's okay, that this place is only the past. That I'll protect him now.

He falters, breathing for a few heartbeats before meeting my eyes. 'Sierra, I can't keep lying to you. I can't keep lying to myself.' He reaches out and swings the door closed, clears his throat again, and suddenly all the nervousness leaves his face. He gazes at me with such intensity I nearly fall back. 'You aren't just another crew member to me. I don't just *like* you. I don't see you as my ally or my friend. Surely you've noticed what's between us? We became close despite all our hatred and history. There's something about the two of us, something that works. Our bodies certainly know as much. There's something that connects my heart – no, my soul – to yours . . .'

'*Arden*. Are you in your right mind?' I have to stop him, because if this isn't one hundred per cent true, I won't be able to take it. I can barely take it as it is. 'I know you're upset—'

'Stop. Listen. I can't explain it. But I know you feel it too. We're meant for something more. Every time I try to stop thinking of you, or to hate you, it's like fighting fire with fire. I only care about you more and more. I can't think when I'm not around you. Sierra, tell me you feel it too.'

All the blood rushes from my head so fast I could faint. Can he really mean it? Is he really saying, admitting . . .

No. Not Arden. Not *him*. I— What am I doing? In his child-hood home, being kind to him, wanting to protect him? This isn't me. This isn't how any of this was meant to go.

'I'm not lying,' he says. 'I wish I was, but I'm not.'

'Please.' I want to push him away, but I catch his eyes and instead I crumble. How can I lie to him now? 'When I was hurt after touching the sword,' I say softly, 'when I turned into the swan to heal . . . I didn't want to come back. Sometimes I find it so hard to become human again. It's like the swan is taking over. And I was so afraid of being hurt again that I nearly disappeared.'

'*Sierra*.' His brow is furrowed as he watches me.

'But I heard your voice. You were calling me, and I saw you, and I knew you, and I knew myself, and I came back. I came back for *you*.'

He steps in front of me, peering down at me with an affection that, for the first time, he doesn't try to mask. I let him cup the back of my head with one familiar hand, and tilt my chin up with the other. I stand dead still, my body flaming and frozen. Our breaths come heavy, warm, deep. His eyes half-close and he leans down, his lips almost on mine.

'For me?' he whispers.

I sigh deeply. This must be the worst timing, and the curse is always a risk when it comes to kissing, but I *can't* make myself push him away. We kissed once and the world didn't end. Of course, that was only lust. There weren't all these . . . real feelings. I can't let what happened with Zeus happen again. But with Arden, I'm utterly powerless. It's like we're magnets, and no matter what's between us, we can't stay apart.

I unfreeze, run my hands around his waist, as if saying *yes*. I lean forward and—

The door bursts open.

We break apart and I lift my fists to my face. Arden whips his knives from his belt. We are once again feral and violent and not soft and not kind and not, *fairies forbid*, kissing.

The man from the wanted poster stands in the doorway. Arden's father. His face is a storm of years of anger hardened into lines in his skin – and a new shock. Blue magic blooms at the tips of his fingers, a swirling water-like light.

Fairies. Arden pushes me behind him, and I let him, but I squeeze his hand.

'How dare you show your face here,' hisses Bart Lacerta. His voice is nothing like Arden's. Not smooth and gentle, but scorching and rough.

'What, Dad,' Arden says, dropping into nonchalance – because like me, he can't show weakness, not to his family, 'you aren't going to welcome me home?'

CHAPTER
TWENTY-ONE

SOMEWHERE, SOMETIME...

Arden had spent his entire life waiting for the day the Reeds were finally beaten. He never expected he'd be the one to do it. And yet, when the opportunity came, he knew it was his duty. They had taken everything from him, and from so many others. He would happily be the one to make them pay.

It wasn't as if he *ever* could've suspected he'd fall in love with one of them.

He stood with his crew on the *Neptune*, ready to sail into the waters they knew would be guarded by the tyrannical sisters he would free the people of Grace's Territory from. But Arden didn't want them dead. He wanted to stop the Reeds, of course, but that wasn't enough. He wanted to *disgrace* them.

This was for him, for his territory, for the world.

For Kyla.

It had taken Arden months to accumulate the amount of power he had now, all of it simmering in his heart and under his skin, stirring with his hatred to form something unstoppable and terrible. This magic, this curse, would be so strong, so intense, that no Reed could escape it.

They spotted the Reeds' ship, and the *Neptune* powered towards it. Upon the ship were seven sisters trained from birth to be the best fighters in the world – to be able to use any weapon, defeat any opponent, and most importantly, do it all on even the stormiest waters.

No more.

Only the deadliest of the pirates – or the stupidest – went up against the Reeds. Few survived. Which meant their terrible odds gave Arden and his small crew the advantage of surprise. What would they have to gain from such a battle?

The women all but waved them past with well wishes.

But with the full moon shining above, not yet dulled by dawn, the pirates braced themselves to attack. Arden nodded at Opal, who sent an arrow flying at the closest sister. The *Neptune* increased its speed, sidling right up to the Reeds' vessel.

Fiery and filled with adrenaline, Arden led his crew as they burst into action and jumped over. They were outnumbered by one. The youngest Reed was on the ship – she usually wasn't – and Arden hadn't accounted for that. His confidence faltered for just a moment, but then he grinned with determination.

Good. He'd get her, too.

One Reed was already stumbling from Opal's first arrow, which lodged itself into her calf. Opal howled as the Reed screeched.

Arden pounced at an older one, grabbing at her hair so she'd fall backwards. But she was too smart for that move. She took his arm and flipped him over, loosening his grip. His back hit the wooden deck with a painful crash. She leaped on top of him, sword swinging, before Opal managed to get her in the sword-wielding hand with a lightning-fast arrow.

He had barely a second to take in the fight around him. Opal up high, raining down arrows to keep the Reeds off the pirates. Levi grappling with the youngest one. Ebony slashing another with a knife before being pushed back enough for her weapon to transform into a sword, which the Reed parried with ease. Lark and Wren back-to-back, fending off three Reeds with surprising skill. Ebony had been a great trainer for all of them.

Unfortunately for Arden, the Reed on top of him was barely fazed by the arrow in her hand. She simply shifted her sword into her left and swung with just as much skill. *Fairies.* Arden knew he was outmatched – she was toying with him, each swing brushing air across his face – and fear seeped through his hardened layers of rage. The magic within him was bursting, ready to explode out of him in attack.

But it wasn't time, not yet. He needed them weaker. He needed to make sure they were all here. He needed to do this properly. If he messed up now, there would be no second chance. Besides, part of him just wanted to fight, hand to hand, real weapons clashing. He wanted to know what it felt like to pummel a Reed with his own fists.

Droplets of water appeared on his skin as a *splash* sounded near them – the youngest Reed had thrown Levi over the side of the ship. Arden gasped. Levi, the biggest and strongest of the crew, couldn't fight the *least* experienced Reed?

He shook his head – he knew what they were facing, and his secret weapon hadn't been revealed. Arden did his best to fend off the woman atop him, struggling maniacally as she arced her sword down and opened a gash on his forearm. He cried out and she sniggered.

Arden distantly registered Ebony falling, knocked out by the oldest Reed. Without the pirates' best fighter to distract her, the woman sprinted in his direction. She took over from her sister, and he barely dodged the kick she sent towards his stomach. The one he'd been fighting ran towards Opal, who was exposed with only a few arrows left. Opal could fight with her fists, but she wouldn't last long.

They were losing the fight. Hopelessly. With both Levi and Ebony taken out, Lark and Wren tiring, and Opal posed to fall next, Arden's heart raced. They were being picked off one by one. But this was what he expected. He stared into the eldest Reed's eyes, and fury engulfed him like flames.

Wren screamed in the distance; the youngest Reed pulled the knives from Wren's hands, slashing her own fingers in the process. She sneered at Wren with no mercy.

And that was all Arden needed to see.

Sapphire magic began bleeding out of his hands, then pouring from his skin all over. It floated around him, rising as if it were air in water. The gash in his arm healed. The energy in his body was restored. The anger within him was palpable, no longer locked beneath his skin.

The eldest Reed scrambled back. 'Thief!' she screamed. 'You are not worthy of Grace's magic.'

Arden laughed and gave her the smuggest look he could muster. 'That's too bad.'

Ebony had gotten up and was wrestling one of the girls. And Levi must have climbed his way back onto the deck; he was soaked in water and punching one of the Reeds in the head. The pirates finally had the upper hand.

The eldest Reed began to plead with him – she knew, now, she was beaten – and Arden was overcome with joy, the feeling of absolute power.

He pictured Kyla's face, her soft eyes; he tried to remember her laugh. He remembered her playing with her doll, splashing in the dirty lake water, tickling Arden as he pretended to fall prey to her tiny hands. He couldn't bring her back, but he could give her a legacy.

For my sister.

But before he could act, he was struck with a memory: his last conversation with his father. It centred him as reality slowed down, validating his every move as he readied his magic to curse the Reed sisters.

+ ◊ ⁺ ○ ⚔ ○ ⁺ ◊ +

Arden's father always haunted him like a vengeful ghost. The lines on his face, too many for a man of his age. The yellow teeth and fingernails. The emotionless black eyes.

'We're selling the ship,' Bart said, his tone unceremonious, as if such a thing wouldn't ruin both their lives. He was already several drinks in for the day, on his last bottles before he wouldn't be able to afford any more.

Arden's heart raced as he shook his head. 'What are you talking about? What do you owe?'

His father had already taken enough from him – his only sister, his life – and he wouldn't let him take any more. He was about to turn fifteen, and he already ran a successful – albeit dirty and illegal – business in the slums of Grace's Territory. No way was he giving up the magical ship that made it possible. No way would he let his father sell the *Neptune* so Arden would have to move back home and live with the man who let Kyla die.

His father's voice was aggressive and final. 'We're selling her, son. The boat's mine. Not yours.'

'No,' Arden stammered. 'I'll get you the money you need. Just tell me how much. You give the *Neptune* up and we'll lose everything I've built.' He tried to keep his voice flat, but it shook with fear. His father was a lightning storm; Arden never knew how, when, or where he would strike. Sometimes he would only thunder. But sometimes, he could tear a roof off a building with only a shout.

'I don't need *money*.' A look of shame – if only for half a second – crossed his face. 'I bet the ship.'

Arden's chest shattered. 'My ship? You lost my ship? There's no way out—'

Bart slammed a fist on the table. They were in the small house; Arden had received a message to visit his father. Since Kyla died, Arden had all but run away. He saw Bart as little as he could, only once every month or so to check he was alive. Someone had to look after the man. '*My* ship, Arden! Mine!'

'Well, it certainly isn't anymore!'

Bart's nostrils flared. 'Do not speak to me that way.' The quiet threat in his tone made Arden want to run. When he was younger, when he'd heard his father's voice go that way, he was helpless. He had to accept any punishment inflicted. Now he was older, and stronger, but his father still terrified him.

This was the Reeds' fault. Their fault no one in the slums could ever get out, because *they* made sure only their friends, Grace's Territory's richest, could make any money. They would kill anyone who tried to move against them. It was their fault that he and Kyla's mothers hadn't been around. It was their fault his father had turned out this way. Their fault Arden had to turn to crime to survive, to live a life like this, barely a life, while the Reed girls lived in a mansion, met with those descended from royals, and sailed their ships knowing whoever fought them would always lose.

It was their fault Kyla was *dead*.

'One day,' Arden promised his father, 'I'm going to make enough money to get you better. I'm going to be more powerful than anyone. You'll care about me then, Dad. *Fairies forbid*, maybe you'll even love me.'

'What are you saying?' His voice was a quiet rumble, the calm before the storm.

Arden straightened his posture. 'You. Can't. Have. My. Ship. You try to take the *Neptune* from me, and you'll never see either of us again.'

Bart's fist flashed in an arc that barely missed Arden's face. The intoxicated man only made himself trip over his own feet, which infuriated him even more. 'You're nothing,' Bart spat. 'You . . . You . . . Your mother died, and I took care of you. I raised you. I let you play with my ship, let you dally around. I let you keep your blighted sister around despite the money she cost to keep. No more. You think you're smart? You're not. You're nothing, just like me. And it's about time I exercise some control. You don't just do what you want. You answer to *me*.'

Arden's eyes filled with tears, which he quickly blinked away. He wasn't sure why he still cared about his father, but he was his only family. Kyla would want them to stick together, wouldn't she?

'Like I said.' Arden turned. This was the last straw. He couldn't do this any more, even for his sister. 'I'll be back one day. Victorious. You'll be sorry then.'

He flew out the door, knowing he would not be returning for a long time.

◆ ◊ ⁺ ○ ⚔ ○ ⁺ ◊ ◆

Time snapped back into action, and Arden used his magic to lurch the ship to one side. Everyone went flying except for him. Screams, thuds, the creaking of wood. And Arden laughed, covered in a blue so bright he was almost blinded. He pulled himself to his feet and climbed one of the sails, one arm wrapped around rope while his feet found a part of the wooden row to steady themselves on.

He picked the Reeds out of the crowd of fighters, and the lake of blood, and focused his magic towards them. *Swans.* They would become vicious, beautiful water birds. Not so different from what they were now. But they wouldn't kill anymore, and the world would laugh at them. At their family, their legacy, at Grace herself. It would make them all sorry for corrupting their power in such a way.

He closed his eyes, let the curse spread over the ship, meeting its targets, changing the women from the inside out. Curses cut deep, and they could not be taken away. Not easily.

When Arden finally opened his eyes, Opal was beside him, clapping him on the shoulder, laughing wildly even as her side bled alarmingly. The others joined them, circling him in a wet hug as Levi wrapped his arms around the group.

Arden panted, exhausted, watching the white swans waddling about the deck of the ship. The sun had risen – he hadn't had a chance to notice. Their white feathers glowed in the early morning light. The full moon had finally dulled, watching the dawn.

'Hold on,' Lark said. 'There's only six.'

Wren shrugged. There were bruises forming around her neck. 'One probably flew off.' She pointed, her small fingers coated in blood, and for the first time Arden wondered if bringing his friends into this vendetta was the right thing to do. 'Over there.'

Arden looked out to the water to see a single black swan. It had to be the youngest Reed, the girl who seemed to be about his age.

Something had gone wrong with her curse, he knew it. He could sense it; she wasn't on the ship with her sisters.

But it would be fine, wouldn't it? What was the worst that could happen?

They'd *won*.

◆ ◊ ⁺ ◯ ⚔ ◯ ⁺ ◊ ◆

For the next year, the black swan followed him like a shadow, sometimes gone for weeks or months, but always reappearing. He knew it had to be her. It didn't matter if it was the brightest day or darkest night – the shadow would not disappear.

Strangely, he began to miss her when she wasn't around, wishing she would appear. She could hurt him, but instead she just watched. Plotting his murder, maybe. He didn't mind. He wasn't sure why he wished for her to be human again, to really speak to him.

Had he been falling in love with her even then?

Where her sisters seemed to be completely animal, the black swan had an intelligence in her. He did not know, yet, that the curse only held her from dawn to dusk. But he thought that maybe, ever since the day he cursed her, they were connected. He knew she wasn't like the other Reeds.

Was it really that she wasn't on the ship when he cursed them that made her different, or had he done something to lessen her curse? Did he see her youth and see some of himself in her?

He wished to speak to her, to find out. Was she really different, or were his fantasies running wild? As much as he longed to finish what he started, as much as he would always resent her family, he just wanted to talk.

Then, one day, she really did appear. She was both like her sisters and completely other. She was not just the swan, but the woman, too. And as much as Arden tried to hate her for being a Reed, as much as he wanted to blame her for her family's wrongdoings, he could not.

Arden fell in love with a woman who understood his soul unlike anyone he'd ever known.

CHAPTER
TWENTY-TWO

Bart Lacerta lumbers into Arden's childhood bedroom reeking of alcohol. Icy blue magic curls around his fingers, and it takes all my strength to stand tall and not back away with each clumsy step he takes towards us. It takes even *more* strength to keep myself from launching at him.

This is Arden's fight.

Bart sneers. 'What makes you think you have any right to show up here,' he spits, 'and bring that snake with you. A Reed, of all people, into *my* home.'

I cock my head. 'I wouldn't call this place a home. But I'm honoured you know who I am.'

'Stop,' Arden says, his voice weak. The fear in him makes my own veins run cold. 'Don't start with each other. Bart, we're dealing with this between ourselves.'

'Dealing with what, exactly?' The man crosses his arms. He's well dressed; despite his face and hair looking like he crawled out of a dark cave filled with rodents, his suit is pressed, and he wears gold chains around his neck and wrists. 'How you're going to repay me for stealing my ship? For getting me in so much trouble for not handing it in that I spent two years in jail?'

His bad fortune elicits a smile from me, and I'm tempted to tell him we don't care, but I follow Arden's wish for me to stay out of it. I simply give Bart my signature venomous glare.

'You still want money from me?' says Arden. 'Clearly working for Lire is paying you well. Especially when you have magic. *My* magic.'

Bart laughs. 'It does pay well, though I don't know how you know about it. Haven't you learned to stay out of my business, son? And I don't know what you mean about *your* magic. Last I checked, you weren't a fairy.'

Arden steps forward, his face only a few fingers' width from his fathers; the two are the exact same height. I can't see Arden's face, but I hear the harshness in his tone as he says, 'We know you stole my magic. Don't lie.'

Bart lifts a hand and lets his blue magic circle around it. 'This was gifted to me by Lire herself. If you were stupid enough to have your magic stolen, that's your problem.'

I clench my fists. He has to be lying, but . . . as I try to get a sense of his power, I feel nothing linking the curse within me to it. I thought the swan would *know*. I thought *I* would know, that it would feel like fate to reach the magic that can break my curse. But there's nothing. Could Bart be telling the truth?

'I don't believe you,' Arden says, his voice low. 'I lost my magic the last time I saw you. We've been searching the world, *Dad*, and all the evidence points to you.'

'Tsk. All that magic wasted,' Bart says. 'And of course on a failure like you. That's why Lire would never want you on her side.' He raises his chin. 'Not like me.'

I snort. 'Right. Because Arden is so upset that he isn't helping bring about the downfall of humanity.'

Bart sneers at me again, shifting like he wants to attack. I look him right in the eye, dead still.

Arden raises a hand to block his father. As he turns, I see his face again; his eyes are glassy. 'Give me back my magic.'

'I can't,' Bart replies. 'And you're not having any of mine, either. You're not taking anything of mine ever again.'

'Oh, no,' I say. 'We aren't offering you a choice.'

'Really, princess? Then you'll find yourself in a bit of a pickle, won't you? Because I'm the one with the power here.' He raises his second hand, more of that Grace magic whirling around us.

Arden finally falters, putting a hand on my arm. His touch is firm, both leaning on me for strength *and* being protective. It sends goosebumps along my skin.

'You can't fight me,' Bart says. He has Arden's black eyes, but on him they aren't beautiful. They're lifeless and bloodshot. *Fairies,* I wish I could wring this man's neck until his eyeballs burst out. How dare he even be a fraction of Arden? 'Even if my magic was once yours, you wouldn't be strong enough to get it back out of me. You're as weak as your sister.'

Arden lunges into an attack but he's thrown back by a wave of blue. He lands on the bed and it snaps apart under him. He coughs, winded, eyes wide and afraid like a child's. Kyla's doll is still gripped firmly between his fingers.

I ball my hands into fists and growl at Bart, ready to commit what in my mind feels like an *extremely* justified murder. Unsteadily, he readies to hit me with his magic, so I kick him in the chest before he has the chance. He drops to the floor, kicking and screaming like a giant baby. The magic grows larger and stronger around him – so much more magic than I expected – and my heart skips a beat.

Then Ebony appears behind him with the iron sword held out. Bart's magic dissipates like water turning to steam. 'On your knees,' she orders. 'Hands behind your back. Now. And we'll consider letting you live.'

Bart pales, eyes rolling back. 'What . . . is . . . that?'

Arden stands, clutching his chest. I take hold of him so I don't fall; the iron's proximity immediately makes my head spin and my limbs go weak. Arden and I lean on each other, and even as weak as we are, we snicker as we watch his father going queasy on the floor. Well, me more than Arden. Still, with Ebony here, Arden's confidence returns. The scared boy disappears as the pirate captain returns.

He teases, 'Oh, Dad, you don't like our little sword? It's only the weapon that's going to win us the war. And yes—' he peers at his father through narrowed eyes '—you should be very, very afraid.'

Bart's bottom lip wobbles as the others step inside. Levi stands behind Ebony, and Opal watches Bart with the look of a shark watching its prey. Lark and Wren keep their distance, standing by the door.

Bart knows he's outnumbered, that he is ours, and that we are *angry*. He shudders. 'How did a tiny crew of runaways get a weapon like that?'

'None of your concern,' I say, before anyone starts boasting. Anything we say to this man could get back to Lire. She'll already know we have the sword now. Unless we kill him, which I'm still very much up for. Oh, I'll be dreaming of that murder for weeks to come. 'You know you're powerless against us, so hand over the magic before we have to use the sword.'

'But my magic isn't yours!' He waves his hands frantically, and Ebony presses the sword closer to his spine. 'I'm not lying! I swear – you don't want it – it'll only put a target on your back!'

'Why won't you stop lying!' Arden shouts, and Bart flinches. That vulnerable boy who told me about his little sister, barely ten minutes ago, might never have existed. Arden is pure thunder, barely human, as he seethes at the man who let Kyla die. 'How about we start with something a little more easy, then? Tell us where Lire's iron stores are. Tell us where to get more weapons.'

Bart laughs, the sound guttural and horrid. 'You think she'd tell me?' His expression shifts into icy victory as he notices the doll grasped in his son's hands. Eyeing it, he coos, 'Ah, my sentimental little boy. Not as tough as you pretend to be, are you?'

Arden's face falls and he inches the doll behind his back while his friends look on in confusion.

'Bart,' I hiss, trying to change the subject before the others realise what it means. 'Answer the question. Where can we find Lire's iron?'

Bart begins rambling on about nothing – spinning lies about how we'll never defeat Lire, even with the iron – and I think I've saved Arden from having to share this terrible secret, but Lark is still peering between him and the hidden doll. He glances at Wren, frowning, and his jaw drops.

Fairies. Of course Lark of all people would see what the others don't. He's the only one who knows what it's like to raise a little sister.

Arden shakes his head slowly at his friend. Brows turning up in the middle, Lark swallows, nods, and turns away.

Luckily, Lark also knows how to keep things to himself.

Arden crouches, level with his father. He gives him a cold look, but the hand holding Kyla's doll trembles. Only I can see it. 'If you don't start making yourself useful,' he says, 'that sword is going to hurt you a lot worse than it is right now. Mercy is not something we *pirates* are known to have very much of. Or patience.'

Bart's eyes meet the ground and, coward that he is, he breaks. 'There's an abandoned castle north-west of Bearra, before the border of Adella's Territory. She keeps her weapons in a crypt underneath. But going would be suicide. It's so well guarded you have no chance of getting in. And you can't use magic there.'

'*That* we can count on,' says Ebony, twisting her sword. Its reflection makes light shoot across the ceiling. 'Which means Lire will be at her weakest if she tries to stop us.'

'Pfft. A bunch of girls aren't any match for Lire's soldiers.'

'Now, now,' Opal says, placing an arm on Ebony's shoulder before she gets distracted trying to argue with Bart, which we *all* know she will. 'You're looking at some of the best fighters in the world. We have a Reed on our side, for fairies' sakes. This "bunch of girls" are hardly afraid of some soldiers.'

'That's right,' Levi says. 'This "bunch of girls" is . . .' He glances at Ebony. 'This bunch of *women* are to be *feared*.'

She nods seriously in response.

'How do we find this castle?' Arden cuts in, and I realise we definitely should have thought this interrogation through more. Bart is going to tell Lire our exact plan. And to my absolute despair, I can't see Arden letting us murder him.

Bart shakes his head. 'I suppose sending you and your weapon to your deaths isn't the worst idea.' He purses his lips before saying, 'You follow the main river from Darraport towards Adella's Territory. Eventually you'll pass a mountain. When you see a river that goes back towards the south-east, follow it. Don't go all the way to Bearra. You'll know the place when you see it. The rivers and terrain have been cursed to stop people coming through. And if you make it that far, you'll be killed by soldiers. Bye bye, pirates.'

I smirk. Doesn't he realise his warnings only make us want to do it *more*? A perilous journey to reach a hidden weapon . . . There is nothing I'd prefer to do right now.

'Well if that's all we need, what are we doing with him?' Ebony asks Arden.

Kill him!

Arden's expression is stone-like. 'We're taking my magic. Then he can crawl back to Lire and tell her what he lost. She can decide his punishment.'

Oh.

'It isn't your magic!' Bart yells again, so loud I wonder if the rickety old house will crumble. 'You can't have it!'

'Give it to me.' Arden grips his father's wrist. 'Now. Or the iron sword goes right through your back.'

Bart shakes his head. 'You won't kill me.'

'And yet I'm not against hurting you. Badly.'

I raise a hand. 'I'll kill him.'

Opal runs a finger down her bow. 'Me too.'

'Okay!' Bart screams. 'Fine! Have my magic! But Lire will be coming for you! There's a lot you children think you can survive, but you *cannot* survive a fairy.'

'We'll do our best,' says Arden, taking his father's other hand. They lock eyes, and the blue magic billows around them, leaving Bart's body and seeping into Arden's. Clouds and clouds and clouds of it, sapping the oxygen from the air – how did he have this much?

This . . . This is the magic I need to save my family. Our magic. It's here. If Bart wasn't lying, at least.

I expect a glimmer of hope, and instead I'm met with anxiety. Facing my family again. The Reeds back on the water, protecting . . .

But they won't be protecting Grace's Territory, will they? They'll be guarding it. Making sure people like Bart stay poor and people like them stay rich.

Pirates are bad. They do awful things. Normal, helpless people need protecting from criminals. That is the duty I have always stood by.

But the Reeds' way of doing things? Arden was right. We don't help people. I was lied to. My sisters might not be worth saving. We are trying to stop a war, to save the world.

Why am I wasting so much of my energy on people who would never do the same for me?

Fairies.

Arden shakes as the magic encompasses him. As the last shreds leave his father's body, Arden lets go and Bart drops in exhaustion. Drained. The others watch with curious gazes. Arden only looks sad. Is the iron already hurting him?

I take a step back, and he meets my eyes, his irises glowing navy.

Was I wrong to make him do this?

CHAPTER
TWENTY-THREE

The *Neptune* senses our urgency. Arden's magic, blended with the ship's triarue, helps to counteract the effects of the iron sword, allowing us to move quickly again. The two don't cancel each other out, exactly – the iron still makes him sick – but Arden has a deep connection with his ship. The *Neptune* can listen to him clearly again, and that's enough to get us racing towards the rivers where my sisters were last seen.

Huge waves rock against the ship as it cuts through the water. The clouds have cleared from earlier, leaving the night vibrant. And I feel so, so very free.

Opal stands by my side. 'After today, you can finally have your wish of killing us all.'

I laugh, though I'm not sure if she's being funny or snarky. '*Finally.*'

Arden broods separately from us, examining his hands as his magic dances across his fingers. Thinking. He always seems to be thinking, more than anyone else. Probably about his father, or having magic again, or breaking the curse . . . I never know what's happening behind those eyes.

Maybe he's thinking about *us*. I hate to admit it, but I hope he is. I hope I haunt his every thought.

I watch him for a long while, but when we reach the lakes, I begin scanning for my sisters. The stars are bright, reflecting and shimmering in Grace's clear waters. Midnight is always a magical time to be here. I don't let my guard down, though. The night we were cursed felt just as beautiful as right now.

Unfortunately, it doesn't take long to spot the six swans floating peacefully in the crystal water they once killed upon.

I stretch my arms, my stomach stirring. Should I have flown one last time before Arden breaks the curse? It doesn't please me to admit it, but there are parts of the swan I'll miss. Very soon, I'll forget what it's like to spread my wings. To dive under the water and catch fish in my beak, or to spot an enemy from high above.

Can this really be happening, tonight? After a year of fighting for this, it feels too sudden. But I can't put this off. I can't live this way forever. I know that the next time I transform could be the end of my human life.

I can't miss the swan, not after all it has done to me.

'By the beach!' I force myself to shout, and the *Neptune* powerfully halts itself and moves towards the lake's shore. It does that now – listens to me, just like the others.

The rest of the crew come quickly. Levi and Ebony ascend from below, leaning into each other to fight the night air's chill. Lark and Wren watch me with wide eyes.

Arden nervously wrings his hands. 'Sierra,' he says when he reaches me. 'Are you sure about this? I still don't know how to undo a curse. I could hurt them more. I could hurt *you*. And we don't know what might happen when . . . when they're themselves again.'

'*Fairies*,' Opal says. 'Here I was worrying about Sierra killing us once she gets what she wants. But it isn't her we have to worry about. It's her family.'

I exhale impatiently. 'Arden will still have magic,' I reassure her. 'He beat us with it last time. And this time, unfortunately, you also have me.'

The swans have begun to shift around, noticing our presence – and making me all the more nervous.

'You'd fight them for us?' Levi asks, a grin playing at his lips. The moonlight makes his light complexion pearl-like.

I grimace at him as the realisation of what I admitted turns in my gut. 'As much as I love fighting, I would first attempt to use *words* to diffuse the situation, since I wouldn't want any of you to be hurt. But, if I *had* to, yes, I'd protect you.'

Levi pats my shoulder. 'I would protect you too. If you ever needed it. Which you don't. But I would.'

I shake my head and turn around. The six white birds – with their long necks and black eyes and pink beaks – paddle closer to the ship, watching curiously. But there is no recognition in the way they move;

no telling they were ever human. They're just swans, the women they once were hidden away deep inside.

But somehow I can sense that this isn't just any flock. They're the Reeds.

And I, the sister they always wished didn't exist, have come to save them. My hesitation mixes with pride as I let myself relish in what's about to happen. They will finally have me to thank for something. They will finally owe me. My parents will allow me to come home. Maybe even love me this time.

'Arden,' I say, because he's turning green with anxiety. 'Just do whatever you feel makes sense. You managed to do a very effective curse, so I trust your abilities to reverse it.' I stand in front of the group and force myself not to close my eyes. I clench my fists so they can't see I'm trembling. 'Whenever you're ready.'

'Remember,' Arden tells me pointedly, 'if this goes wrong, I tried to warn you.'

'Next time,' I say with a snarl, 'don't curse someone, and you won't end up in this situation.'

The strange thing is, I do trust him. I may not feel ready, but I wouldn't want anyone else pointing magic at me in such a way. We aren't testing this. We're going for it. We're breaking the curse all at once. No questions, just action. This is who we are, and I know that whatever happens, we'll survive it together.

Arden nods, and swirls of sapphire materialise around him. His eyes narrow in concentration and he bites his bottom lip so hard it turns white. The waves of magic amble first around my body, then slowly flood over the edge of the boat, towards the swans. I can't see them, since I'm facing him; I don't let my gaze waver from his eyes.

I gasp as the magic seeps into my skin, crawling towards my heart. It's ice, the opposite of the feeling I had when I touched the iron, burning from the inside out. But I'm not afraid. Not at all. Because it's *him*, and I know he would never hurt me.

I am about to be saved.

Ebony mouths, *Okay*? and I manage a nod in return.

But anxiety strikes me suddenly, starting in the depths of my stomach, then constricting my breaths. Despite all the magical energy running through me, my head goes light. The swan is making herself known, not wanting to go away. As the magic works its way into each cell of my body, all I feel is the cold. My arms stretch out like wings, my hair floats around me, and the magic washes through me—

But there is no change. It doesn't get *close* to touching the curse.

Arden keeps focusing, brows knotted, but he seems to be struggling, confused. I want to say something, I think everyone does, but I'm scared to break his concentration.

Finally, he stops himself. 'It isn't working!' He rubs his palms on his shirt, as if brushing the remnants of magic away. 'I tried everything, thought of all the things I could think to . . . think. Nothing changed. Sierra, what did you feel?'

I heave as the magic slowly leaves me. I fold over and knead my temples. 'Like your power tried to touch the curse, but it couldn't.'

'Because it isn't the right magic.' Ebony sighs, tapping her weapon – in the form of a short knife – against her palm. 'Bart was telling the truth. This isn't the magic we used for the curse.'

Of course, this is the *one* time that liar would tell the truth?

'You're sure you aren't just doing it wrong?' Wren asks Arden. The night sky casts her face with shadows that make her look older. If even she's doubting her captain, things must be hopelessly dire. 'Why don't you try again?'

'It would only be a waste of effort,' I say, lacing my voice with disappointment to hide my slight relief – and my refreshed anger. It was so much easier to suppress my resentment of Arden when I thought we were close to fixing the wrong he did against me.

But in this failure, it all comes back. I look at him and I'm reminded of what he did to me. That this is his fault, whether I trust him now or not. We may be friends – or more – but the damage between us feels irreparable.

I've been living in delusion. Utter delusion. And as I return to the reality that no one can help me but myself, I just want to curl up and cry.

The six white swans paddle away from the beach, towards the horizon where the lake touches the stars. Bored of us, and none the wiser about what just happened. About their doom.

I slump on the deck. Place my head in my hands. To my surprise, Arden sidles down beside me. Then the others. In a circle, all seated in an array of unknowable emotions. It's so late. We should all be sleeping.

But with them near me, at least I'm warm.

'We still have magic again,' Opal says. 'Better us than Bart.'

'I don't even want it,' says Arden. 'It's useless to us. All it does is remind me of my father, and it'll only make me weaker when we go to Lire's iron stores.' He looks ready to scream, to hit something, but he doesn't. He holds himself together; I know if it were only the two of us, he would let himself fall apart. 'We've failed.'

'The magic must still be out there,' Ebony says. 'We'll keep looking.'

Arden and I stay silent while the others argue, and eventually I zone out completely. My eyes threaten to close permanently for the night. 'I'm going to bed,' I say, pushing myself to my feet. 'I need to . . . to think.'

Think about what this means. Think about what's next. Think about what I want.

I wish Maya was here. She would understand. She would be on my side, no matter what. Maya might be the only person in the world that I truly trust. But she's somewhere far away, probably suffering as much as I am.

I just want someone to tell me how to feel, because I don't know anything anymore.

CHAPTER
TWENTY-FOUR

SOMEWHERE, SOMETIME . . .

Maya sighed as yet another aristocrat appeared in the throne room to offer Dawn something they claimed she needed. Unfortunately, Bearra needed many things. The kingdom was struggling more than ever. But nothing came for free – and Dawn had little to give.

Maya's long dress itched, and her neatly-pinned hair tugged at her brain. Well, it had been pinned back neatly; she'd been pulling at it all day. Teddy sat beside her, to the left of the foot of Dawn's throne, in a suit that was too old-fashioned – *Bearran* – for him. If Maya was being honest, however, it not being his style wasn't the only reason she wished to tear it off him.

If only there were more time for that, but with their new duties, leisure was rare. The last few months had come with far too much questioning about why Maya and Teddy were always with Dawn – and where the queen and king were. So, the princess made her friends her official advisors. It was a great honour, apparently. Maya wasn't so sure that looking and acting the part was worth it.

This was the least they could do for Dawn, but it took so much time and energy, and Maya was *restless*. There had to be something they could do other than sit and scheme all day. What was happening with Sierra? Had she broken her curse? Had she found the iron, the weapon they so desperately needed?

Did any of it even matter? Next time they went up against Lire, they wouldn't be so lucky. Last time Maya faced the fairy, the only reason she survived was because of the enchanted crown. If Lire returned before Sierra, before they gained their advantage, there would be no chance. And even if Sierra was successful, could some metal alone really defeat such a powerful being?

Maya, Dawn and Teddy were spending every moment trying to hold together a kingdom that didn't have a future. It broke Maya's heart to know after everything she did to help her family, they may not even survive the fairy war. Especially considering that Maya's actions seemed to have set off the chain of events which led to the world's current state.

It wasn't like her to lose hope, but she was losing *herself*.

Teddy nudged her and cleared his throat. Maya turned to him, having already stopped listening to the conversation between Dawn and a jewel-dripping woman who morbidly reminded Maya of her late aunt.

Her heart constricted. Hadn't Maya won? When would the horrors *end*?

'Follow me,' Teddy whispered in her ear, his warm brown eyes suddenly twinkling. Yes, those eyes were always beautiful, inviting, glowing – but they only *twinkled* for her. When he stood quietly and sauntered out of the throne room, taking a corridor to their left that was usually reserved for servants, Maya did not hesitate to scurry behind, polite manners forgotten. Dawn shot them a betrayed expression, but could not berate them for leaving her. She, at least, had to save face.

Maya shrugged a half apology to her and rounded a corner.

Teddy grabbed her arm and pulled her into him, eyes half closed, his hands moving to her waist as he backed himself against the wall. She gasped, looked around, but the dim corridor was empty.

She smiled, heart jumping. 'What's this?'

Teddy stared at Maya with his mouth agape. 'I couldn't be in there a second longer. I thought you might . . .'

'You would have been correct.' She longed to touch Teddy. There was so much she wanted from him. *Love* – there was no doubt. She still hadn't said that word, though he had. Even with all the family dinners, the endless nights they spent together, the stolen kisses in dark spaces in the castle, she found it near impossible to tell him. He'd broken her trust more than once, and Maya did not easily forgive.

Even if things had worked out in the end. Even if he had saved her in so many more ways than he'd hurt her. Even though she loved him so, so desperately.

Love could alter a lot about a person, but Maya was who she was. Untrusting, unforgiving, and deadly stubborn. Teddy would never be able to take back his actions or change who and what he was, either.

With all the stress of the oncoming war, she wasn't sure they would ever be able to have a normal relationship. They didn't get many chances to talk, and when they did, that was the last thing they wanted to do. Any tension between them was hastily put aside for . . . *other* kinds of tension.

In moments like this, she did not care about her apprehension – she only cared about getting her hands all over him.

A red-haired maid shuffled past them, giggling, and they burst into laughter as soon as she was gone.

Teddy kissed Maya quickly, his hand cupping her head in a way that made her swoon. But there was something urgent about the way he kissed her, too, like he was afraid he might never get the chance again. A few heated moments passed before he broke away and gave her a serious look. 'Maya, I'm worried.'

She responded with an impatient expression. They were always worried. Why had he stopped kissing her?

But he went on, whispering, 'Dawn is at her breaking point. I don't know how long we have left before she snaps. I trust her. I always have. But lately I . . . I'm afraid she's going to do something reckless and desperate.'

Maya swallowed. *Would she?* 'Even if she did, what would we be able to do?'

'What if she decides to side with Kara, or the Ice Empire? Or worse. We would have to do *something.*'

'No. Dawn wouldn't do that. She knows that kind of alliance would be bad for us.'

'But if losing Bearra's future is enough to save its present, she'll take her chances.' He rested his head on her chest, as if closing his eyes against her might make all his worries disappear.

'I trust her to make the right decision,' Maya whispered, and she meant it. She brushed his hair gently with her fingers. 'We'll put out the fires we create when we have to. Right now we just need a spark to keep us all alive.'

Checking again that they were alone, Maya placed a hand under his chin, lifting his head back up to hers. An anticipating smile played across his lips, and she kissed him softly.

He laughed and spun her around so she was against the wall. His hands trailed through her pinned hair, ruining it completely. She couldn't make herself care. He used magic to dull the sounds around them; the murmured words from the throne room disappeared. They were in a world of their own.

All they could hear were each other's breaths, each other's laughter. For a few sweet moments, they were able to forget. Forget that Teddy's mother, the world's most powerful fairy, was preparing for war against them. Forget that Maya's family, along with all of Bearra, were still being threatened with starvation. Forget that in the next room, Maya and Teddy's best friend was fighting for her life against people who only sought to take advantage of her, while her parents slept all day and night as if they had never woken.

Maya's hands travelled beneath Teddy's expensive blazer, aiming for bare skin.

Then a sound cut through the magic – a woman clearing her throat.

Maya groaned and opened her eyes, then gasped. Teddy spun so he was beside Maya. With a hand held across her, he blinked at the intruder. Then blinked again, loosing a breath.

'Sorry for interrupting, my loves,' said the rainbow-winged fairy. 'I thought it was about time I came to check on you.'

Teddy broke into a grin and leaped to hug Amora. She giggled, arms around his waist as her wings fluttered.

Maya stood frozen for a long moment, unable to place the fairy here in Bearra. She wasn't unhappy to see her, but her presence felt like a bad omen. Surely she wasn't just here to see Teddy.

'As glad as I am to see you,' Teddy said to her, apparently thinking the same thing, 'are you sure you should be in Bearra? Displaying any kind of loyalty to us could be dangerous. If Lire found out—'

'I'm aware of the political nightmare we're in.' The fairy of passion's face was gaunter than Maya remembered it. Tired and marked with concern. Maya still thought her strange; the fairy didn't look much older than them. All fairies had an ageless, slightly inhuman appearance. And yet Amora had been like a mother to Teddy. More so than the fairy who really was, impossibly, his real mother.

'So why take the risk?' Maya questioned.

'I'm yet to pick a side,' said Amora. 'Lire wants me, as do the others. Grace and Rhiannon's alliance is strong – they have often found themselves on the same side. Kara seems to be allying with the Ice Empire. Soon they'll have wrapped themselves around the circumference of the world, and they'll strangle us as they force their way inward. Muse will side with Lire. Adella and I are left. We may be the least wanted, but we could tip the scales.'

'*Amora*,' muttered Teddy. 'That's why you shouldn't be here. I couldn't stand it if anything happened to you. The world couldn't take losing a fairy. Especially not you.'

She cupped his cheek. 'Don't think I'm not taking every precaution. I am far older and wiser than you, my love.'

Maya's head spun. She knew a war was coming, and that it would be bad. But she had seen it as between Bearra and Lire – not the entire world. Hearing this from Amora herself made it all far more real, more frightening. When fairies were scared, humans should be terrified. 'What will you do?' Maya asked her.

'I've come because I want to help you,' she said. Teddy's eyes lit up, but she shook her head. 'Don't be too enthusiastic. There's only so much I can do without hurting my own people. And I must protect my own territory first. I can only help you in secret. I wouldn't even do that much if it weren't for you, Teddy. But I know you won't leave Maya, and Maya won't leave Bearra, so I'll do what I can to protect this kingdom.'

Teddy nodded, his eyes turning red. 'We'll appreciate anything, Amora,' he replied, gripping her hands.

Amora tilted her head, her long brown hair draping over her floor-length pink dress. She glanced at the door to the throne room. 'We should speak with the princess. Can she be trusted?'

'She can. Should we bring her here? Find somewhere else to meet? We have to make sure you aren't seen.'

'Bring her to me.'

Maya went to fetch the very confused and irritated princess, and Dawn rubbed her neck as they entered the corridor. 'I have people waiting, so I hope this is . . .' She trailed off as her eyes glanced up at Amora's brilliant multicoloured wings. Dawn quickly righted herself, wiping the awe from her face. 'Amora. You haven't visited Bearra in a long time.'

'More than one hundred years,' said the fairy. 'And it's lovely to see how you've grown, Princess Dawn. You're as beautiful as they say.'

Dawn ignored the backhanded compliment – even Maya thought it unfair for Amora to praise her own blessing on the princess. 'What are you doing in my kingdom?' Dawn asked with harsh diplomacy. 'I wish I could welcome you more . . . festively, but in these times, a visit from a fairy is more a threat than an honour. Especially an unannounced visit in a servants' passageway.'

'Dawn,' urged Teddy, 'she's here to help.'

'I certainly hope so.' Dawn gave Teddy a stark stare. It was unlike the princess to be impolite, but Maya knew how important it was for her to appear strong – and not be undermined by her own advisor.

'You are right to be cautious,' Amora said. 'The world is remembering this kingdom, and despite it still being very difficult to get in or out, you don't have long before attacks begin. Right now, everyone is against you.'

'Thank you for the reminder,' Dawn snapped. 'What is your proposal?'

Amora's wings stretched in a way Maya thought to be intimidating. 'I will arm your soldiers with magic, help you grow more food, and offer anything else my magic can do for you. Your people could use uplifting. This place is quite miserable. But you must find a story that makes it believable that I am not involved. You absolutely cannot tell anyone you got the power from me.'

Dawn stood still and emotionless for a few moments. 'They'll know it's your magic from the colour. Besides, our people are not accustomed to magic being readily available. They will be scared. They will ask questions.'

'But everyone else in the world has magic,' Maya said. Maybe Teddy was right – was Dawn's decision-making off? Would she refuse this help? They couldn't afford to pass up this kind of alliance. 'Well, not everyone, but almost anyone can get it if they want. Dawn, Amora is offering Bearra a way into the modern world. And we can tell people the magic was stolen somehow . . . that a spy went out and took it.'

'And if we have to roll it out slowly,' Teddy added, excitement in his tone, 'that's what we'll do. We can start with small things – getting our carriages enchanted, improving our infrastructure, rebuilding the wards that Lire let down when she left. Then we can begin sharing magic with the people, only in small batches, and see how we go before arming all our soldiers with it.'

Dawn's hands trembled, just slightly. 'This seems too dangerous.' Her honey-brown curls had begun to frizz after the long day. 'I can't have magic rampant in the streets. Our people will become unpredictable. And if we really want magic, we always have Teddy.'

He almost laughed. 'I don't have that kind of magic, and I wouldn't share it regardless. The less of my mother's power out there, the better.'

With a muffled gasp, Maya remembered the one time Teddy did share his magic – with *Kara*. In all the chaos of their quest to get the crown, she'd forgotten how significant that could be. She would talk to him about it later; she wasn't sure she should share this before getting his opinion.

Dawn sighed, so Maya stepped forward and asked the question she could tell her friend was dreading to. 'Amora, if you help Bearra, is there something you want in return?'

'Well,' the fairy said, brushing her hair over a shoulder so it fell between her wings. 'I would hope, if I put myself and my people at risk by doing this, that Bearra may find themselves doing me a favour one day if I needed it. I don't know what that might be. I just ask that you keep myself and my territory in mind after the war.'

'That seems reasonable,' Teddy said. His eyes darted between them.

'*I* will determine what is reasonable,' said Dawn, and for a moment Maya could see a little of Lire in her. She had somewhat raised the princess, after all. *Fairies.* Maya hated when she saw the fairy in Dawn and Teddy. It reminded her how separate she was from them, how dangerous they could be.

'So?' Amora asked Dawn. 'Will you accept my help?'

The princess glanced down the corridor, surely thinking of the people ready to talk her ears off for hours, wanting to get everything they could from her, taking advantage of her desperation.

Allying with a fairy was dangerous. Maya trusted Amora, because Teddy trusted her, but she could understand why Dawn would be so hesitant. Especially after what happened with Teddy's brother, Jacob. Dawn knew the worst of fairies and magic. But it couldn't be denied that they needed this.

'I'll accept your help,' the princess finally said, her tone dark. 'But it will be on my terms, and you would do well to watch your step.'

She lifted her chin. 'I have duties to return to. You organise what you must with my advisors.'

Amora laid a gentle hand on Teddy's shoulder. 'We will make this work. We can win the war.'

Maya was not so certain.

Chapter
Twenty-Five

My head pounds the moment I open my eyes; only a crack of sunlight weaves through the small window of Arden's cabin and into the triarue closet.

We're nearly at Lire's iron stores – at least, if Bart didn't lie about their location – a week after confronting him. Everything has been awkward and depressing since. Tension is high. Morale is low.

Arden and I can barely look at each other. Between his shame and my anger, there's little room for the *feelings* that nearly led to a kiss in his childhood bedroom. There's no longer much hope of ever getting the magic back to break my family's curse. We all know it. No one says it. Our one lead was wrong. I'm no closer to saving my sisters or myself.

I'm not sure exactly when we decided to go straight for the iron stores instead of going to Bearra first. I suppose we're all so desperate – so hopelessly beyond the point of caring – that we just want to do this one thing. Who cares if we get hurt? We're still the most capable people to do this. The only problem will be getting the iron on the ship, but we can deal with that later.

We're pirates. Recklessness is part of the job. It almost sounds fun, the way Bart described it. Wards, guards, obstacles and excitement. It's just a game to be won, another enemy to defeat. That, we can all do.

We have an enchanted ship and a captain with magic. What could go wrong?

Except, the magic hasn't helped very much so far. On the third night after seeing his father, Arden brought pillows and blankets into the triarue storage room and made a nest for himself across from me. He's as sick as I've been from the iron, if not worse. Now I fall asleep to the sound of his breaths, resisting the urge to lie pressed against him, to gently kiss the backs of his closed eyes.

Some nights, when I fall asleep as myself and accidentally wake up as the swan, it's only Arden's presence that brings me back. His hand against my feathers, his fingers stroking my neck. His voice whispering my name.

And yet, in the light of day, we couldn't be further apart.

This morning, as I slowly come to, hushed voices hum in Arden's room. I peek through the closet's ajar doorway – Lark and Arden sit on the bed, Lark's hands over Arden's.

'. . . didn't want you to worry about it,' Arden whispers. His words are choppy and crackling; he's holding back tears. He glances over to me and I squint my eyes, pretending to still be asleep. My breaths are steady, though I'm burstingly curious about what they're discussing.

'We can talk somewhere else,' says Lark. 'If you don't want to risk her overhearing.'

Arden shakes his head. 'It's okay if she does. She knows.'

Lark's face falls. 'She knows? Her, and not me?'

'I'm sorry—'

'I'm not angry with you, Arden.' Lark squeezes his captain's hands, sniffling. 'I'm angry with myself. I should have known. I should have seen it. And you should have felt like you could tell me.'

'*Please*,' Arden says, his voice breaking. His shoulders rock with gentle cries. 'This is why I didn't tell you. I didn't want you to feel . . . I just wanted things to be normal. I didn't want to make you carry my grief. The only person at fault is my father.'

With a shiver, Lark whispers, 'We should have killed him.' Then he exhales, calming. 'I can't imagine. Your *sister*. No, I *can* imagine – that's the problem. You should have let me help you. You know I understand.'

Arden rests his head on Lark's shoulder, their hands clasped in his lap. They cry together, Arden letting out years of pain as he sobs into his friend's arms. Tears prick at my own eyes as I watch them, and I bury my nose under my blanket in case I cry. *Fairies*. I shouldn't be watching this. I shouldn't be listening. But I can't stop.

Lark's face is red when he pulls away. 'That's why . . . with Wren. You couldn't stand the idea of her leaving. Any of us.'

'That shouldn't be on you. If you want to leave, you shouldn't stay just for me.'

'No. *No*. When I said I wanted better for us, I didn't mean I would leave you. I will never, ever leave you. It's all of us or none of us.'

Arden lifts his head and gives Lark such a hopeful gaze that I nearly break.

'You're my brother,' says Lark, 'and I will protect you, and hold you, and love you until I die. Do you understand? I want what's best for Wren, but I will never leave you to do that. You and I are in this forever. Wren has the two most loving, protective older brothers in the world. I will never stop being grateful for that, because I couldn't do it alone. Never think you have to hide anything from me. Never again.'

Arden crumples into his friend's lap.

Later that morning, I pretend to wake knowing absolutely nothing of the conversation I overheard. Arden and I saunter up to the kitchen together, but I make a show of not walking too close behind him.

The warm, cinnamon scent of Lark's famous waffles travels through the musty air, and we sit and eat them with honey and fine sugar that melts in our mouths. The seven of us lounge around the long table, which is clean now we're no longer scouring books for clues.

The wood is dark and clean, the temperature is cool, and just a little sunlight peeks through the windows. We aren't quite at the treacherous waters leading to Lire's iron stores. We're treating this morning as a last moment of peace. I take long breaths and allow myself the pleasure of resting with my friends.

Only Ebony and Levi seem uneasy. They shift and start, rub their eyes and play with their food. I don't think they've had an argument

– they seem fine with each other. I try to catch Levi's eyes, but they keep darting around, unable to focus. There's no point trying to eye Ebony into a confession; I know she won't tell me anything unless she wants to.

Yet once everyone is finished breakfast, Ebony speaks, her voice quick and uncertain. 'There's something Levi and I need to show you all. On the deck.'

My stomach bubbles with anxiety. Ebony is never troubled like this, never afraid. She doesn't dally around the truth.

'Sure . . .' Opal says. She's wearing bright red pants today, with a white silk top. Her hair is in its usual two braids, tied with red ribbons. And I'll admit it – I'm jealous that I have barely any of my clothes from home. In another world, we could be best friends, dressing each other up in the finest materials. But this is our real life, and the rest of us wear dark, comfortable outfits. It isn't that I want to dress colourfully – but a silky black dress could go a long way.

Ebony and Levi stand awkwardly, waiting for the rest of us to follow. A sense of something heavy and foreboding hangs in the air. With all these people around me in a small space . . . It's like the emotions seep into the atmosphere, infecting everyone around them, until there's a swirling storm of moods in my head.

My palms go sweaty as we make our way up to the deck, into an overcast but warm mid-morning. We're close to Bearra, and the dry climate around us reflects that. But the water is lovely. I'd be tempted to go for a swim if I wasn't worried the ship would carry on without me.

'To the back of the deck,' Levi says, taking us to a shady spot where a messy mountain of cushions lays on the wood like piled autumn leaves. 'We . . . We thought it might be nice to spend some time up here . . . Enjoy the day.'

'Surprise!' Ebony says, failing to show enthusiasm.

No one seems convinced.

'Okay,' Arden says. He stands next to me, between myself and the others. Is he worried that whatever this is could be an attack against me? *Fairies*, could it? Is Ebony going to stab me? And if she did, *would* Arden protect me? 'That's . . . nice.'

'We need more cushions,' Ebony says. 'You all should sit down. Arden, you come with me to get the cushions. Sierra – you just stand and wait for a minute. I have a special one for you.'

I open my mouth to say something, but I'm lost for words. What on earth is happening? Am I about to die?

Wren jumps onto the cushions, sinking as she lays back and tilts her head up to the sunlight. 'You're right, this *is* nice.'

Opal follows, plopping down beside Wren with a confused smile, and Levi sits beside them, covering them with a blanket. Lark walks towards his sister.

With a dizzy turn, I suddenly realise what's wrong: the iron sword is hidden beneath the blankets. The others can't sense it, of course. Can Arden? Is that why Ebony told him not to sit? But she told *me* not to sit either. So why did they put it there? Are they biding their time, waiting for me to relax so they can *stab me*?

Ebony stops, Arden pausing beside her in confusion, and she watches as Lark descends towards the pile. Why is she watching him and not me?

Unless . . . Unless it isn't a trap for me. Unless it's a test. *Fairies*, what is Ebony thinking?

Wren passed. Opal passed. Levi passed. Ebony uses the sword enough that I know it has no effect on her. Why does she want to know if one of us secretly has magic?

Oh, no. *Fairies*. My gut drops to my feet and Arden puts his arm across me; he must realise at the same time I do.

Lark kneels on the cushions, about to poke Wren's nose. But he leaps up. '*Fairies!*' He spins around, stumbles away and vomits over the side of the ship.

It happens so fast I barely register it, and I blink, trying to make sense of this. I saw it coming, I saw Ebony's plan, but . . . *No*. Not after this morning. How could he . . . How could—

'*Lark*,' Arden whispers, shuddering. 'Why . . . How . . .?'

I can only stand and watch, shocked mute. Lark? *Lark*? Waffle-making, shy, overprotective *Lark*?

The young man turns, wiping his mouth. His face is pink, his green eyes bloodshot. While Wren and Opal stare in confusion, the rest of us move into defensive positions. Levi immediately puts himself in between Wren and her brother.

'No,' Lark says, voice weak. He holds his palms out in front of him, hands shaking. 'This isn't – it isn't—'

'What's going on?' Opal asks, shifting. She and Wren stand, both of them tense with confusion. 'Someone tell me what's going on.'

Arden steps forward, his voice deep and cracking like thunder. 'Lark has magic.' I can't read his expression; he's like stone, eyes trained on Lark. On the man who just this morning called him a *brother*.

'How would you even—' Opal starts, then she feels beneath the blankets and pulls out the sword. It almost slices through the material. 'You set a trap? For him? Why would you even think—Why?'

She pushes the sword towards Lark, where he stands with his mouth open, back against the side of the ship. Ebony takes the sword and swings it near him. He flinches, and blue sparks of magic – so faint in the sunlight they're almost clear – sweep off his body as he squirms as far from the iron as possible.

Wren's hands fly to her mouth and she stumbles. Levi holds her up. And that's when Lark really breaks. He tries to say something, but he falters, unable to form words.

It's true.

Ebony's face is downturned – she has no excitement for the success of her ploy. 'I've been suspecting him since we got the sword,' she explains. 'He would never be near it. He always left the room when it was out. He'd try to hide it, but he was sick like Sierra. It became so obvious. Who could have taken Arden's magic except someone who was on the ship that night?'

Levi gives Lark a furious – yet mildly afraid – expression, his arms still over Wren. 'We didn't want to expose him like this, but we didn't want to share that we suspected him in case we were wrong. All we can't figure out is why he did it.'

I go faint, dizzy. Well, fainter and dizzier. I could throw up over the side of the ship too. A swim seems more appealing than suffering through this.

Lark. *He's* had the magic we've been searching for all along? It was always right – *fairies forsaken* – here? He could have saved me, but he didn't. I've been suffering for so long because of him.

I thought he was my friend. I protected him, and he made me waffles and pancakes and soup, and— My chest heats with anger, and the sun is glaring, too bright, and my clothes feel too tight, my legs too heavy. I want to punch, and scream, and swear.

But I see the heartbroken faces of the people around me. They aren't mad. Not really. They only feel betrayed by their friend, and they want to know why.

So I inhale, exhale, and take a step backwards.

Wren begins shaking her head, and she sprints to her brother. Levi tries to hold her back, but she's too quick. 'You're *wrong*,' she seethes, arms outstretched in front of Lark. He winces, his head hanging. 'How dare you accuse my brother of this? How could you ever even think . . . Ebony, I thought you were our friend!'

Ebony recoils, her jaw slack, but she doesn't find the words to comfort Wren.

'If he wants to tell us the truth,' Arden says, still coldly eyeing Lark, 'I'm sure our *friend* has an explanation.'

'I'm sure we could throw him off the side of the ship,' mutters Opal, but her words have no edge to them. She doesn't mean it. Her glassy eyes betray her devastation. 'We never should have trusted a Musan.'

'Stop it,' Ebony warns. 'Give him a chance to explain.'

But Lark won't meet anyone's eyes. He keeps starting to talk, stammering, then changing his mind. Eventually his shoulders fall, and he lands on, 'I'm sorry.'

'Don't,' Wren tells him. 'Lark, you didn't do this.' Tears drip down her cheeks. And all we can do is watch. Watch her heart break.

Still woozy from the sword, I fall back on Arden, and he grips my arm in a way that I know is for him as much as me. After this morning, after Arden poured his heart out to Lark, I can't believe *this* is our reality.

'You didn't do this,' Wren pleads. 'Please, please, please. Tell me this is a misunderstanding.'

He shakes his head. 'It's too late to keep lying.' He takes her hand, kisses the back of it, then points back to the cushions. 'Go and sit down,' he says so quietly I'm not sure we're supposed to hear it. 'I know they won't hurt you, but I don't want you in the middle of this if they . . .'

Fairies, what does he think we're going to do? Fight him? He's *Lark*.

Still, Wren steps away, all the energy gone from her small body, her face ashen and her steps dragging. Levi places a hand on her shoulder as she goes behind him, falling and pressing her face into the cushions.

I feel as if I should go to her, comfort her, but between the iron and the shock, I can barely keep myself standing. I . . . don't know what to do, how to react.

'Explain,' Opal demands of Lark. 'Before our special sword goes through your lying chest.'

Lark tucks his hands non-threateningly behind his back and looks at us sincerely, apologetically. 'I-I did it to protect us.' The water beneath the *Neptune* trembles and shakes us, this ship's magic reacting to the turmoil on board. 'I'm so sorry I lied. But after we cursed the Reeds, people knew we had magic, and they were going to come for us, and I didn't know what to do. Arden was drunk on power. He was ready to get us into even more trouble. Someone had to . . .'

He breathes shallowly. 'Someone had to put a stop to it before it got too dangerous. *I* had to put a stop to it before my sister got hurt. So I waited for the right opportunity to steal the magic, and made sure the blame would fall on Bart. I swear, I haven't even used it. I've been trying to find a way to get rid of it. But when Sierra showed up . . . I didn't know what to do, but I did know I had to keep it secret or she might *kill* me. I promise, this started with me trying to do what was best for us all, but I got caught up in my own lie . . .'

I unclench my jaw enough to speak. 'This is why you suggested we use iron to suppress the curse? You knew we'd never break it? I nearly *died* because of you, Lark. We went through so much for no reason, all because of *you!*'

'You don't know what magic does to people!' Lark shouts at me, the outburst so uncharacteristic I nearly drop. He shakes his head and drops his voice. 'You. Don't. Know. My parents . . . They were like Arden. They got magic and went insane with power. Muse put a stop to them.' Wren looks at him with impossibly wide eyes. *She didn't know.* 'That's why . . . That's why we were orphans, and why, when Wren couldn't behave at school, they decided she was a danger just like our parents and wanted to— We weren't perfect citizens of Muse's Territory, and Muse couldn't have that, so they were going to kill her. Magic is why I had to uproot our lives and run away. Magic is why we'll spend our *lives* running. I watched one family fall apart because of power, and I was not going to let it happen again. Not to me, and certainly not to my sister.'

'Tell me what happened,' Arden says, rubbing his temples. 'The night you took it. Explain it to me.' He finally seems to have softened – a little. But it isn't fair; Lark is using Arden's shame against him. Blaming him. He isn't wrong, he isn't lying, but he's still using his Musan ability to spin words against us.

Lark takes a breath, his eyes on the deck. 'I saw my opportunity after you bumped into your father. I encouraged you to go out and drink, to forget. My plan would only work if you were blacked out. I waited up here, watching for your return. Saw the young woman you were with leave you nearby, watched you stumble back up to the ship. You passed out. Everyone else was asleep. That's when I took the magic. I didn't even know how to do it. I just thought about it, and . . . it came to me. Maybe you were more willing to give it up than you realised. I carried you to bed and knew you'd wake up blaming only yourself for being careless enough to lose it.'

Arden goes pale. To have one of his best friends use his insecurities against him like that . . . How could he forgive Lark, even if he thought he was doing the right thing? I hold Arden's hand. Try to tell him that I'm on his side, that I understand. Even if no one else does.

After Kyla, Arden let his every mistake drown him. And while Lark posed as a friend, a brother, he was only another weight pulling him further underwater. How many other lies have there been over the years they've travelled together?

Lark has always put Wren first. I understand that. He'd do anything for her – betray anyone. Knowing he did this both makes me respect him more and fear what else he's capable of.

'Clever, Lark,' Opal says. 'Very believable. But isn't it suspicious that you held on to the magic all this time? And that you refused to give it up, even when Sierra was on our ship *threatening our lives*? How about all the times it would have been helpful? *You* . . . How are we supposed to understand this?'

I stop listening as their arguing continues, retreating into my mind. My arms wrap around my torso.

We . . . have the magic. We thought there was no chance. We thought it was over.

We have the magic.

Finally, without a doubt, the curse can be broken.

Fairies. Why do I wish we didn't have the magic at all?

CHAPTER
TWENTY-SIX

'It just makes more sense if we all have some, instead of me having all of it,' Arden whines. With his original magic now taken back from Lark, *and* the magic we stole from his father, he's overflowing. And he hates it. It isn't just the power that frightens Arden – the iron sword is making him so nauseous he can barely stand. 'Please? Just take a *bit*.'

'Well I don't want it,' I tell the cowering captain. He's been asking for days, but even as he begs now, on the deck under the starlight, I will not be swayed. 'Never needed magic before, don't need it now. Besides, when we go to get the iron, I don't want to be even more vulnerable.'

'I'm with Sierra,' Ebony agrees, and Wren and Levi nod along. We don't say it, but the sentiment is: *It's your problem.*

Opal ruffles her blue tulle dress. 'I'll take some off your hands.'

I cringe and kick at the floor, not wanting to be the one to tell her no. Surely we can all agree we can't trust Opal to be made even deadlier.

'Oh,' she groans, seeing our apprehensive looks. 'I'd be good. Promise.'

Ebony tosses her enchanted weapon – currently a knife – and catches it. The iron sword is tucked away safely in her room. 'Hold on to it for now, Arden. When we get to Bearra, we'll donate the magic to their soldiers to help them fight.'

I frown, because I should expect regular genius from Ebony by now, but that is . . . *smart*. If only she'd come up with it days ago, to stop Arden's complaining.

'You could always give some back to Lark,' Levi mutters under his breath with a laugh. Ebony taps him with her knife and shushes him.

Lark has been hiding away in his room since we took the magic back from him. We didn't lock him up or murder him, or torture him, or even be particularly nasty to him. No, I don't entirely trust him – he's a Musan after all, and I don't like the way he spun the blame onto Arden – but we know he isn't a real threat, and he was only doing what he thought was best for Wren.

Still, we all resent him, and the lies have created a huge divide between him and us. We can't trust him; even Wren has moved out of their cabin and into Opal's, taking the hammock I slept in before the iron sword forced me into Arden's triarue closet.

She'll forgive her brother eventually, I'm sure. She'll see he did this for her. And I hope she does, because if she can be grateful for what he did, maybe that will make it okay. Maybe, then, the rest of us can forgive him too.

Besides, we need him back so he can cook, because the rest of us have been trying, and it is *not good.*

I just feel so stupid. How could I not have known the magic I needed to break the curse was with me the entire time? How did I not see all the signs? Ebony did, so why not me?

Unless I didn't want to see. Unless the love I've gained for this small crew of pirates is stronger than any hate I ever felt towards them. Unless I began to love the part of myself that was cursed – the part that was free, the part that separated me from my family.

Unless I began to hate the Reeds so much that the thought of their acceptance was no longer something I even wanted.

Unless I started wanting all of the things I longed for from my family from the pirates instead.

And they might actually give me those things willingly.

A few weeks ago, I would've enjoyed killing Lark for what he did. But now that I know him and his sister, I can understand his reasons. Besides, Lark is impossible to hate. If only because he's the one who feeds us, we're all a little in love with our golden boy. We can't be *without* him. We're a team of seven, no matter what, and when one of us is gone, nothing is right.

The others slowly disappear, back to their rooms, across the deck, into the kitchen, or overboard for a swim – until only Arden and I are left. We stay silent for a long time, standing side-by-side, leaning against the side of the ship and looking out at the water rippling beneath us.

It's been a few days since Lark's betrayal – since Arden told him about Kyla – and I still can't begin to imagine the whiplash Arden feels. So much has happened so fast. I used to be okay with that, trained for that. But now I carry the weight of six others with me, and all their grief is mine too.

Fairies, is this how normal people feel, always crushed under the pressure of those they care about? Life was so much easier when I hated everyone.

Arden clears his throat, shocking me back from the dark depths of my mind. 'I know we're not in a good headspace to make this decision,' he says, 'but we need to choose what to do next. It's either back to Grace's Territory to find your sisters and really break the curse, or continue on to the iron stores. Or we could go back to Bearra first.' He looks away, his eyes glazing over as he overthinks. 'I don't know. Whatever you want, Sierra.'

My poor captain. Before we discovered Lark's secret, we were in a bad place – though not as bad as *now* – with lost hope after Bart's magic failed to reverse the curse. At least then, we were sailing directly for the iron stores. Now the ship has been almost idle, stopping and starting, going forwards and then backwards, because we're all so confused.

It seems impossible. I've never had so many thoughts and emotions before. I think I finally understand Maya and Teddy's dilemmas. They seemed silly to me before, but that was when I always had an unwavering goal and only myself to take care of. Now everything is complicated. I don't know what I want. I only know who I want to protect.

'Arden,' I whisper, my words barely carrying over the waves. 'I don't think I want to go home anymore. We should go to the iron.'

He turns to me, frowning. 'But we have to break the curse.'

'Do we?' I meet his eyes, a flutter of hope in my chest.

Because Arden was right, maybe about everything. I didn't understand it until I knew him. I didn't think it possible. But my family aren't who I thought they were. I thought we were warriors, but the Reeds are just killers. I don't want to be that anymore. I want to be like him. Free.

Damn the magic. I *like* being cursed. It's the best thing that's ever happened to me. Without it I would never have seen the truth. I would never have learned how love feels. Now I know, and I wouldn't change a thing.

The Reeds can squawk for eternity. I want my true family.

Arden doesn't catch my meaning. 'Of course we need to break it. What are you saying?'

I look out at the water. The night has turned dreary and the river is rough and grey, but stars peek through scattered clouds. 'When I was seven years old . . .' I start, then stop. It's embarrassing to talk about my past, but with him, I want to share everything.

'When I was seven,' I force myself to say, 'I first realised I was an outsider in my family. I had a friend, then, if you would believe it. My parents had sent me to a small school for my education, rather than have me tutored. Anything to get me out of the house and away from them. I met a girl there who had wealthy, important parents like me, so we understood each other. It was the first time I'd known someone who actually wanted to hear what I had to say. Who liked having me around. I wasn't sure what to do with that. So, one day I visited her house. She had a large family like mine. I . . . They cared about each other. I watched the parents kiss the children's foreheads and hug them goodnight, tuck them into bed – even though they had maids for that.'

I glance at him, expecting a dazed, bored expression, but he gives me wide-eyed attention and nods for me to continue.

'I watched as the children all played together, sometimes fighting but almost always laughing,' I say. 'Sharing, listening, just enjoying being with each other. It was the first time I ever saw love. I didn't understand. In my family, all I knew was violence and coldness. My birth took my mother – a Reed as powerful as any of my sisters – off the water after fighting with her daughters for years. I was a sick child, Arden, and it was a bad pregnancy. The only reason my family kept me was because Grace insisted they do. Even before I was born, all I did was burden everyone.'

I pick at a splinter in the ship. 'I never spoke to that girl from school again. Knowing the truth hurt too much. When I got older, I thought maybe if I could just show my family how skilled I was, they would start to love me. When I realised that would never work, I decided that if I couldn't get their love, I would settle for their acceptance. And still, nothing. I tried to become better than them. To show them how great I could be, out of spite. Even that didn't work.' I blink. A long blink, a swallow, a breath.

'Arden, when I'm with you, when I'm on this ship . . . I feel the way I did that at that girl's house all those years ago. But I don't just feel as if I'm watching. I'm part of it. I hate to say this, I really do, but you were right about my family. They aren't worth saving. Maybe even

311

I'm not. But you? The world deserves Captain Arden Lacerta. Lark was wrong when he blamed you, when he said it was your fault he had to take away your power. You were right to do everything you did. You were right to show me a better way. You should be powerful. You're strong and kind, and it doesn't matter that you make mistakes, because you're—'

He gives me a quizzical expression, just a hint of a smile. 'Please, don't stop.'

'That's not the point. I'm saying that I choose you. I'm saying that if my sisters are left as swans, maybe that isn't the worst thing. I can go to Teddy, and maybe he can make me better, stop the curse from taking such a hold – he's changed it before. This is a power I want to keep. I can use it to help fight in the war. We— We mustn't break it.'

Fairies, I don't think I've ever talked this much in my life. Let alone been listened to. I catch my breath, nervously awaiting his response.

'I don't know what to say . . .' His hands grip the side of the boat, and he leans over as if he's motion sick. 'You think . . . You think I'm right about something?'

I roll my eyes as I realise he's only feigning shock. 'Don't start giving me second thoughts.'

'Okay, okay.' He takes a breath. 'Thank you, for telling me all of that. I . . . It means a lot to me. And you know I'd be happy to leave your family cursed. But are you sure you don't want me to take the swan away for your own sake?'

'I'm sure,' I say, and I really mean it. There's never been anything clearer to me. Yes, it's a risk, with the iron, with the swan getting stronger, but I'm happier than I've ever been. 'I'm better the way I am now. A better fighter, a better person. I don't want to go back. I don't want to see my family again. I have a new family now. A family that makes me strong, instead of trying to make me weak. A family that has done so much to help me – if only because I threatened you, but—'

'If I had known you before that day,' he says, his voice low, 'you wouldn't have had to threaten me. I would do anything for you, Sierra.'

I soften all over, inside and out. I'm *melting*. 'I spent so long uselessly hating you. Someone I didn't even know. You did make it easy, I'll give you that, but . . . *Fairies*. Everything has changed. And I'm so happy that I get to—' I nearly throw up in my mouth, but I force out the words. 'I get to love you now, Arden, and that's all that matters to me.'

He stands up straight. 'You get to . . . to *what*?'

I groan. Step forward. I've never been good at subtlety, never been good at lying, except to myself. I am *always* one hundred per cent, in or out, happy, sad, angry. Whatever it is, I feel it fully. My goals, my dreams, I pursue them fully and never waver. I can love and I can hate – nothing in between.

I've spent years pouring my heart and soul into hating, because there's always less damage. Because when I love, I can't love softly, I can't love halfway, and I can't love safely. When I love, I do it with my entire being, and I always, always get hurt. As much as I fight to hate, I fall for love every time, and it destroys me.

From the moment I met Arden, I've been drawn to him. And I can't hate him anymore.

I meet his eyes. 'I'll never understand you. Do you realise that? I don't have a single clue what's going on in your head. Ever. It drives me insane. And yet I am entirely bound to you.'

'Are you sure you're in your right mind? Are you drunk? Is it the iron?'

'*Fairies*, I could kill you.' Before he can respond, I wrap my hands around his neck and pull him into a kiss. It is – *oh, to the power of all seven fairies* – magic. The good kind. All the good kind. He leans into me, and it's nothing like our first, lustful kiss in that cave. This is . . . caring, and it is joy, and it is *everything*.

He breaks away for a second. 'If I haven't made it clear enough,' he says, catching his breath, 'I am falling in love with you, Sierra Reed. It makes me sick to my stomach, but it is what it is. I wouldn't change it. Because I am insane for you.'

'Shut up. Keep kissing me before I kill you.'

He leans back in, his lips soft but fast, his hands warm on my face. We curl into each other, getting closer and closer even though at any moment someone could see us. I don't care anymore. I don't want to keep my feelings for him a secret any longer.

But something shifts, my hands turning cold. *Fairies*, the curse! Have I already turned him into a swan?

As I gasp, I feel a pull in the pit of my stomach, a seizing throughout my body, electrifying my limbs. Blue magic courses over my skin, swallowing me like flames.

'Arden!' I scream. Nothing is happening to him – he isn't turning into a swan – so what's happening to *me*? This didn't happen when I kissed Zeus. 'What are you doing!' For one terrifying moment, I wonder if this has all been a lie. If he's snapped and he's finally decided that now is the time to kill me.

But I can see the fear on his face as he pats at my skin like it's a fire he can put out. 'This isn't me!'

A pained cry escapes me as an inferno shoots through my body, like my skin is being ripped off from the inside, like my veins are seizing, like every muscle is exploding.

I try to turn into the swan – anything to stop the pain – but nothing happens. I try harder. Think as hard as I can. Imagine how it feels to not be in this body. *Finally* I manage to shift. Arden jumps back as my wingspan nearly knocks him out.

But this is *worse*. My body cracks and creases, burning and whirling.

Eventually I must pass out, because when I next open my eyes, I'm human again, and laying on the floor. The pain is gone. The blue waves leave my body, floating into the night air like rising smoke. I breathe, and breathe, and breathe. Arden grabs my hands and I cling to him like he can save my life.

'Are you okay?' he asks. The other pirates are surrounding us, all looking down in concern. Even Lark has made an appearance. How long was I unconscious?

'You must have done something.' My voice is weak, my body exhausted. 'With your magic.'

'I swear,' Arden says. 'I didn't do anything. I would never.'

I breathe again, just let myself sit and *breathe*. 'No . . . You didn't.' Of course he wouldn't. I let out a sigh of relief. 'It came from within me,' I realise. 'It was like . . . like . . .'

Ebony appears in front of me with the iron sword, making Arden turn green, but he doesn't leave my side. 'Reach out to it,' she orders me. 'You don't have to touch it. Just reach.'

Sensing her train of thought, I put a hand forward hesitantly. And – *nothing*. No pain. I don't even feel nauseous at the iron's presence. It could be any kind of metal, any regular sword. Even my blessings don't seem to be concerned with it. They must be such a small amount of magic that it doesn't matter.

Which can only mean one thing.

Ebony answers the group's unspoken question, her expression a mask of confusion. 'Arden removed the curse.'

'No – I did not—' Arden gawks at me with pleading eyes, grabs at my hands. 'I didn't do this. Sierra, please believe me. I did not do this. I wouldn't do this to you. I wouldn't hurt you again. Never again.'

'I believe you,' I whisper, my eyes filling with tears. For once I let them fall, and I let the others watch as I pull my knees to my chest, bury my face in my arms, and sob. Arden's arms wrap around me and I lean into him.

I reach for the swan, but she isn't there. She's no longer part of me.

They let me sit for a long while, all of us in silence. Together. No one asks me questions. No one offers me pity. They just let me grieve what I've lost, they stand with me, and that's all I could ask for.

'I just . . .' I say eventually, my voice hoarse. 'I can't believe, after all this time . . .' I try to understand it, this new reality, but I can't. It's so sudden, it's so awful. Part of me, the part of me that changed everything, is *gone*.

'You'll be okay,' Arden whispers. 'This was meant to be. The curse couldn't last forever.'

I cradle my head in his lap. 'But I don't know how to be human.'

'We're going to help you figure it out,' Ebony says. The sun is rising behind her head, haloing her, one of my best friends, and I feel as if there really is magic between us, knowing she really means it. She'll help me. Someone is going to *help me.*

Wren says, 'The good news is that now you can help us when we reach the iron stores.'

I manage to wipe my eyes and smile. No, this isn't so bad. Not if I have them with me.

Levi kneels beside me. 'We're here for you, Sierra. Anything you need. But, uh, not to make this situation worse, but . . . do we think the curse was broken for your sisters as well?'

I nearly faint at the thought. 'I suppose we'll find out eventually.'

'We should go back to Bearra,' Lark says. 'Take Sierra there to rest and tell them where the iron is. Our job is done.'

'No,' Wren argues. 'We've come this far. And Sierra can go near iron now.'

The group begins to bicker, but I barely register it. I feel both as if a huge void has opened within me, and as if something has been filled. I feel strong in my body, more real, more solid, than I have since I was cursed. But I also feel like I'm missing something as vital as my lungs.

I try to transform again, one last desperate attempt, but there's nothing to even reach for. That part of my life is over, thanks to Arden. Because . . . because of a kiss? He isn't a prince. I'm no princess. We kissed once and nothing happened, but this time, after I told him I loved him . . .

Was it his magic at all, or is the legend that the love of a soulmate can break a curse *real*?

Could I ask for better proof that whatever is between us is . . . true?

'Oh, *six territories*,' says Opal, swinging her bow off her shoulder. She points an arrow upriver. 'What is that?'

Arden stands, pulling me up with him. Levi notices the gesture and smirks, but I have no time to sneer back at him, because in the distance is a vast glimmer of yellow magic. It's coming towards us, fast. We haven't even made it to the iron stores, but it's too late to flee now.

My heart races with anticipation. At least we're going to have an extraordinary finale.

Is this what Lire was counting on? Was it always her plan to send her sister to stop us right before we thought we'd won? How long did it take Bart to tell her everything?

Muse soars above her ship, rising with the sun, her wings glimmering like stars. She's so bright that even the sunrise can't silhouette her.

There is no more time for me to mourn or panic. I can worry about the curse, about *love*, later.

The fight has come to us.

And I'm going to kill a fairy today.

CHAPTER
TWENTY-SEVEN

Muse's ship rushes towards us with enchanted power.

Arden readies his blue magic. Opal fetches her bow and arrows. Ebony holds the iron sword in both hands, her enchanted weapon tucked into her belt. Levi stands tall beside her. Lark has his own sword, and Wren has her knives out, surveying the ship like a cat about to pounce.

Meanwhile I – still weak from the curse being broken – am pushing my limits just to stand upright and try to *appear* strong.

So much for all those treacherous obstacles Bart warned us about – and I was looking forward to that. Our enemy stops us in our path before we even get close. The land around us is sparse and dry, but the wide river glitters under the rising sun. Fish dart away as the *Neptune* rushes past, the waves we make creating chaos on the shore. But even we are nothing compared to the fairy-led vessel coming our way: huge, bright yellow, and glowing with magic.

Clearly, Lire knew we were coming. She wouldn't allow this to be on unfair ground, near the metal that weakens fairies. Here, in the open, magic has all the power.

But whether Lire was too unbothered to deal with us, or too cowardly, she hasn't even shown up to her own fight. Instead she's chosen the most powerful ally of hers, the ally that scares us the most. The fairy of life and song: *Muse*.

A compliment, really. She could send an army our way, but Lire knew only a fairy could defeat the crew of the *Neptune*. Lire may have hurt Maya and Teddy, and I may want to wring her neck, but I have a score to settle with Muse. All of Lark and Wren's suffering is because of her. She won't get away with that.

My weakness ebbs as my blood churns with anticipation. I cannot *wait* to annihilate this fairy.

'Arden,' I say, trying to stop my voice trembling even as the wind whips my hair and threatens to buckle my knees. 'You have to curse me again.'

He spins to face me. 'No!'

'Why?' Hot air rushes against my ears. 'You were *more* than happy to do it the first time. Now I actually need it! I can't fight without the swan.'

'Sierra, you know why!' He throws his hands in the air. 'I'm not risking it. That curse was flimsy to begin with, and you only learned to use it to your advantage after your half-fairy friend altered it. I could hurt you more this time. I'm not taking that risk. And not right now, of all times!'

Opal groans. 'We have enough magic on this ship for a small army, and no one knows how to use it. We're about to be demolished by a *fairy*! Someone better come up with a plan. I give us five minutes before we're all dead.'

'Curse me!' I shout.

'No!' Ebony shouts back. 'Arden is right. We don't have time for a risk like that. You're more useful to us at your weakest.' She hands me her weapon, and it changes into a shining sword in my hands, the perfect size and weight for me. Deadly sharp. 'We are going to fight. Even if we all die here, if all we've done is weaken her army a little, decrease it by one soldier, or better yet weaken Muse herself, then we've done some good.'

Fairies. If I'd simply not kissed Arden for just a few more hours, everything would be fine! But *no*.

No curse. No swan. No power.

I look to him, and he gives me a lopsided smile with his hands on his knives. He juts his chin in Muse's direction and draws a finger across his neck. With a wink, he mouths, *Let's kill her.*

A shudder wracks through my body. He has never been more attractive. I could kiss him again right this second. Take him down into his room and—

And I need to pull myself together. I'm being weak, and nervous, and getting distracted by him – which isn't a bad thing, but now is definitely not the time. I'm Sierra Reed. I'm a warrior, a pirate. I'm not afraid of a fairy, I don't need a curse to win a fight, and I'll deal with Arden once we've won the battle.

I breathe, focus on each inch of my body: the muscles in my arms, the skin on my calloused knuckles, the power in my feet. I remind myself that my strength stems from the very core of my being – I'm not just powerful, I *am* power. And with my crew by my side, there is no being strong enough to stop me.

I release the ship's railing and stand tall. This is where I'm meant to be. The sway of the *Neptune* on the river, the wind in my hair, the scent of freshwater in my lungs – the river itself invigorates me.

Today, I am going to murder Muse. Tonight, I'm going to spend every last second in Arden's arms. It is going to be *fairy's forsaking* magical.

'I have an idea,' says Wren. We all peer over our shoulders to the small girl. 'We keep going towards the iron. The closer we are, the weaker she—' She squeezes her eyes shut for a moment, the yellow glow of the distant fairy bouncing off her eyelids. 'If we're closer to the iron stores, Muse will be weaker.'

Lark nearly chokes. 'We would be heading right for her!'

'No, Wren is right,' I say, nodding to her. 'We go right past them, and we'll get ahead while they turn to chase us. Even if we're still hours away, the closer we are to the iron, the better. We just have to keep fighting until we're near enough that she can't continue.'

'Or until we die,' Opal offers. As luck would have it, she's already in her favourite fighting outfit – a silky purple dress with matching ribbons in her braided hair.

'Muse won't want to get her hands dirty,' Lark says. His eyes keep darting to his sister, his shoulders set tight. 'She'll let her soldiers fight first, and wait to attack. If we can keep them busy until we get close to the iron stores, we could survive. But if she does use all her power to strike . . .'

The shouts of Muse's crew begin travelling through the wind. They're not just ready for a fight – they're ready to show their dedication to their fairy. That's what scares me most. Last time I saw the fairy, in her capital city with Maya, her people ran through the streets with tattered clothes and bleeding feet just for a chance to lay their eyes upon her.

These aren't just soldiers. These people are entirely under Muse's enchantment. They don't have minds of their own, and they won't hesitate to fight to the death.

'So that's our plan?' Opal says. 'Just . . . try not to be killed by one of the most powerful beings in the world?'

'If it helps,' Arden tells her, 'you can take whatever you want from them. Stealing and killing may be exactly what we need most today.'

She sighs. 'It's always *stop stealing things and killing people, Opal,* until everyone's lives are in danger.'

'Everyone. Focus.' I hold up a hand. 'We need to get the *Neptune* moving as fast as we can. Arden, put some magic into it. We all stay on board, okay? No one get excited and jump onto Muse's ship. Ideally we won't even get close enough that it's possible for either of us to strike as we pass.' I glance around to make sure I have everyone's attention. 'Plan A is to lose them and race to the iron stores. Plan B, if we don't make it that far, is to take a stand and fight. But if we do, this is going to be the biggest fight of your lives. We have to stick together. For once, we can't be reckless.'

I'm partially lying, because if I get a chance to kill Muse, I'm not going to *not* take it. But as for the others, I need them safe.

'Yes, captain,' says Arden, with a small smile.

My heart skips a beat. If we get out of this alive, I'm going to kiss him until my lips bleed.

The *Neptune*, listening and obeying as always, speeds through the rough water, right towards Muse's ship, even as the saffron magic glows around it menacingly. Our boat rocks and jumps over waves of brown water, and my body automatically shifts to stay balanced.

Anyone not used to being on the water would stumble. But we are pirates. And I *love* this.

Arden pours magic into and around the deck, its blue sparkling around us like water on a stunning summer's day. We're all high-lighted in sapphire, surging through the river. Muse is probably too stupid to be terrified, but she should be.

The soldiers' silhouettes become clearer. The fairy flies above the ship, her starry wings glittering, spilling over with magic. Back and forth, back and forth, with wind in her red hair, and her dress billowing around her ankles. She's breathtaking – but her eyes ruin the image. They're fixed on the Neptune with something between chaos and mischief, like a cat toying with its prey.

My breath hitches. Seeing her up close, my bravery turns to panic, and oh, *fairies,* we are utterly doomed. I'm going to have to watch all of my friends die, if I don't go first. 'I'm sorry!' I shout to my crew. If this is the end, I have to say it. 'I'm so sorry. To all of you. For everything. For being the reason we're here right now. I-I'm sorry.'

Opal wraps her arm around my shoulders – which isn't easy, since she's much shorter than me. Her bow hits me in the side. 'Quiet, Sierra. All of that's behind us. Focus on *now*.'

'Right. Sorry.'

The fear eases from Wren's face as she smiles at me, while Lark and Levi hold in snickers. Ebony and Arden look at me seriously, but I know they understand.

I nod, push Opal off me. '*Okay*. Sorry. I mean, thank you.'

My cheeks are flushing, but it's like a weight has been lifted off my shoulders. Everything is out in the open now. I clench my fists and turn to the fairy. I don't have to be afraid, because even if I slip up, my crew has my back. I have never been more excited for a fight, and that's really saying something, because fighting Teddy outside Maya's grandmother's grave was a highlight of my life.

That's right. I've beaten a half-fairy with an all-powerful crown. Muse doesn't know what she's up against.

Opal starts firing arrows at the fairy, but we're still so far away – and they disappear by the time they reach her. Simply dissolve into nothingness as they pass into the magical yellow light surrounding the fairy. Her laugh echoes down the river.

When Opal realises her arrows are doing nothing against Muse's magic, she wastes no time aiming for the soldiers instead. There must be thirty, forty of them to operate a ship that size.

No matter. I could handle a hundred soldiers. A thousand. It's only the fairy I'm worried about. Clearly, arrows can't do anything against her, and I feel useless just standing here waiting to get close enough to strike. If I still had the swan, I could fly to Muse and confront her before she gets too close to the ship. Sadly, we need to wait for her to come to us.

Come *on*. I'm *bored*.

The soldiers shift and race around the deck as they realise we're coming for them rather than running away. They couldn't have anticipated we'd be *that* insane.

'Follow them!' Muse sings from overhead. I *love* the shock in her voice. 'Stop their ship!'

Arden tries to send lightning-fast blasts of magic towards the soldiers, copying Opal's arrows, but they don't even come close to their targets; he doesn't have the skill to manage it. His hits land on the enemy ship with sparks that flitter out, and the soldiers' shoulders shake as they laugh.

Still, we keep racing and racing towards them, until I can see the wicked looks on their faces: the eyes hungry for violence, the sneering lips.

'Now!' calls Muse. 'Kill them!'

The soldiers jump to action to work the ship, but it'll take them time to turn such a large vessel around. We'll have a short head start, which could be all we need to reach the iron stores before we're slaughtered.

So we rush right past her ship and continue speeding upriver. Arden even uses his magic to block them from turning, sending waves of blue power – so dark it's almost black – to press back at the ship.

Muse catches on and sends an incomprehensibly immense wave of her magic back at us. Shimmering yellow air courses up like a tsunami, swallowing our entire world. I scream and duck. For one horrific moment, my chest pulls tight as I remember Teddy's attack on me in Kara's Territory.

But Ebony races *towards* it. She extends her arms upright, her sword vertical in her hands, and Muse's magic is cut right through by the iron. Yellow arcs around the ship, missing us entirely; it's as if Ebony has split the sun itself, bathing us in darkness.

For a few moments, we're encased in an amber shadow – it reminds me of passing through low, late-afternoon clouds as the swan. Although dizzying, the blindness is also dream-like. The thumping of my heart eases from my ears, and I steady myself.

The better I can focus on getting away from Muse, the faster the *Neptune* will know to go. As Muse's magic fades and we race further away from her ship, we jolt and dip through stormy waters. The rapids are certainly enchanted; the water was soft and still only a few kilometres back. I nearly whoop with delight when the ship goes up a wave so high it crashes down with a splash that soaks the deck.

I take my sword – Ebony's enchanted weapon – and ready myself for Muse's first attack. I can't fight magic, but the moment those soldiers step foot near us, I will relish taking them out one by one.

Muse's ship finally reaches close enough for her to fly her soldiers onto the *Neptune*. They land with amber magic circling their feet, swinging their swords with intention to kill.

The seven of us, the crew of the *Neptune*, become a machine in an instant, back-to-back and ready to fight. Outrunning our enemies hasn't worked, so murder it is. What. A. Shame.

The *Neptune* doesn't stop – it knows we have to continue towards the iron, no matter how bad the battle becomes. Luckily, that means many of Muse's soldiers will be too distracted piloting their ship to properly attack us. A mountain rises in the distance, a gigantic rock jutting out of the ground. The landmark Bart told us about.

We're close.

Swords clang, arrows fly, fists beat. Blood sprays until the deck is dripping with red, and I have to assume some of it belongs to my friends.

But I remain focused. As I cut down a soldier by slashing their sword off the side of the ship and cutting through a soft spot in their thigh, I remember the best way to protect my friends is to keep killing and *not* worry.

My mind settles as my body takes over, muscle memory making my limbs move like lightning and adrenaline heightening my awareness. My Strength and Justice blessings kick in, bringing me extra drive and power.

Halfway through a gleeful laugh, I scream. A sword catches me in the left shoulder, opening a deep wound.

Fairies. All seven fairies. Ah!

I use my right arm only to swing my sword, dipping down and swinging at my attacker with my leg to trip him before burying the weapon in his chest. I yank it out, my eyes teary from the pain.

There's no time to assess my wound. Within seconds, two more soldiers are on top of me – one of them has magic, a swirl of red as bright as the blood around me.

Fortunately, I'm not afraid of a little soldier with a little magic. Truly, I've missed this. I take a breath just to enjoy the moment. The thrill before the kill. Life is wonderful, isn't it?

I boot the soldier in the chest and they fly back, magic sparking out from their hands as they fall. The other takes a swing at me but I jump at their neck and pull them onto the ground, bashing their head into the deck. I run over to the magical soldier to finish them off, but find them already unconscious. I'm *too* good.

I throw both over the side of the ship for the chance to spare their lives. It's severely disappointing, and honestly, I've become too kind, but one look at my friends and I forget my instinct to kill.

It is what it is.

The battle worsens. Weakened and wounded, I almost can't fight off the soldiers that keep coming and coming and coming. No matter how many soldiers I knock out, the fighting doesn't ebb. I'm losing a lot of blood from the gash on my arm, and it's making my head spin. I resort to kicking ferally, lashing and biting like an animal. They can't get their weapons close enough to hurt me, yet, but I'm faltering against them.

As my lungs heave and my muscles strain, a few soldiers manage to surround me, making a loose circle. With a coordinated glance at each other, they pounce at once.

Fairies. There's too many—

One nearly falls on me, an arrow in their neck. *Opal.* For once, I'm grateful for her violent tendencies. The other soldiers' momentary shock is enough for me to get them off me, tighten the grip on my sword, and swing it down on them with unrelenting fatality.

I did try to be nice to them, but it isn't my fault they kept attacking! A few kills each battle is *healthy.* I slice a neck with a satisfying swish, stab a heart with a rib-destroying crunch.

And it's all very lovely, but at this point I feel as if I can barely move. I think, if *only* I could turn into the swan, destroy them as that other version of myself, then turn back fully healed like I used to. If only I hadn't kissed Arden.

I stop dead. *Arden.* I think I— No. I *know* I love him. It all happened so quickly – I haven't had a proper chance to think, to take it all in.

A soldier appears and I punch them in the face, sending them flying over the side of the boat with a scream. How dare someone interrupt my thoughts?

Arden and I are in love. *Love!* And it is real, and true, and . . . it doesn't even make me sick to my stomach anymore. I look around for him, and catch him swinging his knives at the soldiers circling him, while using magic to keep them back.

He meets my eyes, his blood-soaked shirt billowing as the enchanted storm rages around him. He slashes his knives across a soldier's chest, simultaneously blocking a wave of magic from another with his own power. Despite the chaos, he grins at me in a way that makes my heart rush.

Oh, my, *fairies.*

I am so in love. He is the world to me, and I am the world to him, and that is strong enough to break a curse – it is *destined.* Why is that thought not making me want to hurl out my last three meals?

'*Fairies!*' I yell as a wave of pink magic flies towards me. I duck out of the way just in time, and it hits a soldier behind me instead, knocking them unconscious. I glare at my attacker, and go to stalk towards them, but Ebony's weapon turns from a sword to a bow in my hand. An arrow appears and, trusting the weapon's intuition, I pull it tight and aim.

The soldier stops, blinking in shock at the enchanted weapon. With a laugh, I let the arrow fly right into their chest. Any further away and I may have missed – I'm hardly an expert shooter – but they fall with a thump, the pink magic seeping out from their body as their life leaves them.

Yet another smile greets my face. I am having a great battle, I am in love, and I'm sharing a beautiful day with my friends. Life doesn't get better than this.

We're surely getting closer to the iron stores now, because the water is getting rougher with every passing minute. The metallic scent of blood mixes with the stench of muddy water mixed up by the storm. Soon the ship is jumping and crashing through waves so often that the fighting lessens considerably – with most everyone just trying to stay upright – giving me a chance to catch my breath and tear a piece of fabric off a dead soldier's shirt to wrap the wound on my arm. My face feels bruised too, and I'm certain my jaw is bleeding.

No matter.

Arden nods to me from afar, his magic curling around his body as he uses it to send unsuspecting soldiers off the side of the ship. Mostly he's protecting Wren and Lark. I wink in return, but the moment is short-lived, because suddenly Muse is coming right for us. I run to Arden without thinking, knowing only that I have to be by his side.

Why is she already here? Surely she'd love to watch more of her devoted followers die for her first?

Standing back-to-back, we watch the fairy descend, her yellow wings outstretched and beating ethereally. The sight fills me with an intense, animalistic hatred. My fingertips itch with the desire to hurt her.

We're passing the mountain, ever closer to the iron. It's only a matter of time before Muse loses her power. *So she's gotten desperate.* Even as Muse lands, it's clear her magic is a dulled shade of its usual searing bumblebee yellow, appearing instead as a drab mustard. The sun goes behind the mountain, and the fairy becomes the only source of light, dimly glowing against the jagged rocks and storm clouds that appear all around us.

As always, I am incredibly grateful that our ship can navigate itself. As long as none of our intentions waver, we can all focus on fighting, while the *Neptune* works on weakening Muse by carrying us onward.

Opal shoots at the fairy, but Muse only laughs sweetly as her feet touch the deck, the arrow caught in a cloud of magic. Just to be dramatic, she takes it in her hands and snaps it in half. 'So *you're* the pirates who have been working so hard to find a way to kill Lire.' She nods at her soldiers, who stop fighting and run back to surround the fairy, protecting her – as if she needs it. Even as they bleed out around her, they stand straight and hold their focus.

I glare at her. Everything about this *creature* is for show, from the small smile on her lips to her ridiculously monochrome outfit. 'Clearly, we've already found a way to kill Lire,' I spit. 'And you. Unfortunately, you're in our way.'

Muse watches me through her dark eyes. Her red hair trails silkily over her yellow dress. She reminds me eerily of Teddy. What is she, his aunt, or something? Not to stereotype, but every day I'm seeing that red hair is a red flag.

She says, 'Some of you humans are so cocky, for beings so weak. Are you children too young to know that I am the true queen of this world? The fairies are the very foundations of the land you stand upon. We *are* this world. You cannot think to stop us. You cannot even begin to imagine how powerful I am.'

Opal snickers, standing in front of Lark and Wren. 'I can begin to imagine how boring this speech is.'

'Oh, look,' says Muse. 'This one wants to die.'

I step towards the fairy, my feet weak beneath me. 'I know your power. I've bested Lire's son, and you're hardly as powerful as his mother. I see through your disguise, Muse, and I am so very thrilled to have the honour of killing you.'

The fairy's face falls into a scowl. 'Lire is *not* more powerful than me. You would do well not to spread such rumours. Not that you'll make it through the day.'

'Why?' Levi goads. 'Because you don't want people to know that you're only Lire's second in command, while she's the one who'll actually rule the world if she wins the war?'

'How *embarrassing*,' says Wren, chin high as she laughs at the fairy who took her childhood, her parents. 'How weak.'

My palms go cold. I would have preferred a scared, meek Wren to an angry one. She's too much like the rest of us – filled with too much spite and too much confidence.

'Do you think you can stop me by insulting me?' Muse floats towards Wren, her magic snaking around the girl.

'It isn't difficult,' Opal says, only a hint of fear in her eyes as she moves into the magic and pushes Wren behind her. 'You're a hag in an outfit that looks like it's from three hundred years ago. And you're about to lose a war you've barely managed to start.'

Saffron magic curls up to Opal's throat, disappearing from around Wren and squeezing its new target as if the fairy's real hand is choking Opal. Her eyes bulge, but she doesn't attempt to move away from Wren.

I glare at Muse, wondering if this would be the best time to maim her like it's her worst fairy nightmare.

'Stop!' Arden shouts, sprinting to Opal while his own magic floods out of his hands. He reaches around her neck and tries to scratch away Muse's magic with his own, but it's too strong. Even Wren has faltered behind her as Opal quakes, unable to catch any breath.

'Muse,' I hiss. All my pride disappears and I know I'll say or do anything to stop the fairy from hurting my friends. 'Muse! You have nothing to gain from killing us – just stop!'

Muse giggles. 'You're a liar, Sierra Reed. But you are right. I'm wasting my time on this one.'

The magic shifts away, leaking back towards the fairy. Opal falls, coughing and clutching her throat. Arden holds her up, his blue magic softly cradling her like armour. Muse just shakes her head at them, impatient and bored.

We're still steadily headed towards Lire's iron. Why hasn't Muse stopped us? Has she even thought to? Surely her magic could. Unless she doesn't even see us as a threat. She's just having fun. Toying with us. Putting on a show for her soldiers.

If we can keep her arrogant for long enough, play her game until we get closer to the iron—

'Tell me what Lire's son and the Bearran princess are planning,' Muse demands of me, so close I can feel the soft flutter of her wings, her breath on my face. 'Tell me everything you know, or one of your friends really will die. Maybe all of them, if I feel like it.'

'As if I would know,' I retort. I would *never* tell her anything to put Maya in danger, but even so, I don't know anything useful to the fairy. Her magic curls around me and I shake my head. 'They have no plans! They know they have no hope. That's why we're out here trying to find anything we can to help them.' Muse is close enough to reach. If only I had Ebony's iron sword, I'd drive it through her heart right now. 'Unless something has changed in Bearra since I've been there, I have nothing to tell you.'

The fairy scoffs at me, and I lurch back. I've only ever been this close to two other fairies, and I trusted them far more. Grace and Rhiannon may be very different, but they don't lie, and they don't hide. I could anticipate their moves. Muse, on the other hand, is unpredictable and always masked.

'So you're useless to me,' says the yellow fairy. 'You're nothing. I thought . . . Well, I don't know why I expected a crew of lowly pirates could be the key to Bearra's plans. Lire seems to think highly of you, but I suppose you really are just Princess Dawn's dogs, sent out to do what she is too cowardly to do herself.'

'We don't mind,' says Ebony. She smiles through a bruise forming from her right eye to her top lip. 'Someone has to save the world.'

'From what? *Me?*' The fairy laments. 'What do you think killing fairies will accomplish, exactly? The fairy war is about power, the one thing everyone wants. Our world has been teetering on a cliff's edge for a very long time, and Lire has had plans in place for hundreds of years. You like to think you don't need us, children, but you do. This world needs magic, and to get magic, you must have fairies. You need a powerful leader to watch over your land, your societies, and rebuild them in her image. My sisters will either be smart enough to join Lire and myself, or be foolish enough to fight us. Humans will surrender or die. But I can promise that when we win the war, the world will once again have order.'

Opal rolls her eyes. 'Our world may be pure chaos, but taking away our free will is not something we can get behind.'

'And do you think, little Adellan, that if Lire and I die, then all will be right? Without us to keep the Ice Empire at bay, they will take the world. If not them, then someone else. There will always be an enemy for you to fight, always someone hungering for power. At least if it is the fairies who win, we can promise that the world will be a better place.'

'A better place?' echoes Ebony, her sword held high in front of her face. 'Lire cursed a kingdom to sleep for a hundred years. Does that sound better?'

I will my friends to be quiet. Though the conversation is keeping us from being killed *and* keeping us on track upstream, we can't keep teasing the fairy like this. She'll soon lash out again, and I need my friends safe.

Muse waves a hand dismissively. 'My sister doesn't need to convince any of you. Although it would be lovely to have such talented warriors on our side, we do not require you. Killing you is the better choice.'

'Then *try us*!' Wren shouts. Her brother whirls, his eyes begging her to stop, but she shakes her head as her face morphs into deep rage. 'There are enough people in the world to take you down, Muse. Maybe not us, but someone. The Ice Empire, or Princess Dawn, or the other fairies. We all hate you enough. Maybe you'll have to kill everyone in the world, and then you'll finally win. Kill us if you want. You'll only make Bearra angrier. They'll still find the weapons they need, and they *will* pummel your stupid fairy wings beyond recognition. You think you can kill us? We can't wait to kill *you*.'

Muse's neck lurches forward, a snake striking, and Arden jumps in front of Wren. 'She doesn't mean that!' he says. 'We'll leave, we'll go!'

But the fairy's face becomes a dark snarl. We've pushed too far. A ball of power, a glittering star, forms in her hand. She points it towards Wren. 'I will not be insulted by a child!'

Ebony tries to run up with her sword, but it's too late. In an instant that feels like a thousand years, the magic flies in Wren's direction. The girl screams, and Lark is falling to his knees, and my gut wrenches painfully, and Muse's power eclipses us like the sun, and Arden is trying to push Wren out of the way so he can take the hit instead, but—

But Opal dives in front of them both, flying like a swan, a tornado of silk shimmering as the magic strikes her in the heart.

CHAPTER
TWENTY-EIGHT

I'm screaming – we're all screaming – and I drop to my knees. Opal lands on the deck, gasping for breath, coughing up blood, clutching her chest, crying, crying, crying. The magic glides through her veins, yellow crossing her skin like streaks of lightning.

It's awful. So awful I feel as if I'm the one suffering, as if I'm the one whose heart is being shattered. My gut constricts on itself and it's all I can do to keep my last meal in. My best friend, my first friend on this damned ship, she's— she's—

I shake my head, try to clear my mind. It all must take less than two seconds, because the next thing I know, Arden and I are racing over to her. It's as if Muse and her soldiers are no longer here. The fairy has stepped back with a small smile, enjoying our pain like it's sweet honey. It's just us, and Opal, and she's dying, and . . . and . . .

'Opal!' Arden is screaming. He picks up her head, cradles it in his lap, holds her hand. 'Don't close your eyes!' His magic curls around her once again, but there is nothing to be done. Healing magic is complex as it is, and that's for regular wounds. *This . . .*

I watch the blood drain from Opal's face and take her other hand, tears pouring from my eyes so intensely I can't see.

'You're okay,' she says, her voice pitched high, crackling. 'You'll be okay without me. You'll be better without me.' The others gather around, kneeling and sobbing and reeling.

I clench her hand tighter. How can this be happening?

We were supposed to be invincible.

'B-But we need you,' Arden whispers. His flood of tears mixes with her blood as she feebly reaches up to wipe his cheek. 'We— You were my first friend, Opal. You're my family. My sister. I-I will not watch you die. *Opal.*'

She shudders. 'Then you better close your eyes,' she says. 'Don't, though, because this is a lovely dress and I want you to remember how gracefully I—' Coughs steal her words, and Arden pulls her up into his chest.

It's as if my heart stops. The moment seems to last forever, yet it is sand slipping through my fingers as I try to make myself remember Opal's voice, her expressions, try to imprint her memory in my mind forever.

She can't go like this. She can't. Opal accepted me before any of the others. She let me sleep in her cabin, let me borrow her clothes when I had none, teased and taunted me like a sister. And how did I repay her? By never trusting her, by resenting her, by leading her here to . . . to—

'Ebony can have my dresses,' Opal stutters. 'She could really use them. Wren gets my weapons. You can all share my jewels, I don't care. Sierra can have my room, though we all know she'll end up in Arden's soon enough. Wren can have it then. Sierra,' she says, looking up at me through bloodshot eyes, 'don't wear green. It isn't your colour.'

'I never would,' I mutter under my breath. 'Ew.'

She takes a shuddering gasp and more blood leaks from her lips. She continues quickly. 'Lark, you need to pull yourself together. No – the opposite. Let yourself live a little. I'm still mad at you, but I would have forgiven you. Because I love you. All of you. And I know you'll win the war, because you're *you*, and we can do anything.'

Arden presses his head against her chest. 'Stop. Stop saying these things. You aren't leaving us.' But surely even he knows he's lying to himself. He whispers, 'I can't lose you. I can't lose you. I love you. We're supposed to always be together. Me and you and our ship. We were supposed to run away and be free. We were supposed to take care of each other. W-We were supposed to be best friends for life.'

Opal blinks up at him, clenching his hands in hers. Her face is a streak of scarlet blood and saffron magic. 'Arden. Captain. I love you. F-Forever,' she chokes out. 'You are my brother forever, and if there is life after this, know I'll be back to watch over you. You were the first person to love the real me. The first person I ever l-loved. Now do me a favour and do good things, Arden, and just get together with Sierra, no one cares, and defeat Lire, and make Muse pay, and don't let me die in vain.'

Wren's small frame wracks with sobs that should be too colossal to come from her. '*Opal.*' She pushes between us and towards Opal, pressing their foreheads together. 'Why did you do that? It's my fault— You weren't supposed to— It was supposed to be me, Opal, and y-you— *Opal.*'

Opal manages a small smile. 'Wren, my love, you are going to be so much better than me, okay?' She blinks slowly, the life already leaving her. 'You're going to b-be the best of the best. You have the greatest family surrounding you. And— And you are going to live a much better life than I ever could have.'

'I don't want to. Not without you.'

Opal tries to shake her head, but a fit of coughing takes over her body. When she recovers, she looks at Arden and whispers, 'Don't waste your time mourning me.'

'Waste my time?' he replies softly. 'I won't ever forget you. You are everything I ever wanted you to be. You gave me the pleasure of being by your side, and I'll never stop thinking of you. Never.'

She smiles weakly. Final teardrops fall from her eyes, and with a last shaking breath, she goes still.

• ◊ ✝ ○ ⚔ ○ ✝ ◊ •

Muse clears her throat behind us, but I barely register it. My eyes are blurry, and I feel so distant, so disconnected from my body, like I'm floating above, watching this all happen from the outside.

Muse says, in her sickeningly sweet voice, 'That's enough. Do you see *now* that I am serious? Has it really taken watching one of you die to understand the stakes?'

She flutters down to the group, and I'm almost certain all of us are ready to do something completely reckless. None of us are known for our patience or forgiveness. But revenge? That is what we're built for.

First she hurt Lark and Wren. Now she's taken Opal's life.

Muse has so much to pay for.

I want to tear the fairy's wings clean off, I want to wring my fingers around her neck, I want to set her on fire and watch her and her vomit-yellow taffeta go up in flames.

Still, my shoulder is wounded, and as I come back to reality, the pain is really setting in. I'm not accustomed to dealing with this anymore; it's been so long since I couldn't simply transform to heal any injuries.

Arden's shoulders are hunched with grief. Lark walks with a limp. Wren holds her arm close. Ebony's nose is broken, and Levi, at her side, has blood dripping from his lips.

The stormy waters have calmed. We must be close enough to the iron now that the wards have lost effect. Within me, though, is a tempest great enough to shake worlds. I will die before I let Muse leave without paying for her crimes.

Justice. That is what I am trained for, the moral I was raised upon, and the blessing Grace herself bestowed upon me.

Immediately, I lock eyes with Arden. His grief-wracked expression drops for a split second as he listens to my silent words. As he sees that I have a plan. Then he goes back to sobbing, to pounding his fists against the deck as he wails – capturing Muse's attention. The crew senses the shift, something no one outside our unit could possibly notice, and follow along.

Lark, a perfect Musan, drops to his knees right in front of the fairy, begging and pleading to her to spare us, to reverse what she did – *save Opal, please, please can't you?* – while Wren fumes at Muse with clenched fists.

We are a song, each of us in perfect harmony, and how could Muse resist such a thing? Her head tilts to the side as she watches the grieving pirates, eyes brimming with sparkling yellow tears. She did the kill, but our grief is hypnotising.

Good.

Pay.

Blood drips from my fingertips as I stand and sidle up to Ebony, pressing her weapon back into her hands behind us as I switch it for the iron sword, holding it for the first time. It's heavy and warm – blood-soaked – and I wrap my hands around the hilt with no apprehension. It cannot hurt me anymore.

Ebony keeps her face straight, not questioning me for taking it. Her weapon must sense my plan, because it does just what I need and mimics the iron sword perfectly. I keep the real sword behind my back while Ebony catches my ploy and swings her weapon outward, showing Muse and her soldiers that she has the iron. Making sure no one sees that the real weapon is in my hands.

My head spins, but some instinct takes over, guiding me towards the kill I so desperately long to perform.

Muse, still mesmerised, steps slowly towards Opal. The pirates spread apart, letting her crouch beside our lifeless friend. Arden is still on the floor, leaning back with his knees up, rocking himself as he cries. His magic clouds around his hands, directionless.

But I move behind Muse as she watches Opal, leaning down and brushing her hair ever so gently.

She pays us no attention. How could we bring any harm to her, weak as we are?

Unfortunately for Muse, weakness has never been an issue for me. And we're so close to the iron now that *she* is weak too. Even the sparkles atop her pointed wings have dulled, like stars disappearing into the day.

I tighten my grip on the iron sword. My limbs turn to stone, my blood rushing through my veins, my senses sharpening. *This is why I lost the swan.* The curse had to be broken so I could do this. If I can kill Muse, then this is all worth it. For Opal. For the sake of the fairy war. For Bearra.

For me.

If Muse is so arrogant that she would turn her back on Sierra Reed . . .

'A beautiful thing,' she says, brushing a curl of Opal's hair from her forehead, 'the end of a story. The final note of an extraordinary melody.'

I keep stepping closer, letting my sword arm hang, hunching my shoulders. My mouth curls into a grimace but my body hums with anticipation. One iron sword couldn't be enough to kill a fairy, but already weakened by the stores of it nearby, she's finally vulnerable. *This is the kill of a lifetime.*

The fairy's soldiers remain back, not wanting to get in her way even as I approach. They don't know I have the iron sword. They don't know I'm a threat. They probably don't even know about iron, or understand that their fairy is weak.

Muse takes a breath as if to say something, her faded yellow wings fluttering gracefully.

I lift the sword – slide towards her – raise the iron above my head – take aim – take a deep breath—

Slash it right down the centre of her back, tearing open her skin. She screams, her wings seizing as she tries to grab at the wound.

And I laugh, and laugh, a manic joy coursing through me as I watch her spasm in agony.

No one kills my pirates but me.

There is no blood. Just a gaping hole full of yellow magic, as if that's all she's made of. It spills and floods out of her. She falls back, squirming, screeching for her soldiers. They don't know what to do; they run around in a panic, screaming.

I slash at her again – then again – watching the wounds widen, watching the power pour out, watching her wail and writhe.

'So iron really does work on fairies,' says Ebony, no sympathy in her expression. 'Good to know.'

Lark and Wren gaze at Muse with slack jaws, unable to make any sense of what they see. And despite being the one to attack her, I feel much the same – barely conscious of the gravity of what's happening. This is a *fairy*. How am I . . . winning?

'You *dare* . . .' Muse starts, but her words are cut off as she tremors, her hands clutching her back. 'You have no idea . . .' She tries again, with a heave that might be an attempt at a laugh. 'You have no idea what's coming. This will only make Lire angrier. Every creature in my forest is on her side. Including the *dead*.'

'We're aware,' Ebony says, wiping her bloody nose. 'We met them.'

More magic spurts from Muse's mouth, like mist. 'You may not be afraid of ghosts, children, but the dead are no longer dead. Lire made them a promise – fight with us, and they will be resurrected. Already they are all over the world, disguised beyond recognition, with wonderfully unique magic, willing to do *anything* to keep their new lives. Oh, and Lire sent a very special ghost to take care of Princess Dawn. If you make it out alive, you'll just love finding out who they are.'

My breath hitches. The ghosts were bad enough contained to the forest, but *this*? I need to get back to Maya and warn her. But my eyes flicker to Opal's limp body, and I'm renewed with fresh fury. I have a job to finish.

Arden places his hand over mine, so we're both gripping the sword. He's no killer, but of course he couldn't miss this. Not after what she's done. We loom over the fairy. She looks like a flickering candle – but until the flame is *gone*, there's life.

I meet eyes with Arden for a short moment. *Are we really going to do this? We can't come back from it. The consequences could be catastrophic.*

But there is one truth that trumps everything else. *She killed Opal.* Justice can be a terrible thing for those who deserve it.

Muse screams. 'You'll pay! Lire will have your heads for this!'

Wren steps over the fairy, sneering down at her. 'What a shame you'll never get to see it, you sad old witch.'

And silently, with the sun in our eyes, Arden and I together drive the sword directly through Muse's heart, putting out her light for good.

⁕ ◊⁺◯ ⚔ ◯⁺◊ ⁺

'We have to bury her,' Arden says. 'We have to . . .' His eyes are bloodshot, no longer wet with tears, but red from the remnants of them. He holds Opal's still head in his lap.

I can barely look. 'We don't have time,' I whisper. 'We need to get back to Bearra and tell them about Lire's army.'

'Sierra!' Ebony reproaches. 'Bearra can take care of itself. Opal is our priority.'

We're on the deck, sailing slowly through pouring rain that washes away the blood. Washes away the magic, the pain. The soldiers retreated – we kindly spared their lives – but they didn't have a body to return with. Muse's magic misted out of her like steam, leaking into the atmosphere until there was nothing of her left.

Yet while all evidence of our battle is gone, nothing can simply wash away Opal.

I sigh. 'I'm sorry. But where? How? We can't bury her here. We're close enough to Adella's Territory that we could take her body back to her family . . .'

'She would hate that,' says Wren, facing away from the group.

Arden's eyes light up, and I don't like the look. 'We could take her to Muse's Territory. You heard Lire. She's resurrecting the ghosts there. If we bury Opal in the forest, maybe she becomes a spirit, and maybe—'

'Becomes a slave to Lire?' Levi says. 'Arden, you must know that isn't a good idea.'

'But it's *an* idea. Isn't it? Shouldn't we do all we can to bring her back?'

Ebony kneels beside him and places a hand on his shoulder. 'No. We won't do something to her that she would never want, just because we're too selfish to lose her.'

Arden's voice cracks. 'But she can't be dead. She just . . . She *can't* be.'

Seeing him like this makes me want to stab myself through my own heart. There's no easy way to describe this feeling – it's like falling, with no end in sight, through a colourless void. And how can any of us reach to each other for help, when none of us have anything to give?

'I'm sorry,' Ebony says. 'We all are. I would do anything I could to bring her back, too, but we have to do what's right. Opal didn't sacrifice herself for us just for us to lose our way.'

'*Please,*' he begs.

'No,' Lark says. 'This is not the time to do something desperate.'

Arden looks around the group, hoping for just one of us to agree with him, but we each, in turn, shake our heads pitifully. Another sister lost. I can't even begin to imagine his pain. And yet I can, because it sits right in the centre of my heart, right where he does.

I stare at Opal's body and swallow, ignoring the pit in my stomach. 'We should take her to Bearra. I'll make sure the princess gives her the flashiest, most ridiculous grave the world has ever seen. Is that a compromise we can agree on?'

Arden's face falls. 'Okay,' he utters, barely audible.

I drop beside him and wrap an arm around his waist. 'We're going to survive,' I whisper.

I won't lie and tell him we'll be okay, as much as I hope that one day we might be. But we are survivors, and we have a world to save. Sacrifice is nothing new to a Reed and a pirate captain.

The ship begins to turn around, back towards Bearra. We'll return for our iron another time. Right now we have a friend to bury and a princess to warn.

Arden finally releases Opal and curls into me. I hold him gently, promising to never let go, and we cry together until the skies are clear once more.

Epilogue

Somewhere, sometime . . .

In the servant's quarters of Bearra's castle, Relia woke on a hard bed and a scratchy pillow. It still felt strange, to wake and sleep, to fall into dreams, then at once find herself returned to a physical body. A body that wasn't even her own. A room that was still unfamiliar.

She'd spent the last hundred years as a spirit, before Lire brought her back. Those years now felt like a haze, mostly forgotten, a dream; yet she wasn't her old self, either.

Relia was well aware that anyone who had been resurrected would struggle to adjust to a new life, a new body, so she tried to be patient with herself. It was difficult being a maid, though she seemed to be competent enough. It was more difficult being a spy. She did not enjoy telling Lire about Bearra, betraying these people to an evil fairy.

What was most difficult, though, was betraying the princess. Especially when the only reason Relia did all of this was to have one more chance to be near her.

But even if she had to destroy all of Bearra – all of the world – to see Dawn again, she would do it. Whatever Lire's cost, she would pay it. Of course she knew it was part of the fairy's wicked plan. Of course she knew nothing could ever happen between her and her love again.

Still, a century ago, she had naively died for this opportunity, having always known this was her goal. She was given a second chance at life – at *her* – and she would take it. She would not lose her world again.

Sometimes terrible things had to be done. Sacrifices had to be made. Relia had spent her entire life being meek and quiet, kind and sacrificial. She was never able to have what she wanted, because she never fought for it.

Now, she would.

If there was a way to correct her mistakes, if she ever found a way out of Lire's grip, she would take it. She would fall to her knees and beg those she harmed for forgiveness, do anything to make things right.

But love clouded guilt. Relia had lost too much in her life to not give herself this.

She rolled out of bed, stretched her aching shoulders, dressed by herself, and made her way upstairs to find the princess.

Dawn was already awake, sitting at her desk in a nightgown, her hair unbrushed. Even as tired as she appeared, the princess was the most beautiful person Relia had ever seen. Dawn smiled widely when she noticed Relia. 'Morning, Carlotta.'

And Relia melted. How could she do this to her love?

How could she *not*?

Acknowledgments

I never expected people to connect this deeply with my beautifully villainous Sierra, but there's something about a girl so lost and angry that many young women relate to. I kept this in mind as I wrote her book; I wanted her story to be about finding family and love, about vulnerability and trust, and letting go of goals that aren't what we really want. Sierra is for the furious women, the eldest daughters (despite her being the youngest), for those of us who long to be free and loved and valued in a world that wants to put us in a box and trample us. Sierra lives inside my soul and reminds me to be strong, to be powerful, to say no to things I don't want, and yes to things that scare me. I hope she can live in your hearts and hold your hands too.

Creating and publishing book two felt very different to book one, both easier (because I understood the process better) and more difficult (because there's so much pressure to do what you've already done, but better). Still, one thing remains clear: I couldn't have done this alone.

So I don't simply copy and paste the acknowledgements I wrote for book one, I'll keep it simple and say an overall thank you to all my family and friends. Much love to you all. Your support means the world.

To anyone else who has supported my work by either sharing it or buying it (or offering advice and encouragement), thank you. To those of you who have reviewed Woken Kingdom so kindly and have been eagerly awaiting book two, thank you.

To my authory coworkers. My beta reading team, who are so encouraging but always honest: Angie, Emma, Savannah, Zinnia, Madi and Emily. To my editing team, who I can't imagine doing this without: Pauline, Ellyssa and Lizzie. To Haylee Buswell for the book design (both the cover and the lovely illustrations within).

Finally to my grandfather, Robert Ixer, for the stunning artwork, and for showing me that a life in the arts is possible. You didn't get to see this one published, but I hope you would've liked it.

◦ ✦ ◯ ⚔ ◯ ✦ ◦

Can't wait for more Woken Kingdom? Follow Relia and Dawn's quest to save Bearra in *Haunted Princess*, coming early 2024.

Follow @PoppysVintageBooks on Instagram and TikTok for Woken Kingdom content, and sign up to the Poppy's Pages newsletter for sneak peeks at upcoming stories!

poppyspagesediting.com/newsletter-sign-up

About the author

Poppy Rose Solomon's YA novels reflect the traumas and lessons she experienced as a teenager, and she loves creating 'unlikable' characters who learn to heal themselves. Evoking inspiration and escapism is the goal of her storytelling. From her home on the Sunshine Coast, she freelances as a YA editor and coach through her business Poppy's Pages, and runs the Writing YA With Poppy podcast. Woken Kingdom is her first series, with plenty more to come.